"In *The Girl in His Shadow*, Audrey Blake takes the reader on an exquisitely detailed journey through the harrowing field of medicine in mid-nineteenth-century London."

—Tracey Enerson Wood, international
bestselling author of *The Engineer's Wife*

"Fluidly written, impeccably researched, *The Girl in His Shadow* is a memorable literary gift to be read, reread, and treasured."

—Gloria Goldreich, author
of *The Paris Children*

"With its strong woman protagonist and authentic period detail, this is the best kind of historical."

—*Library Journal*

PRAISE FOR *THE SURGEON'S DAUGHTER*

"In Nora Beady, Blake has created a truly captivating heroine, for then and for now."

—Sally Cabot Gunning, author of
The Widow's War and *Painting the Light*

"History comes to life in the dramatic account of Nora Beady's ascension in the medical world of Bologna."

—*Booklist*

THE WOMAN WITH NO NAME

A Novel

AUDREY BLAKE

sourcebooks
landmark

To Stella. Because she asked.—JF

To Imogen, Vaila, and Ingrid—fiery little women. —RS

Published by Sourcebooks Landmark, an imprint of Sourcebooks
P.O. Box 4410, Naperville, Illinois 60567-4410
(630) 961-3900
sourcebooks.com

Cataloging-in-Publication Data is on file with the Library of Congress.

Printed and bound in the United States of America.
LSC 10 9 8 7 6 5 4 3 2 1

PROLOGUE

"MAMAN, TU NE LE CONNAIS PAS." MOTHER, YOU DON'T KNOW HIM.

Silence on the line. I hugged the receiver to my ear, curling against the telephone niche built into the wall. Still nothing, so I glanced down the hall at my daughter, Jacqueline, sitting quietly in the salon. She was small for six, even tinier folded up in the great armchair, a book spread on her lap. Slowly, she turned a page.

Damn. She was listening. I strode as far as the cord allowed and pushed at the door with an outstretched foot. It swung most of the way shut.

An exasperated sigh filtered down the line. "I said the same thing to you, Yvonne, but you were determined to marry him."

"Yes, but—" I bit my lip. *My mistake.*

"A wife belongs with her husband. You've been away long enough. You must go back to London."

"Alex doesn't want me." And here, in Paris, Henri did. My life had luster again—except when I spoke with my mother.

"Yvonne, it's been months and you spend all your time running about with that man. Your husband will know."

"So?" Alex didn't hide his feelings for the widow across the street. "I want a divorce."

"Your husband will never agree to that."

"He'll have to if I stay in France."

"And you think Henri will marry you?"

"He wants to," I retorted. "But I have to lose Alex first."

"It will never work."

She'd said the same thing about my marriage. "I'm not—"

A car horn hooted cheerily from outside. My heart jumped. "I have to go, Mother."

"Yvonne—"

"Bye." I wasn't six anymore. I set down the receiver and reached for a new ivory cloche trimmed with wide brown ribbon. "Jacqueline! Get your coat." In the mirror, I inspected the diagonal fall of my skirts.

"Mummy?"

I answered in English, sensing this wasn't the time to argue about speaking French. Eventually, she'd tire of people not understanding her. "What is it? We're in a hurry, Jacqueline."

"I miss Daddy. Can't we go home?"

I turned around and found myself confronting a miniature Alex, complete with folded arms and frown. I took a moment to collect myself.

I crouched down and picked up Jacqueline's hands. They were small and quick, like my own. "He doesn't want us," I said quietly. "I know it's hard, but—"

She blinked twice, her lips pursing. "He wants me. I know he does."

This was no time to point out that it had been six weeks

since he'd sent her a letter. "We both love you very much, pet. Let's talk about it later. We can't let worries spoil our drive, not on such a beautiful day." I guided her arms into her coat, worried she'd refuse. Henri was wonderful with her, but it was natural for her to be standoffish. In time, she'd warm to him, but for now, I didn't want to keep him waiting.

"Quickly, love."

She tugged her knitted cap onto her head and stomped outside.

"Darling, how are you?" Henri called to me. As usual, Jacqueline was ignoring him, climbing into the back seat of the open-top car with as much enthusiasm as she'd show for a trip to the dentist.

I adjusted the angle of my hat and smiled up at Henri, kissing both his cheeks.

"Trouble?" he asked in an undertone.

"It's nothing," I said.

"What do you say to an ice cream, Jacqueline?" Henri asked, helping me into the car. "Right sort of day for it, no?"

"My name's Jackie," she reminded him.

At least she'd replied in French. Henri didn't speak English. "That's just what your schoolmates called you," I said. "You'll have new friends and a new nickname this year."

Jacqueline scowled at her knees.

"Definitely ice cream," Henri said, shifting the car into gear. "Hold tight, Jackie!" He took the corner at speed, earning laughs from both of us. Standoffish or not, Jacqueline loved going for a drive, especially when Henri put a little thrill in it.

We left the suburbs and whizzed through Maisons-Lafitte, the town where I'd been raised, and tore down roads walled on both sides by impenetrable masses of green, the forest of Saint-Germain.

"What's for lunch?" I asked.

"Bread, brie, pâté for me, and tomatoes for you, darling, since I know you don't like it. Some pears, a very nice bottle of chardonnay, and a ginger beer for Jacqueline," Henri said. "A plum tarte tatin, which I think you will like, and a thermos of coffee."

"Sounds wonderful," I said.

"There's a turn a kilometer or so away," Henri said. "We'll take the footpath into the woods until we find a place to picnic, then after we sleep off lunch, we can walk back to the car and, on the way home, find our ice cream." He grinned at me.

I returned the smile, then glanced back at Jacqueline. "That sounds perfect, doesn't it?"

"What kind of ice cream?" Jacqueline asked, still needing convincing.

"Whatever you like," Henri promised grandly.

"From what they have in the shop," I amended and turned my attention to the scenery.

"Help me watch, darling? I don't want to miss the turn," Henri said, passing me a well-used map without taking his eyes from the road. I unfolded it awkwardly, struggling to keep it from flapping in the breeze. We rocketed down a straightaway.

"Maybe slow down a little," I said. "This thing is going to fly away or smack me in the face."

"Other way up, darling," Henri said.

"Yes, I know. Just give me a—"

"Merde!"

I slammed into the dash as Henri stomped on the brakes. A deer bounded off the road and into the trees. The back of the car fishtailed, swinging right, left—

"No!" I shouted as we veered toward the edge of the road.

The car didn't hear me, skidding inexorably and spraying up gravel.

"Hold on!" Henri shouted. I twisted to reach Jacqueline and found myself hurtling through the air. I crashed to the ground and lost my breath in a shatter of glass.

"Yvonne!"

I lifted my head, spotted Henri on my right crawling through high grass over a loose tire.

"Jacqueline?" I gasped soundlessly.

Henri bent over me, his hands hovering anxiously. "Are you all right?"

"Where's Jacqueline?"

This time he heard me and scrambled to his feet.

I seized his hand and hauled myself up.

The car was at least ten meters away from us, upside down, stopped by a thick stand of trees.

"Jackie!" I lurched forward, desperate for a sight of her blue cap.

"Jacqueline!" Henri was faster on his feet. My legs weren't obeying. "She's here," he called, bent at the back of the car. "She's—"

I staggered closer and saw her, beneath the car, with blood on her skirt and her blue knit sweater. Breath left me in a rush and I sank to the ground, gathering up her limp form with arms that felt like ribbons, choking on each breath. "Baby. Baby," I sobbed. "Please, please, please."

———

"Her leg will be scarred for the rest of her life." Alex spat each word at me. They might have hurt if I hadn't loosed them at myself dozens of times over the past week.

I'm so sorry, Jackie.

My eyes swerved to our daughter, sitting in a wheelchair in the hospital garden. My hand rose, pressing against the window glass between us. It hurt having her even this far away. I'd held her hand in the ambulance, keeping her in arm's reach from the moment she came out of surgery. It was only her second visit to the garden. I wanted to be with her, but Alex had words for me, and neither one of us wanted them overheard.

His arrival the night before, delightful to Jackie, was torture for me. We'd smiled and made the best of things in front of her, but there'd been no chance to talk. What could I possibly say? This was my fault. I gave thanks every hour for her life, for her two legs, still able to walk.

"I'm taking her home with me," Alex said.

"You can't." I said it as solidly as I could. "I'm her mother."

"I'm her father. She needs me. Look what happened when I left her with you."

"It was an accident," I said, knowing Alex would never agree. Sure enough—

"Accident," he snorted. "Negligence is more like it. Look how happy she is to see me."

"Of course she's happy. She thinks this means we're a family again."

His nostrils flared.

"A girl needs her mother," I said.

"Like you need yours?"

I kept my hands still. Maman and I seldom agreed, and Alex never fought fair. "Jackie and I are staying here," I said. "You know we can't live together." If Alex cut me off from our joint checking account, I'd do what had previously seemed unthinkable and ask to live with my mother.

"Maybe you and I can't, but Jackie and I sure as hell will. I'm not leaving her with you and that man who almost killed her. Or whoever you find next month or the month after that."

I stiffened. I wasn't talking to him about Henri, who'd retreated the moment I received Alex's telegram. Since the accident, I wasn't sure how to look at him. I didn't know how to look at myself either, so I avoided the mirror. Alex had pointed that out too, annoyed by my tired face and untidy hair. "I've told you a hundred times I want a divorce," I said tightly.

Outside the window, Jackie leaned forward in her wheelchair, chatting animatedly with my mother.

"She looks better since I came," Alex said, joining me at the window.

I wished I could deny it.

"She wants her home. That's London," Alex asserted. "If you try and stop us, you know what I'll have to do. No court will let her stay with you, not if I say no. Not after this."

I closed my eyes. "You can't take her from me. Please, Alex. You know you can't look after her. You're never home."

"I've never come within an ace of killing or crippling her."

Hold your tongue. Hold your tongue. Hold your—

"I'm sorry." Alex sighed. "That was unfair. *You* weren't driving."

Even though you chose the man who was, I added silently, finishing the sentence for him.

He tapped the pane of glass, telling me to look with him at the dark-haired girl smiling in the outdoor sunshine. I did, painfully noting the brightness in her eyes that hadn't been there yesterday.

"Of course she wants her family," he said gruffly. "All children do. And you're right. I can't be mother and father to her."

I waited.

"For her sake, we have to tackle this sensibly."

When had I ever been sensible? It was one of his chief complaints, though years ago, I would have sworn it was why he loved me. Then, I was delightful and spontaneous. Now, I was impulsive and irresponsible.

Perhaps we wouldn't kill each other if we each had a little distance, but we didn't even like each other anymore. I couldn't go back to England. I'd suffocate. France was my home, where I could have a new life, not a dead one.

But if I couldn't have Jackie…that wasn't much of a life either.

I turned to Alex, barricading myself behind my folded arms. "What do you propose?"

His eyes were fixed on Jackie. "Come back to London. We'll work something out."

CHAPTER 1

---

*There are vast numbers, not only in this island but in
every land, who will render faithful service in this war but
whose names will never be known, whose deeds will never
be recorded. This is a War of the Unknown Warriors; but let
all strive without failing in faith or in duty, and the dark
curse of Hitler will be lifted from our age.*

—Winston Churchill, 14 July 1940

LONDON, 5 JULY 1942

"Everything's in order—now," Vera Atkins said, latch-
ing my suitcase with a snap. "But you can't take this. You know
better, Yvonne."

"Jacqueline," I corrected, reminding her of the name on my
carefully forged French identity papers. "Jacqueline Viallat."

"Yes, for now," Vera agreed. "You'll go through a good
many names, I expect." Normally brisk, her face softened as
she set aside the old-fashioned silver locket she'd removed from
a rolled-up pair of brown stockings inside my suitcase. She
peered at the little girl in the photograph taken fifteen years
ago. "This is her, isn't it? Your daughter, Jacqueline?"

"She goes by Jackie. She's entirely English." Jackie's frequent assertion jumped out of me, a reflex. I'd heard it so many times. I told myself just as often Jackie didn't mean it as a rejection of me.

"You don't have to go," Vera reminded me, her voice soft.

I frowned skeptically. She had to say that. After months of training—shooting, bomb building, coding, crafting convincing lies—this one was too incredible.

"Truly," Vera said, her voice slowing and dipping lower. "You know all this is voluntary."

"I'm not afraid." My left eyelid, twitchy from lack of sleep, didn't betray me.

"I know. But if you wish to reconsider, now's the time. If your family—"

I shook my head. "I'm going." Vera knew I had a daughter but not that she was grown, married, busy with a life of her own. Alex, my estranged husband, wouldn't notice I was gone.

"Then you must leave your own life behind." Beneath dark, perfectly sculpted brows, her eyes questioned me—full of the same doubt I'd confronted for months. *Can she do this?*

Very well. The break shouldn't be hard, considering. "You'll keep the locket for me?" It hadn't seemed too much, just that one photo and the necklace I'd bought with two months of back pay once I passed training and they'd belatedly commissioned me an ensign with the First Aid Nursing Yeomanry, or FANYs. I trusted Vera. She'd sent many men to France already.

But not a woman—not yet.

"Of course I'll keep it." Vera tucked the silver necklace into her uniform pocket. "I have keepsakes and instructions from plenty of others. If you want to leave letters or…"

I shook my head.

"You met with the attorney I mentioned? Wrote a will?"

"Yes." Again I kept my thoughts to myself, ashamed of the truth. I owned nothing besides this suitcase filled with French-made, French-labeled clothing, the fighting knives, a gold compact, and a silk scarf printed with a map of the Loire made up of branches and blossoms instead of plainly marked roads, towns, and villages—all government issue, all made for Jacqueline Viallat. My new self. "Everything's taken care of."

"Good." The faint crease vanished from Vera's brow. "I'll drive you out to Tempsford. Good luck, Jacqueline."

I grinned and shook her offered hand. "Thanks. You too." I'd always been too good at dreaming, wanting the impossible, the implausible, the untrue. Until now, I had absolutely nothing to show for it.

But tomorrow, I'd fly to occupied France.

CHAPTER 2

ENGLISH CHANNEL, 6 JULY 1942

"Rum?" the man yelled over the noise of the plane.

I forced a smile and shook my head, absorbing another jolt. We sat on freezing bare metal in the tail of the plane. Cords and wires, taped together in snaking bundles, ran colorful patterns along the steel walls. I had orders to not speak to the three agents huddled beside me more than necessary, but from the hue of this one's pale face, I guessed he needed the alcohol.

Remembering Vera's final instructions, I studied my knees, avoided looking at my fellow passengers, and strove to be as faceless and forgettable as possible. *Stay quiet. Stay calm. Be innocuous.* It ought to be easy after the last fourteen years, but those had never felt easy either.

Sunlight barely penetrated the partition separating us from the cockpit, leaving only narrow beams that leaked through the joints of the fuselage. I sniffed my collar to see if the strong smell of oil had infiltrated my blouse.

Was a plane supposed to shake this much? The two men across from me, unperturbed by the rattling, leaned back against the riveted wall. If there'd been light enough, they'd probably have pulled out books. Were they pretending, or had they flown before?

One of the men in training told me he fell asleep every night picturing bullets tearing through his torso. *If you die every day, it takes out the fear of it. Gets almost boring after a while,* he'd confessed. Perhaps he'd taught his technique to these fellows.

"Oh God," the man beside me murmured, wiping his forehead.

In actual fact, flying was far less glorious than what I'd imagined—limbs turning weightless and hollow as we soared into the air. Instead, from our first lurch off the ground, I felt yanked toward the earth as never before, and now I was a pebble, tossed in a tin can. One of the crew picked his way toward us, bent almost double, steadying himself against the fuselage. He waved and shouted something inaudible.

"Come again?" I called back.

He came closer, crouching near enough to kiss me, but there was nothing intimate about the way he bellowed into my ear. "Skip says we can do better for our lady passenger. You'll be more comfortable up front. Take my seat."

My eyes went wide. I'd finally tamped down my nerves by locking myself in place right here.

He misread my hesitation as shyness. "It's all right, go on."

Abandoning the urge to explain, I forced a smile and accepted his misguided chivalry. Maybe this was the crew's attempt at an apology. They'd been surprised when I walked up to the plane this morning with the other three agents, assuming I was someone's wife come to say goodbye. When Vera explained I was the fourth agent, two of the flight crew argued she'd made a mistake.

"I don't look like a spy," I'd admitted to the loudest naysayer. "That's why I'll be great at it."

"Please," the crewman shouted in my ear. "We can make you more comfortable." He took my hand and helped me up, steadying me as we both wobbled forward. "It's a great day for flying," he told me. "Unlimited vis!"

Whatever that means. Careful of my stockings (sturdy wool, but war had taught me to guard my clothing), I shuffled past the partition, squinting as I moved from the dark belly of the plane into the blinding glare that reflected off instrument panels and the Perspex dome.

Another jolt. I clutched the empty seat beside the pilot.

Sit, he mouthed, gesturing to the chair.

I balled my hands to keep from touching the wrong thing. Hundreds of wrong things—dials, knobs, levers. Moving like a toddler clinging to furniture—in this case, the copilot's chair—I eased myself down and studied the pilot's harness until I figured out how to strap in.

Once safely seated, I pulled my legs back so I wouldn't jar anything important and shaded my eyes against the intense light.

"You'll want these," the pilot offered, passing me a limp leather helmet with hard circles over the ears and a pair of goggles.

I tugged them over my head and the glare dissipated, allowing me my first real look. I gasped. The pilot, understanding, finally offered some words. "Nothing like it, is there, love?"

His voice burst in my ears through the radio, crackling over the engine and propeller noise. A smile canned and packaged, sounding of tin. There was a snap of static, then another voice, not the pilot—perhaps the other one, who'd given his seat? "You like the view, Jacqueline?"

I nodded, unable to speak. Eye-shattering blue above and below. A sea of rippling silk, bordered by crescents of white beach and miniature cliffs that rose to a patchwork of fields and lanes, dotted by clusters of rooftops: barns, houses, and the pin-prick spires of churches. It looked so peaceful and perfect—no signs of bombs or antiaircraft guns or blackout shelters.

"Absolutely gobsmacking. I've never seen anything so wonderful."

"You picked the right day for it," another voice said through the radio. "This one is right out of Hollywood."

The pilot pointed and named the controls, the technical descriptions sliding past without leaving a trace. The stunning beauty shouted down everything else, even his tinny voice in the radio.

He gestured to a ribbon of cloud streaming toward the horizon, and the navigator changed course, angling east, over the Bay of Biscay. The flight crew were chatty, ribbing one another about how they would spend their days of R and R in sunny Gibraltar. I leaned back, cushioned by their voices, imagining myself a film star flying for a holiday—or a movie shoot—in Algiers or Morocco. Cool drinks at the seaside, a man in a fast car and a suitcase of slinky gowns to wear at casinos... The vivid pictures evaporated as fast as they came, no match for this impeccable blue. "I don't know how you can stand to go back to the ground," I said.

"Well, not every flight is like this one," he explained. "There are plenty when the ground is all you want. But I know what you mean. Moments like this, it's easy to think you can conquer the world."

His smile never faltered and his hands stayed relaxed on the controls, but a familiar restraint shadowed his words. He hinted only obscurely at bad weather, bombing raids, or the many men in his squadron who'd taken to the skies and not returned to base. People were the same everywhere.

I did it too, talking about the comedy of setting out from my bombed London house with two pillowcases and my daughter's long-abandoned, worn-out teddy bear, with barely a change of clothes. Maintaining the cheeriness exhausted us all, but the alternative…

"Thank you," I told him. He might not fully understand, but it was enough if he thought I was only referring to the view.

"Least I can do. You are all"—he jerked his head backward at the partition—"terrifically brave."

That was as close as we came to the issue. He pointed out more features along the coast and told me facts about the plane, a Whitley Mark V. I nodded, pretending to be as keen as the boys who spent afternoons peering through binoculars and listening to the BBC each evening for RAF/Luftwaffe tallies like they were football scores.

A pang of sadness tugged inside my chest but softer than usual. I was, after all, sailing like a god through the heavens and finally, finally about to do something to help fix all of this.

I heard a chuckle in my ear and realized I was humming. *Blue skies, smilin' at me, Nothin' but blue skies—*

"You like Sinatra?" That was Hutt, the navigator, from his map-strewn station beneath the observation dome.

"Too much," I admitted, laughing guiltily. "But I better stop. If I do this in France, I'll be found out."

"Better get it out of your system now," chimed in one of the gunners. *"Blue days, all of 'em gone, nothin' but blue skies from now on,"* he crooned in an off-tempo baritone, swinging precariously off the higher notes.

"Hutt," the pilot—Skip—chided. "You're worse than the static."

Laughter filled my ears and then more voices, singing much better than Hutt, managing something like harmony. I joined in.

Never saw the sun shinin' so bright,
Never saw things lookin' so right—

"Skip." The gunner's crisp voice cut across the lyrics. "Looks like a Heinkel coming up on our tail."

My eyes jumped to Skip's face. His gaze didn't leave the sky, but his mouth tightened for a heartbeat. "Livingstone's notorious for pranks. Don't worry. He's stringing me along because you're here."

I swallowed, the wide-open sky no longer so welcoming, every pilot interview I'd read in the papers rushing into my mind. Their incomprehensible, sexy slang describing enemy planes bursting out from the sun's glare, how they raced for cover in the clouds.

Outside the cockpit, there were no clouds, nothing but some jagged islands scattered in the sea far below and the impossibly distant, blurry horizon. We buzzed on in silence, the song forgotten. I waited, but Livingstone didn't laugh, didn't own up to the joke.

I bit my lip, afraid to speak, when a shattering crack erupted beside me, a flurry of brilliant flames arcing past the observer's dome. Curses and barked orders rattled through the static as the plane jumped sideways and dove. Tracers, I realized, and the percussive snaps were bullets—hitting us where? The left engine? Or punching through the duralumin fuselage and killing the crew? My stomach climbed to my throat and my spine fused into the back of the pilot's seat as we plummeted toward the rippling water.

"We've got another," Livingstone barked. "Not Heinkels. Arado 196s. Must have spotted us while on patrol." His next words were obliterated by a burst of machine-gun fire.

"What should—" I gasped, clutching at the buckles trapping me in the copilot's seat.

"Don't move," Skip barked, and I clamped my lips shut, terrified that another word would divert him, with disastrous consequences, from the fighters on our tail and handling our shuddering plane. I'd never made a practice of watching air battles in deck chairs in parks and back gardens, but I'd seen enough to know our Whitley—an older, wide-winged, and long-bodied bomber—wasn't nearly as fast or nimble as a fighter, capable of the aerial acrobatics of a mosquito.

"We've got bigger fuel tanks," Skip muttered. "We just need to fly out of range." I didn't know if he was talking for my benefit or the crew's. Could they even hear him over the gunfire? Far away, the horizon was a white-blue blur.

O Mary, Mother of God… The prayer in my mind wasn't my voice. Instead, I heard the measured, even tones of my mother.

…shield and save sinners who fly to you…

I held perfectly still, as I had as a child, sentenced to pass an hour confined to a sitting room chair for some rambunctious misdemeanor. But this was no sitting room. We vaulted, spiraling at the sun, racing for the western horizon. I didn't even breathe.

Miles away, where the sea touched the sky, a bank of clouds rose. It might as well have been illusion because death sang at my shoulder in the roar of the pursuing fighters and the scream of the tracers cutting apart the sky.

"Hang on," Skip gasped as he yanked on the controls and forced the plane into a roll.

My hair floated off my neck as we tumbled in painfully slow circuits once…twice…halfway around, climbing upside down in a wide curve… A bright silver plane flashed in front of us, spitting bullets, then vanished into the sun's glare.

"One's in a dive," Livingstone gasped. "We lost him."

"Hit?" Skip asked.

"No smoke. Can't say."

"Two o'clock," Hutt said, his voice high and tight. "It's Fritz coming back for another pass."

More tracers, more hits, and the thunder of the fighter drawing closer. Another roll in the opposite direction. Skip was leaning so hard on the controls, I feared they'd snap off. Then, as I stared out the cockpit, bracing for bullets, for explosions, for the sudden plummet of our beleaguered plane, everything disappeared. At first, I thought I'd been hit, then I realized a cloud had swallowed us. Someone cheered, Skip yanked hard right, and we emerged from that blank, white world on a new course.

"Did we lose him?" Skip asked.

Hope crackled along the static. Finally, "No such luck. He's spotted us," Hutt said. "Coming around on our six."

I didn't know what that meant, but it didn't sound good. "Bugger." No one noticed my curse, but I felt them all thinking it.

"Come on," Skip said, glancing over his shoulder, then back at another towering cloud, still out of reach. "We've got to be out of your range by now." We brushed past the fringes into smothering white, and he let out a sigh. "Not much of this," he commented, veering back into blue seconds later. "But with luck it will be enough."

We hopped from cloud to cloud, the same way I'd learned in training to dash from tree to ditch to riverbed, keeping cover.

"Can't see him," Livingstone said as we plunged into another, thicker stack. Skip's hands loosened on the controls, and his breathing flowed easier. He changed direction once more before the white vapor slid off our wings, then turned east, leveling off.

"Think we lost him," Hutt said. "He'll never make it back to Brest from here. We still have enough fuel for Gibraltar?"

"Plenty." Skip's retort was terse. But really, even if there wasn't, what would he say? I eyed the gauges, then thought better of it. After watching the scene outside the cockpit and the dancing needle of the altimeter, I preferred taking Skip's word for it. "Main thing is we're clear. Keep watch. Don't let them catch us again."

Quick as the flick of a light switch, the crew started chattering again. If anyone noted the feverishness of their ribbing asides, no one said anything. Hutt read out a new course, and though Turnham, the copilot, pointed out that we'd be cutting across neutral airspace, no one suggested altering direction. I let their banter soak into me until the shaking in my legs subsided. Relaxing again, Skip spared me a glance. "You've some nerve, love. I figured you'd have been screaming our ears off. Glad I was wrong."

"I'm full of surprises," I said, flashing a smile.

"So I see. You'll do, love. You'll do."

———

We landed in Gibraltar with a bump, which Turnham said was due to the short runway and not any fault of Skip's. I didn't care. Any landing was perfect.

"You're a queen, Miss Jacqueline," Skip said, offering his hand to help me down the ladder. His leather flight glove closed around my fingers, firm and reassuring. "Cool as ice the whole time," he informed the crew over his shoulder.

My feet settled on the ground before I noticed Skip still had hold of my hand. I wasn't sure if he was obliging me or the other way around. Had I clung too long? If he detected my residual trembling—and surely he did—he gave no other sign. The other three agents disembarked, rumpled and shaken. One looked as if he'd aged a decade during our hours in the air.

"So this is Gibraltar," I said. On the side of the runway, a car and driver waited. Maybe my movie-star fantasy wasn't so far off.

"And you've a new story to tell—chased by Nazi fighter planes for miles and not even a flinch…" Skip's eyes drifted over my shoulder and his voice trailed off, the flirtatious smile gone. I whipped my head around.

Above us, the propeller sported an inches-long gash. Scattered pockmarks marred the fuselage. Livingstone, coming up alongside us, whistled. "Close shave," he murmured.

"Maybe we'll get an extra day of R and R?" Hutt suggested.

"Don't count on it," Livingstone said. "The mechanics do their jobs too well to do us any favors."

Skip turned to back to me and squeezed my hand tighter. "Thank you for your bravery. It's been an honor."

Instead of releasing him and offering a decorous goodbye, I stepped forward and kissed both his cheeks.

"Thank you for saving my life," I murmured, then repeated myself, realizing belatedly I'd spoken for the first time in French.

Skip, ignoring whoops and cheers from his gunners and the ground crew, beamed, then drew me close for another kiss, this time on the lips. "My pleasure, Jacqueline. *Bonne chance.*"

The flight crew invited us for drinks, but this was negatived by our anxious-looking handler. Sweaty and balding, with limp strands of hair plastered against his forehead, he hurried us to the car waiting next to the runway. "Have to get you to the safe house without being seen," he huffed. "Don't even think about going out. There's Nazi spies everywhere."

Crowded in the back seat, we bounced over rough roads. Twice I nearly ended up in another agent's lap. He smiled apologetically at me and did his best to give me some space. With his listless brown hair and roundish forgettable face, he had no trouble keeping the directive to blend in. The car lurched, pressing me against the side door. "Back here first thing tomorrow morning," the handler said, pointing at the docks sliding past my window. "Shipping out before dawn." He applied his foot to the accelerator, pressing us back into the seats. "Your boat's... No, not that one." I followed his finger along a line of shabby fishing boats, depressingly small, tamping down the curl of unease in my stomach.

"There. See it? Red hull. Near the end of the line."

I ducked lower to get a better view, then choked off my exclamation—no one else was saying anything. I waited, sure I wasn't the only one dismayed by the sight. Rusty—not red—with tatty sails and years of grime on her. None of the men said anything.

Vera said we'd be landed in Marseille by boat, and I'd taken her word for it.

Turns out we were traveling by tub.

CHAPTER 3

THE CROWDED MARKET BUZZED, A HIVE OF SINGLE-MINDED shoppers pushing to their destinations despite the late hour. "Pardon me," I said, trying to edge my way through a barricade of men's backs surrounding a tea canteen. They posed a formidable obstacle. At best, the top of my head was level with the shortest man's shoulders.

"Excuse me," I repeated. "Will you let me by?"

A thin-lipped woman wheeling a pram surged in front of me, barreling toward the back of the queue. She must have deduced I was also heading to Mazzochi's stall, which always offered the best produce. Briefly I considered some sort of protest, but in the end, I simply fell in behind her. If her conscience didn't make her squirm over the next several minutes as she stood next to me, nothing I did would make any difference.

Ignoring me, the harried mother made nonsense talk with her baby until it was her turn, then asked and paid for a bunch of carrots, half a dozen apples, and two cucumbers, which she dropped in the pram before gliding away without a sideways glance.

Breathe and release.

"Good evening." Joe Mazzochi, the grocer, had a smile for everyone, but the one he bestowed on me said he'd seen what happened. "Haven't seen you yet this week, Madame Rudellat." He always leaned heavy on the last syllable of my name—*Rue-da-LA*—to show he'd mastered the French pronunciation, though I'd told him more than once he was welcome to use my first name, Yvonne.

"Evening, Joe. How's Tillie?"

"Very fine, very fine. She found some canvas today and managed to patch our broken windows." His voice sported a pleasing mix of cockney and Italian. "What will you have?" he asked.

Not the tempting plums in their neat wooden basket. Too expensive. "A bunch of spinach," I said, my eyes skimming over the string-tied bundles to the neat rows of cabbages. No. My purse wasn't that lean yet. "Two tomatoes and"—I searched the bins in vain—"a cucumber?"

Joe's face fell. "I'm so sorry, Madame Rudellat. I just sold the last ones. From Brownlee farm, in Kent. They've been very popular today."

"No more in back?" I asked instinctively, though I knew Joe wouldn't hold out on me. I'd bought his vegetables for almost fifteen years.

"I'll have more next week. I'll set one aside for you," he promised.

I thanked him, handed over my coins, and deposited the spinach and tomatoes into my string bag.

———

The blank, busy noise of other people's unconnected lives greeted me when I arrived at the boardinghouse: a snatch of indistinguishable words and the muffled strains of a gramophone, wafting above the lingering smells of someone's fry-up. I descended to the basement flat, my tired eyes trailing over the scuffs left in the walls, the traces of dozens of tenants, coming and, in the end, always going, moving up in the world or down or simply to other places.

"Evening, Alex," I called after a tap on the door.

"Door's open."

Alex was in the kitchen, sprinkling herbs on a cutlet of veal sizzling in the pan. Even when we lived together, this had been his domain. All I managed at the stove was burning things. The sound and the smell told me he was being improvident with his butter ration (the Ministry of Food authorized a miserly two ounces a week) but he almost never took an evening off. Might as well enjoy it, I supposed.

"Just leave it on the table," Alex said, not looking away from the pan. I pulled his wholemeal loaf from my bag and put it down next to the open newspaper. He wasn't finished reading yet, but since he was still occupied at the stove…marking his place, I flipped to the horoscopes and today's prediction.

Queer indications in force this day. Might well prove a fateful weekend for the world at large, especially the European World. For luck this day wear or use: purple, brown, 3, amethyst.

"Well, that explains it," I muttered, glancing down ruefully at my suit of charcoal tweed.

"Eh?" Alex called over his shoulder.

"Nothing," I said and let myself out, climbing the two

flights to my flat, a bedsit with a shared bath. Putting me up was, Alex believed, still cheaper than a divorce. And with so many fleeing London, he had plenty of empty rooms.

I had spinach and tomatoes for a salad but couldn't make myself eat. Nor could I muster enthusiasm to resume my neglected yoga practice, a habit I'd maintained for years after learning from a long-ago tenant, a gentleman from Chennai. My small black cat watched from his perch on the corner of my bed, in case I did something interesting.

"No news. I just read the horoscopes tonight, Bones." His ear flicked at his name, but he rolled his head to the side and closed his eyes, unconcerned about the stars' predictions. Besides the horoscopes, I couldn't bear to look in the newspapers. The plucky optimism was as defeating as the headlines. Each day the brave words grew more flimsy and transparent. But then, so did I—not just thinner from the stringent fat ration, but waning as threadbare as the stubborn British resolve. When my only contribution was to eat less, it didn't bode well for me or the war.

I stared too long at the faded walls, listening to the lives of my neighbors. My own possibilities—an overdue library book, a creaky gramophone, a half-done crossword—only depressed me. The best I could manage was to root through my drawers and the rumpled clothes at the bottom of the wardrobe until I found an old lavender night dress. It would count as purple, like the horoscope directed.

Lord knows I need the luck.

———

The moment I slipped into unconsciousness, sirens wailed through the black London air. With a groan, I rolled over, straightened my lavender night dress—it always twisted, which was why it languished at the bottom of the drawer—and consulted my bedside clock. Quarter past two. I'd snatched some sleep after all, however vehemently my fuzzy brain and sore limbs denied it. I rolled onto my stomach and pulled the pillow over my head to block out the noise.

At first, I'd gone to the tube stations during raids, until Alex cleared out the coal cellar to use as a shelter. While many still spent nights in back-garden Anderson shelters or underground, according to the newspapers, more and more elected to stay in their own beds, no matter what might come down from the sky. I'd joined this faction a fortnight ago. If bombs could reach twenty feet below ground (and some certainly had), it wasn't worth spending a sleepless night in a tube station or crouched under a blanket in our grimy bomb shelter.

Of course, staying in bed didn't equal sleeping: the sirens could be ignored with practice, but once joined by the distinct whistling of the falling bombs and angry rumbles of impact, I sat up, my eyes searching the dark room. I pushed off the sheet and groped for my dressing gown, trying not to trip in the dark.

Reminding myself I had fortune on my side, thanks to my lucky lavender night dress—if not a sensible outfit—I went to the window and parted the blackout curtains. Bright arcs of antiaircraft fire sliced through the dark sky above the opposite row of houses. In the distance, the firebombs' glow bounced down from a thick ceiling of smoke. Nothing I hadn't seen before.

A minute later though, flames roared to life a few streets over. The bombs often caught one or two houses, leaving the next ones almost unscathed, but I took defensive measures, donning a cardigan and shoes, because those fires were beacons, telling the next wave of bombers to drop their bombs over the shops and apartment houses of Pimlico.

No one tried to explain why German bombs fell here. They couldn't. With no factories, government offices, or any kind of military targets, Pimlico consisted of only people. Families with sons, fathers—and daughters too, like the grocer's four girls with their curly hair and dancing black eyes. The fire came from their direction.

My eyes swiveled to the ceiling, where my daughter, Jackie, and her husband were staying in the rooms above mine. As soon as the all-clear sounded, Jackie would be expected to report to the ATS. To fight back. I'd begged to join, but they'd asked my age and given me a firm, disdainful shake of the head. Forty-four? If I wanted, they'd give me the name of an agency that would help me find a safe billet in the country.

I had nothing to do but wait and pace alone.

Mrs. Madhukar banged about below, rousing Alex to take her to the shelter. I hoped he'd do so with good grace. Mrs. Madhukar was a good sort, but Alex didn't like spending hours in the cold when his bedroom was nearly as deep as the shelter.

I groped my way to the sitting room, located the hot plate, and reached for the kettle. My hands caught only hot, empty air as the floor jerked away, my body thrown against the wall with a nauseating crack.

I gasped, too confused to know what had happened. It couldn't be a bomb—I hadn't heard anything—no blast, no warning shriek as the deadly cylinder raced down to devour the earth. Nothing in my ears but a high buzz, blocking every other sound: my breath, my pounding heart. I tried to move, but grit and pinpricks rasped my palms. I pushed myself off the floor, away from the shards of glass, and rubbed my hands on my night dress, discovering it was just as gritty as the floor.

A bomb.

"Jackie!" I screamed noiselessly, deafened by the relentless ringing. I coughed and crawled to the doorframe, remembering belatedly that doorframes were stronger when a building collapsed. The fires down the street were the only light illuminating the thick clouds of dust swelling through my broken room.

"Jackie!" I heard myself this time, but no answer came, or at least nothing audible over groaning timbers and falling masonry. *Don't think about them. Move!*

I picked my way through a jumble of furniture and broken plaster into the hall. No sign of Mr. Fawcett. "Go to the shelter!" I shouted, banging on his door as I limped to the stairs. "Jackie?! Ronald!"

The door to the stairs didn't budge, so I threw my shoulder against the wooden panels once, twice, again, still shouting their names. I rattled the handle, flinching at the heavy thuds falling just behind me. A glance back at the window on the opposite end of the hall showed the blackout curtains gone, along with the windowpanes. Filling the space was an amber glow streaked with shadow and smoke.

I'd walked past enough battered husks of brick and stone, climbed over enough rubble scattered like toys across the street to know this house might collapse or catch fire at any moment.

Every second counted. I couldn't afford to stand here, shouting and beating fruitlessly against the door. I needed something heavier to hurl at it. I stumbled back to my room, one hand braced against the wall, but got no farther than a single step inside. My chair, formerly in front of the fireplace, lay in pieces, the plaster falling in chunks from the wall. There hadn't been enough light to see the devastation before.

I coughed, blinked, then reached into the dust-blanketed jumble. My fingers closed on the fire iron. Maybe there wasn't enough time. I didn't care. The next instant I was back at the door, slamming it between the jamb and the door handle.

"Get back!" someone rasped behind me. I ignored them, throwing my weight at the fire iron again.

"Yvonne!" A hand seized my shoulder, but I jerked away and struck the implacable door again.

The second time, the hands held me firm, arresting my next stroke. A familiar curse dug through the dust clogging my ears. "Jackie and Ronald came down through the window. They're in the shelter."

The fire iron clattered to the ground as I turned to Alex. He might have been made from chalk; he was that gray from socks to eyebrows. It was only his voice I recognized, the frayed one he used under greatest duress.

"They're both safe. You're the last one in the house." He shook his head, exasperated, reminding me, without words, of the hundreds of times he'd called me foolhardy and stubborn. "Bloody hell, Yvonne. If you'd just think."

Succumbing to the pull on my arm, I followed him to the cellar as an orchestra of explosions shook the ground beneath my feet.

CHAPTER 4

SO MUCH FOR THE DREAM OF A FILM-STAR LIFE. I SPENT THE night in Gibraltar playing cards with an elderly minder, giving myself stern lectures on bravery and boats, and trying to sleep until we were summoned, well before dawn. I rejoined the three men from our flight outside the shabby seaside inn and followed yesterday's handler to the dock, the sharp smell of fish and salt intensifying the morning cold. The thick dew settled inside my bones as much as it clung to the grass and shrubs. I trained my gaze on them, avoiding the pitifully small sailboat tasked with carrying us 771 nautical miles to Marseille. While the other agents walked to the edge of the dock, I sidled up to our handler.

"Mr. Evans." Of course this wasn't his real name, but I remembered the one he'd given all the same. "There's no other..." I stumbled under his gaze—watery, impatient, implacable—and pressed on. "There's no possibility of another boat?" Or I could travel overland through Spain. It was even possible, I'd heard, to land in France in very small planes. Anything was preferable to that rusty tub on my left, bobbing gently in the water.

"Thought this would happen." Evans's voice was clipped.

"No, there's no other boat, but the plane's still here. You can go back."

I recoiled at the suggestion and the way Evans took my faint heart for granted. Surely, as an intelligence officer himself, he had some idea of what I'd been through just to make it here. Shouldn't he want to help me achieve my mission, adapting my transport (surely not an impossible request) if that's what I needed to continue?

Not at all, it seemed. My request was unreasonable, and I was a mistake.

"I won't go back," I told him, but my stomach quailed the moment I turned my eyes to the boat.

"You'll be fine," Evans snapped. "She makes supply runs to the CARTE network's Marseille cell all the time."

I wanted to believe him, but my brain couldn't convince my body this tiny craft would make it past the harbor. "Fine," I ground out and marched myself forward.

There will be life preservers on board, I told myself, then nearly vomited at the thought of myself, alone in the water, clinging to a rubber ring with no land in sight.

"In Marseille, you'll connect with a local resistance cell called CARTE," I murmured under my breath, grounding myself by rehearsing my mission orders. They came to me easily, memorized exactly from the typed brief that I'd dissolved in a glass of water and then flushed down the toilet.

We supply CARTE's network, but they don't take orders from us, and so far they are only operating within Vichy France, the unoccupied zone. We need you to go north, to

*Tours, into the heart of German-occupied territory. Build
up resistance there. Make life hell for the Germans.*

I couldn't do that from here, so I had to get into the bloody
boat.

Two of my fellow agents were already aboard, talking to
a sailor in a green sweater. Another man, busy on deck with
something mechanical, saw me and waved.

"Come aboard." Even in the shadowy light, his blue eyes
gleamed like they had collected the midday sky after years of
floating beneath it. Fair hair complemented his beautifully
curated features.

"Captain Buchowski," he told me as he reached across the
boat's edge and the end of the pier to take my hands. Clasping
both, he drew me aboard as if reeling in a fish.

Here goes.

"Everyone calls me Boo." His accent was something between
German and Russian. I only smiled because containing my panic
left nothing for words. Perhaps the man sensed it; he was gentle,
asking if I'd be more comfortable on deck or below.

"Waves are rough today," he said with an apologetic smile
when I couldn't produce an answer. "We've got a fetch. That's
an evil wind that takes no breaks. We'll move slow until we get
across the anti-submarine net, and then we'll open sail. We are
a Spanish fishing vessel for this first part of the journey and a
French vessel for the second."

His calm patter followed the rocking rhythm of the boat. I
braced my legs wider to keep steady.

"Below, I think," he said, deciding for me. Instead of sparking annoyance, this made me unexpectedly grateful. Below, it might be dark and rocking, but I wouldn't have to see. "This way." He motioned me to a small opening. Three steps took us into the hull of the boat. It was as shabby inside as out. Two of the other agents were already huddled inside. The one who called himself Charles gingerly lifted a hinged seat, revealing a cache of guns and ammunition.

"I never said we fish with nets." Boo raised his eyebrows and his blue eyes flashed. "Find a place to settle in. Make sure it's secure." His gaze roamed back to me and hovered.

I sat down in the farthest corner and folded my legs atop the bench, making a tidy package of myself. As the gentle swaying of the boat grew to jittery bobbing, I closed my thumb against my index finger, weaving my attention inward with the movement of my lungs.

"You all right?"

I blinked and focused on the fellow beside Charles, the dark-haired man who'd aged visibly on our plane journey.

"Just fine."

"What are you doing?"

"Nothing. Meditating." I'd purposely positioned myself in a relaxed half lotus, used to others' skepticism, suspicion, or more likely, complete ignorance of the practice of yoga. "It passes the time." *And takes my mind away from the water.*

"Huh. Where'd you learn that?"

"You'll find a good bit of everything in Pimlico," I said, reluctant to elaborate. "I've had neighbors from everywhere."

He left me alone, returning to the more lively, conventional conversation with Charles and, a moment later, the fourth agent, who joined us below. I went from silently reciting a calming mantra to rehearsing the horoscope I'd read before the flight—the last I'd see for a long time to come. R. H. Naylor's predictions weren't published in French. *Propitious morning for unusual ventures.*

It had held yesterday. We hadn't been shot down, and it would do again for today. In spite of this rough sea, Naylor promised we'd not be drowned. France waited ahead, reaching out her arms and beckoning me home.

When night finally fell, most of the crew joined us in the hold for miserable, crowded sleep. "Calm seas," one said by way of explanation, seconds before he dropped off. I ought to be tired, but sleep was sure to elude me, packed in here. Outside, I'd have to face the water, something I'd only managed for brief moments throughout the day, but the thought of even one more hour trapped in this stuffy corner drove me to my feet. I ventured on deck, gripping the rail, drawing welcome breaths of cool air without the taste of diesel. Above, the stars burned holes through the night. The captain, satisfied with our course, briefly gave up steering across the dark water and lowered himself beside me, leaning against the cockpit wall.

"You see? It's not so bad."

"As long as I keep my eyes up."

He chuckled. "If it's so difficult, why are you here?"

I shrugged. My reasons were my own. He had no right to them.

"The Germans slaughtered my entire family in Poland."
The murmur of the waves matched his voice. "So I volunteered.
I wanted the most dangerous job they could give me. Anything
except parachuting. That's unnatural."

I rubbed my thumb along my folded fingers. "I wanted to
parachute in."

He laughed. "Then why aren't they letting you?"

I shrugged. "They said my bones were too fine." No reason
to admit they'd said I was too old. Yvonne Rudellat might be
forty-five, but I was Jacqueline Viallat now, my forged identification papers declaring me a spry thirty-three. I smiled to
myself. Twelve years of my life back in the double tap of a typewriter. Vera's idea, once she saw the result of my dyed hair, the
vivid white streak now hidden under a glossy chestnut. Starting
with a younger age gave me more flexibility with identities—
later, in France, if I found myself short of dye, I could become
someone older.

"They told me last night we'd be ferrying over a woman,
but I didn't imagine they'd send such a tiny one." His smile took
the sting from the words.

"They didn't think I could pass training."

He huffed. "And I gather you did."

"Easily." There'd been nothing easy about it, but I'd kept
my promise to myself not to balk, shirk, or flinch. "I know three
ways to kill you right now."

He gave a burst of delighted laughter and pulled a Fairbairn-
Sykes knife from his pocket, the same kind I'd trained with.

My hand shot out, stopping just short of connecting. "And
that is how I'd disarm you," I said.

"Easier said than done," he teased. "But not at all impossible. I've killed fourteen."

I tilted my head, examining him more closely, but he bore no scars on his skin or his spirit. I wasn't sure I could report my eventual tally so blithely, though I'd been schooled to accept it as a necessary cost. I looked away, up at the stars again. "And this is the most dangerous job they could give you?" I asked, comparing fourteen knife fights to this tranquil glide through the dark.

He answered with a finger pointed to the distant side of the sky. "Look. She's up."

The glowing body surfacing across the waves was too massive and golden to be the same moon I saw every night. It pulled itself higher, its crater eyes surveying the water.

"And yes, this is the most dangerous," he said tersely. "These waters are full of submarines beneath and Italian patrols above. Not to mention the planes. We survive on luck and hope no one feels too threatened by a fishing boat powered only by sail."

"You have a motor," I corrected. I'd listened to it all day carrying us at unnatural speeds for a sailboat.

He grinned and touched his lips.

I laughed silently, my speeding heart sloughing free from the cares that normally tangled around it. "Will they challenge us?"

"Time will tell." His words, and the accompanying shrug, were fatalistic. Unlike in the skies, floating here, our cover story was our only protection.

We waited, watching the submarine slumbering on the surface, shrinking as we sailed along. "I see why they chose you," he said.

"I speak French."

He shook his head. "You have nerve."

"I hope so," I said, remembering my cowardice confronting the water.

"I'm certain of it."

I smiled thanks, and we fell back into a companionable silence that made this perhaps the loveliest night I could recall. For the next hour or so, I drank the rushing air, the soft voice of the captain reciting stories of his family and their demise. Even his cold hatred of the Germans sounded poetic in the vast emptiness of the scene. The only hint of civilization was the shadowy outline of Majorca in the distance.

At two in the morning, Boo called down to his sleeping crew.

"Wake up. We're almost passing the submarine base."

One man appeared with a tattered fishing net and a sheepish grin. "Disguise," Boo explained. "Just in case."

I retreated into the hold, thick with the smell of diesel and—I grimaced—vomit from someone incompatible with the increasingly rough sea. Until now, I hadn't realized how little it was troubling me. I tried not to smile when I saw that it was Charles. He was curled up in my former corner, pale and sweating.

As I found a new seat, a loud hum rose from beneath us, coughed once, and fell silent. Boo hurried into the hold and threw open the motor hatch, his eyes large and startled.

"No noise," he instructed us in a strained, low warning. "We just lost the engine."

"At the submarine base?" I hissed, unable to keep panic from flavoring my words.

"My luck is good, except when it's catastrophic," he said philosophically. Another crewman rushed quietly to his side with a heavy bag of tools.

The cabin was too small for all of us. I crept to the deck, pressing against the cabin wall, looking for shadows to sink into despite the bright wash of moonlight. When a third crewman disappeared below, two of the other agents joined me—Charles and another one who called himself Jean.

The boat bobbed as the tinny sounds of clanking tools beat a staccato in the night. The open water carried the thin sound, and I flinched, imagining the submarines gliding beneath us, coming and going from the nearby base.

"Hell of a way in," Jean murmured next to me.

"I told them we should parachute," I muttered.

"We're bloody sitting ducks out here," Charles fretted. "If they can't get that engine working, we're done for."

"Don't scare her," Jean scolded.

"I'm not panicking," I retorted.

"True enough." Jean nodded and lapsed into quiet.

Four hours passed before the sun turned the black coffee night into a weak gray tea and then a flaming punch of burnt orange. I crept back into the hold, tucking into another corner as the crew spoke Polish and sweat beaded on their desperate brows. They repeated one word so often it either meant the wrench they were passing back and forth or a Polish curse. Either way, I liked the sound of it.

The four crew members gritted their teeth, their sentences growing shorter and sharper. Two rushed upstairs with pails and I followed to see what they were doing. They pulled out paintbrushes, rigged a pulley, lowered themselves over the side, and started slapping green and red markings over the side of the boat.

"*Wloski*," one of them tried to explain to the other passengers.

"That's means *Italian*," Charles said. "They're making us look like an Italian boat."

"How does that work when an Italian patrol stops us, and we don't speak Italian?" Jean's sarcasm was dry and scratchy in my ears.

"If they stop us, we're dead anyway. Italian markings might keep them from trying it." Charles checked his watch. "It's nearly ten o'clock. Why haven't we seen a single patrol? We've been drifting for eight hours."

And every minute, completely nerve snapping. A grinding sputter, unnaturally loud in the barren expanse of water, made us jump, followed by a cry from the cabin. I let out a breath of relief.

"Did they get it?" Charles asked, his voice rising with hope.

"We're going!" Boo cried from inside. His flushed face emerged, the hours of muttered curses and strain erased by the flash of his blue eyes. "*Vive la France.*"

"*Vive la France*," we volleyed back.

I rolled my shoulders, trying to shift off a brick load of tension. The movement helped a little, but my body felt broken. I couldn't imagine bending down to my toes without snapping, and normally I could flatten both palms on the floor.

An hour past the submarine base, Boo relaxed enough to distribute rations of rum and pickles. Charles didn't retain his, but the rest of us coped better. Still, by the following night, when the repaired motor rumbled us slowly past the sweep of Marseille's searchlights, we were hungry and tense and tetchy as arthritic cats.

On shore, the shaggy trees painted a landscape of shadows and wafted the smell of cedar and pine across the salty air. My heart thrummed in tune with the wind and relentless waves.

France.

CHAPTER 5

MARSEILLE, 10 JUNE 1942

MAX KLEINMAN WOVE THROUGH THE CROWD AT THE TRAIN station with the tired, stoop-shouldered shuffle of a man twenty years older. In truth, he was only thirty and used to wearing a gray, crisply pressed uniform, not the frayed trousers, baggy coat, and cap of a French laborer. But he knew how to make the disguise fit him and how to pass unnoticed, even in a filthy place like Marseille, a nerve center for a particularly trouble-some French terrorist group.

They called themselves CARTE, and Max's latest infor-mation, gleaned from an informant who missed his comforts (chocolate, coffee, butter), indicated they'd reached out to the British, who helped them funnel supplies and saboteurs north, into German-occupied France. Max was here to stamp out the trouble—and he'd just picked up a lead.

His quarry was twenty yards away, carrying a suitcase to the ticket window. Max had tailed the suspect from a known safe house. He'd been watching the place for a week, and last night, four people had hurried inside, shepherded by the lanky barber who kept the house.

So far, only one person had come out.

With shadowed eyes and the stiff gait that came from days of traveling, the suspect hadn't noticed him, but Max held back, joining the line three people behind. Far enough not to be noticed but still close enough to overhear:

"One way, please. The Paris express."

Max hid a smile. The occupied zone. Until now, he hadn't been sure.

It was no longer necessary to keep his target in sight. Max let his quarry proceed to the platform. He bought a matching ticket, then ducked into the men's toilets to reverse his jacket and change his cap. He knotted a dark scarf around his neck and washed his hands, drying them thoroughly. Back on the platform, he stuffed them in the pockets of his loose trousers so his manicured nails wouldn't give him away. The resistant was waiting, shifting nervously.

Max studied the posters on the station noticeboard, wishing he could have a cigarette.

When the train pulled in, he lingered on the platform, watching the resistant playing the game: walking the length of the train, biding time, waiting to choose a railcar until the last minute.

Too late. I've already found you, he thought.

The last whistle shrilled, and the resistant boarded the train with one last furtive look. A second later, Max leapt onto the car just behind. It smelled of stale smoke, armpits, and diesel. Understandably, there were plenty of seats. Max took one by the window, just in case the resistant climbed off as the train pulled away.

It was good tradecraft to change cars—to disembark and

use another ticket purchased by an ally and passed invisibly within the waiting crowd. Not that it would help. If the resistant jumped off, Max would simply proceed to the engine and radio his men waiting in a car outside the station.

But the suspect didn't even try. It was almost disappointing. He'd expected more from an agent trained by the British intelligence service, worrying about what they might do when put in charge of these disorganized, ill-equipped Frenchmen who thought it worth their lives to resist.

Well, it never paid to become overconfident. Max lit a cigarette to keep himself awake.

The journey was long, with few stops. After Lyon, Max moved up into his quarry's car, choosing a seat across the aisle and three seats behind, still unseen. His quarry was focused on the pages of a magazine, propped against a cheap cardboard suitcase, head nodding with fatigue.

Stilling anxious hands, Max watched the resistant's head droop lower and lower. Finally, surrendering to the pull of sleep, the agent stood and placed both suitcase and magazine on the overhead rack. Max hid a smile behind his hand, planning the report he would write, the arrests he would order, the train journey out of France and back to Berlin—too late to salvage his marriage but his mother would be relieved to have him close. Confined to a wheelchair after an attack of polio, she worried about Max and his younger brother, posted with the sixth army on the Russian front. In Berlin, it might be possible for Max to arrange Christof's reassignment.

The woman behind him stood up and left the car. Max glanced at the black outside the windows, at the other passengers: hats lowered, heads bowed over books or leaned back in fitful sleep. The resistant slumped against the window, eyes closed, jaw slack, draped in a dark wool coat.

This is your chance.

Max stood, stretched, then walked softly up the aisle, lifting the suitcase off the rack as he passed by. The sleeping resistant didn't stir. Max was ready to run, but flight was unnecessary. No one stopped him, no one questioned him, no one called for the porter. Max walked the length of the train, up to the first-class compartment, where he showed the scowling porter his Abwehr pass.

"This way, Oberstleutnant," the porter said. "There's an empty compartment right here."

Safe now from pursuit and scrutiny, Max rid himself of scarf and cap, and opened the case. Beneath a drab set of clothes, he found what he was looking for. And more. After a full minute of bafflement, Max leaned back and lit a cigarette. It would do for now. Later, he'd break open a bottle of champagne.

At Sens, Max disembarked and found a public telephone. He rang the number in Paris, glancing over his shoulder. The contents of this case might as well be dynamite. He couldn't afford mistakes, not like that resistant in the third-class carriage.

"Send a car," he ordered. "I'm at the Sens station. I need direct transport to HQ on Avenue Foch. You won't believe what I've found."

Even staring at the papers in his hands, he couldn't believe his luck.

"Have the police waiting to apprehend a suspicious passenger. Gare de Lyon. I'll give you a description. She'll be getting off the train from Marseille."

CHAPTER 6

———

I CHECKED AND DOUBLE CHECKED THE SIGN AT THE RAILWAY station. Tours. Pushing to my feet, I retrieved my suitcase from under the seat. The journey from the safe house in Marseille had been mostly uneventful. For five minutes, walking from the barber's home to the train station, I thought I'd picked up a tail, but I'd lost the man by cutting through a baker's shop, boarding a bus, and doubling back. I'd had to catch a later train, but it was best to be careful, so the instructors always said. At any rate, practicing my evasion skills couldn't hurt.

Riding the train from Marseille to Paris to Tours, I'd been too anxious to sleep, afraid of muttering something in English or of someone stealing my luggage, with three sets of identity papers and a fortune in counterfeit currency. I'd kept it between my feet the whole way, unwilling to risk leaving it on the luggage rack. I gripped the handle now like a lifeline and stumbled with stiff legs off the train.

With fatigue pressing palpably on my forehead, I surveyed the busy platform and blinked dry, gritty eyes, scanning for the nearest hotel. I needed to find the closest bed quickly, before I did something stupid, lost in a fog of muddled thoughts.

There.

Mesmerized by the tall white sign with red letters, I crossed the square to Hotel Chloe and fumbled through the necessary exchange with the concierge. The woman flipped through my travel permits, identity card, and bank statement while I forced myself to stand without fidgeting. If all was in order, it was thanks to Vera Atkins, not me. How on earth did she know, from her London office, how to get everything right? I readied a dozen explanations while monitoring the concierge's frown.

It was almost a shock when she folded up the papers and returned them to me with a brass key. "This way."

She showed me to the room herself. Clearly, not the Ritz.

Then again, I wouldn't have protested if she'd taken me to an unmade bed with crumbs on the sheets. As soon as the door shut behind her, I shot the bolt and flung myself down to sleep.

———

I woke with a jerk but came to myself slowly, cataloging the details of the little room. This wasn't Pimlico and the now nonexistent house on Warwick Way. Not the improvised dormitories of Garramor and Beaulieu either. I was in Tours, in a tired hotel room, drapes still open, the light outside a warm amber. From the color of the sky, this was probably evening, the golden hour. A telephone sat on the writing desk below the window. I wasn't supposed to use it until I'd been awake at least a half hour—tales of agents being captured after answering the phone or door with a groggy "Good morning" instead of *"Bonjour"* haunted me.

I made it. I smiled at the ceiling. Now I could get to work using the skills I'd spent months practicing: surveillance, fighting, laying ambushes and explosives. Yes, I had plenty of specific instructions, but they all led to one thing—Prime Minister Churchill's directive to me and to all the agents of SOE: the order to "set Europe ablaze." Though I'd read it in a memo, I felt the command as if he'd spoken it to me personally.

First things first. My precise orders were slightly different.

Upon arrival in Tours, contact your network leader, code-named GASPARD. He is in contact with us via wireless and knows to expect you during the 10–15 of August. He'll approach you within those dates, during the afternoon, in the square by St. Gatien cathedral. Use the SOAPTREE alias and wear a green scarf. GASPARD will assist you in finding a safe house and establishing a cover. Together—

I turned my head, relishing the crisp cotton beneath my cheek.

Together, we'd recruit and train an army, harassing the Germans at every turn, readying every loyal French citizen for the Allied landings that would send the Germans to hell, or at least back where they belonged. Unfortunately, I'd slept through the afternoon into the evening. I glanced at the desk calendar—August 12—and returned my gaze to the ceiling. I still had three days to make contact, but I wished I hadn't slept so long.

Well, I could get up and make a preliminary survey of my surroundings, inventory dangers, and look for targets in the local infrastructure. Unfortunately, a ferocious hunger gnawed at my middle, forcing me to kick off the covers and sit up.

The room tilted, the corners turning dark, and I braced my arms on the edge of the bed until the feeling passed. A good meal was definitely in order. Then, when I could think straight, I would begin.

Three blocks from the Hotel Chloe, I found a small brasserie with wicker tables and chairs waiting beneath an orange-and-white awning, within sight of the cathedral. Plenty of diners filled the establishment, chatting, smoking, sitting back, and sipping their drinks, but not with the easy enjoyment I remembered from years before. A cold undercurrent muted conversations and pulled down mouths, eyelids, and shoulders. A gray-haired mother glanced sideways and nudged her twentysomething daughter to be quiet as the waiter brushed by. Old men muttered in a shady corner, instead of joking and enjoying their drinks in the last hour of sunshine. Clearly, their conversation ran to more somber topics than who had thrown a lucky shot at their last game of boules—but were they grumbling about neighbors who listened to the BBC or the latest outrages from the Germans, *les Boches*?

I shivered. This wasn't a training exercise. Though I was full of grand plans, the danger here was real. Impossible to discern a collaborator from a friend with only a glance. Ignoring the strain in the faces around me, I sat down and turned my attention to the menu, grateful to duck behind the tall page.

Most of the more luscious dishes were crossed out with scratches of black ink. Only a scanty selection remained. I ordered brown bread and a bowl of vegetable soup, relieved when the waiter brought it quickly. The smell rose in spirals of steam that dispersed against my face. My mother made soup like this, swimming with carrots and cabbage and broad beans, and my usual worries for her resurfaced just like the celery leaves floating atop the broth. *Is she safe? Does she have enough to eat?* Somehow the uncertainty was worse now that I could confirm the answer in one short train ride.

After draining my small bowl and leaving my coins on the table, I ventured out, mapping the town, looking no different than the other women quietly completing their business before curfew. I found the town hall and the Gestapo headquarters, bleeding long red banners, the swastikas like targets against those scarlet fields—and they would be, once I connected with GASPARD.

———

For three days, I set out with the green silk scarf identifying myself as SOAPTREE waving around my neck. I stayed in the same hotel, ate at the same brasserie, and lingered in the square. But three days later, I remained alone, no contact from GASPARD.

Where was he? Had he been arrested? How could I possibly carry out my mission alone?

My guarded inquiries to the hotel staff garnered nothing. No way to know if they were reluctant to talk or completely ignorant of recent arrests.

For another week, I watched people when I ate and walked, but everyone kept to themselves, afraid to speak where a stranger might overhear. If I passed GASPARD or any other resistance fighters, they were camouflaged in the dreary scene of frightened citizens.

And wisely so, but how was I to find them? A bombed-out widow, like I pretended to be, couldn't afford a hotel indefinitely, and finding a room to rent wasn't difficult. I'd looked at several, and there was one in the old city, by the Church of St. Martin, with large floorboards for a hiding place and a handy fire escape. Only I'd counted on contacting GASPARD by now. This wasn't a holiday; I was here to work, but I hadn't been instructed or equipped to do it alone.

I tried to follow orders but was quickly seeing that, cut off from London, I'd have to invent some of my own.

With no other options, I took the room in the boardinghouse. The landlord, Monsieur Caye, received me warmly enough but adhered to each new Nazi decree with paranoid caution. Worse, my clothes had been refolded twice while I was out. I'd stashed all my contraband beneath a corner floorboard, but it seemed he suspected everyone, even the grieving single woman in his corner room.

I'd have to move as soon as I could without arousing suspicion.

In the meantime, I bought myself a bicycle and spent my extra hours acquainting myself with the streets of Tours and the surrounding country lanes. I bought a camera and took surreptitious photos of power stations and army installations, trusting that eventually I'd find a way to send them to London. If necessary, I would simply have to journey back to Marseille and ask the CARTE group to relay my predicament to the powers above.

"Where are you off to again?" M. Caye asked, catching me on my way out.

I smiled, lowering the handbag I'd clutched to my chest. M. Caye often caught me by surprise, appearing from nowhere, stopping me or his other tenants with a remark or two when we passed.

"Just cycling. It's too nice to stay inside."

"I've never known anyone with such a penchant for the sport as you. Do you never sit still, Jacqueline?"

"When I sit, all I do is remember," I said, not untruthfully, and the inquisitive tilt of M. Caye's eyebrows softened with sympathy. As far as he knew, my son was a prisoner of war (which gave me an excuse to visit the local Red Cross office and the town hall) and my husband had died when our house was bombed.

"Did you hear?" His eyes, half-concealed by folds, flashed unusually bright.

I shook my head. "What happened?"

"More of those idiots. They were caught trying to break into the telephone exchange with canisters of petrol. Why, I ask? Does it help to burn our own buildings? Of course they failed, but they say two of them got away, and now the mayor must give up twenty hostages to the Germans." He shook his head. "Can you imagine? How awful to have to choose between people you've known for a lifetime."

And send them to their graves, I silently finished. Though I hadn't met anyone besides M. Caye, the newspapers were instructive. For every act of sabotage—or terrorism, according to the Germans—local hostages were taken and killed in reprisal. If the local commandant was feeling merciful, they might be lucky enough to be sent to a work camp.

"It must be hard for you, seeing the lists, filled with names you know," I said, swiveling my eyes to the staircase he blocked. "I'm still a stranger here."

He nodded, his worn fingers weaving together.

I needed to find the people with the petrol.

"I might stop at the Red Cross and help make up packages this afternoon," I added, hitching up my handbag and checking my watch. "Do you want to come?" I might have better luck sounding out strangers if he was with me.

"Too busy," he said quickly. He hardly left the house, even to buy food.

As if sensing and defying my haste, he threw his eyes to the battered book protruding from the top of my bag. "Is that one any good?"

I'd bought three from a secondhand stall a week ago, excuses to sit outside waiting and watching, but the prospect of another afternoon wasting time "reading" in a public square made me want to blow up something more than ever. I huffed out an impatient sigh and hoped it passed for grief. "It's better than thinking my own thoughts. Would you like to borrow it when I finish?"

M. Caye shrugged noncommittally and shadowed me to the front door. "Your hat, madame. And...I almost forgot." The words fell clumsily from his mouth. "This came for you." Along with my brown felt hat, he passed me a postcard of a large church.

My heart jumped as I turned it over. M. Caye had read it, of course, but the message was innocuous. *Saw this church Tuesday last. You'd have liked the stained-glass windows.*

I studied the date scrawled at the top. The part no one pays attention to. *JUne 27,,*—two capital letters meant *tomorrow*, followed by two commas for *noon*.

"Anything important?" Mr. Caye leaned closer.

Contact, from someone using an SOE emergency protocol. Maybe GASPARD.

I molded my mouth into a rueful smile. "Just a message from my nephew. He considers himself something of a historian and thinks I share his hobby more than I do. But it's good to hear from him, know he's safe."

I'd have sung hallelujahs if it weren't conspicuous. Instead, I tucked both hat and card in the bicycle basket and took off, the breeze ruffling my hair, straight for the telephone exchange. I parked my bicycle and took a seat at the bus stop across the street. Besides a few bullet scars on the walls and a broken window, no signs remained of the failed attack. And why petrol? It was hard to find, heavy, and all but useless in small quantities. The conspirators either had no supply of explosives or didn't know how to use them. My lips pressed together. If I'd been with them, we could have flattened the building with a few time pencils and sticks of gelignite.

The postcard signal meant GASPARD wasn't in prison—in theory—but the clumsiness of the exchange attack showed me exactly how much work there was to do and reminded me to be wary. So far, few things in France had been as I'd expected.

———

Eleven o' clock the next morning, I arrived at the rendezvous having cycled twenty warm, long kilometers to reach the low-roofed stone buildings and narrow streets of Savonnières. I settled into yet another café directly across from the church in the postcard, my cardigan unbuttoned at the top to show my green scarf. When a wheezing bus pulled to a stop, I watched three passengers disembark: a young mother toting a baby, a man on crutches wearing a striped pullover, and an older man in a homburg and a dark overcoat.

The fellow with crutches, probably. Those were a good disguise, and M. Homburg had already hurried down a side street. I waited, sipping a cup of roasted barley that valiantly tried to pass as coffee, but the man in the stripes was soon joined by a young woman and together they left the square, leaving an unusually cheery trail of laughter behind them.

I fought the urge to drum my fingers on the tabletop. I didn't mistake the code. Before leaving London, Vera Atkins quizzed me on emergency communications protocols. I'd answered every question right—use dead-letter drops for routine communications, postcards in an emergency, with the location of the meeting in the picture and the date and time specified in the way the date and time was written on the card. A simple code, almost impossible to blunder, so by the time M. Homburg reappeared and walked nonchalantly to my table, I gave him a frown I'd learned from my perpetually disapproving mother. He removed his hat, and I recognized the black hair and heavy brows above a commanding nose and prominent ears—I'd seen this man at least twice in Tours, lingering at the newsstand nearest Saint-Gatien Cathedral, while I had sat nearby, scanning faces and pretending to read detective novels.

GASPARD.

I opened my mouth to ask him why the hell I'd cycled all the way to Savonnières, why I'd been watched from afar for over a week and left to my own devices. He hadn't been arrested. He'd been right there in Tours the whole time.

He quelled me with swiftly narrowing eyes. "Jacqueline?"

"Monsieur?" We couldn't talk business until we'd exchanged codes, so he launched into the SOAPTREE identification sequence, an idiotic exchange about a novel by Balzac. I gave my coded reply, but if he relaxed an iota, I couldn't tell. He didn't even seem glad to have found me.

"We'll walk while we talk," he said, his sentences stunted and nervous. "My name is Raymond Flower."

The coffee substitute in the sturdy brown mug in front of me was nothing wonderful, but I was loath to abandon it. "Why don't you join me, monsieur?" I suggested, but his lips tightened in such a way, I knew better than to remain in my seat. I deposited some coins on the saucer, gathered my coat and handbag, and followed him down the promenade. His long strides forced me to hop to keep up.

"We cannot meet in Tours," he informed me, a slight snarl in the way he curled his lip. "You've made yourself far too conspicuous. And as a safe house, your apartment is totally unsuitable."

Criticisms from the man who failed to contact me? "I didn't have any help," I snapped. "But I can move. I'm only renting week by week. If you can suggest a better place—"

"No, I can't. London told me you'd be able to take care of such things and that they'd supply you with your own money." He looked me over, his message clear. I'd find no help from him.

"I can and they did. But my money won't last indefinitely.

When is our next supply drop?" I asked after a careful scan of the street. No one in sight.

"I can't reveal that information."

I stopped, stunned. "But—"

"They said you'd be my courier." He hadn't stopped walking, so his muffled voice struggled to reach me. Even from the distance I caught the emphasis on the last word. Someone to run his errands.

"That's a poor description," I insisted as I sped up to catch him. "I'm trained. Fully trained. I can help with—" His sharp glare stopped me, though I knew better than to say anything indiscreet. "Plans. And I can teach the network. As long as we have supplies." I lowered my voice. "As far as I can tell, nothing's been happening. Nothing but that failed attack on the telephone exchange and—"

"That wasn't my network," Flower said.

Then what were he and his network doing? "Do you know who did it? If the Germans didn't catch all of them, we could recruit them."

He stopped. "You"—his forefinger stabbed the air between us—"are not to recruit anyone." He looked up and down the street of rowhouses before he turned into an alley of rubbish bins and reached into his overcoat for a packet of letters. "These are the messages I need delivered. You can contact me through a dead-letter drop behind 14 rue Ampère. Look low on the bricks and you'll find it."

He touched the brim of his hat.

"Wait!" Wasn't there more? Plans? Pending operations? What about setting France ablaze?

He glanced sideways, clearly impatient to be gone, but I persisted. "I want to pass a message to London. Who's our radio operator?"

He jerked his head, a sharp negative. "Too risky. You can't know that. London knows you've arrived. Anything you need to know, you'll hear through me."

"Not if you only contact me through postcards for meetings once a fortnight outside of Tours," I snapped back. Unwise but I couldn't help myself.

He bristled. "This is not a game, Jacqueline. And I'm in charge. Do what you're told, or I'm cutting you loose."

Loose? He hadn't yet brought me in!

"London gave me orders as well," I hissed in an angry whisper. "I need contacts."

Flower's black eyes glinted; his hair tossed by a stiff wind that blew the stench of garbage our way. "I have lives to protect. Anyone truly on my side would respect that."

"Your side? I've risked my life more times in the last two weeks—"

"We'll see." He cut me off with clipped words.

I clutched the letters to my chest, watching him stalk to the corner and out of sight.

CHAPTER 7

———

LONDON, 11 AUGUST 1941
ELEVEN MONTHS TO DEPARTURE

THIS WAS DESPAIR. HUDDLED BENEATH THE RUINED HOUSE with my fractured family, almost as loose and unconnected from them as I was with Alex's collection of tenants, I watched a trail of dirty water, thick with ashes, drip down the cellar wall. It pooled, morphing from wet spot to spill to puddle, thickening the smell of the extinguished fires. Extinguished like me—clammy beneath soiled clothes, feet numb from crouching, and still trembling. Even small movements ached, my muscles tender and protesting, but this was no time for complaints.

A fast series of bangs shook the door, and our pathetic bunch of mismatched people moved in unison, heads rising.

"You're safe to come out. You'll have to clear the premises. Better make it snappy."

Alex scowled. Clearing out meant the fire warden declared the house no longer safe. Home and income blown to rubble in one night.

"Mum." Jackie nudged me. "Didn't you hear? We're safe to leave."

The others shuffled forward, scraping open the door and clearing debris.

Concern in Jackie's eyes and a wary distance. An old dance we'd stepped through for decades. Ever since the car crash that had scarred her leg, she'd been wary with Alex and me, needing us but afraid to show it or trust we'd stay.

I rose with an inward sigh and stepped outside. This wasn't my street. Or my country. I tucked my face into the collar of my dressing gown but still choked on the hot brown air. Before me rose the remnants of our home—the top floor gone entirely, as if a giant had cleaved the highest blocks off a child's tower.

How did we all make it out?

Two sooty stretcher-bearers knocked into Ronald, not stopping to pardon themselves as they kicked their way through the rubble.

I stepped in a puddle as I made room for them, wincing at the red stain in the water. Brick dust, not blood, I told myself. I moved forward, compelled toward the wreckage, to salvage some remnant of my broken life.

In my room the dresser lay on the ground, its contents damp with the same ashy water coating everything in sight. I crouched and rattled the drawer of my nightstand until it shimmied loose, revealing my precious sheets of paper dry and intact. Lifting them gently, I inhaled the smell of smoke on the pages of music notes. As the all-clear sounded dismally outside the shattered window, the lonely waltz played through my mind, slow and mournful.

The music Henri had written for me.

Every beautiful woman should have her own song. This one is yours.

Mine.

In the wreckage that was my closet, I ran my fingers along the linens until they brushed the baby-skin softness of embroidered French pillowcases—the only fine things I possessed. They slid from the shelf, releasing a snowfall of plaster and dust. I tugged a small battered suitcase from the bottom of the closet and laid it open on the ruined bed, placing the waltz carefully against the bottom, where it wouldn't crease, before covering it with the pillowcases. The vacant recesses of the camel-colored luggage stared up me, judging the emptiness of my life.

There was nothing else that mattered anyway, except for— where had I put it? Scrambling back to the closet, I brushed away the plaster until a black glass eye came into view.

A sigh of relief rushed from my chest as I retrieved the threadbare lump of fur. Jackie's old teddy bear, Benny. Without another glance at the room, I tucked him into the case and closed it firmly.

"Mummy!" Jackie's screech ripped through the jagged window glass. She hadn't called me by that name or with that pleading voice in ages.

I stumbled into the street, where Jackie curled around a bedraggled bundle in her arms, tears drawing pale lines down her gray face. A plaintive cry made me suck in a breath. She lowered her arms to let me see black fur lost beneath a dusting of gray.

"Bones?" My heart lurched.

"He's burned." Jackie choked out.

A woman with a Red Cross cap appeared. "Thank God. I thought you had a baby," she said with relief I couldn't share.

"Best to end its pain. There's a vet putting down injured animals next street over."

Ronald swore as he looked away from the charred cat, one eye unable to open. "I'll go with you."

Desperate, numb, it didn't take us long to find the miserable queue; neighbors held whining dogs and barely conscious cats as they stoically shuffled forward, their faces frozen in grim acceptance. One man held a green budgie, stroking its head as he cradled it in a soiled handkerchief, quieting its frantic attempts to escape.

I turned away, watching the parade of ambulances wailing on their way to hospital. Was it self-indulgent to stand here together, while others worked desperately to save the people who'd lived on our street? I only knew that this pathetic collection of brokenhearted Londoners waiting to kill their mangled pets undid me more than the incendiary bombs. People understood what was happening and why. My pitifully mewling Bones did not.

When we reached the front of the line, a haggard, sweating man reached for Bones with a filled syringe. He took one cursory look, said, "I'm so sorry," and he slipped the needle into Bones's burned leg. Before Jackie could ask a question, his needle was withdrawn, refilled, and he was on to the trembling bulldog behind us.

"Is he—" Jackie asked.

"All done, love," another man answered. "I can take him for you."

Jackie turned to Ronald, who enveloped her in his empty arms. He bent his head, murmuring comforts. I stood apart, with nothing to fill me: no home, no loving looks, not even, at the close of each day, the companionship of my cat.

I looked away. Jackie and Ronald didn't need me to help them do whatever they needed to do. Already they were quietly conferring about hotels, work schedules, train timetables.

I patted Jackie's shoulder. "Call me when you're settled."

She nodded absently, and I set off down the street, the need to do something so heavy in my chest I hardly found room for breath. I hurried to the nearest debris pile and began picking up broken bricks next to a man in the Home Guards.

"Oh, no, ma'am. Please get back. It's not safe for you." His gaze swept through me to the rubble behind, as if my grit-encrusted body was one with our blighted surroundings.

"I have to do something," I gasped.

He straightened, reading something in my shattered expression that demanded…exactly what, I didn't want to speculate. "Come along," he said kindly, looping an arm around my shoulders. "Things aren't so bad yet that we need to recruit little ladies like yourself. I'll get you to the shelter. There's a tea canteen."

He left me there with a score of others under the nursemaid-like guardianship of a uniformed girl. Holding a steaming white mug in my hand, I watched him go, wishing I could go with him, even at the risk of being burned or buried beneath the sliding rubble.

———

Four months later, with Christmas looming, I still had little more than my almost-empty suitcase. Alex had found me a place to stay, and I'd found myself a job, after being turned down by the FANYs, WRNS, the Women's Land Army, and the ATS—any military organization that might pay me.

Working as a hotel receptionist kept me fed, housed, and clothed, but nothing else. It didn't help. I spent my wages as quickly as I earned them, not trusting the world or myself enough to look beyond the next days and weeks. But today at least was Friday, and Jackie would be expecting my call. I fumbled in my pocketbook and stepped up to the phone box across the street from Chelsea Barracks, not far from my job at the Ebury Court Hotel.

"You don't mind?" A young man stepped in front of me, a soldier in uniform with a pleading smile. "It's an emergency."

I nodded and he darted in front of me into the telephone box. Shifting my tired feet, I turned my attention to the passersby on the street, hurrying home before blackout.

"Hi, doll." The soldier drawled into the telephone receiver, loud enough to carry past me and down the street. "You coming dancing tonight?"

I pressed my lips together and blocked out his voice, but when he placed a second call, using almost the same words, I stepped forward and rapped on the glass. "Nice emergency, Tommy. I've waited for this telephone ten minutes already."

"Find another one, then." He turned away, giving me his shoulder.

The room where I was staying was little more than an enclosed porch and had nothing as convenient as a telephone. I stepped around the box, back into his line of sight, and glanced conspicuously at my watch. Tapping my foot, I held my ground for ten minutes, until he finally rang off for the last time and loped away.

"Tosser!" I shouted after him, but he didn't look back.

Tamping my thrumming frustration, I placed my call. As it rang, another soldier exited the barracks and took up position outside my box. My huff joined the alarm-like ring in my ear. He'd have to wait.

The call connected with a click. "Mill House," announced a clipped, cheerful voice.

"Hello, Mrs. Bunhill," I said. "This is Jackie's mother, Yvonne."

"Oh, I'm sorry, dear. She's not in. You know they keep those girls busy in the ATS."

I did. Jackie was in a hurry every time I called, driving fuel to airfields and shuttling pilots. Last time we spoke, she'd closed with, "I'm fine, Mum. Stop fussing."

I couldn't convince Jackie to confess her worries to me, but—"How is my Jackie?" I asked her landlady.

Mrs. Bunhill's voice softened a degree. "As well as ever, Yvonne. She'll be sorry she missed you."

Rote words that didn't ring entirely true.

"She's hale and happy and a favorite with the other girls," Mrs. Bunhill continued. "Shall I tell her you phoned?"

"No, no. Thank you." I didn't want to *fuss*. "Please promise you won't. It will only annoy her."

I studied the receiver, then hung up and slipped past the impatient soldier. It had been over a fortnight since anyone called or wrote me, and I couldn't convince myself that was only because so many were shiftless, struggling to keep up with the work of living. My reception work kept me busy enough during the days, but the off-hours were silent, interminable voids. I didn't even own a radio. Nothing about my improvised, empty room called me home.

A walk then, even if it was only a walk to nowhere.

The Thames nestled in the hollows beyond the street, swirling in the growing darkness, more heard than seen except for pale reflections of a misshapen moon obscured by half-hearted clouds. A familiar silhouette beckoned in the distance—the Chelsea Bridge. I steered my feet to its sturdy, rough-edged outline, my shoulders rounding under the weight of nothingness, the unrelenting load of bleak and worsening tomorrows. I paused near the middle of the bridge, leaned my elbows against the wall, gathering strength and peering into the silken darkness below.

I hated water, especially rivers.

I shuddered in the quiet air, eyes closed. When I opened them again, nothing of interest presented itself. Limestone. Rusted trestles. The perpetual coat of grime on the walls of the embankment.

I rubbed my tired eyes, whispering French to someone loved and long gone—my papa, who died when I was twelve. Not by drowning, though I blamed the Seine for killing him.

None of it turned out as we hoped, Papa. I peered down at the colorless water, my hand pressed against the frantic butterflies swarming my stomach.

Breathe. Pull the air into my nose—the cold, stale smell of fish and mildew—release over my lips, chin quivering. Too much work in exchange for so little. *It's all right,* I told myself, *to just decide to stop.*

The rail bit into my stomach as I leaned over. No one in sight but a solitary man on a boat, the colors of the sunset bleak and passionless in the distance. And on my left, footsteps— another evening walker.

With tense shoulders, I straightened and set my gaze to the water so I needn't make eye contact. Digging in my pocket, I retrieved a cigarette. Not yet blackout hour and always the perfect excuse.

"Mrs. Rudellat?"

I dropped the match. The man added something in cultured syllables, but I was busy beating my hands against my skirt, fearing I'd burned a hole through it.

"I'm so sorry for startling you." He held out a lighter.

Noting his civilian clothes, I relaxed and dipped my head, holding the end of my cigarette to the wavering flame. No uniform meant he wasn't a bearer of bad news. Tired bags under his eyes and a soft mouth gave him a sympathetic look.

"I'm Captain Jepson." He smiled apologetically. "I'm afraid I followed you. I'd hoped to catch you at work, but they said you were gone for the day. The other receptionist did tell me though that you usually walk this way. I spotted you at the phone box. Lucky for me or I'd never have caught up with you."

My eyes sharpened into slits, but my curiosity flamed. I folded my arms. "Well, you found me."

"Yes. And forgive me. I hate to spring at you if this is a bad time." His eyes crinkled with concern. They were kind but sharp and evaluating, the sort of eyes I avoided. "Are you all right? Forgive me, but you look rather down."

I drew my arms tighter. "Who's not down these days?"

"Indeed," he said. "As a matter of fact, that's why I've come. Your name was recommended to me for a job. War work. I'm hoping you'll be interested." He held out a card.

I took it without thinking, my stunned brain belatedly catching the words. *War work.* I glanced down at the card.

Captain Selwyn Jepson, it read, with an address in neat black letters, one I recognized. I'd visited three times, applying to work with every war department I knew of—and some I didn't.

"Your people said they didn't want me."

His smile emerged again. "This is for very different work. And you are uniquely qualified. Would you like to know more? You could be a great help."

I nodded, wondering if he saw how hungry I was for it. Normally, I was better at keeping things in, but he'd caught me off guard, uncomfortably exposed without my usual defenses: a light laugh, a quick smile, a silly story.

"Come to my office tomorrow," he said. "Ten o' clock."

CHAPTER 8

———

I ROSE UP ONTO MY BICYCLE PEDALS, PUMPING UP THE LAST rise of the hill, lungs and legs burning, sweat pooling between my shoulder blades and sticking to both layers of my clothes. "Damn you, Jepson," I muttered, timing each syllable with a pedal stroke. "And damn this wool underwear." The day felt cool when I set out, but I hadn't expected so many hills. Though I was better at getting up them now than when I started working as a courier two months ago.

I'd put the thick ugly knickers Jepson had chosen despite my complaints to good use by securing my messages beneath the elasticized cuffs that came halfway down my thighs. The road—rutted, dry—curved as it rose, disappearing coyly behind thickly clustered trees, their yellowing leaves waving cheerily. Breathing hard, I forced myself up, counting each turn of the pedals. Not much farther. I'd rest at the top, then coast downhill to the farmstead where a man and his wife waited for Raymond Flower's message. I paused at the crest, moving aside for an ancient lorry to bump past.

Resting by the road awhile, I let the sweat dry on my back. Before the crispness in the air began nibbling at my fingers,

I mounted my bike again and sailed down the hill, my heart speeding as the tires bounced along the ruts and the rocks strewn among the gravel.

Humming under my breath, I swerved off the road onto the narrow track marked by a sign for *Ferme de Flamencourt*, the Flamencourts' farm. The buildings sagged, in need of new lumber and paint. I leaned into the curve as the drive turned sharply toward the front of a faded but neatly kept house. I was halfway off my bike, singing out a greeting, when I saw the motorcycle parked almost out of sight between house and barn.

I retreated three steps, but a spate of roughly accented French stopped me. I froze, torn between hiding and approaching beneath a veneer of false calm. Too late. A skinny boy in uniform balancing two loaves of bread and some paper-wrapped parcels shouldered though the door. He spied me and flinched, his hand jumping to his sidearm as a cheese fell to the porch and rolled down the stairs into the dirt.

"Who are you?" he demanded.

"A friend of madame's," I said in the coolest voice I could muster. I showed my hands and stepped backward until his shoulders unknotted and lowered. "I brought her a book. Marguerite? Are you all right?"

The soldier flushed as a shapely woman with blond curls and brown leather high heels appeared in the open door.

"Where is Edouard?" I'd heard enough stories to know what might happen to a woman alone.

"Inside. Helping this gentleman's friend with more parcels."

I nodded, grateful I'd memorized their names. But M. and Mme. Flamencourt didn't know mine, and though they were expecting a courier, they hadn't known exactly when, and I couldn't have picked a worse time. Mme. Flamencourt's hands, hovering above her chest, betrayed fear, and while a visit from pilfering Germans ought to explain some of that, I didn't want her to panic or the Germans to grow curious. Raiding French homes was common but only occasionally dangerous.

"I suppose you want to see my papers," I said to the soldier, wearily pulling out my card and the book I'd brought. "I'm Jacqueline Viallat." I scooped up the cheese he'd dropped and placed it on top of the other packages. With his hands occupied, I held out my carte d'identité. "We share books. I've got the one I promised you, Marguerite."

Frowning, he pushed the food into Mme. Flamencourt's hands and snatched my papers.

He was young, with an upper lip flecked with pale-gold fuzz. Sent to collect food for the officers, most likely. He shifted his feet and tried to look stern. "Everything seems in order," he said.

"Thank you." I turned to Mme. Flamencourt, moving half a pace away from the German. "May I help?" I gestured at the parcels.

"No, we're nearly done, I think." A second soldier, similarly laden, appeared in the doorway. The young man frowned, his teeth clenched in embarrassment as he backed away. Somewhere once, his mother had taught him not to steal. Seconds later, the motorcycle gunned to life and roared away down the drive.

Mme. Flamencourt sagged with relief.

"That was unlucky timing," I said. "But no harm done, I think." I tilted my head at her. "Do you like detective novels?"

"That's Edouard's department," she said, pointing at the man just coming through the door. She loosened a little, her voice pitched to carry to me and no farther. "Come inside and have a drink."

Over glasses of homemade wine, I unpicked their story. Their teenage daughter was missing, gone south to fight with the maquis, and the last news of their son, not even in his twenties, placed him in a German prisoner-of-war camp.

"We fight because there is no one else," Marguerite said, shrugging.

"We *want* to fight," Edouard corrected. "We've done nothing but hide refugees yet."

I held out the sealed message. "Flower has orders for you."

His face stiffened as he read, and he finished by tossing the letter aside. "Watch and wait." His breath escaped in a puff of exasperation. "Always the same!"

I shouldn't have cracked a smile—it wasn't called for and might be misinterpreted, but I couldn't help it. I was always thinking the same. I gauged the urgent creases on their faces, weighing risks, too impatient to consider them for long.

"We could do something." Even without supplies, it was dangerous. Wire cutters and a saw weren't efficient ways to cause damage, but—"Do Germans often use this road?"

Marguerite nodded. "They come this way to the airfields. It's a quieter road. We see the lorries. Sometimes small parties like the one you saw come and steal from us. They used to come in packs. Now they send the scrawny ones alone to rob us into starvation."

"What kind of tools and equipment do you have?" By now, I was desperate enough to use petrol if I had nothing else.

The Flamencourts shared a glance.

"You can trust me," I said. "They sent me to help. From London. Even if all we have are basic tools, I know how to—"

"What's your code name?" Edouard said.

"Soaptree." I gave the first sentence of the bit about Balzac, my stomach soaring when Marguerite, astonished, began the patterned response.

I leaned forward. "Who told you that?"

"Flower," Edouard stammered. "He wanted Marguerite to contact a new agent months ago, but at the last minute, he changed his mind."

"The agent—is that you?"

I told myself not to mind that Marguerite looked so disbelieving. "I'm Soaptree. But call me Jacqueline. Just wait and see what the three of us can do. Your tools?" I prompted again.

Marguerite relaxed a fraction, even as her brow wrinkled. "But—Flower didn't tell you?"

I glanced at them both, reluctant to admit Flower only saw fit to send me biking about with messages, usually just to dead drops.

Edouard leaned forward. "We have supplies here." He licked his lips nervously. "Guns. Ammunition. Explosives."

"They've been here for months," Marguerite whispered. "Every time the Germans come, my heart nearly explodes."

I pressed my hands to my knees to still them. My skin prickled with excitement. They'd trusted me so far, but... "Show me."

———

I laid a cylinder of a common plastic explosive, 808, wires, and a detonator on the Flamencourts' kitchen table. "This is all we need." Though they had more, a saboteur's treasure trove, in their hidden cellar. "With this, we can bring down a power line or blow up a lorry." And Flower said to watch and wait. I almost snorted.

Edouard was too stunned to reply, but Marguerite gestured helplessly. "We can't possibly. We don't know—"

I fought to slow down, to be patient with their self-doubt. I'd felt the same often enough. But now I was giddy, electrified by the ready supply of ammunition and explosives. "It's easy enough. I'll teach you."

Their lack of response told me they needed to learn more than how to use the matériel in their cellar. No one had taught them to be bold—unsurprising, with Flower as their leader. "You want to fight," I reminded them. "We've waited too long already. We'll begin right now."

"Now?" Edouard looked like he might choke.

I nodded, sure with each passing second that this was the right decision. France needed people with courage and determination. Edouard had felt both moments ago—now was the time to show him how to deploy them.

"Are you certain you know what you're doing?"

He wanted more reassurance than that, but I couldn't promise they'd be safe. No one could, so it wasn't worth saying. I knew my orders, and I knew how desperately I wanted to succeed. I needed the Flamencourts and their supplies. "Edouard," I said patiently. "I'm a demolitions expert."

"Forgive me, but you don't look like one," he admitted.

"I expect in a few months, people will say that about you," I told him. "But by then, Edouard, both you and Marguerite will be. Come on."

—————

I explained what we would do over and over, but they weren't persuaded. They didn't trust me enough yet, I realized. Fair enough. "You don't have to come with me," I said. "Just give me a time pencil and a single cylinder of 808." Both small enough to fit in my pocket. "I can bring it down by myself."

And they would see that they could do the same, every day of the week, in between visits to town, to see neighbors, on the way to the bank. The start of dozens of tiny fires that would have the Germans not knowing where to look next.

They'll demand more hostages. I glanced at Edouard and Marguerite, wondering if they were contemplating the same thing.

"All right," Edouard said.

I stuffed the materials in my pockets before they changed their minds. "You could hide these in the middle of a loaf of bread, in a hollow book—almost anything," I told them. "For me, today, this is good enough."

"Be careful," Marguerite told me, her fingers tight on the pearl necklace at her throat.

"Of course," I promised. "In an hour, cycle toward the airfields. By then, you'll see what I've done. Call me tomorrow. We can plan our next action then." Hopefully, my example would strengthen, not destroy their resolve.

Edouard passed me a pencil and I wrote M. Caye's number on the flyleaf of the detective novel I'd brought. I passed it to Marguerite, grinning at them both. "My landlord isn't friendly, so ask for me and say it's about the book. And let me know what you think of the story."

At the end of the Flamencourts' drive, I turned westward, farther away from Tours, too excited to regret the extra kilometers. Twenty-five minutes down the road, I found an ideal place, far from any buildings, the road running through thick woods. I hopped off my bicycle and propped it against a tree that leaned over the road. Once felled, it would stop anyone traveling to and from the German airfields.

It took less than a minute to lay the 808 and set the time pencil; then I was pedaling home, glancing frequently at my watch.

I'd given myself ten minutes, but time pencils weren't exact; nine minutes after I'd left, I heard the explosion, like a firework from far away.

CHAPTER 9

———

MAX ENJOYED JAZZ, THOUGH IT HAD LONG BEEN BRANDED "degenerate art," and this Paris club had a particularly good band. Beside them onstage, a gorgeous woman with an even lovelier voice launched into another hit song. Recognizing the melody, Max nodded along.

You're the tops, you're a German flyer
You're the tops, you're machine-gun fire

"So what's next for you?" the man at his elbow, a junior officer named Richard, asked. He was a former policeman from Alsace who shared Max's office. Max liked him, though other officers questioned whether he was German enough.

"Hopefully a few more days in Paris," Max said. Even after another round of arrests there, he'd rather not travel again to Marseille, which was still hot and stinking, even in October. Nor did he enjoy the headaches of dealing with the Vichy government, nominally French but subordinate to Berlin. Not every police officer and government functionary there understood that, and Max had little talent for diplomacy. Wrangling concessions that should have been understood slowed him down, besides being downright infuriating. Although he'd jailed half a dozen terrorists on this last trip, the three he wanted to question were in still in French hands, in a French prison where, so far as he could see, no one did anything whatsoever. The fact that these three had assisted in the landing of British agents was even more frustrating. Though he wasn't proud of the water baths and thumbscrews his colleagues used to extract information, collecting the names and descriptions of these British spies before they could inflict real damage was vital.

Four had entered the safe house that night—three men and one woman—yet somehow they'd escaped unseen. They could be anywhere by now, and Max, unlike some, was not reassured by their apparent lack of action. They were up to something, even it wasn't obvious yet.

Max set down his glass and signed to the bartender for another French 75. In spite of these difficulties, the information from the stolen briefcase had helped him dismantle another network of underground hostage couriers—so no more Jews, Allied pilots, or escaped prisoners of war would be funneling from that particular house to Spain and Gibraltar.

"You'll receive another commendation, surely," Richard said.

"That was mentioned," Max admitted with a smile. But no transfer to Berlin. As he reached for his new drink, his mother's latest unanswered letter nudged from within his breast pocket. She'd be disappointed he wasn't coming home.

"Congratulations," Richard said.

Max took a sip of champagne, gin, sugar, and lemon, a kick

he felt down to his toes. "You'll have your own by the end of the month," he promised. If they tracked down those agents.

Since he fully intended to do just that, Max couldn't complain about remaining in France—the occupied portion at least. Acts of resistance were down, thanks to the intelligence he'd gathered and widespread reprisals. For now, it would be foolish to ask for reassignment, with his career flourishing. Better to return after he'd climbed another rung or two up the ladder.

Exasperations aside, this chase was too exciting to miss.

CHAPTER 10

———

Two days after felling the tree with my first explosion, I pedaled the same road, my legs pistoning, racing the dusk.

Marguerite and Edouard waited at our meeting place, a sharp bend of the road about three miles from their farm, bordered by thick towering shrubs. A thin brown-haired woman wearing knee-high boots, a man's button-up shirt, and well-cut trousers crouched beside them. "This is Souris," Marguerite said.

The nickname, Mouse, was one of my favorite French words, as soft and playful as the animal it described. *Soo-ree.* And it seemed strangely appropriate for a woman who at first glance betrayed intelligence in her sharp black eyes but made no sound. I liked the look of her, dressed like Marlene Dietrich but lacking the film-star face. More importantly, her presence proved Marguerite and Edouard trusted me, not only with their lives but with the lives of their friends. A humbling realization, that.

"I haven't worked directly with the British before," Souris said coolly, like I was twenty years younger, interviewing for a job as her personal secretary. She wore her confidence as casually as her man's shirt. Someone else might have been put off by it, but after my weeks at Garramor and Beaulieu, convincing instructors I wouldn't lose my head or my nerve, I understood.

"Souris hides downed pilots," Edouard explained. "And works with us to get them across the demarcation line, out of occupied France."

Souris acknowledged this with a barely visible nod. "But that's not enough to stop the Germans. Marguerite and Edouard tell me you are the person we need. *La meillure.*"

The best. Her eyes flicked at me then, just a shade uncertain.

"And so I am," I said just as coolly. "I didn't fight my way here just to run messages."

I wished Flower were here, listening.

"Souris offered to help me keep watch," Marguerite explained. "That way there will be two of us. You'll be less likely to miss the signal."

Hardly any chance of that.

I couldn't help grinning at the shrewd woman. She'd come to see the new agent.

Any vehicle would need to slow down to negotiate this curve in the road, and though the track wasn't well used, we couldn't risk detonating the explosives at the sound of the first engine. It might easily be carrying French civilians. Marguerite—and Souris now—would watch farther up the road and warn us of the Germans' approach with three bursts from a battery-powered torch.

Hopefully we had enough time for Edouard and me to lay the explosives in the hollow we'd dug earlier, cover it with dirt, and race back to the ditch before any Germans approached. The moment the first lorry crossed over the bomb, I'd activate the switch. Then we'd run like blazes.

That was the plan at any rate.

It would work brilliantly for a single German lorry, but a convoy posed problems. Even if we succeeded in destroying the first vehicle, there'd be no damage to those following. Within seconds German soldiers would fan out, hunting for culprits. We'd have only a moment's head start. Better to set the bomb off remotely from a safe distance but impossible due to other complications: unpredictable variations in the lorry's speed or size. This action required eyes on the target, a last-minute scramble, and a long wire to trigger the blast from the ditch.

"Do you have a hat?" I asked Souris after scrutinizing Marguerite's nondescript clothing and the dark scarf tied over her bouncy blond hair. Passing Germans would be unlikely to recognize or remember her in the aftermath. I wasn't willing to bet the same for Souris. "If we pull this off, you don't want to be identified. Someone in the convoy might remember you were in the vicinity."

"They won't see me. I'm a hunter." As she spoke, she shrugged into a men's gray overcoat and reached for the rifle resting beside her. I'd thought it belonged to Edouard, but she handled the weapon with a fondness and familiarity that made my mistake clear. I suppose I shouldn't have been surprised.

"Good." I glanced at Marguerite. "I brought two pistols. Do you want one?"

She shook her head. "I won't be any good with it." Despite the shadows, I caught the way she gritted her teeth, biting down on her resolve to keep it from fleeing.

"Next week I'll teach you," I promised and offered the gun to her husband instead. He took it with the right degree of respect but more uncertainty than I liked. He probably had only a nodding acquaintance with handguns, but tonight that would have to do. We needed to stay close to detonate the charges, and if Edouard and I ended up in a shoot-out against the Germans, there wasn't much hope we'd escape. We'd take some down with us, though. More importantly, they wouldn't take us alive. Souris and Marguerite, whose chances of escape were better farther away from the blast, could claim ignorance of the operation afterward, so long as we weren't in prison saying otherwise. Edouard kept the gun pointed skyward, his eyes distant, as if seeing the same shoot-out scene I'd imagined. In spite of his desire to fight, until now, he'd only stored illegal equipment.

I squared my shoulders, calculating the distances from the road, the signal sight, our escape route. I'd set charges like this half a dozen times before and practiced with dummy explosives until I could wire them in my sleep. But tonight, with armed Germans drawing nearer every minute, and Souris, Marguerite, and Edouard trusting me to lead them, the seriousness of what I was about to do tightened like a noose at my throat. This time counted. Praying for luck, I inwardly promised to make no mistakes. "Hide the bikes here, and let's go."

Edouard nodded and reached into his knapsack for the bundle of explosives as Souris and Marguerite stashed the bikes in the brush and slipped away in the dark.

I'd wired this bomb two days ago, using it as an opportunity to teach the craft to the Flamencourts, but I checked the connections now, staying low in the ditch as Edouard kept vigil and held the torch. The tall grass grazed my face, and I jerked when something skittered over my arm.

"Everything looks fine." I carried the tightly wired 808 cylinders to the hollow we'd deepened just shy of the center of the road. Nerves stiffened my usually agile fingers as I attached the detonator, unspooling the wire behind me as I made my way back to the ditch and then into the tree line. Edouard covered the evidence as best he could by smoothing the dirt back into place with the back of his spade before joining me.

"We'll give these Boches some sausages for supper," he said grimly as he adjusted himself behind a rough-barked tree.

"They call sausages *bangers* in England," I told him. "These will certainly do that."

He grunted a laugh, a comforting rumble in my ear.

I frowned as I studied our work from a distance. It was impossible to make the marred road look perfectly natural—the surrounding dirt was hard-packed and weathered from years of passing tires and seasons. In the dusky light I couldn't see anything overtly suspicious, but when passing headlights swept their white glare over the disturbed spot… Hopefully our target would approach too fast to notice anything unusual. This was a routine run for them. They might only be carrying stores, but with any luck at all, we'd destroy a load of weapons, fuel, or ammunition.

"Now the tricky part," I told Edouard as I edged out of our hiding spot back to the side of the road. He followed, clutching his gun. "We need to stand here, watch and wait, and try like anything not to miss Souris's signal." A second of inattention would bring all our work to nothing. The sound of an approaching vehicle would warn us, but without the signal, there was no way to know if it was Germans coming or a French farmer with a load of chickens or milk.

I stared so hard into the gathering dark my eyes watered.

A lorry rumbled toward us. I tensed, ready to bound into the woods like a deer, but no lights flashed from the bend. I riveted my eyes on the distant undergrowth where Souris was waiting. Still nothing. At the last second, we retreated to hide out of sight in the bushes.

The lorry bounced past, and I tensed as the wheels steered perilously close to the charge of 808. Beside me Edouard let out a breath. "That's Louis," Edouard mumbled. "He's a bricklayer. Lost his son last year."

"That's why this charge is wired," I whispered hoarsely on a sigh of relief. "And why we use watchers." And why I wasn't trusting Edouard with the detonator yet. Even after months of practice, I was too jumpy to fully trust myself, and tonight, I couldn't make mistakes. Lives like Louis's depended on it.

I blocked my unsteady breath in my throat and sent it through my lips in a smoothly murmured mantra. *I am here. I am enough.*

The dust settled and the dark thickened. The night birds stopped singing. In this blackness flashlight signals would announce our presence like a neon sign, beacons in the dark alerting the Germans. Edouard consulted his watch again. "They're late," he said.

Or maybe not coming. We'd laid our trap based on what the Flamencourts had seen week by week, but schedules changed. Any number of things might cause a delay. "Keep watching," I said, caressing the detonator in my hand. Still no light winking from the trees.

Edouard shifted his feet and unleashed a thin rambling

whistle, some aimless tune I didn't recognize. I kept silent, though the melody made my eyes want to wander more than ever—if only to shush him with a glance.

"There," I whispered. It was so dark, I caught a distant flicker—Marguerite—before another, nearer, flash through the trees. Edouard and I retreated behind the thickest trunks and lowered ourselves to the shadows. The headlights swept around the curve and cut two bobbing circles of light through the dark road.

"There's two of 'em," Edouard whispered as a second pair of headlights followed.

Perfect. Six or seven lorries with German soldiers would be too many for us to evade, but if each lorry had only two soldiers and two were incapacitated—it all rushed through my mind in the seconds as I lined up the distance, estimated the time left, accounted for the trigger delay.

Steady.

The explosion came a breath later than I expected, a brilliant blossoming flame, bucking the back of the first vehicle into the air, and blowing one tire far out of sight.

"It worked," Edouard whispered.

"Yes. Let's hurry." I pulled him by the arm, detaching him from the ground. We raced uphill. Looking back was an unaffordable luxury, though I burned to know how much damage we'd done, what kind of cargo we'd destroyed or delayed—more importantly, how many soldiers now pursued us.

German shouts thundered behind, followed by a spatter of bullets covering the sound of our racing feet. But the shots were a wide, untargeted spray, ricocheting in the far distance. Another closer volley and Edouard inhaled sharply.

"Quickly," he panted, but I was keeping pace with him, so the command was likely for himself. I had no time and no right to reassure him. We clambered over a fence, fought through a tangle of scrub, and raced across an open field, sprinting for the copse that held our bicycles as the shots and the shouts faded. They were tending their injured or guarding the cargo instead of searching for us.

We didn't slow or stop until we made it to the bicycles and threw off the branches covering them. Souris's and Marguerite's were gone already. A trail of dark liquid dripped down Edouard's handlebar as he rolled his bike to the nearby road.

"What happened?" Had he torn his hand in the woods? There were sometimes stray remnants of barbed wire.

"Think one of 'em got me," he murmured through clenched teeth. "Not serious."

I bit my lip. No choice but to take his word for it. The ride home was complicated now. If we were stopped on the road, in the dark, after curfew, right after an explosion, Edouard's bullet wound proved our guilt.

I pulled the scarf off my head and handed it to him. "Wrap it. Quick."

The sound of an approaching vehicle rumbled through our chests, made our eyes mirror pictures of panic. "Off the road," he said as we both yanked our bikes back into the woods, leaving them and retreating for thicker cover. A motorcycle and sidecar roared past, the riders easily identifiable as Germans by their helmeted silhouettes.

"Through the wood. We'll walk. Follow me." Edouard led the way through the disorienting forest until it thinned near his home. The light inside told us Souris and Marguerite had made it safely. "Thank God," he whispered.

We opened the back door into the kitchen.

"Did it work? We heard the explosion," Souris asked just before Marguerite caught sight of the bloody scarf.

"What happened?" she cried.

"We hit the target. Didn't wait around to see results. One of the soldiers started firing." Edouard lifted his wet red hand, and I got my first glimpse of the wound, a graze from a nearly spent bullet or a ricochet from a tree trunk or a stony bit of ground. It had cut through the side of his hand just below the little finger, taking a semicircle of flesh with it. I smiled weakly—the blood making my head float up off my shoulders and hover in the vicinity of the ceiling—and silently told myself what we were all thinking: *A hand is much better than a heart.*

Marguerite covered her mouth, but Souris advanced. "We need to wash it and have a story in case the Germans show up," she said. "Too bad it's so visible. You'll have to wear gloves as much as you can until it heals completely."

As she thrust his hand under the faucet, the blood multiplied, running rivers along the white sink. "Do you have any bandages?" she asked Marguerite.

"Yes. Iodine too," Marguerite said, hurrying away on unsteady feet.

Edouard cursed enthusiastically when Souris poured disinfectant into the wound, but only her wrinkled brow betrayed sympathy. Calmly, she packed a roll of gauze into the missing flesh. "All the way through the fat and muscle. It didn't break any bones, but it will take weeks to close without sutures."

"I can't wear gloves everywhere, every day," Edouard said. "Might as well just admit I have something to hide."

My eyes flew around the kitchen until I caught sight of a long rasp for sharpening knives, just the right size.

"Hold his hand over this," I directed, bloodying the tool, as well as a short fat knife. "If anyone comes tonight say you were sharpening the knife and it slipped. You gouged your hand on the rasp. The blood on the tools should convince them."

Edouard gave a short laugh. "I won't have any trouble convincing them it hurts like hell."

Souris lifted the bandage for a quick look. "It's too clean. The rasp would have shredded the edges."

"You think they'll examine it that closely?" I asked, my eyes narrowed.

"No. But whatever doctor we take him to will. They all know a bullet wound from a mile away. It's too dangerous."

"There must be a friendly physician," I pushed.

"One, too far away to reach tonight. But I have daughters who know their way around a needle and thread." She gave Edouard a tight smile. "You're not the first one we've patched. Those pilots aren't downed because they ran out of petrol."

Edouard grimaced. "Your Moune is going to sew me up?"

"The sooner the better. I wish we could go now but it's too dangerous." Another lorry sped down the road just outside the house. "We'll stay here and use the knife accident as cover if anyone shows up to question us. If they don't, we hunker down and go early in the morning. We'll keep it as clean as we can until we can close it."

She pulled his hand above his head and held it there as we

watched the gauze slowly change color, red advancing across white, no matter how many times we changed the bandages. After an hour, no one had stopped at the house and no more vehicles had passed. Souris decreed another fresh dressing was in order.

"The bleeding hasn't stopped," I said, peering over Souris's shoulder at the fresh blood still seeping from the deep wound. Edouard looked away, grimacing as Souris wrapped it tight and tied another knot.

"It needs stitching. We'd better leave now," Souris announced as she rolled up the unused gauze. "We'll take the back way to my estate and avoid the roads. Jacqueline can come with us. It's on her way back to Tours."

Estate? There were, I knew, several châteaux nearby. Souris must be referring to one of them. I looked her over again—her man's shirt stained with blood and her slacks wrinkled from crouching in the woods and on the Flamencourts' kitchen floor. But her damaged clothes were beautifully cut, the fabric thick and soft. I'd noticed their fineness but hadn't interpreted it correctly—or correctly enough.

"You said it's too dangerous to go out," Marguerite objected.

"Nothing's happening now except Edouard soaking through all the clean linen in the house," Souris said. "But just in case, you stay here. If the Boches come, tell them about the knife and say Edouard came to my house to ask for more bandages because he was too stubborn to go to the doctor."

Marguerite sucked in a breath. Traipsing through the woods after curfew or having the Germans find her alone in a blood-soaked kitchen? I didn't envy her choice.

"If anyone questions you, send them straight to Nanteuil to verify your story. It will all check out."

Silence, as Edouard and Marguerite weighed their options. Marguerite spoke first. "Souris is right. It needs stitching. Go. I'll be fine until you come back."

Edouard nodded, but this time when they separated, he left a kiss on Marguerite's lips—swift, natural, almost too brief to see, but not something I'd seen him do before. He opened the door slowly, listening intently before leading Souris and me out.

CHAPTER 11

———

LONDON, 12 DECEMBER 1941
SEVEN MONTHS TO DEPARTURE

AT TEN MINUTES TO TEN, I PUSHED THROUGH THE USUAL MOB in Trafalgar Square and the barriers of precisely stacked sandbags, repeating Captain Selwyn Jepson's words: *You are uniquely qualified… You could be a great help.*

I glanced at my piecemeal reflection in a grid-taped glass window, trying to convince myself he could be right. The utter ordinariness of the woman looking back defeated me. *You? Help this disaster?* her frown said.

I straightened my skirt and propelled myself inside—the new sign over the revolving door of what once was a posh hotel said simply War Office.

Too bad I didn't have real stockings. Leg makeup just wasn't the same.

The lift, creaky as an old woman's knees, chugged up to the second floor. I squeezed my fingers, wringing out the tension, then forced myself to be poised and still. When I emerged from the elevator, Jepson was there, waiting.

I resisted the instinct to check my watch. I wasn't known for punctuality—which drove Alex mad—but today I wasn't late.

"Madame Rudellat. Good to see you again." He stepped forward, taking my hand in a firm grip. "My office is this way."

He led me into a bleak room with hardly any real furniture, only a metal filing cabinet and some chairs. The desk was a trestle table covered with a gray army blanket.

"My colleague, Colonel Buckmaster." Jepson motioned at a man seated in the corner.

He stood and offered his hand with a perfunctory smile that, a moment later, resettled in a grim frown. "Thank you for coming today." Words as bland as porridge from a face with eyes that didn't blink.

"My pleasure." Ignoring my speeding heart, I sank into the offered chair.

Jepson took one behind the desk. "On your FANY application, you indicated you speak French."

"I am French," I said.

"Where were you born?"

"Just outside of Paris. Maisons-Lafitte."

"I've been told by friends who've stayed at Ebury Court where you work, that you speak frequently of your desire to help the war effort. And France."

My lungs swelled, suddenly elastic and filling to capacity, light and easy. I hadn't felt this way in ages. *Careful, Yvonne. Not too eager.* I crossed my ankles and pressed my shoes to the floor to still my restless feet.

"You heard correctly."

"What of your family? I'm afraid the work entails relocating, but I think the chambermaid said you live alone?"

Those keen eyes. He must have watched me for some time.

Even collected information from my fellow employees at the Ebury Court Hotel. "The only one who might have noticed my absence was the cat, and the Boches murdered him in the bombings." I smoothed my skirt, trying to make the words come off lightly. "I'm free to go where I please."

Jepson tilted his head, studying me, while Buckmaster's full lips curved into a deeper frown.

"As I said, there are…" Jepson paused. "Unique opportunities for those of French language and birth. If you'd be willing—"

I leaned forward. "I'm willing."

"You don't know what we're asking," he countered. "This isn't serving sandwiches at the village hall or working shifts in a factory."

"Good," I replied.

Jepson scanned my face, his own grave and focused. "I am speaking of duties behind enemy lines, where there is no one to help you if things turn dire."

An icy thrum ran under my skin, pushing up gooseflesh. I nodded, afraid they'd mistake a quaver in my voice for fear instead of the heady thrill of excitement.

"Mrs. Ru—" Buckmaster began.

"It's Madame," I corrected. "Madame Rudellat."

Buckmaster hesitated, assessing. "Your desire to help is very brave, Madame Rudellat." His accent, like Jepson's, was impeccable—but cold. "We may have some work for you but can make no promises. Our requirements are very specific." He smiled thinly. "You have already passed our security check, and your answers tally with our information on all points. But I cannot overstate the danger of what we're suggesting."

Jepson cleared his throat. "In fact, we have not considered women for this line of work before." He glanced sideways at Buckmaster, who deliberately folded his arms.

"And the idea hasn't been approved yet."

I sputtered, stymied by my own eagerness. "I'm willing to face danger. I told you, I have no one to be careful for."

"Indeed," Buckmaster said dryly. "Well, let's not get ahead of ourselves. Your service is your own choice and fully voluntary, but if the department is to make a reasonable decision, we must first see if female candidates have the necessary skills."

"To be seriously considered," Jepson put in, "you are required to pass training."

I nodded.

"It will be arduous and exhausting. You will need to learn Morse, to swim, to live in conditions of extreme hardship— perhaps spending days without food and warmth, sleeping on bare boards or even the ground."

Swim? I kept my hands still. "I'll do it. I care nothing for comforts." *Liar.*

"I don't think you fully comprehend," Buckmaster said. "There is danger even in training."

"That changes nothing for me." I smoothed my skirts again, frightened by the pounding of my heart.

"You should take some time to consider," Jepson said.

"I don't need time to consider," I insisted, meeting their eyes levelly. "You want me to join the resistance in France." I knew I ought to continue, grave and sensible, but a smile tugged at my mouth. "I can do it. I want to do it more than I want anything else. And I'm not afraid to parachute."

Jepson coughed. The blighter actually reached for his hand-kerchief to conceal his laugh.

"That is how you send them, isn't it?" I demanded.

"Forgive me," Jepson said. "A woman of your spirit and determination is just what we need. But in your case, jumping from planes will not be necessary."

CHAPTER 12

———

"I've never been to Scotland." But I certainly liked the views. Mountains and sea, sky and heather, and a handsome Scot to complete the picture. His name was Gavin Maxwell, and he'd introduced himself as Garramor's chief instructor. With windblown hair, a commanding nose, and the breadth of shoulder beneath his knitted jumper, he looked like a mountaineer from a magazine.

I wondered if he'd killed any people. If he had, I wasn't going to let it spoil my first day.

"It's a rugged place." Maxwell looked me up and down again, as if surprised so little eye movement was required. "And I'm to train you." He shook his head and blew out a cloud of smoke. "At least you've only the one case."

We weren't off to the best start. Some communications error had him thinking I'd come a day early. I tried a disarming smile. "I didn't expect my arrival to pose so many challenges, but I suppose it's just as well. There will be women here after me." *So long as I don't fail.*

Maxwell grunted. "We've only the one bathroom."

I peered up at the gray stone walls and steep slate roof. "Where I'm going, I don't think we'll have all the modern conveniences."

He barked a laugh that sounded like a knife being sharpened. "Probably not at that. Come on, then."

He led me down the grass alongside the house, past the untrimmed, shaggy flower beds. Walking below an open upstairs window, a sharp, bitter scent made me wince. "One bathroom will be sufficient," I observed. "Your other pupils have been pissing out this window. I won't be doing any of that."

He took a drag from his cigarette. "You expect a little more decorum, hmm?"

"Not in the least, Mr. Maxwell. I'd use the window too if I could, but someone would have to hold on to me, so I don't fall out—no doubt a terrible inconvenience."

"Terrible indeed," he said, holding back a laugh. "But we don't teach decorum or convenience here, Mrs. Rudellat."

"Yvonne," I corrected. "And I'm counting on it."

"Actually, that name won't work either," Maxwell said. "We don't use real names here. You won't need your own for a good long while." He consulted the letter from London I'd presented on arrival, still clutched in his free hand. "Orders are from now on, you'll be known as Clotilde Viallat."

Clotilde? "That's a name for a black-garbed widow with thick ankles and a basket of knitting!" I'd never learn to answer naturally to Clotilde, but if anyone called my daughter's name I'd turn instantly, on reflex. "I'd like my given name to be Jacqueline."

He regarded me as smoke looped between us.

"Well then, Jacqueline, how did the powers in London dig you up?" His arms folded across his chest.

I shrugged. "I'd like to know myself. I speak French. When I came for the interview, I thought they'd offer me a job translating." Or typing.

"And what did they tell you?"

"I know what I'm in for," I said. "Do you ask the men that?"

"I do," Maxwell returned evenly. "And if I don't like their answers, I don't want them here. No matter how hardy they are. You—"

I resisted the urge to snap at him, wanting to make a good impression. Jepson had offered me the purpose I needed, but everyone else, from Buckmaster to Gavin Maxwell, thought I couldn't do this. "I want to help," I said tightly. "France is my country."

"Not for more than twenty years."

I glanced up, surprised.

"They have people who check," he told me. "I have a whole report. So don't think you can keep things from me, Jacqueline." He leaned on the alias heavily.

I bit down on my lip. Impossible to confess the truth. That I was made specifically for this mission because I was lonely and desperate and determined enough to throw caution completely to the winds. I'd waited fifteen years for a new life, and this was it. I suspected, though, that these weren't on the list of approved reasons. "I need to help," I insisted. "I know the training will be hard, but I'll surprise you."

He took another pull on the cigarette and exhaled a thick stream of smoke. "I certainly hope so."

———

Maxwell took my case and left me in the hall, but I soon grew bored studying the faded seascapes on the wall. Had he forgotten about me? Or was he busy in all the opening and closing of doors and general bumping about happening on the upper floor?

I smoothed my hair and ventured up the wooden stairs to the upstairs corridor, lined with a threadbare runner, where two shirtless men loaded down with cases almost knocked into me.

"Sorry, princess," one of them muttered.

The other vanished into one of the rooms, reappearing in a shirt.

I frowned at the pile of luggage blocking the hall. "What's all this about?"

The two men hemmed and hawed, but before a scowling third could enlighten me, Maxwell appeared and explained.

"They're clearing out to give you a room."

There were more heads now, peering into the corridor, men leaning against doorjambs in fatigues, in wrinkled shirts, in underwear. Though this house was large, it wasn't large enough for this many. Easy to see, from the men's expressions, who was being displaced.

"This one?" Without waiting for an answer, I walked into the room where the luggage had come from. It must have been nice once—charming paper and a lovely view from the two windows—but it was crammed with four iron bedsteads and one remaining trunk.

I shook my head. The other trainees had little reason

to like me already. If four of them ended up sleeping on the floor… "This is ridiculous," I said. "No need to rearrange on my account. I'll manage elsewhere."

"There aren't any other beds, Jacqueline." Maxwell cleared his throat. "You should have your own room."

"We'll find something. Show me around."

He shrugged, agreeing because my challenge amused him. Several of the other trainees came along, probably expecting me to back down. I hoped my determination didn't result in me sleeping in a tent or a cupboard.

Maxwell was right—with so many rooms given over to instruction, there was no space left. The tent was seeming more and more inevitable.

"And here's the library," Maxwell said.

"What about here?" I pointed at the couch.

Maxwell scanned the room. "There's no doors."

"Hang a sheet if you must," I suggested.

"People are often coming for books," Maxwell warned. "It's a special collection. Focused on spy craft."

"I'll change in the bathroom," I said. "And they can have their books…if they can get past me."

The men snickered at my bravado. Maxwell just ignored it. "See about bringing a pillow and some sheets for our new trainee."

"Yes, sir." But the man paused on the threshold, turning back to me. "I'm Gerald. Welcome to Garramor, Jacqueline. SOE training center and one-star hotel. You know what SOE stands for, right?"

"Special Operations Executive? That's what I was told."

"Stately 'omes of England," three of them answered in weary chorus.

Gerald wasn't finished. "*Stately* means poorly heated, with unreliable electricity..." He glanced at his companions with a faint suggestion of a smile. "And too many ghosts."

Ghosts? I filed this away for later, unwilling to take the offered bait. "When do they give me a gun?"

"Not yet," Maxwell said, unamused. "Start by unpacking. Then join us in the mess hall."

―――――

By the time I returned downstairs and found the dining room, everyone was already seated, eating as if their lives depended on it. Gerald had saved me a chair. "We get better rations than civvies," he told me. "Eat up. You look like you need it."

I glanced at the table. No salad. The only vegetables nestled in a stewpot between hunks of lamb. I took my time unfolding my napkin and sipping water while I debated. In the past five years, I'd only occasionally tasted fish, never any other meat, but I told myself war wasn't the time to insist on a special menu. Maxwell saw me as an inconvenience already. If I wanted to go to France, I'd have to learn to eat whatever was available.

By the time I drained the last of my beer, half the men had left the table. Though the others had all finished, they lingered, talking, some of them fixed on a worn deck of cards. I didn't recognize the game, and no one had invited me in any case.

"Tired?" Gerald asked.

I nodded, smiling guiltily.

"If you head up now, I expect you'll be able to wash without a wait."

"How long do I have before the crowd comes?" After a day of travel, I longed for a bath, but that was hardly fair. A sponge at the sink was all anyone could have if we all wanted a turn before midnight.

"Brown and Dubois will probably talk some of the others into a late-night swim. I wouldn't worry about taking too much hot water," he said with a conspiring smile.

Hot water. Magical words. I pushed my plate away and rose from the table. "Carpe diem—or carpe hot water taps, I suppose." Grinning thanks, I hurried from the room.

"Wait, Jacqueline—"

I turned, just in time to see Gerald thunk another man's head. Whatever he'd been about to say, the blow appeared to change his mind. His cheeks flamed, and he stammered, "Pipes here are noisy. Don't mind 'em."

I lingered at the door, suspicious of the aborted warning, but they all turned back to their conversation and cards. I wanted my share of the hot water, and the only alternative to Garramor's plumbing was a freezing swim. I'd take a chance on the noisy pipes.

I turned for the back stairs I'd seen some of the men using earlier—unlit but with just enough light seeping in from the window on the upstairs landing to navigate. If I'd mapped the house correctly, it was the shortest way to the library.

I plodded up to the second landing—and screamed as the ground tilted beneath my feet. Pitching wildly, I reached for the wall—a bomb? This far north? A white shape, round and heavy, hurtled from the shadows and I screeched again, raising hands to ward off the blow, but it caught me on the shoulder, shoving me back, off the landing into nothingness, tumbling down half a flight of stairs.

Heart thudding, I picked myself up.

Not a bomb, I realized, but it took a dozen repetitions before sense regained hold. A booby trap. The trick panel in the floor was wildly askew, revealing hidden springs, and a lumpy canvas bag with a childishly drawn face, complete with toothbrush mustache, traced arcs in the empty air, just where my head and shoulder had been. My bottom, elbow, and shoulder ached from the fall, but those were trifles next to the rage licking up from my belly into my lungs.

I shoved the dummy Hitler with enough force to smash him into the wall, then marched back downstairs and barreled through the door—right into a crowd of chortling, snickering idiots.

I pressed my lips together and drew a deep breath. Much as I wanted to, I couldn't shove them. "That wasn't funny."

Gerald smirked.

I looked away.

"You aren't hurt?" This from the one who'd tried to warn me. From his guilty expression, you'd think I was made of glass.

So instead of shouting, I snorted. "I was bombed three months ago. Of course I'm not hurt; you morons almost gave me a heart attack."

The snickers stopped. "Sorry, Jacqueline," someone muttered. "Wasn't us."

"It's the instructors who rig 'em."

"Any more of these booby traps I should know about?" I demanded, as if making a list for the market.

"*We* had to find them the hard way," Gerald told me, the challenge written in his eyes.

"Then it's only fair I do the same." I wheeled around. "Enjoy your swim, fellows."

I stalked off, refusing to limp, and collected my things before I shut myself in the bathroom. The old chipped tub was easily big enough for three, but the hot water held out only until it reached halfway up my hips. I didn't feel the least guilty for taking every drop of it and scooted down onto my back, the water lapping against my stomach, my hair floating in waves around my face.

Next time I discovered a trap, I'd be damned before I screamed.

CHAPTER 13

————

I BLINKED AWAKE, PUZZLED BY THE UNFAMILIAR WINDOW. Tall tapestry curtains let in a green and strangely quiet light. I turned my head, surprised by the softness of the pillow and the floral paper making a garden of the opposite wall. Without the grinding gear sounds of the early morning bus and the smell of M. Caye's last dinner (always vegetable soup), I couldn't place myself. I stretched up and ran my fingers through my hair. When my gaze fell on the borrowed nightie, I remembered: our carefully executed explosion, the burning lorry, flying bullets, and two hurried flights through the woods thanks to Edouard's injured hand. He'd needed stitching, so we came here, to Souris's home, an honest-to-goodness château. And Souris, as it turned out, was an honest-to-goodness countess.

I had better get up and check on my new friends.

I slid out of the strange bed and found the nearest bathroom, where I washed and dressed before exploring my way to the room assigned for serving breakfast. Souris had shown me last night. She was already there, dressed for riding, drinking coffee beside her husband and her daughter Moune. I wrinkled my nose. I didn't like to be last to anything.

My eyes continued their scan, and I started, trying to hide it by reaching for an empty chair. A stranger sat at the table: a small man, thin, with dark, neatly combed hair above round shiny spectacles. He sported a horrible toothbrush mustache that made him look like a genial Hitler who worked at a library. I kept my eyes on him, my lips tight. No uniform but such a straight back only came through military service. A German government worker? I lowered myself cautiously onto the edge of my seat.

"Good morning, Jacqueline." Moune, the daughter I'd seen last night, but not really met—she'd set to work on Edouard the moment we'd arrived—smiled over her coffee cup, either not worried by the man or an excellent actress.

"Pierre is a resistant," Souris explained quickly. "We are safe with him. Pierre, this is the lady I was telling you about."

I stilled a twitch and an instinctive look over my shoulder. She, Marguerite, and Edouard trusted me last night; it was my turn to trust them, so I reached forward, holding out my hand. "Jacqueline."

"Pierre Culioli." A long, shallow dimple appeared for an instant when he gave me a cursory smile, but his face fell instantly back into grim watchfulness. He was equally wary of me. I liked that.

Miss Cox, the family's English nursery governess, who'd introduced herself to me simply as Nanny, nudged the marmalade close to my china plate. "You may have missed this," she murmured in a mishmash of Anglo French.

"Thank you. I've never cared for it," I said. "Margarine, if there is any, and coffee."

Moune quickly supplied both, and the coffee was real. "Where did you get this?" I asked, reverently inhaling the steam. "We still have some in reserve," the count said, smiling. "From better times. We bring it out for special occasions." He raised his cup, silently toasting his wife and me in turn. "Pierre is from the French infantry," the count continued. "He escaped from prison camp and heard that we helped people on the run."

"I have papers now, so I'm not in hiding. And I haven't given up fighting the Germans. It's why I contacted Raymond Flower," the little man—Pierre—said. "But his *network*"—he used the English word, revealing contempt or perhaps his knowledge of Raymond's true nationality—"isn't worthy of the name. He's done no *work* at all."

"That's why I asked you to come this morning," Souris said. "Tell him about your work last night, Jacqueline." Something in her manner made me think she wanted me to impress him.

I hesitated.

"Pierre is a trusted friend," the count put in.

Still, I toyed with my fork, deliberating. This man seemed to know Flower. He was friends with Souris. "Come over here," I said.

Ignoring the stares from the rest of the table, I motioned him with me to the fireplace, beneath a pair of mounted antlers. "Do you read Balzac?"

The tightness in my chest eased when he gave the code words. He could still be a double agent, but at least I knew he was, in fact, a member of Flower's group. I gave the required response.

"Nice to meet you," he said with a smile, and we returned to our seats.

"All of us need to be careful," I said. "Keep your circle small and always use code words."

The count nodded. "Of course. I should have thought of that."

"Now will you tell him what you did?" Souris asked.

"What we did," I corrected, picking up my toast. Between bites, I explained. "It was a relatively small operation. Nuisance level but with impact. We used some of Flower's supplies to destroy an enemy vehicle. Unfortunately, there was no opportunity to determine the cargo or number of casualties." As I spoke, Pierre grew grim, but he nodded tacit approval. "My priority, naturally, is safeguarding resistants so we can make more attacks. The operation itself was relatively simple. The key is repeating it as often and in as many places as we can—bleed the Germans from a thousand tiny cuts."

"And much more effective than your friends' attempt," Souris put in.

I raised my eyebrows.

"A few weeks ago. A failed attack at a telephone exchange," Pierre admitted tersely.

My skin buzzed, my muscles as tense as a gambler watching a roulette wheel. I wanted this man. I wanted Souris and her family and the Flamencourts.

Don't get careless, Jacqueline.

"It's a shame you didn't have proper explosives," I said. "If you'd had grenades—you must have trained with them in the army—it would have come off better. But still, in my mind, not as good as a package of 808."

He studied me. Everyone at the table, even Souris, who struck me as hard to impress, eyed me with respect.

"Grenades would have helped," Pierre admitted. "Firearms are no good, even if we had them—plenty of us know how to use them, but we're outmanned and outgunned everywhere. I never learned to use sabotage explosives."

I nodded. "We have to depend on Flower and his wireless operator." For now at least. But he didn't trust me with either.

"I like Marcel," Pierre said.

I stared innocently into my coffee cup to avoid betraying my sharpening interest. *He knew the radio operator.* With Flower cutting me out, I had no way of contacting London, but if Pierre could connect me with the British agent, I could transmit my own reports. I had my own requests—and complaints—to make.

"Flower will not be pleased when he hears of the explosion," the count said.

"I'm not worried about pleasing him, Berbert," Souris said. She took a sip of coffee. "These thousand cuts you speak of— could it be done with the matériel at Marguerite and Edouard's?"

"Code names, remember?" I said, glancing from her to Edouard, but he waved my objection aside.

"Pierre already knows my family and me well."

I suppose it was unavoidable that existing networks had sprung from personal connections. It was hard to change old habits but important.

"Can it be done?" Souris repeated before I could embark on another scold.

"Yes."

"Is it difficult?" Moune's eyes sparkled.

"Is it dangerous?" Nanny asked through a downturned mouth. Moune was only sixteen.

I took another bite of toast. A decision, thick as a gathering storm cloud, hovered over us. I hoped none of us would have cause to regret it. This was, after all, exactly what I'd come for.

In spite of Raymond Flower, I could do some real damage with the help of everyone at this table. They knew the danger and were still listening.

"Dangerous if you don't know what you are doing," I said. "But not difficult. Not at all."

CHAPTER 14

———

RAYMOND FLOWER CHECKED THE CLOCK ABOVE HIS KITCHEN table and clenched his teeth. *Late.* Despite that, he stopped in the bathroom for another antacid tablet, downing it in a fizzing gulp that made his tongue curl. He washed his hands and dried them thoroughly on his threadbare towel, not once but four laborious times. With a sigh, he pulled his hat low and stepped outside with his chin sunk in his collar.

Last night, some fool had blown up a German lorry without consulting him, an act of sabotage impossible without demolitions training and explosives. And his courier, Jacqueline Viallat, had passed tantalizingly near the ambush site just days before.

The messages he'd tasked her to deliver to Edouard and Marguerite Flamencourt were meant to assuage them more than anything else. And to keep Jacqueline busy, away from him. He hadn't ordered anyone to *do* anything. His orders were, emphatically, to wait for reinforcements from London. Right now, they were too exposed, too vulnerable. He needed to be ready for a drop of cash, supplies, and another two agents within a fortnight. There was no point stirring up a hornet's nest before then.

And now they were in the thick of it, thanks to Jacqueline. Warily, he burrowed past the door of the seedy basement bar, looking for his radio operator, Marcel Clech.

Clech, hunched in a far corner, barely visible through the drifting, stale smoke, brushed the side of his nose with his thumb—a sign to Raymond he'd examined the building and ensured a clear emergency exit. With one foot, Clech pushed the neighboring chair out from his table.

Flower acknowledged the invitation with a nod but went to the bar first and ordered a soixante-quinze. As the bartender mixed his cocktail, Raymond made his own assessment of the room: crowded but not distressingly so, with a good level of noise to bury his and Marcel's conversation.

He carried his drink to the table.

"I need you to get a message out to the parents," Flower said without preamble. Code for London.

"They'll be pleased to hear about the upset on the road to the airfield," Marcel said. "Kudos to us and all that." Even in French, Marcel couldn't divorce himself from his university slang. Raymond considered it excessively irritating and an unnecessary security risk, but in other respects Clech was a fine officer. He could transmit and receive Morse at over thirty words a minute and was unusually scrupulous with his selection of transmission sites, a defensive strategy Raymond heartily supported.

"Wasn't us. At least wasn't supposed to be."

Marcel's eyebrows vaulted upward, emphasizing his sharp widow's peak. "Then who?"

Raymond gave the room another once-over—no one close

enough to hear their tight-lipped conversation. "It's the woman they gave us. She went rogue."

Marcel's full cheeks widened with a smile. "Jacqueline? The little one you had me watch? She pulled it off alone?"

"I doubt it," Flower sniffed and sipped his drink. "Must have dragged in some of my contacts." He knew better than to mention Edouard and Marguerite Flamencourts' names. "Now they can expose us all."

"Well, she got clean away, and the Germans will have to waste soldiers guarding that solitary road now. Good distraction."

Raymond slammed his almost-empty glass onto the table, causing a smattering of men at the bar to look over, so he waited a moment before picking up the hanging thread. "She's a fool and a nuisance, Marcel. I want her out. Send word that they can have her back. I won't be responsible for her."

Marcel's smile retreated. "She's done well in my eyes."

"Then get your eyes checked." Impossible to raise his voice here. He settled for a cold glare. "Send the message. That's an order." He looked over to the bar. The walls of the room compressed, smaller than when he'd entered. It was the same everywhere—the trees, the sky, all persistently inching closer. Even his ribs—he hadn't managed a full breath in months. He needed out of this oppressive, smoky hole. "It's for your good too," he mumbled to Marcel.

Forcing measured steps, he escaped outside, glancing both ways for signs of Germans or French traitors. A man stood smoking in the darkness between streetlamps and Raymond crossed the road where he could keep him in sight as he retreated home.

That stupid woman—her name left a sour taste in his mouth—had no concept of discretion or danger. It was fine for her to get herself killed, but she wouldn't cost him his network, especially when the success of the upcoming drop depended wholly on remaining hidden.

CHAPTER 15

TYPEWRITER KEYS CLATTERED, PAPERS FLEW IN AND OUT OF manila folders, and heads dropped, sheltered in work or low-toned conversations with a telephone receiver. No one dared be caught relaxed or unoccupied, not with Major Boemelberg plowing past rows of desks like an ocean squall.

Max, waiting outside Boemelberg's office, considered him the most self-important, pigheaded man he knew, not excluding the intransigent Vichy officials who still stood like roadblocks between him and the Marseille terrorists he wanted to question. But form must be observed. As Boemelberg strode past, Max clicked his bootheels and offered the straight-arm salute, then followed and shut the door. Though tempted to shout, it was more important they were not overheard. "I have just spoken to General Hochmeister," Max began.

"Yes, yes. And the report from Petit Aunay?" Boemelberg asked.

"One lorry destroyed by unknown terrorists. A second vehicle sustained minor damage. Two men killed."

"Regrettable, most regrettable. But surely, in the vast theater of war, this is a minor concern." Boemelberg smiled, an expression that always put Max on the defensive.

"We lost a vital cargo of fighter plane parts. General Hochmeister says more than a dozen of his planes are grounded indefinitely. He demands to know what we intend do about it."

Boemelberg sorted through the papers on his desk, unperturbed. "Tell the local mayor to give up twenty hostages. No work camps this time. Shoot them in the town square where everyone can see."

A typical response. Max understood the value of reprisals as a tactic, but Boemelberg hadn't been on the receiving end of Hochmeister's phone call.

Max's shoulders bunched. "With respect, Major, I believe we can do more. Without fighter escorts, the Luftwaffe cannot deploy their full strength in the bombing campaign against Britain. Nothing is more important than—"

"I decide what is most important here, Lieutenant."

"Yes, Major." Max stood a little straighter, though it cut against the grain. "May I ask why we have not deployed more of the intelligence I collected? Or pushed our Vichy colleagues to give us the prisoners from Marseille? This unfortunate attack might have been prevented."

Boemelberg looked up. Scowled. Before the war, he'd been a professional policeman, just not the kind who walked a beat. Not like Max, who'd worked his way up the ranks, spending months at a time undercover. Boemelberg was too fine for work like that, padding his pockets, waist, and ego as a German delegate to Interpol.

"We can break these networks," Max went on. "We have

the names." Pages and pages of them, neatly transcribed in a lined notebook and trusted to that idiot courier he'd robbed on the Marseille-Paris express.

"None of the names on your list are within two hundred miles of that explosion," Boemelberg said. "That whole region has been admirably quiet until now. This attack may not be linked to your suspects—and that is what they are until we have more intelligence, Max. Suspects."

True, this could have been the work of unknown terrorists, but… "Where do average citizens get plastic explosives? They must be connected to a network with Allied backing. If they aren't known suspects, they will be linked to them. That list of contacts is the best place to start looking."

And terrorists could take trains just as well as the next person. Someone from the CARTE group could have come north.

Boemelberg returned his attention to his desk. "This wasn't the work of CARTE."

Max reined in his temper. "CARTE's people will know who they are. No matter how tenuous, there is always some connection." There had to be, to smuggle explosives, guns, downed pilots, and refugees the length and breadth of France.

"Precisely," Boemelberg snapped, stunning Max, but only momentarily. "No, I'm not giving you leave to begin wholesale arrests. Not yet. CARTE is useful to us and doing no real harm."

"Until now, they have only had loose links to the British. This attack, which almost certainly relied on British-trained demolition experts and matériel, indicates that—"

Boemelberg snorted. "You're overreacting Max. These are amateurs. They can't do any serious harm."

"General Hochmeister begs to differ."

Boemelberg set down his pen, exactly parallel to the edge of a sealed folder. Not even the telephones outside were audible through the heavy oak door. Max kept his face still, though his heart chugged faster, gathering speed.

"These networks are more useful to me where they are, Max."

"I beg your pardon, sir?"

"You aren't thinking. We could discover who did this if we arrested the people on that list and pressed them for names, but they are not harming us, not really. In the grand scheme, this is no more than an inconvenience. I want these terrorists confident. That way, when the Allies plan their invasion, these little mice will know. They will plan and make ready—and that is when I will close the trap. I can't conduct policy around one load of airplane parts."

"If not for a last-minute change, it would have been a troop transport," Max reminded him. "And what if the leaders at CARTE guess we stole their information? The longer we sit on it, the less useful it will be."

"That would be a concern, but contrary to your belief, you are not the only agent who's busy. Six of the persons listed now work for me. Apparently, the leaders of the CARTE circuit have accepted the loss of that suitcase as an unlucky theft. Do you know why, Max? Because I didn't immediately send out our men to arrest all of them. Bags go missing on trains, after all.

"I've allowed the arrest of one or two cells to keep Berlin happy, but these terrorists are no real risk to us. They are our window into the planning conferences of Churchill and Roosevelt." Boemelberg folded his hands. "And so my mandate to you and to every officer will only be observe and infiltrate.

And we wait. I want to know where and when and how the enemy invasion is coming. You want to shake the apples loose now, but this tree has so much more to give."

It's too much of a gamble, Max wanted to say, but Boemelberg's glare precluded any criticism. They exchanged stony glances until Max said, "Forgive me, Major. I didn't know."

"I didn't wish to tell you," Boemelberg said. "Unfortunately..." He opened the sealed report on his desk and pushed it a few inches forward. "I discovered this."

Blood rushed from Max's head to his feet. *His memo.* "It's only a draft, sir. I never sent it." He never should have committed his criticisms of Boemelberg to paper. "I was frustrated. I didn't understand."

"So I see." Boemelberg closed the folder and shut it in the drawer of his desk. "Is it all clear now?"

"Yes, sir."

"Good. Because now that I have confided in you—a matter of highest secrecy—should my plan fail or my double agents be discovered, I'll have to make you responsible. It happens, you know. Leaked information from bitter, disaffected subordinates." He smiled, took out a key, locked the desk drawer, and returned the key to his pocket. "Is that also clear?"

There wasn't a curse expressive enough for the turmoil in Max's head, but experience had taught him how to retreat. Though it chafed, for now he must appear to salute and submit until he saw a better chance. "I understand perfectly, Major."

In this business, sometimes you went further taking initiative where no one could see. And only he knew exactly what he did undercover.

CHAPTER 16

———

I LEFT SOURIS'S HOME BUOYED BY OUR SUCCESSFUL EXPLOSION, by Edouard's safely stitched hand, by the new contact between Souris, Pierre, and me. Soon, I'd locate the wireless operator, and that would change everything.

But there was a postcard waiting for me when I returned to Tours, an angrily scrawled summons from Flower.

"From that nephew of yours?" M. Caye popped out of the pantry before I managed to escape to my room.

"Probably. I've had no time to look at it yet." *Unlike you.*

"I think he delivered it himself. A tall man with dark hair. He was annoyed to have missed you. I let him wait in your room." Caye slowed his words, studying my eyes as if searching for clues.

"Why is the card here, then?"

If Caye felt the sting in my question, he ignored it. "I brought it down after he left. I didn't want you to miss it, and you always check the mail basket on the sideboard when you come in."

"That's very kind of you." The edge in my voice said other-wise—if he had the subtlety to hear. He didn't. "If anyone comes by again, I'd rather not have them waiting in my room. I might have left stockings on the chair or underthings on the bed."

I would have, in London, but I was always tidy now, except for the markers I'd learned to leave on purpose—papers at carefully "random" angles, hairs trapped between my closed drawers.

"Oh, I made sure it was presentable," M. Caye said. "But I'll remember next time. I figured, since he was the right age and had brought you another postcard...that was him, right? Tall, with"—he waved his hand by the side of his head— "prominent ears?"

"And annoyed at waiting?" I forced a carefree grin. "That's him."

"He's lucky to have avoided the call-ups to German factories," M. Caye said. A true observation, but I didn't like the way Caye's eyes hung on me, like fishhooks digging beneath my skin.

"He had polio," I said. "But if things go on as they are, I'm sure they'll use him eventually."

M. Caye shook his head and rearranged his face into an unconvincing expression of pity. I stuffed the card into my skirt pocket, but before I could wish him a good afternoon and be free of him, he said, "You didn't come home last night."

"Flat tire. I stayed over at a friend's house and had it mended this morning. We collected these." I passed him Marguerite Flamencourt's mushrooms. "Good with tonight's soup, I think. You still have some onions?"

His face softened into a smile, his questions forgotten as he turned the brown heads reverently in his hands. "I do. Herbs too, and a little cabernet." He smelled one, closing his eyes as if imagining them fried with bacon fat or butter. He'd have to settle for margarine and perhaps some dry sausage.

"We'll have a fine supper tonight, then." I smiled back, feigning enthusiasm. "Don't let Madame Bouchierre eat all of it."

His other boarder liked to take more than her share. I left Caye still considering recipes and stole upstairs. A quick glance at the postcard told me I had only an hour left until our meeting time.

My room appeared untouched at first glance, but Flower—or possibly Caye, considering his curiosity—had disturbed every marker: mattress lifted, hairbrush taken apart and reassembled, even my underthings refolded. My fury didn't reach full pitch until I opened the second drawer and discovered an ugly lump misshaping my spare pullover. I reached for it and met the cold metal and rough grip of a pistol.

With tight lips and furiously trembling hands, I unloaded the bullets, dropped the gun into a rubber boot, and hid it in the cistern of the toilet. This wasn't an accident. Flower meant for Caye to discover it and betray me to the Germans. He wasn't careless. He was dangerous.

"A sleeve?" I demanded as I took a seat next to Flower on the bus stop bench. I used the Beaulieu code word for the pistol. Guns were sleeves, a play off the word *arms*. Explosives were cats. Parachute drops were lanterns.

Raymond Flower flinched, and a hot rush of satisfaction flooded me—he'd not heard me approach.

"Jacqueline." He glanced at a waiter setting up tables across the quiet street and a shopkeeper unwinding his faded green awnings. Nearly fifty yards away, both of them, and too busy to mind us, but Flower glared at them as if they wore the long black leather coats favored by the Gestapo.

I forced his attention to the issue at hand, the unwelcome parcel I'd discovered in my room. "You left a sleeve in my drawer where Caye could find it. Do you want us all exposed?"

"Don't lecture me about exposure." His black mustache leaked a sheen of oil onto his upper lip. "Not after the stunt you just pulled."

"It came off all right," I asserted. "But I don't like your present. Think I might give it back." I trained my eye on the robin's-egg blue of the sky above the zigzag rooflines of Place Plumereau.

He blanched, moving his hand deeper into his coat. A knife? A gun? It was unwise to be conspicuous with either. I tensed anyway, just in case.

Face pinched with frustration, Flower snapped, "I left it because you'll need it next week."

A poor excuse, but my heart jumped. "A lantern?" I asked to make sure. Supply drops only worked on nights with a full moon. Training habits kept me mindful of changes in the sky— the prime nights were coming. I'd been growing antsy, wondering if nothing was planned or if Flower didn't trust me enough to include me. "I can help. Just tell me where and when."

He gave a harassed nod. Clearly, he felt he had no choice. "I have reservations about the location."

"We only get so many chances," I reminded him. "We have

friends who can help." Edouard and Marguerite would be more than willing. So would Souris and her family if Flower could be persuaded to trust them.

He blew out an annoyed breath. "I have people in mind. I don't need you improvising. There are written instructions in the box on Rue Carnot. You'll need to distribute them tomorrow."

That was a tall order, given how widely spread his contacts seemed to be, but I nodded, glad to know there was more purpose in my courier runs than delivering messages to watch and wait. "Anything else?"

A woman with a heavy bag wandered too close, and I cut myself off as her eyes traveled over us. I made a show of scooting awkwardly away from Flower as if I didn't know him and wasn't enjoying our encounter. It required very little theatrical skill. The woman, not needing the 8:15 bus, averted her eyes and walked on.

"Do as you're told. No more, no less," he snapped once she was out of earshot. "You're under my command. I know London made that clear."

"Your people trust me," I told him. "You should too."

He didn't reply. Scowling, he rose and stepped to the curb, just as the grimy bus wheezed its way over. It sighed and stopped, and he climbed aboard. Through the dusty windows, I watched him find a seat behind the driver, mouth pressed into an almost invisible line, angry pink spots on his cheeks.

———

"Merde," I gasped, as I bounced over a rut in the road that nearly wrenched the handlebars from my grasp. Recovering with a wobble, I turned my eyes to the track ahead, away from a dinner-plate moon that seemed to float just beyond my finger-tips in the night sky. No clouds tonight, and no wind but a tired sighing that ruffled the trees every now and then, just to prove it was there. Perfect conditions for a parachute drop.

I'd been obedient to Flower's commands. Perhaps that would convince him to trust me, though I had my doubts. Our mutual dislike couldn't be allowed to compromise a vital mission, so I followed his instructions just as he wanted, no more, no less.

As I cycled to the rendezvous, I wished I'd done more. A drop like this was a major operation. Flower had confided nothing to me besides where and when. All communication had been by dead-letter drop, and so far as I could tell, I'd delivered no summons to the Flamencourts, Souris's family, or Pierre. So I didn't know who was helping tonight, and I was uncomfortable contemplating an operation of this size and significance with strangers. I'd practiced parachute drop receptions dozens of times at SOE finishing school, but what about the men and women Flower planned to use tonight? Were they trained? Trustworthy? What was Flower's plan to move the goods and people who fell from the sky?

Pushing anxiety down as I pedaled, I reminded myself to look ahead—not just at the dark road. My goal tonight, besides the drop, was a word or two with our wireless operator. I turned down a narrow lane, avoiding the lights in Chambord. The rendezvous wasn't much farther than the town, just past the grounds of the nearby château, temporary headquarters of the local Gestapo.

So I cycled the long way around just in case.

Though Flower had left me specific written directions to the site, I'd come on my own yesterday to survey the ground in the daylight. The site was good, shielded from the road by a thick wood, far enough away from Chambord and the château that the engines of the passing plane wouldn't excite much notice. Bombers often passed, and our single plane would be smaller and lighter. A car waited at the edge of the wood, just where I'd left the road to beat my way through the trees yesterday afternoon. Dismounting, I kept my bicycle close, wary of the round dark automobile and the occupants hidden behind the glass. The tick of my bicycle chain and the crunch of my shoes on the gravel blended with the discordant cries of unseen insects. A man stepped from the driver's side and I recognized Pierre, more by his shortness and slightness and the sheen of his round spectacles than his shadowed face.

"Pierre?" I whispered, abandoning the prescribed recognition sequence.

He turned, bringing his face into the moonlight. "Jacqueline!"

Warm relief rushed into my cheeks. "Am I first?" I was early but not by much. I'd delivered messages to six boxes, hoping at least some were meant for more than one recipient. Six people weren't enough to handle all the supplies in a heavy drop, not if we wanted to clear the scene quickly. Lingering in a drop zone only magnified the danger of what we were about to do.

"So far it's just you and me and Roger," Pierre said, leaning back to show me the man in the passenger seat.

"I didn't know you had a car," I said.

"This is Berbert's," Pierre admitted. "Flower told me to find transport. I had to reach a little farther than he would have liked. Souris and Berbert have been officially inducted into the network. I'm playing fast and loose tonight, bringing in my own contacts." His brow creased. I wasn't the only one worried.

"Where is Berbert?" I asked, peering down the road.

"Dining at the château."

My mouth fell open with a garbled question.

Pierre added laconically, "Nazis like mixing with aristocrats. Makes them feel important. And sometimes Berbert hears something useful."

I swallowed my sharp reply. So long as the information flowed only one way. But the count and countess had as much to lose as I did. More, I decided, remembering their two daughters.

He'll be discreet. I repeated it to myself, making it a mantra.

"Flower wasn't too pleased with our field," the other man put in. Roger. "Said we're too close to the Gestapo." He jerked his head in the direction of the château. "But it's hard to find decent sites. This was the best I could do in such a short time."

"If we do our job right, we'll be gone in a couple of hours," I said.

We set off over the spongy ground, moving slowly to mind our footing. Away from the road, the cooler air smelled of moss. Roger slipped climbing over a wet log, saved from falling only by a steadying hand from Pierre.

"Careful," Pierre warned. "You don't want to get stopped on the way home looking like you've been crawling through the woods."

It took ten minutes to reach the clearing that would serve

as our landing field, barely big enough for our purpose but far from the road and well concealed. That had a downside, though. We'd have to hunt through the surrounding tangle of woods if any parachutes drifted. Stray packages posed one of our greatest dangers—one misplaced crate would alert the Germans and make it impossible to ever use this field again. And I hadn't begun to give them the trouble I intended, not by a long shot. "I hope the others aren't far," I muttered.

"See anyone?" Roger hesitated at the edge of the trees.

I shook my head. Pierre cupped a hand to his mouth and released a mournful birdcall that was our signal—no movement, no answer.

"Where are they?" He checked his watch again and scanned the sky.

"There's time," I said, reassuring the three of us. I willed my eyes to adjust to the darkness pooling between the trees. "Whose land is this? Does it belong to the château?"

Pierre shook his head. "Bois Renard belongs to the mayor of Mer. He's on our side."

I lifted an eyebrow, but he rejected my caution with a quick nod of his head.

"He is. I know. He's family."

I pressed my lips together. Personal connections again— easy links for outsiders to follow. I hoped Pierre was careful with his confidences.

A movement and flash of weak light across the clearing caught my eye—a slight figure emerging from the trees. No, three people, all female, all in trousers—Souris and her daughters, Moune and Bette. A troubled frown accompanied my low sigh. We couldn't mess up now. Not with Souris and Berbert's girls involved.

"Souris has a pass because of her Red Cross work," Pierre reassured. "She'll draw less attention than most if she's caught driving after curfew."

I nodded. "Do they have the lanterns?"

Pierre shook his head. "Those'll come with Marcel."

"I have a torch," I murmured, half to myself, "but I don't know tonight's signal pattern."

"There." Pierre pointed over my shoulder. I looked and saw another light bobbing through the woods. Pierre hooted softly and a baleful coo replied, loosening the trip-line tightness in my chest. Slowly, the shadowy figures resolved into Flower and a second man, lean with light hair that receded at the temples. He carried a bulky rucksack.

He must be Marcel Clech, the radio operator. The one I needed to befriend.

Flower started by hushing Souris and her daughters, extinguishing their low-toned voices with a command to not make extra noise, though they'd not disturbed anyone else. Marcel bent and opened his pack without a word, removing eight lanterns. He passed the first to Roger.

"Take your positions no more than two meters from the trees," Flower said, his shifty eyes roving the huddle but never venturing beneath anyone's forehead. "Stay close to cover. Listen for the plane but do nothing until you see my signal. This is the pattern." Signing for us to look, he took out a folded sheet of notepaper and held it beneath his torch. I edged closer, peering between Roger's and Moune's shoulders.

"When we hear the plane, we'll take positions so our lights make a triangle shape, like this," Marcel said. "Flower and I will be here, and you'll take these other positions. You can see from the letters in each spot what color lens to use. The pilot won't drop his cargo unless the signal is right. We don't want our weapons falling into the hands of Germans. They've found other fields, you know, and set out decoy reception teams."

Had they only captured weapons? Or had new agents, fresh from England, catapulted into their clutches as well? Marcel didn't enlighten us, and I wasn't sure the others realized the ramifications of his words.

"So it's essential we get both the shape and the color pattern right," I said.

"Just follow these instructions," Flower snapped. "We must clear the field within an hour of the drop."

Biting my bottom lip, I studied his diagram of lines and letters in the wavering torchlight. A triangle, with corners and sides in yellow, white, and blue.

Souris, chosen with Flower's vehement index finger, was handed a lamp and assigned the position at the top of the triangle.

"You have a yellow lens?" I whispered, catching her by the arm before she set off to the opposite end of the field.

"I checked them," Flower hissed.

Souris glanced at him, then flicked her light on and off, releasing a burst of bright yellow and blinding me with dancing afterimages. "Yes, I have yellow," she confirmed.

The torches were battered and dusty, bare bulbs sitting in bowl-shaped reflectors and fixed to short handles.

Interchangeable colored glass lenses slid over the top. I attempted to catch Marcel's eye to exchange at least a smile, but he was fiddling with the buckles of his rucksack.

Roger, Pierre's friend, took his lamp and set off for his position (B, for *blanc*). Moune and Bette both checked theirs before slipping away.

"They better know what they are doing," Flower muttered to Pierre. I blinked away another bright haze as Pierre flicked a torch on and off, and readjusted my eyes to the dark.

Flower saved Marcel and me for last. Only two lanterns remained. "Marcel and I will run this point," Flower grumbled through set teeth. "You're the other white light. Twenty yards that way should do it."

I reached forward and turned the sheet ninety degrees. "That should be yellow, I think. Didn't you send Roger to that position?"

Flower rotated it back with more roughness than necessary. "Get going," he ordered.

With a tight jaw I relinquished my view of the map and found my place on the uneven ground, my chin level with the high grass. In a wide triangle touching the edges of the field, others briefly tested their lights. The plane should come within the next hour, but I knew from experience it might seem more like five. I balanced my lamp in front of me and retracted my hands into the sleeves of my wool pullover as the wind rustled the dry leaves overhead.

At my right, Pierre approached, coming at me in a crouch.

"What's wrong?" I whispered.

"Has he set us up correctly?"

My fear precisely. "I can't tell." I glanced up, gauging my distance from the spreading branches. "This is your first drop?"

Pierre nodded.

"There's a hundred things that can go wrong," I admitted. "But so long as we have something besides Berbert's car to move supplies—"

"I borrowed a wagon," Pierre said. "Flower and Marcel brought it and left it behind the trees closer to the road." He jerked his head to show me where but it was well hidden. I couldn't see any trace of it.

"Good. All we have to do is wait."

He nodded once, sharply, and crawled back to his position. I rearranged my legs, searching for a position where a sharp clod of dried mud or small rock didn't grind into my bare skin.

Not a bad group. I couldn't make out any of them as the last faint light bled out of the sky, leaving only a few pockmark stars. I concentrated on the zealous flight of a darting bat until a low drone rose over the pounding of my heart. Across the field, Souris's and Bette's lights bloomed. Yellow. Blue.

To their left, blackness. No light yet from Roger. I flicked my switch, shielding my eyes from the burning white glow in my hand. Beside me, a red star flared to life.

"Wrong lens," I called to Pierre. "You need the blue one."

Muffled cursing as the plane's engine grew louder. The light flashed again. Green.

I set my light down in the grass and trotted over to Pierre.

"I don't have a blue lens," he said, panting between breaths. "Give me yours."

"I left my extra lenses behind. Wait here. I'll fetch one."

I reached over and turned his light off. "Better they think we missed a lantern than decide we're Germans setting a trap."

"Hurry," Pierre said.

I stumbled across the clearing. Still no light from Roger, and Marcel and Flower's signal barely peeped out from their position against the tree line. "Move farther out," I called. "They won't see you beneath the branches."

If the plane in the sky was German, it might strafe us as it flew past, but this risky exercise accomplished nothing if we hid beneath the trees.

"What are you doing? Get back!" Flower spat.

"Pierre needs a blue lens!"

The plane hummed urgently, barreling closer. I raced on, ignoring the pain tearing at my side.

Across the field, Souris's and Moune's lights waved in white arcs. The engine roared above.

I thought of the det cord, time pencils, and neat packets of 808 just above us. Stacks of money too, cans of food and slabs of chocolate. Maybe they'd see the pattern was nearly right and drop anyway.

I sprinted faster and begged for telepathy, for the pilot in the sky to understand.

A shadow swept over me like a wave, the ground trembling as the plane buzzed past, gunners certainly poised to take German fire. I closed my eyes and flung myself flat on the ground.

The engines faded to silence, but I maintained my scrutiny of the sky, willing the plane to turn around. Instead, the sound faded to nothing. *Merde.* I braced my hands on my knees and blinked until I could see clearly, drawing air to cool my searing lungs.

Around the field, all the lights but mine went out.

I looked up. "Lights on! What are you doing?" The plane would make another pass—standard procedure, but before I could explain, Flower's shrill voice tore out of the trees.

"Run!"

I threw my head around, my hand jerking to my sidearm.

"It was a German plane! We're betrayed!"

"It wasn't German—" But my words cut off, fear clutching my throat. Had I misread the wing's shape? Did Flower see something I missed?

"Scatter. Abort!" Flower ordered.

"We have to wait for the second pass!" someone shouted.

I spun around. Across the field Pierre's light, still green, flashed brave and clear.

"Wait," I called after Flower, who was already plunging through the woods, beyond reason or reach.

The buzz of the engines grew. I ground my teeth together, but it didn't stop the angry, hot moisture stinging my eyes. This time the plane didn't slow. It blasted dry leaves from the trees as it sped past, the force and noise like a rain of curses from the sky.

In the ensuing silence, Pierre walked to my abandoned position and turned my light off.

"It wasn't Luftwaffe," he murmured, disgust drenching his voice.

"I didn't think so either." Still good to have a second opinion. We weren't infiltrated, but we were failures. I breathed against the hot sting in my chest.

"Who's still here?" I called as loud as I dared.

Roger emerged sheepishly from the woods. Souris stepped forward, Bette and Moune behind her.

"Flower?" Pierre spun in a circle, searching for his target.

"He said it was a German plane," Moune said. "He ran away."

"Idiot! It was RAF. Flower!" Pierre called him forward again like an executioner. I wondered if he'd learned that tone in prison camp.

"He's gone," I muttered. Pierre's palpable anger somehow diffused mine. "Marcel?"

I ventured into the trees but found no sign of him. He must have fled with Flower. Another defeat to add to my tally.

"Gone? Both of them?" Souris echoed, her aristocratic intonation made for this kind of disdain.

"We should clear out," Roger said, glancing side to side.

"Are you sure it wasn't Luftwaffe?" Souris frowned at Pierre.

I shook my head, my earlier doubt gone. I'd studied plane silhouettes and trusted my eyes more than Flower's. "It was Brits, but it's too late now. They're headed back to base." With all our munitions, arms, and money.

Bette's head dropped and Roger heaved a sigh. They looked like I had felt after Bones died.

"It will be all right," I said, straightening. Bette and Roger could be capable fighters if someone showed them what to do. Someone besides Flower. "They'll fly again tomorrow and the next night, until the full moon is gone. All we need to do is hide the torches here. We don't want to be caught with them on our way home." I didn't mention that each consecutive night increased our risk of discovery.

"The bulb in mine doesn't even work," Roger muttered.

"Tomorrow we'll bring extra," I said.

"I can bring bulbs. And maybe an extra light," Roger said. "I run an electrical appliance shop."

I nodded. "Good. And we'll all come a half hour earlier tomorrow. We'll check everything first. Including the lenses." We'd keep a tighter formation too, farther away from the trees, more exposed but easily visible to the plane. The job waited, and we could do it.

"But we can't talk to England," Souris said. "They won't know what went wrong. We have no radio."

"Don't need it," I told her. "Not for this. It's standard procedure for them to return the next night if a drop fails. We'll get it right tomorrow." Maybe they'd drop a new radio—and someone to operate it. So far as I could see, Marcel didn't mind taking Flower's orders, making him an unlikely friend for me. I grimaced, then smoothed the expression into a half-hearted smile. "You'll be careful on the way home?"

Pierre and Roger nodded; Souris hitched her shotgun against her side and winked. "Night hunting." Lowering her voice she added, "They don't find an eccentric countess much of a threat."

I gave a breathy laugh, more to release the tension in my chest than anything else. Pierre's face was dismal, a tragic twist to his lips as if he'd swallowed the dregs of a particularly bitter cup.

"You can't murder Flower," I tried to tease. "We need him." Until I had my own line to London.

"We'll see about that." He kicked a clod of dirt. "Does he

know how hard it is to find a good landing field? I'm never working with him again."

"I'll talk to Edouard and Marguerite," I suggested. With the Flamencourts, we'd manage without Flower's and Marcel's hands tomorrow. But no matter how I wanted to, I couldn't plan further than that.

CHAPTER 17

———

"Don't touch anything yet!" Maxwell barked.

I blinked my eyes to keep them open, trying to clear my head from the morning's run up Forcan Ridge, then another three hours of signaling practice. In spite of our instructors' efforts, I was never going to be a wireless operator. Couldn't transmit fast enough. And though I'd run up the ridge today faster than a third of the men, physical fitness wasn't enough to make me an agent, though it might, perhaps, suffice for them.

Maxwell wanted more from me if he was going to risk sending a woman.

I released my lip from my bottom teeth and refocused my attention on Maxwell and the assortment of objects spread on the tables set up at the far end of the lawn. I needed to be good—no, exceptional—at something.

"The materials in front of you are mostly dummies," Maxwell explained. "Because I'd rather you not blow each other up this morning. Still, I expect you to treat them with the caution such tools deserve. So wait for my say-so before meddling with anything."

I locked my hands behind my back, determined to avoid negative comments on my report. Shifting my eyes from Maxwell, I swept a wary glance over the bits and bobs at my station. Gerald was on my right, and I couldn't risk him meddling. He hadn't forgiven me for taking all the hot water again the night before. Every time I made a mistake, he grinned like he'd scored a point.

"One of your main duties, we believe, will be to take out specific targets important to the enemy. You'll need to know how to handle explosives, create bombs, set charges, and time detonations."

Heart sinking, I surveyed the items in front of me—a child's eclectic collection pulled from wrinkled pockets: stray wires, putty, glue, something long and thin wrapped in waxed paper, a balloon, tape, and a pile of magnets. Jean, on my left and always impulsive, stretched out his hand.

"Barbet, do that again, and I'll relieve you of a finger myself," Maxwell spat. "Don't treat these like playthings. Muck this work up and you'll kill or cripple yourself and who knows how many others."

Jean took a step back.

"The gray putty in front of you is simply that—putty. After you perfect your dummy charges, you can give the real thing a go. You can't afford mistakes with plastic explosives." He held up a small rubbery block the color of weathered brick. "808. In moderate weather, this stuff is relatively safe. But apply heat and it will sweat; only it sweats pure nitroglycerine, not water.

So you can't risk warming it using your own body heat. The chemicals will leach into your skin, giving you a hell of a headache. Or worse. Best to soften and form it with warm water."

I scribbled another two lines in my notebook.

"There's no detonating device attached, so I'll pass this around." He handed the lump to the man at the end of our row, farthest away from Jean Barbet. Like a hot potato, it moved down the line quickly. The stench of rotten almonds enveloped me as soon as I took hold of it.

"Watch the fumes. They can also make you sick," Maxwell warned. "And as you probably guessed, the scent can be a dead giveaway. No matter how well you hide it, there's always the smell."

"Then why do we use it?" Gerald demanded. "There must be better things."

"It's what we have. And it works. As you will soon see." Maxwell, for once without his cigarette, cleared his throat. "Pick up your sausage—that's the dummy wrapped in waxed paper."

I pressed my lips together, imagining real dynamite, not a dummy. No mistakes. I had to get this right.

"Here's your recipe." Maxwell walked along our rows, handing each of us a printed diagram. "This bomb is sized to take down a large tree, allowing you to block a road."

This made more sense to me than the dots and dashes. Even before he finished distributing instructions, my hands navigated the pile, gathering pieces with careful precision. My fingers—restless and fidgeting, irritating to others—were always exact and patient when tackling interesting work. And assembling these pieces—well, it wasn't that different from turning a perfect shoulder seam or fitting a jacket lining. I'd worked for years as a dressmaker, trying to extricate myself from Alex, and though I'd never made enough to live independently for long, I did quality work. This was simply a new kind of tailoring.

I finished, looked up, and found Maxwell standing over me. He pushed another diagram and a packet of materials at me. "Do this one."

Hadn't he liked my first? I knew it was well done. Certainly better than Gerald's haphazard contraption, with untidy wires straggling everywhere. The wires on mine curved neatly around what looked like a compact butcher's parcel joined with lots of clock parts.

I studied the drawing, then reproduced the new assembly, this time with Jean and Maxwell watching.

"There." I said it defiantly because Maxwell had frowned silently over my shoulder the entire time.

"Where'd you learn this? Is your father a mechanic?"

I grinned. "Not at all. The diagram is a dress pattern. I just replaced a zipper with magnets and a wool crepe with gelignite."

"Sewing." He rolled his eyes. "Figures. Well, it pains me to admit it, but you're a natural, Jacqueline. I'd say even better than you are at shooting." He smiled, but it faded within seconds as his eyes swerved away. Instinctively, his hand reached for the absent cigarettes. "Take a look, all of you, and see if you can build something half as good. Jacqueline, report to me at noon tomorrow. You're ready for the real stuff."

CHAPTER 18

WITHOUT RAYMOND FLOWER ALONGSIDE US, SHUSHING AND spoiling the mood, the drop preparations took on the air of a surprise party. Six of us—Pierre, Souris, her husband and two daughters, and me—crammed into Berbert's black Peugeot 202, our moods light as parachute silk. At Blois, a German blockade stopped us and checked our papers, frowning at each of us in turn, but Souris flashed her Red Cross pass and seconds later we rocketed down the road, singing along with Bette's rendition of "*Le Chant de Partisans,*" the anthem of Free France. Berbert's baritone blended with the hum of the engine. Moune, offbeat and off-key, warbled happily and jostled Culioli every few lines for refusing to join in. He resisted the temptation to smile, but his trim mustache wobbled, betraying suppressed amusement. Unlike him, I couldn't hold back, laughing as we sang about sabotage, grenades, and guns, black blood drying in the sun on the roads. I tapped the beat on the back of Souris's seat as she swooped the car expertly around the bends, unsure how many songs were left in my life. Perhaps only this one. Perhaps a thousand. But tonight, even a thousand seemed a meager number, and every verse counted.

We parked behind a large shed at the home of Culioli's contact, the mayor of Mer. As I climbed out of the car, a man emerged from the shed. I was expecting Pierre and Roger Couffrant, but this fellow was taller than either of them—Marcel Clech.

He made a handsome picture standing in the dusky shadows, but that wasn't why my heart started racing. While Souris spoke to him, I sidled up to Pierre. "Does Flower know he's here?"

Pierre shrugged. "I invited him. Flower summoned me today. He told me to stand down, that it was too risky to try again. I told him we need supplies and that I was trying again no matter what he said. Then I told him he's not welcome on my family's land, that we can do this ourselves and we're better off if he stays away."

I blinked, trying to imagine it. "That's quite a conversation."

"He became rather upset," Pierre said, like he was making an observation on the weather. "Especially when I said we didn't need him tonight, not with you to lead us."

A sound cut free from my throat, half outraged gasp, half laugh. "Pierre!"

"He doesn't like either of us anyway," he said.

True, but he was the "man in charge," not one to needle unnecessarily.

"I forgive you," I muttered. "But only because you brought Marcel."

Pierre smirked. "I thought you might. Let me introduce you."

"Jacqueline?" I looked right and saw Marcel already moving toward us.

"I'm glad you're here," I said.

He shrugged a little uncomfortably. "We need supplies. Pierre told me you were trying and said you needed all the help you could get."

"He's right," I said. "Trained help especially. How long ago were you at Garramor?"

He laughed. "Don't remind me. I'm trying to forget."

"It can't have been that bad if you passed the wireless tests," I said. "I never got past eleven words a minute." So he wasn't tempted to underrate me, I added, "My best was explosives, and the shooting course."

His gaze turned more appraising. I wondered if he was here simply to help or if Flower had asked him to keep an eye on us. Either way, tonight I intended to show both of them what I could do.

"Shall we?" Pierre gestured to the wood. "Roger went ahead to retrieve the lamps and check the bulbs."

Marcel hesitated. "I think you should know—we're expecting more than canisters of supplies tonight. Two agents are coming. Women."

My head slewed sideways. "Who?"

At SOE finishing school, after my lonely days training at Garramor, there'd been three other women. All four of us had earned operational approval, though I was first to be sent because HQ refused to send me for parachute training. I counted months in my head. Unless they'd accelerated both the Garramor and Beaulieu training, there was a good chance at least one of my friends would land here tonight.

If more women were coming, London must be satisfied

with me so far, whatever remarks Flower had sent. I ducked my head, keeping my smile to myself.

Marcel shrugged. "Sorry. I just have code names." He passed me a slip of paper. "They need to get to Paris. To this address." I showed it to Culioli, but he just shook his head, so I motioned to Souris.

"Don't know it. Don't know them," Souris said coolly after a brief inspection.

"Then I think it's better we keep away from it. We don't need to know who runs the safe house, and they don't need to know who we are. In training, they call that intentional separation a cutout. For security. We'll take the new agents to friends with a farm. You know the one, Souris," I said quickly. "From there, the new agents can make their way to the safe house on their own."

"You think they can manage—" Marcel began.

"Yes," I said, my voice clipped. "These women almost certainly trained with me. They can handle taking a bus or a train." I turned to Souris. "Do you have enough petrol?"

"To get to Ed—to our friends' farm?" She glanced at me, and I nodded approvingly at her correction. "Yes, there should be enough. There's no way we can drive them to Paris, and I think it would look suspicious, traveling with them on a train."

"I think the cutout's a good idea," Culioli said, and after a pause, Marcel nodded.

"That's settled then." I wasn't used to it, but I was the leader here. Not Marcel. Not Pierre or Souris or her husband. My heart quickened, even as frost crept over my skin.

Think about it later.

"Let's hurry," I said, striding off the lane into the woods. "We've got to set up the signal."

It wasn't full dark, making it easy to pick our way through the trees to the field where we'd been disappointed yesterday evening. Roger had successfully unearthed all the lanterns. Souris checked and distributed them to each member. I snapped a dead stick from the nearest tree and scraped it through the sandy soil, drawing a rectangle. "This is the northern edge of the field." I pointed. "We need a yellow torch at that end. Culioli will take that one. Marcel, you position yours on the far side, thirty meters up." The small group crouched together, heads bowed, studying my crude picture. "We must be easy to spot. If we wait until we see the plane, that's too late. Watch each other and listen. You'll learn to judge their distance by the sound. With people coming, not just gear, there's extra risks."

I wetted my lips. "Approach the parachutists carefully. Until we know they're friends, act like it's a trap. Germans can parachute too." And because of last night's debacle, they might have guessed what was coming.

"Berbert, you weren't with us yesterday, so when the parachutes start dropping, do as we do. Once we know it's safe to move, that's when speed counts. Cut the cords from the canisters. Bury the chutes." I passed him my extra knife. "Careful. It's sharp."

I surveyed their faces—grave, focused. "Bring the canisters here; then we'll divide them between the wagon and the car." Flower hadn't seen fit to tell me where to find his storage caches, but I had my own ideas. In this case, his lack of direction was an opportunity, one I'd play to advantage. With my own stores, I could plan attacks without waiting for permission.

As my team scattered to their positions, an unexpected smile tugged at my mouth, pride in this disparate band—a shopkeeper, a countess, children, an escaped prisoner. One by one they faded into the cover of the trees. Maybe we weren't what Flower and the SOE generals in London wanted, but my heart thrummed with confidence. Not one of my band would panic and run. Tonight, we'd finish the job.

I settled on my back between trees and stared at the sky as night fell, imagining the agents curled up in the back of a plane, remembering the feeling of the buzzing engine and turbulent ride, and the three women who'd joined me for training at Beaulieu—Christiane, Prue, and Denise. They probably had new cover names now.

Despite an undercurrent of competition between us in training—Captain Jepson told us they could only afford to send the best—I liked all three women and I'd seen firsthand what they could do. Once they joined the weak and scattered networks here in France, a female agent wouldn't be so surprising to people. With any luck.

I shifted on the ground, working blood back into my numb feet.

At last, a new sound joined the night insects and restless grasses. I sat up, my ears straining at the discordant hum of a plane, felt more than heard. Across the field, lights flashed on, bright flames beckoning it closer. The plane sailed past, leaving a trail of parachutes in the sky, bursting blossoms of gray on black like explosions in the films of aerial bombings I'd seen in the newsreels. Except I was really here, crouching in the dark, not ensconced in the plush seats of a London cinema. Here, the Gestapo waited a scant mile or two away, the growling engines as audible to them as to us—if they were listening. I pushed to my feet, tracking the parachutes' ghostly descents as they grew larger, my heart pounding. We were committed now; those agents up in the sky—possibly my friends—counted on us.

No sounds of traffic reached us this far from the road. Moune was positioned closest to it—if we were surprised by the Gestapo or the Milice, she was our only warning. We'd have only seconds or minutes to flee, but it was better, I'd told them, not to think of that and focus ferociously on gathering our bounty and getting clear of danger.

With a protest of groaning wood and jostled contents, a container landed twenty yards from me, the parachute melting into the ground. I kept my eyes skyward. Hard to say in this dark, but high above me, a shape—possibly human—drifted soundlessly closer. I waited, knees flexed, like a sprinter anticipating the bang of a gun.

Yes, this was someone, floating impeccably toward the middle of the landing field, safe from the surrounding trees. I trotted along the tree line, refusing to expose myself yet. They somersaulted onto the ground, collapsing momentarily, then rose and detached efficiently from the cloud of silk ballooning behind them.

Dark curls shook free as she gathered the silk into a tight ball with practiced efficiency.

A sigh of relief mingled with excitement escaped my lips. "*Bienvenue à France,*" I murmured in an undertone.

The head whipped around. Absorbed in her descent, the

parachutist hadn't seen me. Now her eyes sought me in the dark. "Jacqueline?"

I knew that voice. "Denise!" I raced over, catching her in my arms, laughing giddily.

She hugged me back.

"So they let you come by parachute," I pointed out with a note of envy. "I had to go by boat. It took forever."

"No way the boffins would let you," she said, mispronouncing the British word in her charming way. "All their experiments parachuting people and things from the sky have convinced them someone your age must have fragile bones." She shoved my shoulder.

Denise often reminded me of a surly boy, and this gesture, more than most, reinforced the impression. But it was an affectionate one, and my heart lifted, floating up to fill the space left by the deflating parachute.

"It's so good to see you," I murmured. "As for my weak bones—"

"You'll show them better," Denise finished.

Knowing we'd wasted time we couldn't afford on words, we fell to work bundling up the parachute of the nearest canister. At least a dozen others littered the field, and my friends shoveled frantically, digging holes and packing them away.

"There are friends not too far from here with a farm," I said to Denise, moving to the next parachute, still attached to a metal container. "You'll spend the night there."

She nodded, satisfied. "Then off to Paris. I'm to bring another radio to Prosper in the Physician network."

I filed the names away. I could cut ties with Flower and his network, join Physician and bring along Culioli and his allies. It might make the powers in London unhappy—they'd assigned me to Flower, after all—but I didn't see how they could stop me. Not being on the ground, only hearing his side, they couldn't know how unreasonable he was. I was confident, in time, my results would speak for themselves.

Except I also didn't know Prosper. He might be just as unwilling to use me as Flower. For now, I might have to pull from his book—watch and wait. I'd give a mailing address to Denise. If she was better received by Prosper than I had been here, I could think about offering to operate as a subcircuit of their network. It kept us under English command and under the nominal oversight of a man, which would look better in London.

"Jacqueline?" Denise shoved my arm. "You used to be faster than this."

She was right. These ideas must wait.

Together, we hefted an especially heavy canister, stumbling a mere ten or so yards before Culioli came to help. "Must be ammunition," I grunted. With three, we toted it over the rough ground more efficiently, but my shoulders burned long before we reached the trees. By the time we collected and loaded all the containers, I'd be exhausted.

"Here." Berbert uncorked and held out a flask. Coffee— cold but I swallowed gratefully, then returned to the field. Every parachute had to be buried, leaving no visible disturbance.

We worked in pairs, sharp spades cutting triangular burrows that swallowed the silk into surprisingly small holes. We interred the evidence of our espionage, scattering dried leaves and sticks, the smell of earth clinging to my fingers.

"Does Culioli drive?" I whispered to Souris.

"Yes, actually he—"

"I think it will be best if he and I take our new friends to Edouard and Marguerite." I pointed my gaze at her daughters. "If you don't mind us borrowing the car. You'll have to wait for morning and the bus, but—" There was danger ferrying these canisters and Denise and another agent every mile of the way to Edouard and Marguerite's. If I was the leader, I would decide who took that risk. I didn't want it to be Souris, Berbert, and their two girls.

"Don't worry about us," Souris said. "We can borrow bicycles from Pierre's friends in town and cycle home." Her eyes, following mine, turned soft, caressing her family. "It's a good idea. Thank you."

CHAPTER 19

"STOP OVER THERE," THE INSTRUCTOR ORDERED, POINTING
to the edge of the lawn, barely visible through the morning's
thick veil of mist. He was unfamiliar, not a man I'd seen before,
but that was not unusual at Beaulieu. There were many houses
in the Hampstead woods appropriated by SOE: ones for Greek
agents, Polish, Danish, and French. Some days we practiced
combat in booby-trapped rooms in the house or deep in the
woods; sometimes we picked locks inside and fabricated duplicate keys. Sometimes we even took the bus into town to practice tailing each other or to spend the evening at the pub, but
heaven help anyone who thought this was a holiday. One man,
who'd started training before me, fell in with a friendly girl
after too many pints one night. Next morning, she'd appeared
at our breakfast table in her ensign's uniform after reporting
to the instructors, and he'd been sent away—not home but to
a holding unit somewhere in the northern wilds—for being
indiscreet.

According to the instructors, we had only three weeks of

training left. Three grueling weeks, but success was in reach. I could feel it.

For now though, I pulled my hands into the sleeves of my cardigan, defending myself from the morning chill. Everything here was a test, and I didn't understand what this one was yet, with no equipment visible through the thinning fog. No ropes or weapons on the cropped grass, no dummy canisters and masses of parachute silk to be concealed with tiny spades.

There were only two people, washed gray in the poor light: a slight man in a suit and a woman in uniform.

"Any ideas?" I whispered to Christiane, one of the three other women who'd joined me in training here, as we loped across the wet lawn.

"Not a thing," she muttered.

Denise, on my left, kept her lips tight, her nose raised like a hunting dog searching for a scent. Prue scoured the distant tree line beyond the pond. *Good idea*, I reminded myself. *Might be a hidden "Nazi" ready to pounce at us, forcing us to take cover.*

The games at Beaulieu wouldn't help if I didn't act like they were real. Soon, if I kept on, they would be.

"That's Jepson," Denise murmured. "And Vera."

I narrowed my eyes. Yes, that was Captain Jepson, the man who'd recruited me. I didn't recognize the woman.

"Flight Officer Atkins," Prue corrected Denise with a sniff. "If you give Captain Jepson his rank, don't take away hers."

My interest in the woman sharpened. She had dark, perfectly set hair and a cigarette traveling from her side to ruby-painted lips. She wore her confidence as boldly as her braid-trimmed jacket. An ideal personality to channel while undercover.

"Good morning, ladies," Flight Officer Atkins called. "We've come from London—the higher-ups want to know how you are faring."

"Famously," Denise volleyed back. "Send us to France!"

We all laughed, a nervous release, like dogs shaking off the strain. "Lovely to see you all looking so well," Jepson said.

I smiled, genuinely this time, amused by the incongruity of his manners and his current occupation. "Lady and gentleman, welcome." I gave a mock bow. "The talented females of Beaulieu are here today to amaze and astound you. For their next feat—" I glanced about me, but there was still nothing, no clues.

"Swimming," our instructor, huffing to a stop beside us, interjected laconically. "Here." He flung out a hand at the neglected pond on our right. Behind the mist, bent reeds and blown cattail husks swung over a void of brown stagnant water.

My blood crystallized into sharp flakes of snow. I'd known this was coming, but my stern, self-administered encouragement had always persuaded me the moment was avoidable or a long way off.

"How many of you are swimmers?" Jepson asked.

I shoved my hands deeper into my skirt pockets, waiting for the others to proclaim their expertise. But Denise was the only one lifting a grudging hand, and she scowled even harder than usual, glaring at the water as if it offended her. Prue didn't make a sound.

My shoulders loosened. This was bearable so long as I wasn't the only one shrinking at the thought of flailing into that water.

Our instructor rubbed a hand through his hair. "This might take longer than I thought." He raised his voice. "Denise, you're first."

Never one to back down, Denise marched on wooden legs to the edge of the water, then hesitated, something I'd never seen from her. "Can't we wear bathing costumes?" she asked.

The instructor shook his head. "In the field you'll be fully dressed and wearing heavy boots, swimming rocky, muddy, or fast-moving rivers. You'll need to practice staying afloat while fully clothed and using your boots to kick up from the bottom. Otherwise you'll only get stuck down there. That's how people drown."

My breath accelerated in time with his words. Beside me, Prue turned a sickly gray.

"So…into the water," he said, rather like a parent confronting a child with a plate of uneaten greens.

Denise sloshed into the tangled reeds, and my heart resumed beating. It wasn't my turn. Yet.

In the water, Denise wobbled, righted herself, and glared at us, safe on the bank, like this was our fault. "It's freezing!"

The instructor folded his arms. Realizing the only way out was in, Denise lunged for the deeper water, submerging with a splash that reached all the way to the bank. She bobbed up a second later, wet hair streaming over her eyes, and began flailing haphazardly to the center of the pond. My heart somersaulted. She looked like she was drowning, but our instructor didn't move.

"She's managing," the instructor told Jepson. "Though without finesse."

"So I see." Jepson made a note on his clipboard.

My breath lagged. How would I manage in that freezing, murky water?

Prue, who was next, made it across the pond with better form than Denise.

"You said you didn't swim," Denise said accusingly when Prue heaved herself up onto the bank.

"I don't. Not if there's any way around it." She was white-faced, shaking. And she'd crossed the high ropes course—forty feet up, no safety belt—without turning a hair.

"Jacqueline?" the instructor called. Jepson hadn't looked up from his clipboard. Beside him, Vera Atkins was lighting another cigarette.

Every other test, I faced squarely, knowing I'd rather freeze or fall or take a hard blow than be sent home with a failing grade. This time, I couldn't even convince myself that I'd face worse in France. All my silent reassurances rang hollow.

I glanced at Christiane, loath to admit my terror of thrashing about, unable to reach bottom...or worse, struggling to keep afloat with my feet mired in mud. If I didn't do something, I'd splinter into bits, whimper, vomit... *Bugger it.*

I took off through the grass, skidding when I reached the muddy bank. Before I toppled, I leapt for the dark water, praying I'd clear the grasping weeds. I plummeted into a chasm of ice, my nostrils filling with water that pushed back into my brain and behind my eyes. Stunned, I sank for agonizing seconds until something—soft as my daughter's baby hair—curled around my arm.

My stomach heaved and I clawed frantically, seeing nothing

but brown water and white bubbles until my head broke the surface, allowing me to sputter and gasp. I worked my arms and bicycled my legs against the weight of my clothes and the sucking pull of the water. A few seconds, a few breaths, but my chin sank lower, water lapping against my cheeks, my lips. I fought to keep my nose clear, but water closed over my face.

Down, down, until my feet squished against the bottom. Moving like a sleepwalker, I pushed up and my face broke the surface again. I gulped air and water, but the next second I was moving down again, my arms and legs heavy. Beneath the ringing in my ears, I heard screaming horses, but both sounds faded, slipping away like the lap of the Thames and the faint rumble of a faraway bus.

I should have known. There's no winning against water.

Something struck my face. Fire blazed along my scalp, dragging me down. Instead of grasping me with soft and squeamish fronds, the weeds were rough and pummeling. Until light blinded me, and I realized, sluggishly, that my face was out of the water, and I wasn't wrapped in weeds.

"Stop fighting! Lie still!"

I froze with shock, then coughed and coughed, submerging myself again. But after a second of terror, the arms around me slipped free and hands closed around my head, beside my ears, bearing me up, keeping my face toward the sun and tugging me along.

"Put your feet down," my rescuer gasped. "It's shallow here. You'll touch bottom."

Coughing, sobbing, I obeyed, my two-ton leather oxfords sinking until I was ankle deep in muck. I turned, expecting to see my instructor but found Jepson instead, in shirt and trousers, flicking wet hair off his face.

"Captain?"

"Let's get you out of there."

My head turned. Here was the instructor, waist deep between me and the shore. His hands closed on mine, and he led me stumbling from the water. At once Prue and Vera surrounded me with a blanket—from where, I couldn't guess. Water still streamed down my cheeks—I was crying.

I gulped but only succeeded in interrupting my soft weeping. It wouldn't subside, for any amount of shame. Blinking in a vain attempt to clear my eyes, I gazed out at the water and saw Denise, struggling to shore, spurning Jepson's outstretched hand.

"I'm fine," she muttered, rising from the water as her feet found the ground.

She'd jumped in after me.

Jepson let her precede him onto the bank, then waded out, smaller than ever under his wet clothes. "That was a near thing," he said, not smiling. "We'd better get you inside. Put some hot tea in you."

The thought made me want to sick up again, but I didn't argue. Accepting Vera's arm, I tottered on trembling legs and let her take me back to the house, pretending I hadn't seen the look, the tiny headshake that passed between them, as awful to me now as the weight of that water.

———

"What the hell was that, Jacqueline? You were supposed to wade in. This is training, not a suicide mission."

"I'm sorry." I stared at the desk, unable to meet the combined gaze of Jepson, Atkins, and the instructor. This was worse than when instructors, dressed as Gestapo, surprised me in the middle of the night, bagging my head in a hood and bundling me down to an unfamiliar cellar for interrogation. I'd passed that but not the pond. My eyes brimmed again.

Stop crying! I shrilled silently, to absolutely no effect.

"You might have drowned yourself—and Jepson and Denise with you." He was in dry clothes now, but wet hair still stuck to his forehead. "Agents must at least consider the safety of their teams. That foolhardy stunt—"

"Was foolish but very brave," Flight Officer Atkins put in.

The instructor gaped at her. Then, "Bravery isn't enough. Without coolheaded reason—"

"He's right."

I looked up, square into Jepson's sorrowful eyes.

"That kind of impulsiveness is too dangerous in the field."

"I'm very sorry, sir."

"I know, Jacqueline." He smiled, as kindly as ever, and my sodden, raspy lungs eased. All would be well if Jepson said so. "So am I," he said.

Instantly, my body was stiff as wet leather again.

"Dismissed."

CHAPTER 20

THERE WAS NO SINGING AS CULIOLI AND I PILED INTO THE DE Bernards' car with Denise and her companion, another woman, one I didn't recognize. Taller than Denise and me but still slight. She gave no name, and I didn't ask.

Most of the containers fit in the wagon, but three had to be wrestled into the trunk of the car, so we couldn't afford to be stopped and searched. Though Souris had handed me a borrowed pass from a doctor friend to justify our late-night journey, I doubted a police patrol would accept that explanation for all four of us.

"We'll keep to back roads," Culioli told me, which helped but was no guarantee. Anyone anywhere might ask questions, and a French collaborator, while not posing the same immediate danger, was almost as bad as a patrol or police. We chuffed along, creeping too noisily for comfort down the rough roads. I had never driven at all before Dubois taught me to drive the lorry at Garramor, but the dragging car and the laboring engine made it easy to feel the difference between petrol and charcoal fuel. It hadn't needled me before, on the way to the landing field, but we hadn't been loaded up with contraband then.

I smoothed my culottes over my knees, grimacing at a tear in my left stocking, and focused on acting calm. My nerves were tight as trip wires. "How far?" I asked Pierre.

"On this road, it's at least another three quarters of an hour," he confessed. "You should have your sidearm ready. If we're stopped, it would be best to shoot first and escape."

Denise, in the back seat, needed no encouragement. She cradled her pistol in her lap, a hunger in the way her fingers curled around the grip. The other woman was subtler, her hand resting casually in her jacket pocket. I wondered where she'd had her training.

Pierre tapped his fingers against the steering wheel as we crept around another corner, pained by our lethargic pace—at this speed, we'd be lucky to arrive before dawn. "We should have asked Berbert for his coffee," I said.

"If that's our worst mistake…" Pierre grinned, relaxing as I'd hoped.

"It will be a while, I'm afraid," I said, talking to Denise and the other woman over my shoulder. "Try and sleep if you can."

The second agent, with straight, smooth brows and a head of dark cropped curls, leaned back and closed her eyes, but Denise balked. "You're not capable of sleeping now. I'm not either."

"You'll regret it," I said with a smile, enjoying my superior knowledge for as long as it would last. Soon she'd be cycling here, there, and everywhere, wishing for a chance to nap a couple of extra hours. Though perhaps she was here in a different capacity. She'd shown talent at forging documents.

"How are you?" she asked, her voice an octave lower. Confined in the car, it was still loud enough for Pierre and the other woman to hear. "If you don't mind me asking," she added.

"I'm well," I said, hoping she'd find reassurance in the way I held her glance. "I've missed you. And the others." Even if it was only a little while, it was an unexpected pleasure, seeing Denise again. And I remembered what I owed her.

"You look marvelous," she said. "Organizing your very own parachute receptions. Of course, I'm not surprised." I glanced at Pierre, but he didn't contradict her. She'd taken me for the leader of our network.

"How are things in London?" I asked, my voice low. She wouldn't have the news I wanted—was Jackie all right?—but any news was better than none.

———

We arrived at the farmhouse just as the sky lightened to a palette of warm pastel. After the bombings carried out on a nearby village last week, I was happy to find little evidence of the war here. Marguerite Flamencourt waited at the window, watching for us, and bustled out the kitchen door as soon as we pulled into the yard.

"Souris telephoned. She told me you'd come." Even in the dim light of morning, her small white teeth shone in her warm smile.

"And that's all right with you? You don't..." The weight of my request ground my words to nothing.

Marguerite didn't notice. Clucking over my torn stockings, the chill air we'd endured—"Terrible for the joints, you all must be horribly stiff"—and the shadows lying thick under Culioli's tired eyes, she shepherded us inside.

The warmth of the kitchen wrapped around me as I stepped in, but that wasn't why my heart leapt. Edouard, still with a bandaged hand, tended a pan on the stove, dressed in his wife's floral print apron. With an expert flick of the pan, he slid a perfectly shaped omelet onto a faded china plate. His face used age lines expertly, crinkling them happily beneath his eyes and framing his expressive mouth.

"Breakfast?" the second agent murmured incredulously beside me.

"Sit down," Marguerite invited, gesturing to the table. No coffee here, but there was a teapot with—guessing from the smell—steaming chamomile tea. She introduced herself to Denise and the other agent, then waved toward the stove. "And that's my husband, Edouard."

"I haven't had an egg in almost a year," the other woman said, still rooted to the floor.

"We keep chickens," Marguerite explained. "The Germans haven't taken them all yet, so this is what we can do for you."

They were, of course, doing much more by sheltering enemy combatants, and my eyes pricked as I slid into the empty chair that Culioli held out for me.

Soon, a small omelet graced every plate. A string of white cheese fell across the faded blue roses of my chipped china dish. I studied it in quiet wonder as I chewed slowly, making the most of every bite, but not as slowly as Denise and the other woman.

"I'd forgotten what real food tastes like," she told Marguerite. "This is a piece of heaven."

Marguerite took a seat at the table but without a plate. "What am I to call you?"

Denise was busy with a bite, so I stepped in. "This new arrival is Denise. She'll be working with a network in Paris and…" I trailed off, looking at the woman I didn't know.

"I won't be in Paris" was all the other woman offered.

"There are beds upstairs," Marguerite said, smiling to show she understood the need for caution. "When you are finished eating, all of you must sleep so you are prepared for travel tomorrow."

I made to interrupt but got nowhere. Her motherly authority was absolute. Through some twenty years of raising Jackie, I'd never once mastered that.

"You too, Jacqueline. You and Pierre must have at least at least a couple hours' rest."

I glanced at Culioli. He shrugged. "We'll have to unload first."

Edouard nodded. "There's room here."

"For now," I put in. "Remember, I'm not interested in stockpiling."

Marguerite laughed, sweeping behind Denise and me, and carrying our empty plates to the sink. She gestured to the two newcomers. "This way." She was smiling so brightly, it didn't seem to cost her, putting strangers in the rooms that used to hold her missing children.

"Come with me, Jacqueline," Marguerite said once they were situated. She led me to her own bed and even lent me a night dress.

"I should help Pierre," I persisted.

"Edouard is twice your size and anxious to help."

"His hand—"

"Is fine," she assured me. She gave me a fleeting wink and closed the door.

When I woke, I found that she'd brushed and aired out my clothes, even darning the hole in my stockings. As we left, she hugged me, the smell of soap clinging to her collared dress. "We'll see each other again soon. Be well."

My eyes pricked at the softness of her cheek, the surety in her voice. "Merci," I answered tightly, forcing the words out around invisible tears.

———

Pierre drove fast and restlessly, glancing at the mirrors and spraying up dust.

"That went well," I said, hoping to draw out his thoughts. More than that, if I was honest. I wanted to share my plan about striking out on our own, without Flower. I needed Pierre and his people for it to work.

"I like the Flamencourts very much," I added. "And the man with the field and the farm cart—you've found good contacts."

"It's taken years," he admitted.

I closed my mouth, his words buzzing in my brain. I'd lived with my head on the block since July. He'd been at this much longer—and, I gathered, without much success unless you counted staying alive. I wasn't sure he did.

"What did they teach you?" He interrupted my thoughts. "Besides landing receptions and blowing up lorries?"

"A bit of everything." I swallowed. "I can kill a man twice my size. I can shoot and hide and climb and use Morse—not quickly, mind you—and, well, you know. The other things."

"I don't." He frowned at the mirror. "I asked for training in England, but they wouldn't take me."

"You're needed here," I said. "Your contacts—"

"Are useless so long as we depend on Raymond Flower. He won't trust them. He won't trust me."

I smiled, pleased to have my wishes handed to me. "I've been thinking the same. Denise is going to Paris. She and I trained together, you know, so it might help that she won't be far away. If Flower is too difficult"—I was sure he would be, but it didn't hurt to be diplomatic—"we can simply start coordinating with Denise's network instead. Call it a company reorganization."

His shoulders loosened, and he laughed. It wasn't the first time I'd seen him chuckle, but the occurrence was rare enough to startle me.

"What?" I asked, nettled.

"You and I are alike."

I frowned at him, dubious.

"Have you thought about finding a new place to live?" he asked.

That, I had no answer for.

"Flower left that gun in your apartment," he reminded me. "And you said you have an inquisitive landlord. Staying there isn't safe."

"I know," I admitted. "But I haven't thought of anything else. Not yet. We've been too busy."

"I'll take you to Souris, then. Until we find something else, you'll stay with her."

Normally I'd have bridled at his decisiveness. I was the trained agent. I could look after myself. But the matter-of-factness in his voice, his confidence that Souris would take me, made my heart speed and my eyes sting. He and Souris and her family were willing to look after me. We were on the same team.

"All right." I rolled down the car window to feel the breeze. "I intend to be busy this next week, you know, showing you all what I can do." Pierre would think I meant attacking the Boches, but I was also thinking of Flower, Denise's network, and London too.

"And don't I love you for it." Pierre grinned and blew a kiss at me.

CHAPTER 21

―

RAYMOND FLOWER RAN HIS HAND ACROSS THE BACK OF HIS neck, trying to swipe away the tension building in his muscles. The window in the corner was opaque from grime but still let in a white glare on sunny days. Clipboards of repair orders hung on nails, their edges black from the greasy hands of busy mechanics, but the place was quiet now. No one worked on Sundays. He paced, fidgeting while Marcel set up the radio.

Radioing London was dangerous at any time, let alone two days in a row. German detection vans could home in on a radio signal in less than thirty minutes. "You're ready?" Flower asked. "You haven't used this location before?"

"If you have doubts, we could wait a day or two," Marcel suggested. "That might—"

Flower shook his head. It was imperative that he contact London immediately. According to Marcel, last night's drop had proceeded without incident, but the supplies were diverted to storage with some of Pierre Culioli's contacts, not to the depots Flower had chosen. And the newly arrived agents, instead of being immediately sent on to London, were holed up in an unknown location. Unknown to him at least.

In all his time running this circuit, nothing like this had ever happened before. He ran a tight operation, guarding against danger and security leaks. Thanks to that woman, his operatives were running about like cowboys.

"Here." Flower passed Marcel a folded message in neat block capitals.

Marcel smoothed the paper against the worktable, read it, and froze. "You can't be serious."

"I'm deadly serious," Flower retorted.

"*J is useless, likely a German spy. Subverts orders, and fraternizes with C, also under suspicion. Both must be eliminated?*" Marcel read back at him. "This is absurd. You can't think that. Last night's drop went perfectly."

Too perfectly. For once, Flower didn't feel the urge to look over his shoulder. Planting his hand on Marcel's shoulder, he squeezed hard. "I'm your commander. If you can't follow orders…" The unspoken threat dangled in the air between them.

Marcel sputtered, trying to squirm free. "I just think—"

"Why did Culioli pick a drop site right on the Gestapo's doorstep? Why didn't they run with us? They knew they were safe because they are on the Germans' side. They're double agents. He is, undoubtedly." Flower punctuated the claim, stabbing the note with a forefinger.

"It just seems—"

"Send the message," Flower ordered, releasing him. "It's not your call to make."

Marcel circled his shoulders. "Yes, sir. You'll keep watch? I'll transpose the message, then set up the antenna."

He scribbled and tapped at the radio, while Flower counted half a dozen passing bicycles and two cars, his muscles coiling tighter with each tick of his watch. This was taking too long. The vans would be here any minute.

"Done," Marcel said with a sigh. "Let's get out of here."

"Let's see it," Flower said, not leaving his post at the window.

Marcel crossed the garage and extended a penciled message with a trembling hand.

Received. Stand by.

Flower closed his eyes, some of the tension ebbing in his forehead. The poison capsules were coming—signaling to Marcel and anyone else in the know that London acknowledged his leadership of the network.

All he had to do now was wait.

CHAPTER 22

———

DENISE WAS WAITING IN THE DORMITORY, SITTING ON MY BED, one knee jumping restlessly.

"What happened?"

"Washed out," I replied wearily, still too numb to feel the effect of hot tea, dry clothes, and warm towels. I fumbled with the buttons of my jacket. It felt like my hands would never be quick and clever again.

"Did they tell you to pack?"

I paused, halfway out of my jacket, reviewing the pained conversation. "I don't think so," I finally conceded.

"Then there's still time. Don't pack yet. You belong here." She tossed her head angrily. "And they ought to know it."

"Atkins said it's essential we know how to swim. They won't send anyone who can't." And they weren't going to let me back in the water. I hadn't known, though I certainly did now, how dangerous a water rescue could be. I'd thought to show them I was brave, determined, willing to do whatever it took to go to France. Instead, I'd proven myself reckless and irresponsible.

"Swimming." Denise snorted. "Tell me how that will kill any Germans. It's your skill with explosives that counts." She frowned. "That and making people like you."

"They don't," I said tightly, reliving the shame of facing the disappointed triumvirate: Jepson, Clark—now I remembered his name—and Vera Atkins.

Denise rolled her eyes. "Everyone does. Maxwell praises you to the skies—"

"He likes that I can shoot. It amuses him."

"Jepson—"

"Is lucky to be alive." I swallowed. "He shouldn't have jumped in after—"

"*Chut!*" The French exclamation jolted me as much as her shove on the shoulder. "We all were about to. It's just that he and I were fastest. He wants you to win. He wants us all to win." Her voice dropped; her hand picked a stray bit of fluff from the skirt falling over her knees. "They need us to."

I nodded, not needing any convincing on that one. "But—"

"Jacqueline. Do you really think they can afford to be choosy?"

"It's dangerous if they aren't."

"More dangerous than pushing us into that pond?"

I paused.

"So why'd you jump?" She tilted her head inquiringly. "Those first few seconds, I was sure you'd drown. That it would take too long to find you in the weeds. Come on, Jacqueline," she prodded. "The truth now."

I swallowed, remembering the interminable time without air, the piercing chill in my limbs, and the burn in my desperate lungs. "I'd have been as scared no matter how long it took me to get in the water," I admitted. "My father died in a flood." Practically. He'd fought for hours against the rising water of the Seine that flooded his stable filled with prized horses. In the end he'd saved every one of them and died of pneumonia soon after. I didn't remember his illness so much as the battle against the river, and there was no point in sticking to the absolute truth. "I was only six." *Twelve.* "Since then, I never go in the water. Not even to wade." Death lurked in the water.

I thought of the night Jepson found me, gazing at the Thames, and shivered.

"I think"—Denise was never sparing with her opinions—"it will be good enough if you can float. Get yourself across a short span of water. And you and I can make that happen. But we'll have to be quick. Clark is furious."

I looked up into brown eyes, calm and steady. I was flailing—and Denise was offering me a life ring. "You think so?"

"You don't?" Her mouth curved, teasing, challenging. "We'll take care of this. Tonight."

———

At night, the woods and water around Beaulieu—lovely by day—became hauntingly beautiful. I hitched my rucksack higher on my back and comforted myself with the sight of the gently bowed moon, peering through the clouds, smiling at me.

"The pond?" I whispered to Denise as we crept away from the house.

"You'll do better someplace else. Fewer weeds and no bad memories."

Bad memories lurked in every kind of water, but I didn't tell Denise that. I needed to trust her confidence. Jepson had pulled me aside after supper and quietly told me to pack my bags. I'd return to London with him and Vera in the morning. I hadn't told Denise that either.

I had to swim if I wanted to stay, and tonight was my only chance.

"We're far enough now, I think," Denise said, glancing over her shoulder. Nothing showed beyond the rampart of trees. I reached into my pocket for my torch. With the lone light as guide, progress was faster now. And it needed to be. The lake lay beside a larger house than ours a quarter mile away. I had only hours, few enough to count on one hand.

"I wish it weren't so cold," I muttered.

"I brought one of those survival stoves—the soup can filled with cardboard and paraffin," Denise said. "Showing them you can swim won't help if we succumb to hypothermia."

Beyond the wood, the lake slumbered.

"See?" Denise pointed. "Not so many reeds here."

Good news but not enough to make me feel better. We advanced to the shore, setting our rucksacks down outside a tumbledown boathouse, a relic of better days. Denise said it would be easier to learn without heavy clothes, that I should never have worn them my first time in the water. I stripped down to the regulation underwear, hoping she was right.

"Do you think they designed these to have no sex appeal on purpose?" The horrible knickers—woolen jersey and elasticized at legs and waist—were about as appealing as the back end of a horse. The camisole—three buttons at the neck and four-inch sleeves—was arguably worse.

"Wool is warm, even when wet," Denise recited back at me, parroting the rationale the instructors gave when I'd complained.

I grunted and stepped out of my shoes, peeling away my socks. Dry clothes would be nice to get into, when—if—I climbed out of the water. My heart skittered, impossibly fast. "If I'm going down, don't come after me," I blurted.

Denise, still unbuttoning her blouse, replied without looking up, "We'll stay in the shallow water until you can float. We have to. I'm not like Jepson. He probably got all his watercraft badges as a Boy Scout."

And Denise could barely dog-paddle. Though she'd come after me when I was drowning, there was no way she'd have saved me. If she'd reached me, I'd have dragged her down too.

"Promise me," I insisted.

Her lips thinned. "Don't think about it. Come on."

I followed her to the water's edge, my stomach churning, my toes curling like they were rooting into the cool grass. Denise went in first, stopping when the water reached her chest.

"Don't be afraid," she said. "It's bloody cold, but there's only pebbles on the bottom."

No weeds. That was good.

"Slow your breathing," Denise said. "You'll faint."

I sealed my lips and huffed slowly through my nose, like I'd practiced for much of the afternoon. *Just get in. Get it over with.*

Cold stung my feet, numbing me to my ankles. I marched

forward, clumsy from the drag of the water, though it was much less without shoes and clothes. My stomach caved in on itself when the water touched it, but I took another step, afraid even the slightest pause would become permanent. My lungs were collapsing, my body trembling, not only because of the cold.

"What now?" I asked when the water slid up to my armpits.

"You're going to learn to float," Denise told me. "Face away and let me hold your shoulders."

I'd seen Denise climb ropes and slash open combat dummies, but her embrace was unexpectedly gentle as I tipped backward into her chest. When the water touched my ears, I faltered, twisting and splashing water into my mouth, but my flailing feet planted firm on the stony bottom. I straightened, gasping as if I'd sprinted a mile.

Denise watched me, waiting for my panic to subside and my breaths slow. "Again. Keep your lips closed," she said. "And don't fight. That won't work here. I have you, and I'm not letting go."

CHAPTER 23

———

A FORTNIGHT AFTER THE DROP, I RETURNED TO THE Flamencourts—not with agents and canisters of explosives this time. Marguerite, I was sure, would prefer the latter compared to what I carried now. This would be the beginning of a new and deadly network—my own.

"What's in the bag?" she asked cheerily, opening the kitchen door as I parked my bicycle.

"Supplies," I said.

"Won't you come in?"

I hesitated. Tonight's work was best done outside, but against the risk of being seen… "All right," I said. "Are Roger and Pierre here?"

Marguerite beamed. "Come and see."

My first thought, seeing her packed kitchen, was flight. There were too many people—had they been vetted? But then—

"This is her?" The giant man, dark of hair and mustache, frowned skeptically, exchanging worried glances with the older woman beside him. She was a titan too: tall, square, with capable hands and iron-gray hair.

"This is Jacqueline." Marguerite drew herself up. "Who ran the drop and blew up those lorries. Edouard heard from an acquaintance that they contained important airplane parts."

The tall man's face slackened with surprise.

"But she's—"

"I'm just as surprised as you," I said. "I was hoping for a room of commandos."

The short, stooped man next to him coughed a laugh, rough as rocks. "What a disappointment."

Certainly, they looked like the worst sort of army, an ill-assorted jumble of ages and backgrounds. The stooped man was at least sixty, and the tall woman couldn't be much younger, though she was certainly in better condition. Behind them, hands folded, stood a neat man in a frayed but well-cut suit. Looking at them, I couldn't think of a single interest that would legitimately draw them together. If the Milice burst through the door, there was no way to pass this off as a party.

"A gathering this large is dangerous. In the future—"

"Jacqueline, we need to learn," Edouard said. "All of us."

I nodded. "One of the most important things is being careful. Remember that next time. I can train as often as needed, but we must keep our gatherings small." I scanned their faces again—abashed but eager. "Where's Pierre?"

If he'd been intercepted on his way here, scattering at once was the safest course. My weight shifted onto the balls of my feet.

"He's safe," Marguerite assured me. "He cycled to Contres tonight to reach out to more contacts. So you can teach them tomorrow," she explained. "Him too. He doesn't want to miss."

Naturally not. Like a coiled spring, he always seemed ready to jump.

"If you will," the stooped man said. "There's no one else—and it seems, no one better either."

I hesitated. But Germans had just invaded the south of France, deposing the collaborationist Vichy regime. And in the east, they'd reached Stalingrad. If we didn't strike out now in every way we could, there'd be no chance of Allied victory.

"At least let us introduce ourselves," the man said.

It was better if I didn't know. Names could be extracted from even the tightest lips and the most determined hearts, with ice baths and thumb screws.

"Just the essentials," I conceded. "So I don't call you all Georges."

The tall woman laughed. "No, that's just him." She pointed at the giant. "Grand-Georges, for obvious reasons. And I'm Armadine. From Neuvy."

"Émile." The bent gray-haired man held out a hand. His jacket opened, revealing a cross hanging from his neck.

"Father." I greeted him as properly as I could now that I recognized his profession, my mind tumbling with possibilities. A priest could travel about, calling on others without exciting suspicion. A new courier. "Do you ride a bicycle?"

"Everywhere," he said, a twinkle of understanding in his eyes. "It was I who delivered invitations for tonight's party."

I remembered the bag hanging by my side. "I'm afraid I'm not as prepared as I'd like. You see, I planned for four."

"That won't matter, surely," Marguerite said.

I smiled guiltily. "Actually…" She'd gather the truth soon enough. "Gather around the table. Lock the doors."

Of course there weren't enough chairs. The man in the suit—a wine merchant not ready to share his name—stood by the sink, keeping an eye on the drive through a crack in the shutters. Grand-Georges, bigger than ever in the crowded room, leaned against the locked door.

I set my bag on the table with a guilty squirm. Marguerite had iodine, but I hoped she also had a bottle of bleach. "We'll start with easy sabotage."

Armadine frowned.

"Don't worry," I promised. "Still effective." I pulled a blue metal tin from my pocket. "There's more of these in the canisters. Looks like face cream on the outside, but inside—" I popped the lid.

"Doesn't smell like any face cream I've ever used." Marguerite drew back.

"It etches glass," I explained. "Easy to carry in a handbag until the right opportunity presents itself. All you need is a minute with an unattended car—it will ruin the windscreen in minutes, and you can leave as soon as the cream is on."

Marguerite nodded. "I passed two cars outside the police station just last week. It was early morning. No one was about."

"You might think a windscreen or two is too small to matter," I said to the room, because Marguerite was clearly planning missions already, ruining the windscreens of every gendarmerie car in the region. "But every time we delay, damage, disable, or waste, we slow the German war machine."

"Loosen enough bolts, and the whole thing will grind to a stop." Grand-Georges smiled approvingly. "That, I can do."

Laughter filled the room. I was silent until Edouard let me in on the joke. "He keeps an auto garage, Jaqueline."

Another circuit closed in my head. More possibilities.

"What else do you have for us?" the wine merchant asked.

"Well." I delved into my coat pocket for my gloves. "Don't be alarmed."

Poor Marguerite. She thought I was teasing. When I reached into the bag and pulled out a dead rat, she went white as fine flour. "Don't faint," I said. "We haven't even started yet."

I laid the corpse stomach up on the table and drew out my knife. "This is just another way of attack. Some plastique?"

Marguerite's chair scraped loudly against the floor. She staggered out of the room, returning a moment later with a wax-paper-wrapped sausage in either hand, her color slightly better.

"This is an ideal way to begin working with explosive," I explained. "Because it doesn't require a detonator. You won't lose arms or eyes or fingers—"

"Or kitchens?" Marguerite put in.

"Making these little gifts for our German friends," I finished with a smile. "Though I apologize for dirtying your table, Marguerite."

"I'll use bleach." She said it with the fervor of my mother with her rosary.

I made a practiced slit down the middle, then pushed the explosive into the rat's abdomen. "It can't look unusual, so it's best to stitch it up,"

No one looked eager for that job. I'd just have to show them. I knew it got easier after watching a time or two and then with some practice.

"Would you like my sewing kit?" Marguerite asked tremulously.
I had a needle and thread in my other pocket, but—"Please."
She fetched it, surrendering the tidy, lace-trimmed basket
without hesitating.

"I'm afraid this part is a little awkward with gloves." I wasn't
squeamish anymore. Not like the first time, when all my determination failed to stop me from flinching. I'd pegged Prue as
the one to faint, but she hadn't. Iron-faced the whole time, our
group had assembled two dozen rat bombs in twenty minutes.

"We slip the rat bombs into enemy coal stores. They'll
be thrown with the coal into boilers, and the heat will set off
the explosive, blowing up the boiler in the process. Trains,
factories—they can be disabled or destroyed this way."

"That shouldn't be hard to do," Grand-Georges conceded.
"And it would be surprisingly effective."

"The rats are like us," I said. "Unimpressive. Unattractive,
even. Deadly."

That earned me a round of laughs.

"The important thing," I said, licking the thread so it would
slide through the needle easier, "is not just to do this. You must
teach it to someone else." Like I was, so if I died or was taken,
these men and women could keep fighting. Caution made me
add, "Just be prudent in choosing your friends."

Quickly, I stitched skin and fur back together, then set the
body aside. "I have three more. Any volunteers?"

———

Rat bombs and ruined windscreens were only a start. Every
few days I cycled out from Nanteuil to my letter box, leaving

dates and locations for upcoming meetings. Abbé Émile, the priest, distributed them under the guise of making calls on his parishioners.

I cycled to Chambord, Bracieux, Neuvy, Contres, Romorantin, and Montrichard, never instructing more than five or six resistants at a time. I'd left training proud of my superior shooting, but we didn't practice with guns. It was my sabotage experience that was needed. Shooting and open rebellion would come in time, but for now, I needed to give my fellow conspirators immediate tactics.

And as much as I felt at home with Souris and her family, I needed to find a new safe house. Flower, as promised, was no help, but he was fast becoming superfluous. I had my own friends, and they were busy—Abbé Émile carrying messages, a grocer from Montrichard (also named Georges, but without with the *Grand* prefix, as he lacked Georges Duchet's impressive height) taking illicit photographs of larger, less opportunistic targets while he ferried vegetables. Souris was hard at work too, carrying messages and photographing German command centers while delivering Red Cross bundles to refugees. Already Amandine had ruined the windscreen of the collaborationist mayor in Neuvy and passed a supply of plastic explosive to her son-in-law who worked at a rail yard, though she made him find his own rats.

I'd managed to establish contact with Marcel the wireless operator, who'd been forced to leave Tours after a near miss from a roving German detection van. He was hiding out now with Abbé Émile, who was firmly on my side. I wasn't sure how often he contacted Flower but told myself not to worry about it.

So even though London had rejected my request for a supply of underclothes (my spares had been left behind with Mr. Caye in Tours), I hummed as I cycled the flat country between Nanteuil and Montrichard, planning how to safely teach wired detonation to an electric company executive, a hairdresser, a poacher, Georges Fermé the grocer, and the wine merchant and his wife. I knew his name now—André Gatignon, married to dark-haired Paulette—and tonight we were meeting in their wine caves.

Pierre was waiting for me, lounging against a lamppost on a side street in Montrichard, nursing a nearly spent cigarette. He tossed it away as I approached. "And how many miles have you ridden this week?"

"Too many," I laughed. Today's ride was two hours each way. Soon I'd need new tires—a real problem. There were none to be found, so that was another request to put to London. I prophesied, darkly, more than a shade resentfully, that they wouldn't be nearly as tightfisted with those as my undergarments.

"You ready?" Pierre asked.

Georges Fermé had ferried the necessary matériel earlier, as arranged. I was here, born again as a person of punctuality; all that was left was for Pierre to show me the way.

"Lead on," I told him, hooking a hand through his arm. Only a friendly touch, but he jumped like the brush of my clothes burned before making himself relax.

"I suppose it is a nice night for strolling," he said, smoothing his awful mustache. Though he wore it ironically, I didn't appreciate the joke. Hitler's mustache was Hitler's mustache, and it was unpleasant on him and everyone else. "Georges seemed distracted today. Is anything wrong?"

"I shouldn't think so," I answered, but my skin prickled like the temperature had dropped ten degrees. Émile had passed my message to him just yesterday, instructing him on which equipment was needed tonight. And Émile hadn't noticed anything amiss—at least, he'd mentioned nothing. "Why do you ask?"

"Felt like he was avoiding my eyes. Maybe I imagined it."

And maybe not. Smothering the tendrils of unease snaking out from my belly, I tried to consider it coolly. I didn't want to think of Georges as an informer. But for everyone's sake, care was essential.

"Let's go," I decided, adding in an undertone, "but watch for anything amiss."

We set off down the road, past ordinary shops and houses. The mother wheeling her baby in a pram, the old man in a beret sitting on the bus bench reading a book, the hurried woman with a net bag full of potatoes, the young man with a bandaged eye and a missing arm—no one studied us with narrowed eyes or ducked away at our approach.

My unease solidified in an icy lump. Thinking I could discern loyalty at a glance, in them or in Georges, was a delusion. In all probability, Georges merely had a stomachache. And there was no more time to consider. Ahead of us, a steep-roofed, timbered building appeared on the side of the road, built at the edge of an abandoned quarry and surrounded by thick trees. "The entrance to the caves is here," Pierre told me.

Away from the road, stuffed out of sight were four other bicycles. I sent Pierre an inquiring glance.

"There's two missing." I expected six for training tonight: Raymonde and Julien, Theo, André and Paulette, and Georges.

"Georges probably walked. He lives close."

I pushed farther into the trees, but all I flushed out was a lone wood pigeon, who cooed mockingly as he took flight.

"Maybe André and Paulette drove," Pierre hazarded. "No reason why they shouldn't. He stores wine here and comes and goes all the time. He gave me the duplicate key." Pierre glanced left and right, peering into the trees. My concern was infecting him.

Better get on with it. I stashed my bicycle, taking the pistol from the basket and stuffing it in the loosening waistband of my culottes. We left the warm evening light and passed through a heavy iron gate into the cold and musty dark of the limestone cave. Accompanied by the sinister sound of our footsteps echoing through a wide tunnel, we turned left, left again, and saw a faint light. "That's them," Pierre whispered.

It was an ideal spot for meeting. Their light was the only sign of human presence, and the tunnel amplified our approach, sounding a warning. If only I felt certain of what we would find.

"I brought two pears today. No figs," I called out in a low voice.

"No figs here either" came the coded reply.

I'd be light blinded the moment we stepped into their cavern. "Wait here," I whispered to Pierre. "I'll go first."

Giving him no chance to argue, I flicked on my torch, shone it at the bare rock in front of me, blinked until my eyes stopped squinting, and stepped into the room.

"Jacqueline!" André Gatignon, seated at a makeshift table of ammunition crates, held up a glass. "Just in time. We're about to toast Theo. Today he blew up a tree and stopped traffic to Blois. It took three hours to get a crew out to clear the road."

Theo grinned, revealing an array of mismatched teeth. His little dog, Louki, held the place of pride on his lap. "A child can manage a time pencil fuse. It was easy." Despite his offhand words and the casual way he ruffled Louki's soft ears, delight showed in his small smile.

"Two more glasses," Paulette told her husband with a nudge.

"Come on, Pierre," I called.

For him, André had only a quick nod, a mechanical smile. Georges stared at his hands, nervously rubbing the stem of his glass.

"This is quite a good vintage," André went on, covering the stuttering pause. "Worthy of Theo and his brave act. Let's not waste it." He raised his glass. "To Free France."

We all joined in, and I added a silent toast for André as well. Long before our group coalesced, he'd floated downed pilots and fleeing Jews downriver in his casks.

"Lost any batches to bad barrels lately?" Pierre inquired.

André's bushy eyebrow twitched. "Not one. I'm a good cooper."

Not a single life lost in his care. He and his wife, Paulette, kept up their work right under the noses of the Germans, while caring for their three young children. And came here tonight, anxious to do more. I sipped my glass, tasting meadow flowers and plump grapes and courage. It took a hard blink to ward off the mistiness gathering in the corners of my eyes.

By the time Theo finished recounting his road sabotage, and Georges reached his third glass, the slight awkwardness dissipated.

"Well done, Theo," I said. "Success with a time pencil fuse means you're absolutely ready for wired detonators."

These were essential when a bomber needed precise control, like the trap Edouard and I had set on the road near Petit Aunay. Wired detonators were also needed for protective measures—booby traps to guard supply caches, safe houses, and meeting places such as this cave. But they required greater skill.

"We'll practice with dummy explosives tonight," I explained. "First you need to learn to wire a circuit and choose a detonator. London has supplied us with a few different types."

Louki the dog was dispatched to a corner. Theo assured us she wouldn't make trouble and that she'd warn us the instant she detected any. I didn't mind. She went most places with Theo. It was hard to imagine the weathered old man without her.

And Theo did well at tonight's work, unlike Georges, who struggled to remember which wires went where. Georges, however, showed real presence of mind in choosing targets, demonstrating unexpectedly creative ambush plans, talking enthusiastically as he worked. There was a sugar factory in the district, he said, poorly guarded, with several large storage tanks. Destroying them would shut down the entire factory.

"Look over the site," I told him. "And if you decide to target it, bring along a friend like Theo. A time pencil should work for that." I didn't want Georges fiddling with wires yet.

"People will be angry," Paulette interjected, "if we stop sugar production."

"When's the last time you had any sugar?" asked Julien Nadeau, the electric company man. "Rationing is a farce—there's never any food in the stores."

"Yes, but some find us easier to blame than the Germans," Paulette said.

"That's what this work is for," I said, patting the dummy bomb she'd assembled. "It's not just about sugar. It's showing people we don't need to be afraid."

"And I'll help," Pierre offered. "If you decide to hit the factory."

André smiled thinly; Georges stiffened again. And though I puzzled over it as we disassembled and reattached detonators—rote practice, like children learning arithmetic—I couldn't think of an explanation. I was on the point of dismissing it all, but as we tidied up and slipped away, singly and in pairs into the night, Georges bent and whispered in my ear as he passed.

"Keep an eye on Pierre."

CHAPTER 24

―――

PETIT AUNAY, 29 NOVEMBER 1942

MAX EXTINGUISHED HIS CIGARETTE AND PICKED UP HIS HALF-empty glass. Beside him at the bar, a thickset rail yard worker shook his head.

"The Germans are crazy, I tell you. I spent the whole day digging through coal stores looking for dead rats."

"Find any?" Max asked.

"Four. Each one was examined and thrown in the trash. Just about broke my back—and for what? None of our trains left on time." He drained the rest of his glass and stared at it mournfully. "It just doesn't make sense."

"I'm sure they have their reasons," Max said, signaling for the barman to refill both their drinks. "Things will get better." Stalingrad would fall. He'd find the criminals responsible for the blocked roads, the exploded boilers, the fleet of police cars with ruined windscreens.

The man frowned skeptically. "Or worse." He held up his hand, stopping the barman from dispensing another dose. "Thank you but no. I should get home."

"You look dead on your feet," Max said truthfully.

"Maybe tomorrow we'll wake up and the world won't be

upside down." The man gave a weak smile and shook his head. "All that shoveling. For what?"

Max, who'd been briefed on the latest memos, could have enlightened him but didn't. The last thing Germany needed was more disgruntled Frenchmen getting ideas.

He exchanged goodbyes with the rail yard worker and watched the man shuffle out of the bar. Stymied again.

Max had followed this fellow from a known terrorist location in Paris, all the way to Tours, hoping to establish a bridge to a nebulous local network who insisted on disrupting the peace with increasing regularity. Police officers couldn't leave their cars alone for fifteen minutes, and now a Reich official was refusing to tour the region without increased protection. And this rat business… When Max considered the lost manpower resulting from high command's warning to be alert for exploding rats, his eye started to twitch, his stomach soured— the first signs of an oncoming migraine.

And it turned out the man he'd followed had actually visited the house next door to the terrorists, delivering eggs and butter to his sister. An innocuous coincidence, not a real lead. Max would have to start again, digging up more clues.

He was beginning to think the cell he was hunting wasn't connected to CARTE or any known networks. It was, he conceded, the smartest way to do it. But their attacks used plastic explosive, so they must be supplied by the British. So why hadn't he found them yet? Angry telegrams arrived almost daily from Berlin. His earlier commendation was all but forgotten. Richard was bitter, grumbling about transferring back to Alsace, and Max couldn't even complain to his superiors, not since Boemelberg had stolen a copy of his insubordinate memo.

"Hard day?" the bartender asked.

"You can't imagine," Max said wearily. He picked up his laborer's coat and cap and set out for the train station.

CHAPTER 25

———

I DIDN'T RIDE HOME TO NANTEUIL AFTER LEAVING THE CAVES. I followed Pierre, my best ally, to his safe house, grimly considering what I must do if he proved otherwise, unable to dismiss Georges's warning.

All the way to Neuvy, he didn't seem to notice, but as I prepared to overtake him on foot, just outside a small hotel, he turned on his heel.

Then he saw my knife.

"What the hell?"

"Shh. Move away from the door." The street was dark, but better if we kept to the shadows. I motioned him into a passage between a shabby cafe and the hotel.

"Jacqueline—"

"Something is wrong. Georges warned me to be careful of you as he left. Why would he do that?"

Pierre flung out his hands, a thoroughly French gesture, but one I'd learned to read as a threat. I raised the knife, and he jumped back. "Be careful with that thing!"

"I am being careful. So explain."

"I don't know! He and I are old friends. And you and

I—Jacqueline, if I was a traitor, why would I have helped with the drop? Why plan it at my family's field? I swear I'm loyal. I shouldn't have to, but I swear it."

I wanted to believe him, but there was a vast difference between knowledge and hope. Hope was dangerous.

"You're staying here?"

He nodded.

"Let me see your room."

I knew perfectly well what the concierge would think, so I pinched my cheeks, working up a blush I didn't feel as I tucked away my knife, then followed him into the hotel.

"You know these people?" I whispered after he collected his key and led me upstairs.

He shook his head. "They think I'm a tax inspector. I was, before."

I stood back as he unlocked the door, my hand on my hip, close to my pistol.

"You aren't seriously going to—"

"Don't be ridiculous, Pierre. I'm simply confirming what I already know." And if I was wrong…well. "Stand over there." I motioned him to the corner, away from the window.

"Go ahead. Look. I don't have anything to hide."

And he didn't. Yes, there was a neat little pistol in a hollowed-out book, but his craft was good. There were no scraps of paper with carelessly jotted information, no typical German gifts. He had a healthy supply of cash, but it matched very nearly what we'd divvied out between us after the drop at Bois Renard.

I sat down on the edge of the desk.

"Trust me now?" Pierre asked sarcastically.

I rolled my eyes. "Yes." Of all people, he should know that. If I didn't trust him, he'd never have reached the hotel. "So what's gotten into Georges?"

———

I spent the night at Pierre's hotel, overcome by the late hour, the hourlong ride back to Nanteuil, my aching legs and restless mind. It would have drawn too much notice to slip downstairs and ask the concierge for my own room—Pierre and I argued over this until I conceded the truth—so he gave up the bed and slept on the floor. I slept poorly, suspicious shadows thickening in my mind. At daybreak, I crept out of bed, dressed, and left Pierre lying on his back on the floor, mouth open, head at an angle he would soon regret. The only trace of my presence was the note on his pillow.

Lay low. I'll speak to Georges.

I found him working in his grocery, exchanging tired vegetables for his dispirited customers' ration coupons. He caught my eye, blinked acknowledgment, then turned back to bagging bundles of carrots and kale. I browsed the baskets of pears, careful not to touch and bruise them, looking for ones with smooth green-speckled skins and the stems still attached. My mother always said that was the trick to finding good ones.

Intent on my study, I counted the jangles of the bell on the door as the early morning shoppers came and went. Finally, the last of the customers left. A weary shuffle announced Georges moving up beside me. "Can I be of assistance?"

"These pears." I turned and presented my basket to Georges, adding in an undertone, "You are alone?" There might be others, in an adjacent office or storeroom, and we couldn't be overheard.

He nodded but still took the precaution of motioning me to the back of the shop, by the tubs of beets and cabbages.

"Why did you warn me about Pierre?" I asked. "He's been nothing but friendly."

"That's what I thought. But…" Georges dropped his voice to the point where I had to study his lips. "We don't know everything. There was a letter from London—"

I'd considered several possibilities throughout my sleepless night. But not this one.

"What did it look like?"

"A brown packet, marked for delivery to Flower only. I don't know who brought it to him, but he showed me the letter. And the capsule."

"Capsule?" A cold fist closed around my heart. I reached for the stacked crates of onions.

"Yes, a little pill—"

"I know what they look like." My free hand closed around my necklace—Vera had confiscated my locket and given me this hollow pendant instead, with orders to wear it always. My last defense. "Do you have it? What did the letter say exactly?" What had Flower said to convince London Pierre was a traitor? Neither he nor they knew more of him than I did.

Georges gave a half-hearted shrug. "Flower showed me the letter, but I don't read much English. I saw *terminate* and Pierre's last name. That's why Flower showed it to me. He ordered me to secretly feed it to Pierre, but I—" His eyes fell. "I said I couldn't do it."

"Thank God," I murmured.

"But then I felt guilty—what if I'm wrong? I thought Flower must have given the capsule to André instead."

Last night's wine. My heart stuttered, stopped, and lurched to life again. "But nothing happened!"

Georges nodded. "I must have guessed wrong."

"Well, so did Raymond Flower," I snapped. Unless they had good reason, London would defer to Flower's orders. But not everyone would say no to him like Georges. "You did right to tell me," I said, hoping to relieve the troubled frown on Georges's face. "It's a misunderstanding. I'll take care of this. Where did you see Flower last?"

His eyes widened. "Jacqueline—"

"Where was it? The bus stop? The café outside St. Gatien?"

Georges shook his head. "It was here. He came to the shop." He reached for me, like he was afraid. "Please don't do anything rash. We need you."

I nodded, only half hearing. First, I needed to warn Pierre. Then—

"There's something else," Georges said. "I didn't mention it last night. Because of Pierre. But I found a target. A good one."

"Look it over with Theo first." I couldn't join every single sabotage mission, and I needed Georges to learn that.

"I did. I've been thinking about it for weeks. Finally figured out a way the other day. We can—"

I held up my hand. "One thing at a time."

First, Pierre. I trained a level gaze on Georges. "Pierre is not our enemy. If I tell him to come here, you'll keep him safe?"

Georges hesitated. "Yes, I can hide him. For a few days. If you're sure."

It wasn't much time, but it was better than none. "Good. I need your telephone."

———

Pierre, mystified by my urgent call to his hotel, agreed to come but insisted on stopping in Romorantin at Duchet's garage first. I tried to dissuade him, but he was adamant. "Grand-Georges is expecting me. If I don't come, he'll worry."

I chewed my lip, more anxious than ever but unwilling to tell him over the phone why he too should worry. I couldn't afford to lose him, but I didn't want him flying off the handle and going after Flower. "Come as quick as you can. Be on your guard. And don't tell anyone. It's important."

It was the best I could do. Replacing the receiver, I turned back to the grocer.

"Will Pierre be safe?"

"Let's pray that he is" was the best I could offer. "Now, what's this target you're so keen about?"

Georges grinned. "You'll like it."

I folded my arms.

"No, really. All trains from Vierzon to Tours have to come this way, through Montrichard. Because of the tunnel."

I shook my head, unimpressed. "Germans will guard it. They always do."

"Yes," Georges conceded. "But—"

"We can't. Not yet. Planning that kind of attack takes numbers, arms, combat—"

"The tunnel has an air shaft higher up the mountain," Georges said. "We can hike up, then lower the charges down the shaft without being seen. But I'm not sure if we can lower them or if someone will have to abseil down the shaft. Only a small person can do it."

His brown eyes met mine.

I considered. Tracks could be repaired relatively quickly. Not tunnels. "Show me."

"I have to wait until lunch," Georges said. "When I usually close up shop. It will take us a couple of hours, longer than I normally close, but—"

"That will be fine." I glanced at my watch. Not even ten yet. Flower and his L pill were a problem, but I preferred fighting Germans to my own allies. The safest place for Pierre, right now, was at my side. He'd be happier with something to do, as would I.

I reached for the telephone, drumming my fingers on Georges's till until the line connected.

"Room eleven, please."

"Again?" The hotel concierge, recognizing my voice from the last call, sounded annoyed. Probably the same pinch-faced woman I'd shied away from last night.

"Yes." I supposed I'd be sour too if I never got an hour away from the reception desk.

The line connected, Pierre's voice cutting through the static. "*Allo?*"

I wondered if the concierge was still listening. His voice seemed fainter than on my first call, though perhaps it was simply a poor connection.

"I need you to bring me a kite. One of the ones we left in the woods," I said.

A long pause, while I prayed he'd understand I meant one of the buried parachutes.

"There's no white ones," he finally said.

"It's the string I want."

"Ah. Anything else?"

"That's all." Everything else I needed was hidden in the nearby caves. I could fetch it while waiting for Georges. "But hurry."

———

Two hours later, Pierre rolled into the plaza in front of Georges Fermé's shop on a motorcycle.

"Fast enough?" He dismounted with a boyish grin and joined me on the bench where I'd been sitting in the sun, eating pears and reading a detective novel.

Gathering myself—he was clearly enjoying my shock—I peered past him at the rusty motorcycle. "New toy?"

He nodded. "Runs on charcoal. Grand-Georges fitted her up for me. That's why I had to stop at the garage."

"No funny looks from him?"

Pierre shook his head.

Anxiety wrenched my stomach as I studied him. Flower's poison pill might be slow acting. "Have you eaten breakfast?"

Pierre gave a quick negative jerk of his head. "Grand-Georges offered, but you said to hurry." He smiled at the bike. "She's fast."

"And loud," I said, concealing my relief. It was clear Pierre was wildly in love with his machine; my surprise had worn off, but I remained skeptical. The motorcycle was useless for after-curfew travel, not like my bicycle. The four black-garbed women who'd stopped to stare at his noisy entrance were only now turning away.

"So what's the matter?" Pierre asked.

I tucked my book into my string shopping bag, along with the turnips, pears, time pencils, and packets of plastique. "I need you for a job. Today. Now. And you were right about Georges Fermé." I jerked my head in the direction of his shop. "He heard something about you that bothered him, but he's all right now."

"Good." Pierre laced his fingers together and leaned back on the bench, turning his face to the bright October sun. "You sorted it."

"Not really," I admitted. "I'll tell you later. After the work's done."

Pierre closed his eyes, experienced enough not to ask questions about the job I was about to pitch him into while we were out on the street. "Everyone's jumpy, these days. Flower probably gave him an earful, is all."

I didn't contradict him. Across the street, Georges Fermé locked the front door of his shop.

"You brought the string?" I asked Pierre, worried because he wasn't carrying a bag.

"Under my sweater," he muttered. "Two kites' worth wrapped from my waist to my shoulders."

More than enough. "Is it uncomfortable?"

"Like a shirt made of blisters."

I laughed. Couldn't help it, the way he kept such a straight face. "Don't complain, Pierre. You did just get a motorcycle."

"I suppose there's that," he conceded.

Georges crossed the street toward us, his crumpled shop apron tucked under his arm. Pierre waved, and Georges replied with a nod and a smile, as if last night's mistrust had never been.

"Finished! For now at least," Georges announced.

"It's a beautiful day. We'll find somewhere to stop for lunch?" I suggested, for the benefit of any passersby.

"First I have to stop at a friend's," Georges said. "Asked me to bring the milk in off her porch. Two bottles, front and back."

My brow furrowed. He'd heard, then, from his friend in the village. Two guards at each end of the tunnel today.

"Better get on, then," I said, my smile intact. The three of us stood in a purposeful triangle, each of our eyes trained over the other's shoulders, alert for surveillance, for any sign of approach.

"Did you find everything you needed at the shops?" Georges asked me, meaning *Did you gather all the necessary supplies?*

"And a bit extra," I assured him, hoisting my heavy bag.

"Let me carry it," Pierre said, but he dropped his outstretched hands when I darted my eyes to Georges.

"You're carrying enough," I murmured. "Blisters."

"We can walk to my sister's house over the hill and enjoy the view," Georges said, taking the bag. Even though there was no one around to hear, precautions must be kept, must be drilled until they became habit.

We set off down the road, chatting as if this really were nothing but a friendly stroll. When the railroad tunnel came into sight, we gave it only passing glances, gathering information without staring. The German sentries at the mouth of the tunnel held their guns close, their stance alert, their eyes pointed down the tracks. It was impossible to guess anything from their toy-soldier stiffness and emotionless expressions, and they spared no attention for the hill towering at their backs. They were either smart enough not to give anything away or didn't guess we were coming.

Georges led us to a path that skirted the hill, out of the guards' line of sight, and we veered off the trail into the press of trees, their branches spread like protective arms over our heads. We climbed the steep incline making very little sound thanks to the undergrowth of ferns and moss. Georges spoke in whispers as I stretched my steps to match his. He was not a tall man, but the expansive sort who somehow took up more space than could be accounted for by his size. Of course, everyone was large compared to Pierre and me. The damp forest soaked its way into my socks as we traveled.

Georges picked his way around a thorny shrub and pointed between two trees to a large black pipe protruding from the hillside, sealed with an iron grate.

"Here." He rolled up his loose trousers and unwound the bandages binding a crowbar and a wrench to his calves. There hadn't been time to stow any equipment up here earlier. Everything we needed we had to carry with us, in plain sight.

I studied the bars and the black void beyond. "You're right. It's small."

Georges pursed his full lips in doubt as he stared down the centerpiece of his grand plan.

It was certainly too small for the barrel-chested grocer. As for me, I wasn't as confident as I wished. Maybe I wouldn't have to go down.

I started explaining, for Pierre's benefit. "We want to lower the explosives through the air shaft and collapse the tunnel from the inside, but there may be a grate at the bottom of the shaft, which could block the charge before we get it deep enough. I brought a torch. Hopefully we'll be able to see."

"Should we wait for dark?" Pierre asked.

"If we do, our lights will be visible from miles away. I think daylight is safest."

Pierre picked up the wrench and hefted it experimentally, shifting his head in that nervous, jerky fashion of his, looking through the trees to the town below. "We may want to wait until there's a train before we start pounding on the grate. The sound may carry through the tunnel to where the guards are standing."

"We could wait," Georges said, doubt creasing his sweat slicked forehead. "But there's no way to say how long. Nothing is regular. Usually there's a passenger train from Tours in the evening, but you know how it is." Civilian transports were routinely delayed and disrupted to accommodate German troops and supplies. "It could be hours. If it even comes."

"The sound won't carry that far," I reassured Pierre as I picked up the crowbar and wedged it between the pipe and the grate. I leaned my weight into it.

Georges looked on with amusement as both Pierre and I tried to no avail, then took my place. "Let me."

It took a half hour, torturing the rusted bolts with both crowbar and wrench, before they gave and the grate lifted. My blouse stuck to my underarms and the small of my back. The iron handle had stained my hands a greasy black.

"Well, let's look." Pierre pointed the torch into the dark recesses of the air shaft. "Merde," he muttered. "Too deep to see. We can lower something and see how far it goes before it's obstructed."

I slipped my head between his and Georges, confirming the diagnosis. The light died midtunnel, telling us nothing.

I lifted the parachute cord, letting the silky rope slide against my fingers. "We expected this. Come on. I'll need your help to fashion a harness."

"A harness?" Georges was as startled as if I'd asked for a ticking grenade. "Not yet, Jacqueline. We can lower an object first." He brandished the wrench.

"That wrench won't tell us details," I pointed out as I made a knot, holding up the cord to test the size of the leg hole I'd just made as if eyeing a sewing pattern.

"It's so narrow," Georges said, studying the shaft with new eyes, gauging it against my size. "I'm not sure anymore."

I pushed away all thoughts of the dark space, the close-pressing walls. There might even be bats. "I can brace myself against the walls." My shoulders gave an involuntary shiver as the thick cobwebs of my imagination brushed over my neck.

Pierre paced two steps, his hand movements sharp, agitated. "No, Jacqueline. I should do it."

I raised my eyebrows. He had the flexibility of a dry oak and shoulders much wider than my own. "Don't be stupid. Hand me the torch." I pulled the harness around me and tightened it, my split skirt bunching beneath the cord.

Reluctantly, Pierre took the other end of the cord, circling it around a tree trunk. "If anything goes wrong, yank the rope and—"

"Just hold it tight," I interrupted. "Nothing will go wrong." During the hike, I'd told him about abseiling steep cliffs in Scotland, and he knew what to do to keep me safe. In theory.

"I'd rather go down," he said. "Have you holding me. What if—"

I silenced him with a hand on his arm, thought about saying something blithe and reassuring, then changed my mind. He was different than me—quiet, intense. He wouldn't be strengthened by casual words. I hadn't understood that before. Instead, I held his eyes, waiting until he made his own decision and nodded, but not without a sigh of protest.

"We have to make sure she fits first," Georges pointed out. "Maybe we can't see the bottom because the shaft turns or narrows."

"One way to find out," I murmured between tight teeth.

I clenched the sides of the pipe and lowered my feet, testing the space for my hips. They slid through easily. My shoulders did the same with enough space for me to wriggle myself into a braced position.

I pressed my shoes against one side of the pipe, my back against the other, unable to tell if it was wet or cold that seeped through my blouse. The tension on the cord cut into my thigh as I controlled the descent. Less than fifteen feet down, the ring of light above me shrank to a dispiriting size. It hovered in the distance like a foreign, mysterious object, while the air solidified around me, still and old.

"I'm fine. Keep going." My voice circled me like a dog panting around its owner, unwilling to leave. Despite my assertion to Pierre, I didn't dare speak any louder. Who knew which direction voices carried in this crypt? And how far? I closed my eyes and took in the powerful smell of mildewed earth and stone. It reminded me of other places; for a moment I imaged the Thames closing over me, dark and rushing, and then the ceiling at my old home falling in a cloud of dust. I let the sensations come deliberately, acclimating myself to danger, making it mundane.

Cold wrapped its clammy fingers around my ankles, my throat. I looked up, the hazy ring of light half-obscured by Pierre's and Georges's shadows. The pressure on the rope changed, tightened. My descent stopped. Before I could wiggle the rope to tell them to continue, a thrum traveled through the dead air around me.

A tremor grew, deep, like the earth beginning a mighty growl. Then sound, like the echo of explosives or thunder concussing a mountainside. The once-dead air pushed up the shaft, blowing past my feet and lifting my hair. Below me, a strip of light ran from one side of the shaft to the other and disappeared as a train stampeded only meters away. I hadn't realized I was nearly at the bottom until the headlight reached my shoes.

I braced my hands on the wall and let the vibration travel through me, overtaking my heart and jarring me until my face shook. Or maybe it was laughter—breaking free while the train covered the sound. For a wild moment I imagined there was no cord; I could let go, plunge atop one of the cars, and set the detonation as it sped on toward the arms of the enemy.

It ended too soon, the earthquake retreating to a wind, to a memory. The rope cut into the back of my legs as the men tugged me back to the surface with a haste that betrayed their worry.

"Are you okay?" Pierre asked as soon as his voice could reach me without shouting.

"I'm fine. Don't fuss. There's no grate. We can lower the charge all the way to the tracks." Doubt assailed me. "That was a civilian train, right?" If we'd missed our chance at a troop transport, I'd throw something.

"Slow engine, only three cars. Looked civilian to me," Georges said.

Pierre gave a flicker of a smile. "They won't walk the track inside to check for sabotage—not when they're constantly guarding both sides of the tunnel. We can lower bricks of explosive and bring the entire tunnel down."

I pressed my lips in doubt. I'd rarely been inside anything that felt stronger or thicker than that tunnel, and we had only six pounds of 808. I wasn't sure now if it was enough.

"If you lower me the entire way, I could look for seams in the walls where I can rig it." *And do more damage.*

"Too risky." Pierre shook his head. "The tunnel's too short. If they look inside, they'll see your silhouette."

"I think it'll be dark enough in the middle."

Georges frowned. "We can't afford to do anything foolish."

"Can't afford?" I huffed. "We can't afford to only inconvenience Germans when we have the chance to hamstring them."

Georges remained dubious, but my complaint convinced Pierre, as I knew it would.

I set to work under the dappled light of the trees shaping the explosive, the foul smell of decaying sweetness overwhelming the fresh scent of the surrounding ferns. I folded the 808 into my pullover to keep it away from my skin and lowered the bundle into my shirt. "Quickly," I said. "Get me back down there." My harness was in a heap on the ground, stained and grimy. I reminded myself to be meticulous, checking every knot.

"Are you sure?" Pierre asked when I was poised above the maw of the air shaft. "If they look inside—"

"I'm not settling for small wins," I said. "Not when there's the chance of a bigger one."

"You're sure the time pencils are set correctly?"

I gave him a look. He retreated, dropping his eyes. "I know. But the thought of you down there is bad enough without a bomb ticking." He was no double agent. Sincere worry tugged at the sharp features of his face.

"I'll be fine," I said, telling myself as much as him. I, at least, was used to obeying these kinds of orders. "Just wait for three tugs."

This time, I passed through the dark without thinking, my mind fixed on the task waiting for me.

I did pause, hovering a moment where I'd found space instead of a grate, peering cautiously into the tunnel. Wide white circles framed the tunnel on either side, like spotlights. At my right and twenty meters away, a pair of German sentries made a blurry silhouette. My hands, slippery with sweat, clenched the rope. It was dark here, but was it dark enough?

Be fast, I told myself. *They'll have no time to see you.*

I shifted my grip and dropped like a spider, flattening myself on the ground. Rope trailing, I groped blindly for the sweater-wrapped bundle with one hand while the other traced rails, stones, dirt, mapping my surroundings. I crawled to the nearest wall, groping for a recess to magnify the percussive blast. It was too smooth. I may as well have been dropped into a bottle.

Fine. I'd settle for the ground, right at the bottom of the wall. If I dug a slight hollow, the explosion should break enough rock to destroy the track and make clearing the line almost as bad as a complete cave-in.

Barehanded, I scraped at the gravel, moving it carefully to avoid the grating sound of shifting rock, sure I must be shredding my skin and nails but too charged up to feel anything. The hole had to be so much larger than I'd thought, and my digging was slow. I wedged the package against the stone wall, then pulled it free, hollowed out another dozen handfuls of dirt, and tried again. It fit. Sort of. Barely. But I'd crouched here long enough. Any moment, one of the sentries might catch my movement from the corner of their eye or hear the muffled rasping of my pitiful excavation attempts. If I did this again, I vowed, I would carry a trowel. Or at least a spoon.

I tugged three times at the rope.

Nothing.

I tugged again. I took two steps, beginning to pace, telling myself to breathe and not panic, when the harness at my hips yanked me a foot in the air. I nearly let out a yelp, flopping like a fish on a line as I jerked upward. My shoulder banged on the tunnel mouth, and I bit my lip hard enough to draw blood. Safe in the tunnel, I let out my breath in a pained hiss, but there was no time to inspect anything. Bracing myself against the walls, I propelled myself up, mostly managing to steer myself away from additional knocks.

"No gaps," I gasped when Pierre's face appeared. "I don't know if we'll bring down the tunnel, but I placed the charge to maximize damage."

"Time will tell," Georges said. "Let's get out of here."

CHAPTER 26

———

"ARE YOU CERTAIN?" VERA ATKINS ASKED. BEHIND HER, CLARK scowled, clutching a life ring like he was afraid of drowning.

"Certain." I wasn't, not really, but Denise and I had practiced last night until we were blue with cold, then huddled by the paraffin burner until warm enough to try again. I could float without sinking now and propel myself through water. Not with style, not easily. But I could do it.

I'd made my case first thing this morning, but Clark wasn't convinced, and Jepson and Atkins were skeptical.

"You don't have to do this, Jacqueline."

I frowned at Vera, surprised. "Of course I do."

This was the only thing to do, the only way forward. Nothing else could have propelled me into the water last night, and nothing less would make me wade in this morning.

Stay calm, I told myself. *Once you reach the other side, you can dream up seven different hells for Agent Clark.*

He didn't think I could do it, and even if I could, hadn't I already proved myself unsuitable?

Aloud, I vowed that I was willing and ready, so the four of us—Clark, Jepson, Vera, and I—had piled into a car and left the New Forest in favor of the nearest village. And the nearest river because that was the stated requirement.

Beaulieu River wasn't that big, and the water certainly wasn't fast. But unlike the lake, it was moving. I wouldn't be able to stay close to the bank, near enough to touch bottom, not if I wanted to prove myself and reach the other side.

"This is ridiculous," Vera muttered.

Maybe so. But if crossing a river was needed… "I can do this," I said. "And I learn from my mistakes. I won't be impulsive again."

The water, spilling sleepily over the mill dam a short way upstream, shimmered in the light breeze.

It can't be more than thirty yards.

Outside my range, though I wouldn't admit it.

"All right. Whenever you're ready." Jepson circled one oar, keeping his little rowboat steady in the water. "I'll only be a few yards away," he promised. "If I see you going down, I'll stretch out an oar." Otherwise, they wouldn't have let me do this.

"Thank you, Captain. But I won't need it." I waded into the water, cold seeping into my boots. Parting the reeds, I pushed farther in, up to my knees, hips, chest. Then I kicked off, my arms and legs churning, my chin bobbing on top of the water, my lips sealed shut.

I thought the current would be negligible, but it thrust me downstream, where the river widened. I'd read books long before yesterday's disaster warning swimmers not to fight currents.

You'll exhaust yourself. You'll need Jepson's oar, I told myself, surrendering slightly. But if this kept up, I'd have to paddle along for forty yards. Fifty.

"Marvelous!" Jepson called. I didn't look. He wasn't here. The oar didn't exist. I cycled my limbs like gear wheels in a mechanical toy, willing the shore to move closer, but it taunted me, aloof, at an impossible distance. Fire flared in my side, and my lungs screamed for more air. I flopped onto my back for a rest, stretching hands wide, struggling to compensate for the weight of my boots. Jepson's shouts fired around me, but I stared at the sky, gulping air for a few seconds, then righted myself again.

Damn. I'd floated downstream. The bank looked even farther.

Push, I told myself, scurrying through the water again. I didn't have to look good, I just had to make it. My boots felt heavy as rocks. My arms burned; there was no way to get enough air through my nose. I gasped through my mouth and choked on a quart of water.

"Jacqueline—"

I closed my ears. *Push*. Another hundred paddles. I counted them out. Once, twice, and again. It was too many, so I told myself to stick it out for another fifty, afraid to risk floating again.

The riverbank looked closer. I was more than halfway. A fallen tree beckoned me, half-in, half-out of the water. If I could reach it... I cycled faster, burning everything I had.

"Not the tree!" Jepson hollered. "The current might sweep you beneath it!"

I was so tired, I didn't know if I believed him, but I knew I had to show caution and presence of mind. Surrendering for a moment, I let the water pull me past. I dog-paddled again, and when my arm seized, I stretched a foot down—nothing—and slipped under the water. But my lips were closed, and I thrashed my legs and fought my way up. *Move*, I told the uncooperative arm. *Move faster.*

Numbed by cold, by the shock of not touching bottom, my ears began ringing.

"Get back! You can't swim."

Papa's voice, right beside me, just as he'd sounded years ago as he'd pushed me away and entered the flooded barn to rescue our horses alone. To die from the weight and chill of muddy water. My limbs morphed into bags of sand, lifeless and heavy.

Will it be fast, Papa?

I shook my head to clear it, repeating my earlier order. *No. Move. Move faster.*

My left toe slipped on mud; my hand flailed for the reeds just beyond my fingers. I sank, floundered, found the bottom, and pushed forward. My next step, both feet sank ankle-deep in mud. My fingers clutched like a baby's around a fistful of cattails. Over my desperate gasps, I heard Jepson cheering as I crawled onto the bank.

"Just breathe," he said, as if I could do anything else. I rolled onto my back. Dark swirls nearly drew the sky shut, but my heart slowed as I drew calm from the firm, rough ground, pushing away unconsciousness. I heard Jepson, leaping from his boat into the water, splashing to shore, but I looked away, guarding this moment for myself, afraid of what might show in my face.

Before, water had tempted me, promising an easy-seeming escape. Now I was a fighter. I'd learned how to swim.

"I crossed. I crossed a river," I gasped.

Jepson beamed, brushed absently at his eye. "You certainly did."

CHAPTER 27

———

GEORGES AND HIS WIFE FED US SUPPER. WE HEARD THE explosion while we ate, but instead of smiling at each other and lifting our glasses, Pierre and I followed Georges's wife's lead, reacting with surprise and leaving the table to watch at the window through a gap in the curtains. As we puzzled aloud what the noise might mean, I wondered if Georges was protecting her or if he didn't trust her. I couldn't tell, and that was the trouble. You couldn't really tell with anyone. George's wife didn't know, and I still hadn't confessed the truth about Flower's poison pill to Pierre.

When we resumed our seats, my shoulders were stiff, my arms wooden, my appetite gone. I worked to move our conversation along, pushing a chunk of brown bread through the last of my vegetable soup.

"Isn't Adeline expecting you?" Georges asked when his wife began clearing the plates.

"I forgot." She glanced at us, then the door. "I'm sorry. A friend—"

"Don't apologize," Pierre said. "We're so grateful for dinner."

"Go on," Georges told her. "I'll do dishes."

She gave me an apologetic smile. "Next time you come, I promise not to hurry off." Moments later, she whisked out the door, a patterned scarf tied around her head and a brown paper package clutched to her chest. "Good night, Pierre. Good night, Jacqueline."

"Old shoes," Georges explained as the door closed behind her. "For our friend's children."

I smoothed my blouse, waiting a few extra seconds to ensure we were alone. Time to tell Pierre.

I worked moisture into my mouth as Pierre stretched and leaned back in his chair. "Do you need a lift, Jacqueline? I can run you back to Nanteuil on the motorbike."

"Don't frighten her," Georges said, his lips twisting in a teasing smile.

Pierre rolled his eyes. "She hopped down that tunnel like she was stepping out to buy milk." To me, he added, "I'm a good driver."

"I'm sure you are."

"I trained as a pilot, you know. But when I asked, England wouldn't take me. Bad eyes." Pierre tapped his spectacles.

I filed away the information for later and mentally braced myself. I couldn't put it off any longer. "We can't leave yet."

"Oh? Another job?"

I shifted uneasily, glancing from Pierre to Georges. "It's Flower."

"Yes, what about him?" Pierre's voice sharpened into the belligerent tone he always used for our theoretical leader. It clashed with his mild appearance. So did his hot temper. I slid my hand to my waistband, just in case he needed extra incentive to stay calm.

"Well?" Pierre prodded.

"It's all a mistake," Georges said. "I'm sure when we tell him…" He trailed off when I shook my head and turned his attention to the tablecloth, tracing the white-on-white embroidery with anxious fingers.

"Flower's trying to poison you," I said. "He asked Georges to give you an L pill sent from London."

Instead of the flash bomb anger I expected, Pierre was eerily, icily still. Madame Fermé's place settings were safe, for now, but I wasn't sure of anything else. "What's an L pill?" His dark eyes flashed to mine, the color of the mahogany bay stallions my father always favored and just as uneasy.

I licked my lips. "Cyanide. Usually. When you want death to come quick."

"I refused," Georges put in hastily. "Even when he said you were a traitor. But when I saw you at the meeting, I was nervous." He twisted his hands, almost writhing in his seat.

"We all are. And we should be all the time," I said gently, thinking of Georges's absent wife. "It isn't easy, deciding who to trust."

"Not when the choice is between Flower and me," Pierre said, his lips snapping shut. "Seems clear enough."

"Why do you think I refused the pill?" Georges's voice rose, a strong wind circling the room.

"I'm going to kill him," Pierre said, his eyes dark and shimmering. His hands compressed into tightly packed charges of fury.

"We're supposed to be fighting Germans, not ourselves," I said softly, ballast to weigh down their foundering tempers. Flower had misjudged his team—again—and this time there was an excellent chance he'd die for it.

"Will you tell Flower that?" Pierre challenged. "I'd be dead if not for Georges!"

"And probably André Gatignon," I put in. "Maybe Grand-Georges too. You saw him at the garage this morning. We don't know how many Flower has approached. But you're alive, so you have trustworthy friends."

"Maybe," Pierre muttered darkly. "You should have told me at once."

"Georges acted prudently. As we all should. And he made the right choice. Orders are—" I waved impatiently, frustrated by my struggle for words. "I'm not saying they aren't important, but they can't be an excuse. We have to live knowing what we've done with the lives in our care, including our own."

"Flower doesn't think that way," Pierre said. "He only cares about his own skin. And your bosses in London only care about keeping the Germans busy enough here to save their alliance with Russia."

I couldn't dispute the claim, knowing it might well be true. I'd heard the disheartening argument before, bantered about in buses and busy cafés. And SOE HQ sent the pill, so I'd never persuade Pierre to trust them now. "I'm not here for London."

"Why then?" Pierre demanded.

"Same as you," I countered. "I'm a Frenchwoman. We aren't meant to lick the boots of Germans." I mirrored his scorching rhetoric, hoping he'd believe it. He wouldn't understand the truth—I'd come here for myself, and I stayed because of him and Georges and Marguerite and the others, like me, who needed ways to use their courage.

"I'm not sure why I bother with London," Pierre snapped.

"How can we trust them?" Georges added. "If Pierre is disposed of so easily, what about the rest of us?"

"They don't know Pierre," I insisted. "And God only knows what Flower's seen fit to tell them."

"You could avoid him," Georges offered. "Perhaps it will blow over if we wait a few days."

It wasn't bad advice. If we stayed out of sight, Flower's poison-wielding friends wouldn't find us, and though I wasn't smoking at the ears with rage like Pierre, control over my fraying temper was weakening. Like Flower, I was also trained to protect myself and my operatives by killing traitors as quickly as possible. Unlike him, that wasn't work I would delegate.

"Where is Flower?" I demanded.

"Don't do anything rash," Georges begged.

Pierre shrugged. "You know the protocol for traitors. Flower had no difficulty applying it to me. Too bad Jacqueline and I will do a better job," he added, in an uncanny echo of my own thoughts.

"No. *I'll* handle this," I told Pierre.

"Not on your bicycle." He pushed up from his chair, starting for the door, but I beat him to it, planting myself in his path.

His palms turned up, supplicating. "I've got to do something, Jacqueline. He's not going to leave me alone. You might be next. There's no love lost between the two of you either." He paused to see if he'd convinced me yet. "And if we aren't here, nothing will ever get done."

As I digested this, he pushed past me into the hall.

I followed, Georges at my heels, hissing, "Pierre, you can't!"

"Stay here. Your wife," I reminded him. She'd worry if she returned home and found him gone.

I grabbed my coat and purse and dashed into the street, already twenty paces behind Pierre, who was striding along, his unbuttoned coat flapping. "Wait! You said you'd give me a ride!"

He slowed, and I jogged to catch up, drawing even with him at the edge of the square. All the shops were closed now. A few children were flying paper airplanes, but the main action was a leisurely game of boules, played by a band of stoop-shouldered men who looked as if they'd played here every night for the past thirty years.

"We won't find him," I said, panting. "He never—"

"Grand-Georges told me where Flower was staying," Pierre said. "It wasn't that long ago. I bet he's still there."

He saddled the bike and started the engine. I hopped on behind, looping one arm around his waist. I wouldn't have chosen such proximity, but I didn't know anything about his driving and didn't want to fall off. Since I couldn't stop him: "We have to be smart about this," I said.

We swung away from the curb and into the street. Pierre cranked the throttle, curving the bike around a lorry loaded with crates. I clung tighter, pressing my face into his shirt.

When the lorry was far behind, I raised my voice to carry over the rushing wind and the noise of the bike. "It's almost curfew. And what about witnesses? If you charge in—"

"That man tried to kill me!" As the bike slowed, Pierre's voice climbed, not a good omen for his ability to silently break into a safe house.

"And if you kill him, the whole network will be training guns on each other. The Germans will be delighted."

I saw the struggle in his tight neck muscles, so I continued. "It's not the job."

"He tried to kill you too. Planting that gun in your room? If your landlord had reported you, you'd be good as dead and all of our contacts endangered. You. Me. Marguerite. Roger. Georges. Souris." Even over the buzz of the engine, his words came out measured, philosophical, almost wheedling. He wanted me angry. If he knew me better, he'd know I was. But I wasn't going to be stupid, not for Flower, not for Pierre. Not for anyone. Wading in, not jumping, was how to start across this river.

"This is bad for the network," I insisted.

"Yes. But Flower is expendable." Pierre pulled the bike over to the side of the road, stopped, and turned around on his seat. "They trained you for this. You know what to do. If I tried it, yes, it would be loud, messy, probably a failure. But you—"

I grimaced, silently finishing his thought. I knew how to kill silently. It wouldn't be that different than the dummies I'd slashed in training. I hoped.

"We'll wait outside his safe house," Pierre said evenly. "Follow him when he leaves and make him disappear. The network will never know."

"You're not thinking straight," I said. "He's a lunatic, but he's a British agent. Georges will know. If Flower approached anyone else, they'll guess. I don't want his death on my tally. And I don't want to alienate London." No matter what Pierre wanted, I wasn't letting this network go back to the days of haphazard, hopeful violence, attacking phone exchanges with nothing but black market petrol. "We need to let them know."

"How?"

"Denise. Or Marcel."

"How long will that take?" Pierre challenged. "He might kill one of us before they respond. Flower has the poison now. God only knows what else he might try. I'm not willing to sit and wait while he paints a target on my back. You can't either. Jacqueline, you're the leader of this circuit now. London might have chosen Flower, but he's unfit for it."

"Don't treat me like an idiot," I said with a snort. "You can't flatter me into this."

"I'm just trying to make you see sense! You have it, usually. That's what I depend on. We all do. Marguerite and Roger and Souris—"

"Shut up." I didn't need him hurling names at me. Again. "I get it. But if I'm leader, we do this my way. We'll find him. But I decide what comes next."

Pierre gritted his teeth. "My way is easier."

"Today, maybe. It leaves us in a mess down the road."

The last burst of sun flared on his driving goggles, blinding me and hiding his eyes. "We probably don't have many miles left on our roads anyway." A wistful hint of regret snuck through his bitterness.

"Maybe not," I agreed. "But I'm planning on outliving this." I would see the end of this war. I'd see the end of bombings and reprisal killings and shortages. I'd return to England and settle in a flat somewhere quiet where Jackie could easily visit. I'd make up stories to account for the time I was missing. A new lover. An assignment as a translator in one of the wireless stations. Anything I came up with would be more believable than the truth. Maybe someday I'd share that too. "You should plan on outliving this, Pierre."

He was young. Married, maybe. Perhaps he had children, though I couldn't imagine that for him, not yet. But someday he might have a child, or a trio of them, little boys with his slight size and serious mien and probably his need for spectacles. The thought made me smile. "Flower is a problem. Let's go find him."

CHAPTER 28

———

A WEEK AFTER MY SWIM, A BATCH OF NEW RECRUITS ARRIVED at Beaulieu. All men from another training facility they wouldn't tell us much about. Denise complained, saying in spite of all the talk and tests, they'd send the men and never let the four of us anywhere near France.

After two days, half the new men were in love with her, including Alain, who was sitting beside me, listening to Denise and looking absolutely gobsmacked. Of course, she was too animated to notice, recounting a classmate's disastrous wall-climbing session with frequent gestures and expletives, at least until Alain stiffened and stopped her with a hand on her arm.

"The Heavenly Twins," he whispered, as two older men in captain's uniforms entered the training room—what used to be the portrait gallery.

"What did you call them?" I asked quietly.

"Heavenly Twins." Alain pinched his lips, his eyes alert, his jaw so tight I hardly caught his words. "That's Sykes and Fairbairn. They look like two nice preachers. Older, soft-spoken, smile almost all the time. But the moment they stop smiling, they can kill a man without making a sound and not think a thing of it."

Denise angled her head closer. "How?"

"They worked for the Shanghai police, secret units," Alain whispered. He shifted away from Denise and me, his eyes never leaving the captains.

"Huh." Denise closed her hands into fists and smiled—a French bulldog, small but with plenty of swagger.

I held my breath as Fairbairn stepped forward. He had a thin slash for a mouth and deep-carved dimples. A man hewn from ice, complete with bleach-blue eyes and silver hair. His gaze fell on me and rested. "Perhaps man-to-man combat instruction was a poor description," he quipped. "These are lessons I'm sorry you have to learn. We are a civilized people embarking on a most uncivil war." He clasped his hands behind his back and stepped forward, his voice hardly loud enough to carry to the back of the room. "I'm here for one reason only—to keep you alive. You must forget the Geneva Conventions, fair play, any high-minded principles. Your duty is to kill them before they kill you. You will not think. You will not hesitate. You will strike and strike to kill. These are the skills you will rely on in moments of greatest danger—and one of the last things you must learn before entering enemy territory."

Without warning, his flat hand shot out at Alain, pushing his head backward, his throat stretched dangerously. Someone behind me yelped. "If I had applied force to this strike, our friend Alain would be lifeless on the ground. The head is a disconcertingly vulnerable piece of the body, hinged precariously and easily detached."

Fairbairn lowered his arm and Alain straightened his neck back to a natural position, his eyes wide. He shot me a baleful look. *I told you.*

"We begin with our version of anatomy." Fairbairn motioned Sykes forward, who smiled at the class and stood, feet apart, hands at his side. "Windpipe, neck, spine, nose, temple, kidney, groin." As quickly as Fairbairn spoke, he slashed his flattened hand through the air, mimicking hits on Sykes's body. "These are the kill spots I will teach you first. But then you must learn how to take a man down using any part of the body, down to his finger."

"This is our first class with women," he added. "This is fortunate for me. I've long said gender and size don't matter. I'd like very much to be proven correct."

Again, his eyes fell on me—an invitation, a challenge, the first to come my way since the river. And I felt different now. "You will, sir," I said.

"*Absolument,*" Denise added beside me.

Sykes was busy beside Fairbairn, stringing up bolsters from hooks in the ceiling. I couldn't help thinking what a travesty it was, putting holes in such beautiful paneling. Meanwhile, Fairburn instructed us to tighten our trunk muscles.

"Your power is here—not just your arms," he said. Our hands must be blades, our shoulders like cannons.

After forty minutes pummeling our bolsters, Alain was breathless and Denise working her tired shoulders.

"Again, Jacqueline," Sykes said quietly. "Right, left, right, right."

I let my hands fly.

"Have you studied before?"

"No, sir."

He looked unsatisfied, but before he loosed his next question, Fairbairn spoke up from behind him, while holding the bolster for another trio. "They told me Jacqueline is the dark horse here. Friendly. Fragile-looking but determined, which makes her unexpectedly dangerous to overlook."

I tried not to blush, but it was impossible, with Denise beaming at me from behind him, mouthing something I hoped was too soft to overhear. It was as satisfying as receiving a medal.

"Just the kind of agent we need." Sykes gave me a smile. "Now make your strikes faster."

I knew without being told that things had changed. The higher-ups had decided—approved. Soon, I'd be leaving for France.

CHAPTER 29

———

IT TOOK PIERRE AND ME TWO DAYS TO FIND FLOWER. Two
days of discreetly questioning contacts, relaying messages, and
watching Flower's cottage. The first night we slept rough in
the woods, shivering and taking turns looking for lights and
movement in the house's blank windows. The second night I
put my foot down and insisted on an overpriced, unimpressive
hotel. But I'd have paid every franc I had for a bed by that time,
so perhaps it was a bargain.

Pierre didn't mention his family again. Or his wife. Had
I remembered wrong when he spoke of his family's land? I
didn't think so, and this conspicuous omission added another
line of concern to my lengthy list. Pierre might, like Georges
the grocer, be shielding Mme. Culioli from danger or hiding
from her. In wartime, these were only two of among a multi-
tude of painful explanations, many much worse. Twice I nearly
worked up the nerve to ask him, then gave up. After all, I didn't
intend to confide anything of my own family. I told myself we
both inhabited different, previously unimaginable roles, and
there was little point going over what had come before. We had
enough trouble to get on with.

When we returned to Flower's cottage the next morning, washed and mostly rested, there were fresh footprints on the front path.

Pierre gave a satisfied nod. "He's back."

I caught up to him just as he yanked the door open, not bothering to make sure it didn't hit me on its rebound, which it nearly did.

Not a stealthy entrance. It gave Flower enough warning to brace himself behind the kitchen table, his trembling hand hovering at his hip. There was a split second of relief when he saw it was us and not Germans, but the blood drained from his cheeks as he read Pierre's furious expression.

His hand darted for his gun, but Pierre had more medieval tactics in mind. He launched himself across the rickety table and tackled Flower, plowing into his stomach like a charging bull. They crashed into a tangled knot on the floor, issuing pained grunts as they scrabbled, knocking against the table and upsetting a metal chair.

Pierre seized Flower's collar and tightened the blue fabric into a near stranglehold. "You tried to kill me," Pierre rasped in a half shout, half winded gasp. His fist found Flower's mouth and came away bloody.

"You recruit people without consulting me," Flower fired back. "No background checks. No clearance. For all I know, half of them are Nazi plants—"

"How could you think I'm one of them?" Pierre demanded. "Those Nazis—" He wanted to say something that refused to come out. A tidal wave of exhaustion crashed over him and he reached to his back for his concealed pistol.

I stepped around the table and raised my own gun. "Pierre isn't a Nazi. L pills are for traitors, Flower, not personal grudges."

His black eyes shifted to me, widening as my aim settled on his forehead. "Insubordination," he rasped.

"Not at all. I'm trained to protect my network. You're the one trying to take out Pierre. You're the one sabotaging our work."

"You can't hurt me," Flower gasped. "London needs me. They've issued an order for my return."

"I don't believe you," I countered.

"The order came from Paris via Prosper yesterday. It was confirmed over the wireless last night. They're sending a Lysander for Marcel and me. Two days from now." His eyes flew to the bread box on the table. "Look."

I motioned with my head for Pierre to investigate, keeping my hand steady despite my skipping heart. He heaved himself up using the tabletop. Beneath a loaf of brown bread, he found a neatly folded paper, the semitransparent kind I'd learned to use at Beaulieu, which could be flushed down a toilet or eaten in a pinch.

"What does it say?" I demanded.

Pierre frowned. "It's from Prosper. It's true. Flower's going back."

I looked down at Flower, his cheek blooming with the scarlet outline of Pierre's fist. He might do us more harm in London, but wasn't my record already speaking for me? A successful drop, a network deploying rat bombs and sabotaging police cars, and the bombed tunnel in Montrichard. London might not want me in charge, but Pierre, Georges, the de Bernards, and the Flamencourts followed me.

Flower would report to Jepson and Vera in London, and they knew what stuff I was made of. Knew too that I remembered exactly what they expected from me. Maybe they were recalling Flower to give me a real chance.

"You can go if you give me the L pills," I said. "Yours and the one they sent for Pierre."

Flower's face twisted. "It's with Rémy in Bracieux."

I didn't recognize the name, but Pierre did, his face darkening. Before he launched another punch, I said, "You'd better get a message to him before you head to the landing field. If you want to get on that plane."

"Jacqueline," Pierre protested. "You can't—"

"I'm not going against London," I warned.

"My L pill is here." Flower gestured with his eyes at the ring on his right hand.

"Give it here."

Flower surrendered the tacky gold band with a black stone to Pierre.

"You'll have Rémy give us the other?" I demanded.

Flower glared at me, whatever he wanted to say almost worth his life. His lips tightened to hold back the tirade so visible in his eyes. He refused to look at Pierre and studied my gun, peering into the black abyss of the barrel.

"I'll explain to London it was all a misunderstanding," he offered.

I wanted to say that he'd better, but instead: "If you're going home, I'm pretty sure they already know."

I held my gun steady while Flower placed the call to Bracieux. "Come on, Pierre," I said, once Flower finished.

With a mutinous glare, Pierre stormed out of the house. I followed, backing away from Flower without lowering my sights.

————

We returned to the Mercure, the overpriced hotel, for the next two nights, until Flower's scheduled return to London. Then we rode the motorcycle to Nanteuil, where our hopes were confirmed. Souris had heard from Denise: Flower was gone, flown back to London on the same plane as Marcel. He'd surrendered the L pill to Souris himself. I told her to keep it. She might need it someday, and I still had my own.

"I think at the last minute Flower realized this wasn't a promotion," Souris said. "But Denise said he got on the plane without a fuss."

"What does it mean?" Pierre said, brow furrowing. "Calling him home?"

"Jacqueline's bosses have finally seen sense," Souris said airily, neatly avoiding any mention of London. "One less worry for both of you." She'd erupted almost as fiercely as Pierre after hearing about Flower's poison pill, but her anger had dissipated quickly.

"And the news from Montrichard?" I asked, stifling a yawn. Souris had a beautiful array of loungers out on her terrace, and the day was unseasonably warm.

"They say the line will be running through the tunnel again in a week," Berbert said.

I pursed my lips. "Only minor damage, then." I'd hoped for more.

"Don't be too disappointed," Berbert said. "I visited the

commandant in Tours yesterday. Apparently, the recent train delays—on all lines, mind you, not merely Tours to Vierzon— are because—" He paused.

"What?" Pierre leaned forward.

"They are picking through all the coal stores, looking for exploding rats," Berbert said. "He's furious. He also mentioned an attack on a sugar factory near Montrichard yesterday. I assume that was you as well?"

I shook my head and smiled. "Not me." Georges. Again.

"We were still hiding," Pierre said ruefully.

"A disciple then?"

I grinned. "Our friends." Georges had mentioned the factory when we'd practiced with detonators the other evening in the wine caves. Just last week, but it seemed so long ago. "They are quick studies in Montrichard."

Pierre sank back onto his lounge chair and closed his eyes. "I wish we had such good news every day."

Pierre returned to his safe house after dinner that evening. I spent the next week dashing from one village to the next, training members and delivering messages. Denise contacted me from Paris, saying her boss, Prosper, was pleased with the recent action in our region and that we were to continue as a subcircuit of his network. Could I please select a code name and send it to him to relay to London?

I showed the message to Souris and Nanny.

"How does SOE pick names? They all seem rather silly," Nanny said.

"They started with plants, then switched to professions," I said.

Nanny snorted. "Juggler is not a job." Not one she approved of at any rate.

"How about Actor?" Souris suggested.

"Already taken," I said.

"Magician?"

Nanny rolled her eyes.

"I was thinking we could call ourselves Adolphe."

Souris met my eyes. "Not after—"

I nodded, my suppressed laughter slipping out. "Pierre's mustache."

"He'll never agree to it," Souris said. "He's proud. And it's your circuit."

I shook my head, embracing her and Nanny with a smile. "Ours. And Adolphe—I think Pierre will like it."

———

Pierre did. By the day I told him, Berbert also had news, arriving in the breakfast room with a somber face. "I just got off the telephone. The local German commandant has asked us to house five of his officers. They're coming tomorrow."

My stomach seized with embarrassment. I'd overstayed and now needed to vacate before Germans filled the house. "I'll go back to Tours," I said quickly. "Find a hotel." It would do until I found another safe place.

Pierre looked dubious. "It's farther away."

"I have a better idea," Souris said. "I spoke to Marguerite. They have a place."

My eyes rose, and the corners of my lips too. "I'd be happy to stay with the Flamencourts." Their noisy chickens and warm smiles.

"Not with them. With a friend of theirs," Souris said in a low voice. "And not just you. Pierre too. We need a safe place for both of you. We've all been worried."

I glanced at Pierre, leaning against the mantelpiece, his face unreadable. "The police visited my apartment yesterday. Luckily, I was out. My father-in-law warned me. That's why I came here." Father-in-law. Still no mention of his wife.

"We'd keep you both," Souris said. "But—"

"Houseguests," Berbert finished, rolling his eyes.

"And you can't just waltz into this place with no cover story," Souris continued. "So you will be married. Bombed-out refugees from Brest."

Pierre's face rearranged fractionally. Still the frown. Still the furrow between his heavy black eyebrows. But his eyes lifted from the ground, roved from Souris to me, his thoughts inscrutable.

"Jacqueline will take your false last name and you will be Pierre and Jacqueline LeClair, childless, homeless," Souris decreed.

Pierre's face relaxed. I couldn't tell why.

"Why Brest?" he asked.

Souris began spreading jam assiduously on her toast. "Because Brest was bombed so heavily, everyone has scattered, and no one can check the story with old neighbors." She paused and grinned. "And because of Jacqueline's accent."

"What about my accent?"

Souris's smile widened at my defensive tone. "It is marred permanently with English. But I think it passes off as the odd accent of Brest."

"My French is perfect," I argued, a hot flush rising in my neck.

"Flawless," she agreed with amusement. "But hopelessly marred. You are neither here nor there." She gave a shrug.

"So I've got myself a lethal wife?" Pierre's eyes flashed behind his spectacles with momentary amusement.

I snorted. "As if you'd be so lucky! If I were foolish enough to marry"—*again*, I amended silently—"I would choose"—I almost said *someone taller* but wasn't sure how touchy Pierre was about his height—"someone without that horrible mustache."

Pierre smoothed it carefully. "Yet you chose it as the name of our distinguished network."

"It means something to us," I said. "We should have a name we all understand, not some meaningless word chosen by London."

"No one will have any trouble believing you're a pair," Nanny said, shaking her head as she poured out another cup of tea.

"Well?" Pierre asked, his eyes turning to me. "It's not a bad idea, really. It would be good for Adolphe."

I considered. I liked Pierre. Trusted him. He'd been difficult to command when it came to Raymond Flower, but otherwise we worked well together. "All right," I said.

He smiled. "Thank you, Mrs. LeClair."

"Excellent," Souris said. "I'll give you the address."

Our host, Marguerite and Edouard's friend, turned out older than expected. Matthieu Toutain was a white-haired welcoming man, who shuffled on unsteady legs. For every ten sure steps, there was one that shook and threatened to overturn him. He spoke in mumbles, punctuated with smiles for us and growls for the Germans. But his home stood in a quiet pocket of trees, and he lived alone with few visitors. Like most of the resistance, he'd offered to shelter agents and soldiers but settled for a displaced couple from Brest. Several times I opened my mouth, tempted to tell him he was part of a network without even knowing, but I couldn't break protocol for kindness to an old man.

I missed Souris and her horses.

Matthieu expected Pierre to be busy, since his cover had him masquerading as a government inspector. My comings and goings were harder to explain, especially as the days grew colder. And it was increasingly inconvenient, traveling back and forth to the Flamencourts' farm or André Gatignon's wine caves for supplies. I didn't dare store explosives, wireless parts, or any of the telltale contraband we routinely used in Matthieu's rundown little house. The closest safe spot to work was an abandoned shed at the edge of Marguerite and Edouard's property. I spent many hours there, wiring, coding and decoding messages, wearing two or three woolen pullovers, depending on the weather.

But then it turned cold, too cold to work long hours in the shed. Through the Christmas holiday, I braided det wires in the privacy of my room instead of holly branches and wrapped pistols instead of holiday gifts. Those who received them appreciated them more than scarves and belts anyway. On New Year's Eve, Pierre, Matthieu, and I kept close to the stove, a huddle sharing small cubes of cheese and guessing at the next moves of the British and Americans.

Matthieu's cloud of hair had grown longer, wisping in comic contradiction to his earnest expression. "The invasion has to come this year. The Russians have the Krauts pinned and there's no reason to wait any longer. This will be the year," he vowed. He threw his eyes to the old wooden-framed clock on his wall. "Well, in an hour this will be the year."

"Is it that late?" I asked, putting down my bite of food. I'd lost interest in it anyway. "I need to finish my washing."

"Water's too cold. You'll chap your hands," Matthieu argued. "And you're too pretty for that."

Pierre grinned like a husband grateful for the compliment to his wife.

I snorted. "Don't be silly. If a bomb can't take me down, I can manage cold water. Besides, I left everything soaking. We need to rinse out the clothes before they freeze." Every morning this week, there'd been frost.

I left the ring of heat and stepped to the sink, turning the handle. Only a few drops fell. I tried the other handle, my brow wrinkling in confusion. "There's no water."

Matthieu stood, momentarily bracing against the table when his leg betrayed him. He stepped beside me and repeated the turning of faucets and opened the cabinet doors to view the pipes. "Must be frozen."

I bit the inside of my cheek. With only one set of clothes, waiting was not an option. I had to finish and get them drying.

Outside the ground was gray white, rimmed with ice, not snow. There was nothing to boil to make more water.

"We could try the well," Matthieu said as he went for his coat hanging on a peg. "It's the deepest one for miles. My grandfather dug it himself. We should find some water down there."

"I'll help," Pierre said, rising and putting on his felt hat and Matthieu's extra wool cardigan. He retrieved a torch from his bedroom and flicked it on.

"Don't let him fall," I whispered to Pierre as the torch beam made a glittering circle on the black night, illuminating the crystal ice on every blade of grass. The frozen air pushed into the house, biting through my nightclothes, prickling my skin.

Pierre nodded. He stepped close to Matthieu, ready to reach and catch if his tricky leg gave any more trouble. I closed the door behind them, watching from the window until they turned the corner. My shivering body pushed me back toward the stove, where I hovered, trying not to let my teeth chatter. I glanced back at the clock: 11:11. Almost 1943 and still alive. A satisfied sigh huffed through my lips. The bomb. The plane. The boat. The checkpoints. I listed every moment the Germans nearly claimed me.

Still alive. And I had every hope that Matthieu was right—this year, 1943, the Allied armies would come.

The kitchen door slammed open. Pierre's eyes searched the room wildly.

"What?" I asked, spinning around.

"Matthieu. He's—"

I exhaled in concern. "I knew he'd fall." I should have

stopped him, but I thought with Pierre nearby... "Calm down."
Hopefully Matthieu hadn't broken anything.

Pierre didn't calm down. "He didn't *fall*," he clarified. "He
collapsed." He sprinted outside ahead of me.

I ran after him, a dull drumbeat growing louder in my chest.

Pierre threw himself beside the dark shadow of Matthieu
on the ground beside the well. "He almost fell in," he said. "It
was close." His voice shook as he trained the light of his torch
on Matthieu's pale face. The old man was tinged blue from the
cold. It was the cold, I insisted.

"Matthieu." I lowered my mouth close to his ear, his name
an urgent plea. I patted his cheek, soft first and then with
more vigor.

"He's not breathing," Pierre said.

A string of curses lurched from my mouth. "Please,
Matthieu." Each time I smacked him, his head lolled.

Lifelessly.

A small gasp escaped me. Despite my training, the explosions
I'd detonated, I'd never touched a dead man. I wasn't nearly as
calm as I wanted to be: my hands nerveless and clumsy, my heart
battering my ribs hard enough to shatter them. Was Matthieu's
skin already rubbery, or was I making it up in my mind?

"We can't be found here," Pierre said. "I don't know how,
but he's dead."

The word thundered in my head, followed by an echoing
silence.

"We need to leave," Pierre said, squinting into the dark.

"And go where?" I asked, unable to let go of Matthieu's
body.

"To Marguerite and Edouard. They need to know."

The cold shook me violently now, making words difficult. "We can't travel at midnight with no cover story."

We both looked at Matthieu, his hair whiter than the frost shining around it like a halo.

"Then we need to bring him inside and put him in bed. They'll think he died in his sleep. It gives us tonight to pack. We'll stash everything in the attic until Edouard can help me move it."

I shook my head. "We can't leave anything here. And the Flamencourts have family staying with them." I groaned and cursed again.

Pierre's hand closed on my shoulder and his steady gaze met my frazzled one. "I'll take his arms and you carry his legs."

He was too heavy to move with any dignity. I managed his legs but couldn't pull his backside off the ground. His body made a dark path in the frost where we dragged him. I ignored the taste of bile in the back of my throat when his torso bumped over the threshold.

In his bedroom, I unlaced his boots, tugging against his unyielding feet, while Pierre struggled to wrestle off his coat. We grunted as we lifted him onto the bed, his damp clothes wetting the wrinkled linens.

I flicked my fingers to clear them of stinging cold and trembling nerves.

Someone needed to close his left eye, which hovered slightly open, a sliver of blue iris shining in the uneven light. I reached out, my fingers caressing the lid, brushing his stubby white eyelashes.

"I'm sorry, Matthieu," I murmured, wishing I knew some appropriate prayer. Wishing I had the right to say it.

Pierre crossed himself and turned away. As Matthieu lay peacefully beneath his wool blanket, we bundled the evidence of our true identities into our bags. I wrung out my clothing as best I could and put it on wet, my skin protesting in an eruption of gooseflesh.

Beneath the stare of the clock I furrowed my brow. 12:44.

How long had we been cleaning up and packing? "Did he make it to 1943?" I asked the empty room. The dented pots glinted from their pegs on the wall.

By the time dawn shed its first frigid light over the trees, I'd cleaned and swept the house, the new year hanging uncertainly in the east, death twenty feet behind us down the narrow hallway.

Always in the middle of the two.

Pierre drummed the table with his fingers. He hated waiting as much as I. "How early do poultry farmers feed the birds?" he asked, knowing we'd look ridiculous shivering in the Flamencourt garden on New Year's Day.

"Maybe the Germans are lazy at dawn on a holiday." Either way, we couldn't stay here. If it wasn't safe at the Flamencourts', we'd find a hotel.

Pierre's fingers traveled to his trousers, where a pleat hid his pistol. "Happy New Year, Matthieu," he mumbled as he rose. My eyes brimmed as I glanced toward the bedroom. No one to mourn the brave, kind man but two displaced agents.

I thought of what Mr. Naylor, the horoscope writer, would have to say about this being the start of my year. *Does not bode well.*

CHAPTER 30

———

MAX WOULDN'T HAVE CHOSEN TO COME TO THIS FLYSPECK village at the back of beyond, not on New Year's Day, not before noon. Over the past month, a steady increase in terrorist attacks, ranging from low-level nuisance operations to a crippling railway tunnel explosion, had earned another serious reproof from Berlin. Boemelberg still refused to change tactics, and Max's covert investigations had brought him no closer to discovering the culprits. As a result, he'd drunk more than he ought last night, as if the solution to these troubles lay at the bottom of the next glass, not at all like someone celebrating. Naturally, he now had the headache to prove it. Even wearing sunglasses, he flinched from the onslaught of wan winter light as he climbed from the car. The local police officer and a young Abwehr officer came out of the run-down farmhouse to meet him. After a brief and, for Max, painful exchange of niceties, they got down to business.

"A neighbor came by this morning. He pays her for extra eggs. No one answered her ring, so she tried the door. Found it unlocked and inside—"

"Dead," interjected the French police officer.

"Murder?"

The Abwehr man rubbed his chin. "It doesn't appear so."

Max frowned. If not for this urgent summons, he'd still be in bed, only communicating with his aspirin bottle and a glass of seltzer water. "Then why—"

"He's old. Known to have a game leg and a weak heart," the police officer said. "But—"

"Come inside," urged the Abwehr officer.

Max stripped off his gloves, tucked them into his uniform belt, and followed the two reluctantly.

"Doesn't look like anyone was here," he said, surveying the kitchen. It was cold, the fire in the woodburning stove starved to ash long since. A lonely plate, chipped and with barely a hint of gold paint adorning the scalloped edge, lay in the sink. "Only one glass," Max murmured.

The muddy footprints scattered about the worn wooden floor were easily attributed to them and the inquisitive neighbor.

The French police officer reached into his pocket and held out a snippet of dark green cord. "I found this upstairs in the other bedroom."

Max examined it. It wasn't rope. The core was solid. "Wire?"

The Abwehr lieutenant shook his head. "Detonation cord. And the neighbor said the dead man had strangers staying with him. She's seen them on the road to the house, riding a motorbike."

The band of pain around Max's temples loosened a notch. "This must be tested. Identified," he said. This house was only a mile away from the sabotaged sugar factory and close to the bombed train tunnel at Montrichard. "I want to know who makes it, where it's manufactured."

The lieutenant nodded.

"Autopsy the dead man. Tear this place apart," Max ordered as he made for the stairs, his heart thumping. "If this was left behind, we'll find more." Finally.

He spent three hours turning over the shabby guest room himself and found nothing, but in the lavatory down the hall, behind the toilet, he found a long brown hair.

He slipped it into an envelope, then propped his notebook open on his knee.

Suspected terrorists in the Sologne:

Man with a motorcycle

Brunette

Experienced with explosives. One of them? Or both?

CHAPTER 31

WE TRAVELED FROM VILLAGE TO VILLAGE, INN TO HOTEL, from one surreptitious meeting to the next throughout the Loire Valley, training, planning, planting traps and explosives, coordinating at least one drop every full moon. I had one set of clothes to my name, a brown leather handbag, a hairbrush, a toothbrush, and a bicycle. Fewer things than I had fingers, and austerity wasn't terrible, though I didn't like getting shabby. Finally Pierre learned of a decrepit cottage barely accessible by roads. A machinist in our network had come across it while repairing a thresher and agreed to ask the local farmer if he'd rent it out to a homeless couple. Us.

The cottage was low to the ground, deep in a thicket of trees, and spartan: two rooms, barely furnished, with no plumbing or electricity. The only water came from an outdoor pump, and we could only cook on a single gas ring. What we lacked in comforts was more than made up for by the quietness and isolation. Austerity aside, it was the perfect place to work.

After a month of rudimentary living, we'd grown almost comfortable, adjusted to sleeping on the floor, skipping meals, and inventing cover stories for trips to network members.

Around us, the worst of winter sloughed off the surrounding woods and crocuses opened white arms in the scrubby garden where we'd planted a barricade of protective explosives.

Tonight, our oil lamp drew shifting orange shapes on the cracked plaster walls and deepened the shadows to pitch. The divot in Pierre's chin was a black pool beneath his still lips as he sat at the kitchen table. He'd stopped shuffling the maps, but I didn't notice until I glanced up from the fuse wires I was stashing carefully into emptied cans of tinned yams. Pierre owned a special blade that took the tops off without shredding the metal. When we seated the lid back in place with a drop of glue, no one could tell they'd ever been opened. I settled the cans quietly on the bench I'd pulled over to be my desk as I worked on the floor.

"Did you hit a snag?" I asked, unnerved to see him so still.

He shook his head once, my voice waking him from distant thoughts.

"I've finished up as well," I told him, brushing my hands together, though I'd done nothing to dirty them. It was simply a signal to me to move on to the next task. Only I didn't have one. There were no runs to make tonight, and the full moon wasn't for another week. "I could go to bed."

"You didn't eat yet today." He turned his head to look at me, which threw his face entirely into shadow.

"Haven't I?" Like me, he never fussed over food, but maybe this was code that he was hungry.

He shook his head. "And it's only seven. You won't be able to sleep yet."

"That can't be right." His watch must have stopped. I turned to the small brass alarm clock on the table only to find I was the mistaken one.

"I could cycle over to Souris and see if she has any news from Prosper."

"She doesn't. I stopped in on my way to town this morning." He stood up and walked to the shelves above the sink. "We still have some walnuts and cheese. You should have some."

I tried to protest but he was already shaking them onto a plate and slicing the cheese. He laid the meager offering on the table between us as he sat across from me.

It was only after I looked up from my plate and found him staring that I ventured any words. "Heavy thoughts?"

His lips tightened as if he meant to refuse to answer, but he tapped a walnut on the table and spoke quietly. "It seems every day is the anniversary of some nightmare."

As well as we got on, we talked little of our lives outside of the network. Certainly no sharing of feelings beyond our contempt for Germans. I'd never heard him approach anything like this. "Is today's anniversary a bad one?"

"They all are. You must have them too. Your house was bombed with your young daughter inside. Your husband left you."

I didn't correct him. I wasn't sure who had given him that information, and frankly, it was most likely some careless lie I'd dropped to throw anyone off my trail. But it was close enough to get on with. I too had made inferences. Pierre had in-laws, but he didn't have a wife, not anymore. We'd worked side by side for months now, and there'd been no unexplained meetings, no extra messages.

He grimaced. "I have plenty. There's the day they refused to let me into the air force because of my spectacles, the day my father died in the first war, the day the Boches captured me." His mouth softened. Or was it the lines of his eyes?

My lips parted in unspoken sympathy, but he didn't give me a chance to attempt a reply.

"What did it feel like to be bombed?" He stared at the wavering glow cast on the wall with an expression begging me to answer and refuse all at once.

Ah. I'd suspected something like this. My throat tightened with sympathy, and I chose my words carefully, like I was dusting the china ornaments on my mother's parlor shelves. "I don't think it felt like anything at all. It happens so fast that your feelings don't catch up with you until much later. If I felt anything in that moment, it was confusion. Adrenaline."

"Was there pain? Fear?" He scrutinized me now, watching for a lie.

"None of that," I promised. I forced myself to think only of sitting in the coal cellar. I told myself it was a memory of boredom. If I recalled the terror, he'd see it.

"Was it your family?" I asked, opening space if he wanted to talk. I averted my eyes to his hairline, where the short dark hairs grew straight up in defiance of gravity.

"My wife."

Just her, it seemed. My neck prickled in the stillness. I wasn't surprised, but I didn't like guessing right.

"A freak bomb in the village. No warning. She was the mayor's daughter. The whole town knew her..." His voice trailed off. "I was in a German prison camp. They had caught me and three others when we tried to escape on a boat. The hull was rotten.

It fell apart underneath us in the middle of the river. Damn Boches pulled us out." He huffed. "I got the letter in camp. We'd only been married three months when I left to fight."

Her shadow moved in his eyes, almost visible. My own filled, but I couldn't let him see. These things called for facts, resolve, or silence, not sympathy.

"How did you get out of the prison camp?"

"I went mad." His gentle frown betrayed no shame. "I lost my mind. Couldn't eat. Fevers every day. They gave me medical release for thyrotoxicosis when I started attacking everyone I saw. I was more trouble than I was worth. Why they didn't just shoot me…"

"What is her name?" I couldn't speak of her in the past tense. I didn't know what it would do to him.

"Ginette." His voice faltered on his own name attached to hers. "Her father is Maurice Dutems, the one who lets us use his land in Bois Renard."

"Oh" was all I managed. I'd met Maurice. This cottage bordered the district where he was mayor. He'd helped haul away canisters at our last supply drop. Pierre and I rode through the village almost every day, but he'd never given any indication he was passing the church where he once emerged in a shower of falling rice. Or the churchyard where his happiness rotted beneath the turf. If they'd found enough of her to bury.

I swallowed. No wonder he spoke so little and worked so feverishly. "I'm sorry."

He shook his head. "Doing something is better than being sorry. All I've wanted since is the chance to kill as many as possible."

I understood that, but it was troubling. This was the same determination that drove me to jump in the pond, nearly scuttling my deployment. "We're doing everything we can to help our people," I began. "But we can't—" As I stacked away the last cans of wires, an owl let out a startled shriek and a discordant crunch of footsteps sounded on the gravel outside. I ducked down below the window and caught Pierre's eye. He'd frozen already. His hand crept to his hip, and he brushed the grip of his gun.

"Move. You're an easy target!" I hissed. Keeping low, I lunged forward and blew out the light, then crawled through the oil lamp's dying smoke to the shelf where my pistol lay, out of sight of the bare window. Whoever was outside had a perfect view of us. The footsteps continued, not stealthy or timid, yet none of my traps went off. Whoever it was walked like someone who knew exactly where we were and what he had come for.

And this wasn't a friend. The few who knew where we stayed knew not to come, that the ground around the cottage was heavily mined.

"They found us," Pierre whispered.

Willing my eyes to adjust to the dark, I cocked my gun just as sharp pounding rattled the door.

"Come out!" someone demanded in angry but perfect French. "Who gave you authority to be here?"

Milice? I mouthed to Pierre across the dark room. Not that they were any better: French militia were just as deadly to us as the Gestapo.

"I know you're in there. Show yourself!" the voice ordered.

Pierre slid behind the half wall of the kitchen and signaled me to the door. I understood immediately: open the door; keep our cover. I flicked the safety and slid my gun beneath my waistband, in the small of my back, the metal against my skin giving a boost of courage as I turned the tarnished handle.

"Bonsoir," I said with a stern frown as I opened the door, revealing a tall glaring man. "What's the meaning of this?"

"What is the meaning of this, indeed? What are you doing on my property?" The broad man stepped onto the threshold, pressing his chest almost to my own.

"*Your* property? I've rented this cottage from the farmer who owns it." I stepped backward, but he followed me, too close for Pierre to have a clear shot.

"Like hell you have. I own this land and this cottage." Dirt mingled with a day's worth of heavy whiskers, and he wore two tattered collared shirts as if hoping the two combined would make one complete garment where no holes overlapped. "That's my farm through those woods."

"Your farm?" I glanced back. "I've been paying Monsieur Fontaine every two weeks."

"Who?" His eyes bulged.

"Monsieur Fontaine," I repeated as Pierre slipped noiselessly around the wall into view.

The man jumped and retreated half a step, but no gun emerged. He was unarmed. Eyeing Pierre, he edged toward the door. It hadn't crossed his mind that I, too, might be armed and ready.

"We thought you were a robber," Pierre answered in a soft voice, meant to soothe. "I'm her husband. What's this about the rent?"

"I saw your light from my field and knew someone was in

my building." He pointed to us to make his accusation of trespassing perfectly clear.

"And what if we had been Germans?" Pierre demanded.

"All the more reason to clear you out!" he thundered.

Pierre's lip lifted on one side and his hand relaxed. "My wife and I are refugees from Brest, bombed out of our home. We came here and contracted for this cottage for eighty francs a week. We've paid it."

"You've paid it to a pirate, then, because this is my cottage and I've not got a centime. Fontaine owns the land behind this and has been stealing your money." His breath smelled of cheap beer and a pungent stink I didn't recognize.

Pierre and I exchanged glances. Marguerite and Edouard wouldn't have knowingly sent us to a crook, but it was possible they didn't know Fontaine as well as they thought.

"We're happy to correct the problem," Pierre said, and reached into his pocket. The farmer flinched, but Pierre merely pulled out his wallet. "Do we have your permission to stay? We want only a quiet place, out of the way, with no visitors. All I ask is that my wife never see one more German in France than necessary." Pierre's free hand rested on my waist, just above my gun. "She hasn't recovered from the bombardment."

I understood his direction. "Maybe they will bomb us here," I said with a quaver in my voice. "We should go hide in the woods."

"No, dear. It'll be fine. We're safer here." Pierre turned back to the man. "She is shell-shocked."

The farmer's rough face creased with pity. "I beg pardon, madam. I misunderstood, but I mean you no harm. Fontaine is a scoundrel, but so long as you're not making trouble, I'm happy to let you stay."

Pierre gave a slight bow. "You are a good man. And we'll happily pay you the rent that we owe. In future, I'll bring it to you. Unexpected visitors…"

On cue I continued my charade. "They bombed us with our daughter inside. The ceiling came in on her." I pictured Jackie, bleeding, covered in plaster, and my eyes brimmed easily.

Pierre gave the man a mournful shake of the head in answer to the farmer's wide-eyed, silent question.

The farmer pulled off a hat that was little more than a rag and wrung it in his soiled hands. "I'm sorry. You're welcome to the cottage. You know there is no electricity and no running water, but the well has a pump…"

"You are kinder than you know. Let me walk you out." Pierre put a friendly hand on the man's arm.

He'd have to steer him around the trip lines in the dark. Whatever luck had spared the farmer from our land mines so far wouldn't last another trip through the yard. My breath left me in a shallow huff. When the door opened several minutes later, Pierre looked as pale as I felt.

"How did he get to the front door alive?" I asked.

Pierre shook his head in thought. "It's more of a miracle that he *left* alive. I've never come so close to shooting a man without doing it."

"Well, we've learned some lessons tonight," I muttered.

"We have?"

"Yes. We need more traps outside. And more importantly, some curtains."

CHAPTER 32

MAX STUDIED THE PHOTOGRAPH. IT WAS BLURRY AND FROM A bad angle, taken across the street from a nondescript Paris café. "Which one visited the safe house?"

The house in question, home to Germaine Tambour, had been under surveillance since the previous August, when her name and address was pulled from Max's stolen list. Since then, dozens of visitors had been photographed and matched to names in the CARTE network. The women in this photograph, though, were new and unknown. Which was why Richard, the former French policeman, had rushed this photograph to Max.

"Her." Richard stabbed a finger at the woman on the left. "But I followed her to this café, where she met this one."

Max grunted and reached for his magnifying glass. Even on an enlarged photograph, it was difficult to make out either woman's features. Both were brunette—the day this photo was taken, at any rate.

"I took the closest table I could get. Couldn't hear their conversation, except when they exchanged greetings. This one"—he planted a square fingertip on the younger woman's chest—"mumbled, but the other woman hugged her and called her Denise."

Max frowned. Probably just two friends meeting to talk. Not everyone who visited the CARTE safe house on Avenue de Suffren was a terrorist. Terrorists had book clubs, doctors, and house cleaners just like anyone else. Both women looked more the house cleaner type.

"We're after a woman bomber," Richard reminded him.

"Possibly," Max conceded. He wasn't going to admit that the det cord and the long hair from Matthieu Toutain's bathroom resided in a brown envelope in his desk drawer. He moved the magnifying glass and peered closer.

Both women were petite, but the one Richard followed from the safe house was noticeably younger. In spite of stringent rationing, her cheeks were round, framing full lips. The other woman was leaner and facing away. It was difficult even to get an idea of her profile, since she was half-in, half-out of the shade draped across their table by the café awning.

"Where did they go afterward?" Max asked.

"I followed the younger one, but I lost her when she turned into a shop," Richard said.

Max rubbed his forehead. Was that mere chance or suggestive? The bomber he pursued was no amateur.

"Make up files for both," he said. "You have copies?"

Richard nodded.

"Good. Leave this with me."

Alone, Max inched his magnifying glass over the sheet. Both women had ordered the brew that passed for coffee in most places. Both had shabby clothes and sturdy shoes. The younger one wore a large, almost gaudy ring. His eyes, and the glass, moved back to the other one, the woman concealed by a line of dark shadow. Without moving his gaze, he adjusted the angle of his desk lamp, trying to minimize the shine off the picture.

Amid the thick hair springing from her forehead was a wide white streak. If he had to bet, Max would identify it as natural graying of her hair, not a trick of the light or a flaw in the film. The corner of his mouth twitched upward.

He couldn't see her face, but he'd found a distinctive identifying feature, something to watch for. Hair dye was hard to come by these days, making it hard to conceal that dramatic white streak.

Max reached into his desk and slid the photograph into the brown envelope. Just in case.

CHAPTER 33

———

I PUSHED MY WAY THROUGH THE HEDGES AND SCANNED THE drive—Berbert's car slept in the sun beneath a light layer of dust. He must be saving fuel for the next full moon. More importantly, the car was alone, not hemmed in between canvas-topped Krupp lorries or polished black cars with new tires. No Germans today.

I stepped clear of the shrubs, mounted my bike, and pedaled the rest of the way down the drive, curving around the house to the kitchen garden, where I found Nanny Cox and Souris at one of the cast-iron tables, arguing over a book.

"I haven't finished it yet!" Souris said, trying and failing to snatch it from Nanny's hand. I smiled. No matter how quickly Souris moved, she'd never outmaneuver Nanny, with her years of nursery experience.

"You left it in the hall yesterday, and now I only have four chapters left. Wait until I'm done," Nanny told her.

"But—"

"Tear it in half," I suggested, amused at the idea of playing Solomon. "Then you can both read." It was only a paperback—Buchan's *The Thirty-Nine Steps*.

Nanny's horrified eyes shot to me.

"Then neither of you will have to wait," I said. "It's a good one." I'd reread the spy thriller myself not too long ago, in my library bed at Garramor.

"You better not be wanting to join the queue," Souris grumbled.

I missed having access to her library. "I wouldn't mind a book if you don't mind lending one, but only in French." Carrying English novels about was far too risky. "It would pass the time in the evenings."

Souris raised her eyebrows. "Are they dull?"

"When I'm not working," I amended. "Pierre is no great conversationalist."

Souris and Nanny exchanged looks.

I rolled my eyes. "It's not like that. We work well together, but there's absolutely no spark."

He was almost twenty years younger than me, not that I'd told anyone that. Not that the age gap was necessarily a deterrent. But he was in love with his dead wife, and I liked being respected for my abilities, without the emotional complications of romance. With work consuming nearly every thought, I couldn't feel bored or lonely. The ups and downs of my marriage and love affairs seemed silly in comparison now that I had a real mission.

"No spark?" Souris asked again, testing me.

"None. Though I like him very much."

"He's a good sort," Nanny said. "And this reminds me—I've something for you." She pushed up from the table, her stout legs carrying her speedily into the house.

"Don't ask me. I've no idea," Souris said, her empty fingers tapping against the tabletop. She missed her cigarettes.

I poured myself a glass of water and downed it in quick gulps, thirsty from my ride. Halfway through my second glass (swallowed with more decorum now I wasn't so parched), Nanny emerged.

"Here. I sewed it for you."

"Parachute silk?" I unfolded the small soft bundle. It was a dressing gown, plain but expertly sewn.

"They didn't send you any new undies in the last drop—"

"Don't remind me," I groaned. Of my many requests, I'd only received a bottle of peroxide to color my hair, so I was still rinsing out my underwear every night and wrapping myself in a blanket when Pierre was around. When he wasn't, I'd sit in my skin until my things dried enough to put them back on. Knowing my wardrobe dilemma, Pierre took care to absent himself frequently.

"I know how often you're washing," Nanny went on. "Figured wearing this wouldn't be so risky if you only wear it in that cottage."

She was probably right. If I could get it there without being searched.

"Since there's no spark," Nanny said, flashing her broad smile, "you might like a little privacy."

I laughed and rubbed the silk between my fingers. "If there were a spark, this would be divine."

"Careful," Souris warned. "Or there might be."

I shook my head. "Thank you, Nanny." It would be nice not to be forced to spend so much time at home in nothing at all or the nearest thing to it.

"Take some books before you go," Souris said. "Since you have nothing better to do in the evenings."

"Thank you, I will."

"Tea?" Nanny offered.

"Please." I noticed, while we'd been talking, she'd pocketed *The Thirty-Nine Steps*.

I left with a Minuit crime novel only two years old and a packet of messages to deliver to the next mailbox, destined for Denise in Paris.

The sun burned fierce, the trees too few and far between to provide more than scattered patches of shade. I drank the last of the water from my canteen and hoped fate would revenge me on Vera, Jepson, or whoever kept vetoing my request for new, lighter underclothes. If not for the risk of being caught wearing them, I'd have asked Nanny to sew me up some camiknickers too.

I pedaled across a narrow bridge and down a street of forlorn shops: a bakery (*fermé*, according to the sternly lettered sign hanging from the door), a cobbler with four pairs of wooden-soled sandal-type creations with canvas uppers in his window, and a shuttered *fromagerie*. The only business that looked even halfway ordinary was the chemist's. But a handful of people shuffled along under the sun, toting parcels and bags. I smiled at a girl wearing plaits tied with string and swerved my bike down the lane that opened right after the bookseller's.

This lane crossed with an even narrower one, running behind the shops and a row of back gardens. At the third house from the end, I dismounted and bent over a loose brick, three in and fourteen up from the ground. There were a few letters, carefully coded and bearing false names, for me to distribute before the next moon and—thankfully—a cardboard folder with the right stamps and a slightly blurry photograph of the new me. I'd had the same identity for over five months now, which made me nervous. It was past time for a change.

Age 35. Flattering. *Height 5 feet.* Not flattering. They'd cheated me of two inches. The letters went into my basket, the card into the battered leather purse hanging across my body from left shoulder to right hip. I jimmied the brick back into place and was pedaling away before I'd counted thirty. The second and third glances I took behind and beside me only proved yet again my complete solitude.

The next box on my route was two miles away. As our network and operations had grown, so had the number of messages—far too many for Abbé Émile. These days, most of us did some courier duty, and this next stop meant pitted dirt roads and one hill that always tried to get the better of me. Not anxious to spend longer than necessary in the sun, I steered toward the next village and promised myself a cold pump-water bath back at the cottage when I finished. I'd save the longer deliveries for tomorrow.

The road wound beside a stream, where spreading trees offered brief relief from the heat. Close to the water, thick ferns choked the ground, the shushing breeze filtering the sounds of gurgling water. I splashed through a puddle in a shade-filled hollow and coasted out of the trees into bright sun, right across from a field of grazing horses.

Foals. I braked and set a foot on the gravel, pausing to watch a black and a chestnut frisking around their imperturbable mothers. Leggy, with bright shiny coats, they lacked the tired look of most farmers and field animals these days. They reminded me of long vanished days with my father, admiring horses not only to decide which ones to buy, sell, or keep, but often simply for the love of it. The steep-roofed house in the distance might even have been—at least to a passing glance—my childhood home.

I pedaled on, but my mind traveled backward, not the road ahead. From the pasture, my thoughts glided into my old home and then from room to room, touching my mother's crystal bowls and inlaid tabletops. In my conjured scene I was sixteen, my blue dress adorned with rows of pintucks and seed pearl buttons. I ran my fingers over the top of the piano, fingering the Burano lace scarf. Heaven above, what I would give for some luxury now! Silk that wasn't cut from a brown parachute or petits fours made with real butter.

Dreaming of sweet cake and thick chocolate ganache, I swung left to avoid another puddle and bounced over a deep rut. Before I managed to steady myself, the angry blast of a horn jolted my body sideways and my attention forward. A black Citroën careened toward me, bouncing on the washboard road. My front tire twisted, and I flew forward, my breath punched out of me as the handlebar stabbed into my abdomen a split second before I landed in a tangle of steel and chain. I sucked in a breath—it brought a barrage of pain, but I couldn't exhale, couldn't make a sound, each part of my body sending competing complaints: fire in my leg, deep and scorching, and a sharper, scalding discomfort in my hand and hip. I gulped air again but couldn't force any out past my lips.

"Madame! Are you all right?"

A gray silhouette against the blue sky. Neat hat, crisp suit.

Now a sound escaped me, something between a squeak and a moan. The man fell to the ground beside me, turning me over, telling me to remain calm, to breathe. His French was rough and sharp cornered.

I closed my eyes and forced away the shakes. There'd not been a car on the road this entire trip. I took in another breath, opened my eyes, my gaze landing immediately on the gold swastika pinned to his collar. "I'll be fine in a minute."

I extricated my leg from the tangle of frame, spokes, and pedals. Flopping onto all fours, I reached surreptitiously for my bag—with Nanny's parachute silk dressing gown inside, concealed in a rolled-up newspaper, nestled next to the smuggled letters—still closed, thank God. I palpated my ribs, feeling for the outdated identity papers I'd had no chance to destroy, still beneath my brassiere. I scanned the ground for loose scraps, but I'd lost nothing.

"Are you badly hurt?" His hands stretched toward me, and I lurched away before he grazed more than my cotton blouse. "I won't hurt you," he said. "Don't be afraid."

"I'm fine." Speaking out loud calmed me, but he wouldn't believe me unless I managed to stand. I took inventory and stood up, staring at the crimson skid on my right leg. My knee protested as soon as I asked anything of it, and an ugly rip, black from the greased chain, shredded the hem of my culottes. I'd have a time finding matching cloth to repair it. But that was the least of my worries. The front wheel of my bicycle bowed left, the spokes broken and bent. I couldn't ride, and my knee shook beneath me. I couldn't even walk. "Let me help," the man said. "You must see a doctor."

Who'd want to see my ribs. Who, before doing anything else, would have to check my papers—if this man didn't do it first. Germans always checked. They didn't need an excuse, and I had two sets of identity papers on me, plus that damning robe of parachute silk.

"I'll be fine," I said, waving him away as I sank back to the ground. "All I need is a chance to get my bearings and catch my breath."

I glanced through the trees, looking for a house. Nothing.

He crouched down beside me but didn't try to touch me this time. "I won't hurt you. And you need help. You live nearby?"

I shook my head. The address on my new identity card was for the cottage. "I'm staying with a friend," I lied. He couldn't know where I lived, and he certainly couldn't take me there. The garden was mined, the door guarded with a bomb that would go off if I didn't disarm the trip wire. On the strength of those defenses, I'd left another half-finished bomb beneath the sink. I had to make him leave me alone.

"I'll drive you," he said, getting up and bending over my bike. "This isn't going to take you anywhere, even if you are fit enough to ride it."

"I can manage," I protested, my voice nearly a squeak.

He shook his head. "My dear madame, you can barely stand. I may be German, but I'm not a monster." He lowered his voice. "You are safe with me. And if it makes it better, I'll let you out before we get to your village. No one will see."

I met his eyes—bright blue, tired, but surrounded by laugh lines—and gulped. I really had no choice. My heart thrummed as I tried to temper the rhythm of my shallow breaths. "All right," I conceded. "If it's no trouble, I'd be glad of a lift to—" I gulped again, trying to pass off my frantic calculations as lingering breathlessness from the fall. "Chavannes." Close by and probably safe. I'd find a café there and call Souris.

Please let it be safe.

He held out his hand, and I took it, praying he wouldn't think why I'd gone cold, why my palm was damp with sweat.

"My name is Jan," he said.

"Jacqueline," I returned, my throat tight.

He helped me into the car and secured my mangled bicycle in the trunk. "I'm terribly sorry. It will need repairs," he said, sliding into the driver's seat. "I'm happy to compensate—"

"Thank you; that's not necessary."

His eyes took in my torn clothes, my shabby dress, and my knotted knuckles pressed even more tightly together. "I wish you would reconsider," he said, and returned his gaze to the road. "I'm very sorry for—"

"I wasn't paying attention," I said, cursing myself yet again.

"Neither was I," he admitted. "When I saw you and tried to brake—" He shook his head. "I'm just glad it wasn't worse. I know better than to drive with my head in the clouds. I was thinking of home though. It's my son's birthday today." His words were suspended in the confines of the quiet automobile. The seats were black vinyl and meticulously oiled.

"How old?" The question seemed required, so I complied.

"Eleven."

"A good age to be," I said, wondering what a small German boy would know of the horrors inflicted on France.

"And your thoughts? Where were they?" He caught himself and swallowed. "If you don't mind me asking."

Small talk? Very well. It seemed safe enough. "Cake."

He flashed me another glance.

"Chocolate," I added.

He nodded, adding fervently. "That I can understand."

I forced a smile.

Jan did not ask for my papers or search the contents of my purse. I asked him questions about his boy and let him give me 120 francs to assuage his guilt over my battered body and bicycle. When I told him I would wait for my friend and have her take me to the doctor, he didn't argue and let me and my bicycle out in the square. No one stopped to stare, but my cheeks heated from the cling of passing attention. I had no contacts in Chavannes, which was why I'd chosen the place. If I was recognized with a German, I wouldn't blame anyone for thinking I'd turned traitor.

"You are sure you are all right?"

"Quite sure."

He didn't offer his hand again, and out here, I wouldn't have wanted to take it.

CHAPTER 34

———

SOURIS'S DAUGHTER MOUNE RETRIEVED ME FROM THE CAFÉ in Berbert's car and took me back to Nanteuil, where Nanny Cox bandaged me. Grand-Georges, hastily summoned, promised to attempt bicycle repairs but admitted morosely there was little to do unless he found a spare wheel—a difficult feat. We enjoyed a moment of comedy as we sat around Souris's table and wondered if London would send us a few bicycles in the next parachute drop. Then we all made jokes about asking Buckmaster to include a few chocolate cakes but keep them in different crates than the plastic explosives. We didn't want our dessert spoiled by the smell. I spent the night at Nanteuil before Pierre collected me on the motorbike.

For two days I hobbled around the cottage with nothing to do but rest and read, not enjoying either. My knee refused to heal. The cuts and colorful bruises didn't concern me—the swelling did. It hardly passed for a knee at all, the usual wrinkles and divots lost under the red, ballooning skin. Pierre frowned at it occasionally but said nothing. When I had trouble making it to the shrubs we called our lavatory, he pursed his lips, his bright eyes grave behind his spectacles.

"We have to go to a doctor. It may be broken."

I didn't have the spirit to argue. The pain kept me awake at night, a deep burning that flamed away my resolve to bear through. "Not a hospital. They're crawling with Germans. We need a quiet doctor out of the way. You'll need to ask Souris."

———

The next day Souris's youngest daughter, Bette, drove me to a small office in Contres, a distant town. "Roger said Dr. Colbert treated their daughter very capably. She's a woman doctor."

"Really?" I asked. Female physicians were rare in a metropolitan area, let alone the French countryside.

Bette smirked and adjusted the rearview mirror. "Says the female undercover agent."

I laughed out loud. "I suppose I shouldn't be surprised. So, what will you do after the war? Physics? Race car driving?"

Bette shook her head, solemn again. We all wanted to believe in life after the war, but often it seemed too far away to contemplate—or only a mirage. "What I'd really like to do," she said simply, "is vote."

"It will come," I said. The war would end. When France had her own government again, they'd never be able to deny what they owed us, the women. "Don't doubt it."

I thought of Bette and her sister and my own Jackie—a woman with her own career in the ATS. I was still contemplating them in the waiting room. It took my mind off the pain as I sat in front of the gray-haired receptionist and tried to imagine what sort of woman became a doctor with her own practice. It only took ten minutes to find out.

The receptionist waved me back with a sharp jut of her chin, and I left Bette and slipped through to the examining room.

The doctor had her back to me, giving me a view of fluffy brown curls and a tweed suit until she turned and motioned me to the padded table. I had to use the step stool for children and hopped up using my good leg.

She was one of those ageless, undefinable sorts, her face too heavy to be called delicate, too young to be called old, and too smart to be considered soft.

"The problem's easy to see," she said in a solid voice, the kind easily heard in a noisy room. "Lay it straight on the bed." As she palpated, she asked, "How did it happen?"

"A German," I said with open disgust. "His car swerved on a corner when I was cycling. I fell trying to avoid him."

Her fingers paused as her eyebrow lifted, all so fast it barely happened at all. But her face tightened. *A collaborator?* My heart picked up speed.

She kept her head tucked, wiggling my kneecap. I sucked in a breath as pain sliced across my leg.

"Where are you from?" she asked, her voice a half note too high to pull off casual curiosity.

"Brest." We were dancing now, two intelligent women weaving through questions and answers, trying not to be caught in one another's web.

"Your accent is curious." She met my eyes, her own hard but not cruel.

"My father was English," I lied easily. I'd used it many times before for people commenting on my French.

"That's dangerous these days. Too many people with English roots signing up with Churchill and de Gaulle," she said grimly. "You've water on the knee. I can aspirate some of it with a needle and relieve the swelling. It will still take several weeks to heal."

She went to the white metal cabinet, plucking out supplies while I tried to parse her response.

"Did you ever live in England?" she asked, still with her back to me.

"No. My father died when I was twenty," I said. "Cancer." Perhaps we just needed to start over. I reviewed every word and action in my mind but couldn't see any place I'd gone wrong. One possibility flashed at the edge of my mind, like a red flame—if our network was compromised and Dr. Colbert was working with the Germans, perhaps someone had given her a description? My hand instinctively touched my white streak of hair, but that was invisible again, mixed in with my bottle blond.

"But you aren't from here." A statement, not a question.

"I don't like the doctor in Saint-Amand-Montron," I said, inventing determinedly. "He touches more than is necessary."

Her forehead cleared a little.

I shifted positions and inhaled. "I've never been to a female doctor before, but I think I prefer it."

She returned to me and set down a tray with gauze, a blue enamel dish, and a fearsome syringe. Without glancing at my face, she prodded my knee with light fingers again. "For your size and your age, you have good musculature. Once this is drained, your recovery should be straightforward."

Stung by the reference to my age—just how old did she think

I was?—I was caught off guard by her next words, sliding in like a knife thrust. "How much are you riding these days?" The real questions were in her face. *Why so much riding? How far?*

"Sometimes I just need the air."

Again, her strange pause. She didn't believe me.

"My husband and I were bombed in Brest." I spoke low, adding a pitiful tone, searching for her compassion. "We lost our daughter. Sometimes I can't be inside, whatever the weather."

At last her face softened. "I'm sorry," she said, then got back to business. "I'm going to palpate your patella to look for the cavity where the swelling is worst. A moving needle is never fun, but it will be much better after." She gestured to my grotesquely swollen knee. "I assume you have someone to drive you home? You cannot walk or drive."

"Yes. I brought along—" I almost gave Bette's name but held back at the last second. "My friend is taking me home."

"How far do you have to go?" she asked as she marked a spot on my knee with a pen. The black circle made a target on my tight red skin. I diverted my eyes as she pressed the needle to the depths of my knee, an electrical pain shooting as it moved. I inhaled, clutching the table and holding on to her question just as tightly while I thought. Every moment a calculation, an equation of lives.

Before I managed to answer a strange sensation of hollowing filled my knee. The syringe filled with a faint pink fluid. I exhaled, the pressure releasing my lungs and my leg.

"That's better already," I sighed, despite the twinge of the needle.

"It will most likely fill again. You'll need to come back." Dr.

Colbert withdrew the needle and we both looked at the welcome sign of a small wrinkle in the skin. At least she'd deflated it past the point of bursting.

"Yes, I'll come back. Thank you so much for your help." I held my smile. I'd never set foot in this office again. I couldn't interpret the doctor's shrewdness, and that made her too dangerous.

"You need to keep that leg elevated. Stand on it as little as possible and be patient as it heals."

My eyes joined my smile, lit by a secret joke. "What is there to do anyway? No radio, no shopping, my home bombed. I'll catch up on my hobbies. Good luck to you, Doctor."

She probably thought I meant needlework or painting. Let her think whatever she liked.

———

The swelling diminished, but the pain in my knee lingered. Even when I no longer hobbled constantly, sudden stabs caught me unawares, making me wince, cry out, even buckle. Pierre ordered me to rest more, so I sketched an elaborate plan for a second attack on the rail tunnel at Montrichard because our first only damaged it. After a week's repairs, the noise of every train carrying German supplies through that tunnel echoed my failure.

Then Pierre informed me the tunnel was now under constant guard, including the air shaft. A second attack was too dangerous.

"I have to do something. I'm going mad here," I told him. "Let me come to tonight's drop."

"Can you run to the pump?"

I tried but didn't make ten paces before crying out.

"Give it a little longer," he told me before whizzing away on his motorbike.

———

I spent the next days pacing, stretching, and testing my traitor joint in as many ways as I could think of, while collaborators and Germans hunted down six fugitive Jews just before they reached André Gatignon. Two of the women killed themselves rather than be taken. André's wife, Paulette, took the news hardest, wringing out my wash with unnecessary force when she came to tell me. I couldn't help suffering the sting of blame. If not for my knee, I might have helped.

Then Marguerite and Edouard's neighbors were arrested for selling black market pork. I sent half our stores (via Pierre) to their teenaged daughters, knowing they'd never be able to afford to buy rations on their own. On my instructions, resistants in Romorantin destroyed a fuel dump near a German airfield, and in response, the Germans shot two dozen hostages.

I wasn't the only one who found that defeat hard to take.

Some friends stopped replying to messages or went into hiding. Most needed to carry on earning wages, caring for aged parents and young children. Tethered to homes and jobs and families, some decided it wasn't worth carrying on the fight. Better to wait for the Allies—if they'd ever come.

If I didn't do something soon—something bold, successful, and unmistakably defiant—our network would dissolve to nothing.

When Pierre returned unexpectedly early from a missed ren-dezvous and discovered me astride my replacement bicycle, ped-aling cautiously up and down our narrow lane, he yelled at me.

"I don't need coddling," I interrupted, turning the bike around and gliding away. "That's not why I'm here." I wanted to do more than stockpile parachuted munitions and blow up power lines when that only put out the lights in the next village for a day or two. "We need to do more damage."

By the time he joined me inside, Pierre had swallowed his arguments. "What are you thinking?" he asked.

I pointed at the map, at a marked location we'd patiently scouted during previous months on the network of rail lines. "We blow them up at night," I said quietly. "When the trains are running. With wired detonators or time pencils set for two minutes. Like I did to that lorry with the Flamencourts."

Pierre folded his arms. "Can we get clear of a crashing train? It's a lot bigger than your lorry full of soldiers."

"That's the point," I said irritably. "We need bigger. It'll do a lot more damage."

"Maybe to us," Pierre countered.

I shrugged. "We'll have a minute or two to get clear." I pointed at a spot on the map, densely wooded, a good dis-tance away from the nearest town. "The two of us could prob-ably manage it, cycling out in the dark." Bikes were quiet, and I couldn't count on more than Pierre and myself right now anyway, with so many of our friends frightened into lying low.

"We wouldn't need a full moon," I said. The less light for this, the better. Once we were away from the town, we could probably get away with using a torch.

"We need something big. It will energize the whole network. Give us new courage." I held Pierre's eyes until he conceded.

"Fine. You want to run this by Prosper?"

I shook my head, though we probably should, for an operation this ambitious. But Prosper and Denise knew about my injury, and I wasn't in the mood for a no. I'd stood down too long already.

———

We left after dark, with the usual complement of wires and explosives concealed beneath trouser legs, socks, stockings, and my fraying brassiere.

"You shouldn't be riding yet," Pierre huffed beside me on a particularly steep hill. The admonition and his tone reminded me of my mother. The incongruity between her lectures on the correct use of a fish fork and Pierre's advice on acts of sabotage made me crack a smile. I certainly wouldn't beat Pierre up this hill, but—

"I can manage," I said, between breaths. My replacement bicycle had a new chain, smooth-running gears, and a coat of dull gray paint. Apparently dropping a bicycle in pieces wasn't too hard a task after all. Vera had faithfully acquired a French model or a reproduction of one, which Grand-Georges had pieced together in no time. I crested the hill and coasted down the other side, a shark sliding noiselessly through the dark.

"Don't you dare fall," Pierre scolded.

"There're no ruts here." Despite the warm night, I'd donned a pair of gloves. I didn't want to risk setting detonators with cold hands.

He consulted the map at a fork in the road, making sure we took the correct turn, and I tried not to betray the pain in my leg or how much I needed the brief rest. He probably knew anyway. "Don't be so careless with the light," I chided. Any visibility threatened us, even on a deserted road in the middle of the night.

Another mile, and we left the road and concealed our bikes. "You are all right?"

The pain in my leg sharpened, but I pressed my lips together, silencing any protest Pierre might have been inclined to make. "It's not far to the tracks," I reminded him.

Soon, they appeared before us, glimmering silver, like the tails of two falling stars. Though I knew the line led to Blois, I fancied it winding quietly into oblivion.

Tonight, it very well might, but the crossing for her passengers wouldn't be as peaceful as the picture before us. It would come in a fiery, tree-shattering crash, as Pierre and I ran for our lives. "This is a ridiculous idea," Pierre muttered under his breath. Already, he'd dug out the time pencils and a wax-paper-wrapped charge from inside his socks. I held out my hand, trading him for the glowing torch, and set to work braiding cord and molding explosive, humming quietly. Properly placed, we wouldn't need much.

Crouched on the nearby rail, Pierre went still. He took my hand and laid it on the cold steel. "Feel that?"

I nodded. The track was vibrating. "They're early." We only had partial intel on troop transport times, piecing together observations from sources in Blois and holes in the unreliable civilian train schedule.

"Give it up, Jacqueline," Pierre hissed. "There's no time. We'll try again tomorrow."

I shook my head and bit down on my bottom lip, extracting another length of wire from my jacket pocket. "Hold the damn light still." I hadn't cycled all this way to duck out now. "There's time." I was nearly done.

Twitching with exasperation, Pierre helped me place the plastic, running the wires into place. "I can hear it now."

I could too, an ominous thrum, stronger than the sound of any approaching plane.

"Hurry!" he snapped.

I had to, but I wasn't going to rush the breaking and placement of the time pencils. Any mistake would obliterate us now and bring this whole scheme to nothing. "Don't rush me," I whispered. "And please stop moving the light."

Somehow, he forced himself still. I jammed in the last pencil, set to its shortest time, and he seized my arm, hauling me to my feet and half dragging me into the woods. "Farther back," I protested. "No matter which side it goes off, the train will go forward."

"The cars in the back could zigzag all over the place," Pierre spat. We scrambled deeper into the trees. Over my pounding heart, the roar of the train increased.

"How long do we have?" he asked, his words broken with the effort of running.

"Two minutes if the pencil is accurate. Let's hope the train is long and slow."

We made it to our bicycles and pumped hard up the silent road to a narrow deer path that cut through the dense

undergrowth. Pierre dropped his bike in a thick spot and signaled me forward. Still no explosion, just the rhythmic push
of hundreds of metal wheels on the track. Before we reached
the ridge with a view of the tracks below, it came, a sharp pop
of explosives, deceptively small compared to the noise of the
train, then an almost animal squeal of metal. The train cried
out, car smashing into car, wheels grappling to hold a track that
no longer existed. From the dark recesses of memory came the
scream of a colicky horse, a favorite of my father's, as he slowly
crashed to the ground. This train was hundreds of him.

We made it to the edge of the trees and tried to make sense of
the black shadows in the night. The lights of the engine glowed
eerily, still upright, but behind it the cars twisted brokenly.

Hissing, pops, crashes, then at last human sounds.
Thunderous barks from the front of the train from those who'd
only been knocked about. Their small shapes rushed into the
night, rifles pointed, expecting an ambush. A volley of bullets
sprayed the air, but we were out of sight and out of range.

And then at last, other cries. Weeping and cries of pain
from one of the nearer cars. Bent backs dragging limp bodies
away from the wreckage.

You did this, so don't think you can look away.

"Time to go," Pierre whispered.

A few gunshots punctured the night, but they were perfunctory, stilted. No one knew where we were. I pictured the
colicky horse again. My fingers curled around the handlebar
as I lifted my bike from the ground. "Those shots…" I couldn't
finish. I saw my father, rifle in hand, lining up a bullet for that
dying, beautiful chestnut. I shivered as we made for the road,

my jaw tight. I wanted to be home under my blanket, away from the cries growing thinner the farther we pedaled.

"It worked," Pierre said, between gasps. "That's what matters."

"It looked like a troop transport." The bodies carried from the cars had worn uniforms. "We killed plenty of them," I added woodenly. Certainly more than the two dozen hostages they'd shot last week. I didn't like to think what they'd exact in exchange for this, but I wanted something for André Gatignon's refugees; for my bombed house; for Bones, my cat; for Pierre's wife, who I'd never meet.

"A good night's work," Pierre muttered angrily, perhaps working out some arithmetic of his own.

The broken cars, burning scrub, and howling bodies flashed before me, forcing my lips into a tight line. This was why I was here. To set France ablaze. Only I wished I didn't have to use the bodies of hapless boys as tinder.

It wasn't until we were back at the cottage, preparing for bed that I noticed the emptiness of my jacket pocket.

"What's wrong?" Pierre asked.

I licked my lips. Took two breaths. Delved into the pockets of my skirt.

"What is it?" Pierre demanded as I turned away to rummage in the handbag I'd left behind during tonight's mission. Not there either.

I pressed a hand to my forehead, hating how it shook. "My identity card. It's gone."

CHAPTER 35

———

PARIS, 8 APRIL 1943

Max waved the telegram under Major Boemelberg's nose. "You cannot keep ignoring this!" Hours ago, a troop train had been derailed, killing over a hundred soldiers.

Major Boemelberg leaned across his desk; Max caught the look in his eyes and cursed himself. Losing his temper with Boemelberg was an excellent way to get himself arrested.

"I am also concerned," Max's immediate supervisor, Colonel Heinrich added. "We cannot afford these losses."

Max's breath leaked out slowly. Thank God. If Heinrich felt the same, he was probably safe.

"If we fail to suppress these terrorists, insurrection will only grow," Max said with all the evenness he could muster. "And forgive me, Major, but so far as I am aware, your infiltration efforts have revealed nothing of the Allied invasion plan." Moments like this, Max felt as frustrated as he imagined the terrorists must be. So much subterfuge and maneuvering and not a whisper of a plan for an Allied invasion yet.

Boemelberg barely reacted to the criticism, his smooth-shaved face still, save for an almost invisible flare of his nostrils, gone in an instant. Max might have imagined it.

"There is much you are unaware of, Max," Boemelberg said. "And I am in charge here. You will leave the matter in my hands. Now, if you'll excuse me, I must telephone Berlin."

Heinrich stared, then wheeled smartly, stalking out of Boemelberg's office. Max followed, imagining the satisfaction of snatching the telephone receiver from Boemelberg's pudgy fist and bashing his skull with it.

"He's a moron," Heinrich muttered outside the closed door. "Obsessed with the Allied invasion." Like Max, Heinrich also had a brother on the Russian front, retreating now, from the failed siege of Stalingrad.

Last year, Max had been confident they could have turned back any attempt to retake France. Now, with their anemic divisions in Russia on the defensive, he wasn't so sure. Which was why it was more important than ever not to cede ground here.

"Something must be done," Max said. "They're getting bolder."

Heinrich nodded. "Leave it with me for now," he whispered. "You should go home. It's late."

Seventeen minutes past three, but Max doubted either of them would sleep.

"Colonel." Sleep wouldn't fix anything.

"Get some rest," Heinrich said. Then, through still lips, he whispered, "You'll need it."

The latent message clear, Max retrieved his hat and overcoat. He walked the long way to his apartment. When he arrived, the concierge had a message for him, made to look just like a letter from his mother.

Inside were Heinrich's instructions.

Leave tonight. Use the enclosed credentials to search the accident scene and call my private line if you find anything. Stay in the region. Build up a cover there, starting in St. Aignan or Chambord or Romorantin, close to the terrorism. The Allies haven't invaded yet. There's still time.

Thirty minutes later, Max set out again, carrying a suitcase. Nestled between his crisply folded shirts was the brown envelope from his desk, which he'd slid into the pocket of his overcoat before leaving headquarters. Not much to go on, true, but after years in the game, he trusted his instincts. This attack had familiar fingerprints all over it: timed and executed to cause maximum damage. Just like that lorry convoy of airplane parts. His enemy's work left a trail, bombed out and bloodstained. He'd chase it until he found her. He'd make this stop.

———

Combing over the crash site the next day, amid bodies and railcars tossed about like the playthings of a tantrumming child, Max sifted through dirt and clambered over the surrounding slopes—for nothing. Until a young French militiaman, just arrived, bent to examine a curling tendril of bombed track.

"Sir? Did you see this?"

"Careful," Max warned. "Don't touch it yet." This close to the blast, any remaining evidence might disintegrate at the gentlest touch. Stumbling with haste, he scrambled across the crater to the other side of the broken rail line.

"You see—just there." The militiaman pointed.

A scorched square of cardboard nestled inside a curve of twisted metal. "There's printing on it," the Frenchman said.

Max stopped breathing, fumbling lightheadedly through his pockets for a handkerchief, tweezers, anything. He found a pen, and the Frenchman supplied his handkerchief. Moving like the scrap might detonate, Max levered it loose with the point of his pen. It fell on the checked bit of linen, revealing an opposite side completely unmarked.

"An identity card," the Frenchman said.

Carefully, carefully, Max nudged the pocket-sized yellow folder open. The scorched side broke off, but even there, shadows of print were visible. Max didn't bother deciphering them. The name would be false anyway. The real prize was on the other side of the card, cupped in his upturned hand: the tiny rectangular photograph of a middle-aged woman with shockingly fair hair curling thickly above dark eyebrows.

He imagined a streak of white combed into the blond curls. It fit, along with the smile and the curve of the jaw.

Logic might have admitted other possibilities, but Max wasn't feeling logical just now.

"It's her," he breathed. "I've found her."

CHAPTER 36

———

THERE WERE NOT MANY DAYS I HAD ALL TO MYSELF—IN truth, not many hours—but when a quiet morning unfurled itself, trailing the scent of flowering vines and new leaves, I indulged in the solitude. Pierre had left early in the morning, in company with Theo Bertin and another poacher, to scout out more landing fields because we couldn't use Bois Renard any longer.

Besides the increasing risk it posed to Pierre's in-laws, last month a plane dropped more canisters than we could carry, and we had no choice but to leave two behind. Before we returned, the Milice found the dropped equipment and turned it in to the Germans like the rats they were. Luckily, M. Dutems, Pierre's father-in-law, had been at dinner that night with a deputation of local Abwehr, and though they questioned him about the use of his field, they believed his show of ignorance and outrage.

Now we needed a new field and had little time to secure one; the next full moon loomed close. With Pierre gone on the motorcycle, scouting possible locations, I took advantage of the opportunity to do my laundry.

With my fraying clothes waving from the line, my hair

knotted up in a hand-me-down scarf, and Nanny's dressing gown tied at my waist and fluttering at my knees, I stretched out a blanket on the floor and practiced my yoga, teasing a week's worth of exertion out of my joints. Kneeling hurt, but otherwise, I was pleased with the recovery in my left knee.

Hands and feet planted, I pushed my rear end up and back and let my breath pour out. I tensed my legs, preparing to spring forward when—

"Jacqueline!" A female voice calling me by name was probably friendly.

I straightened, tugging my robe into place. "Who's there?"

"It's Raymonde." A courier for Prosper and Denise, she often came up from Paris bearing messages, but we always arranged meetings ahead. No one enjoyed surprises.

"Come out and show me the way," she called.

I peered through the window first. Raymonde was alone, so I stuffed my feet into a pair of worn galoshes and picked my way through the minefield we'd laid around the house.

"What are you doing here?" Goose bumps spread down my arms. Raymonde's sunny smile and carefree wave didn't soothe me.

"Is that how you greet a friend bearing gifts?" She grinned and held out a string bag. "I heard there was a parcel for you in one of the lost canisters."

Unfortunately, along with a canvas tent, thirty-four revolvers, and a dozen grenades, the Milice had borne away a package from Vera, containing my bottles of hair dye. Chances were my lost identity card had fallen from my pocket on some back road. If I'd lost it at the bomb site, it would have—I hoped—burned to bits, but I'd changed identities anyway, just in case. I'd changed myself too, not wanting to keep on as a bottle blond. With my hair dye in German hands, the best I'd managed was an ugly auburn from the onionskin dye made for me by Marguerite Flamencourt.

I squinted through the morning sun at Raymonde's string bag and made out a brown glass bottle. "Brown?" I asked hopefully. Raymonde kept a hair salon in Paris so perhaps...

"Black," she admitted. "Dark enough to cover your streak. And..." Raymonde paused dramatically. "I made you a cake."

———

I smelled flour and butter and aniseed the moment she joined me inside the cottage, before she even lifted out the oilskin-wrapped loaf. "I used honey and raisins for sweetening," she explained, but I scarcely heard, too intent on her progress removing the wrapping. Catching sight of the first corner, I let out a wondering sigh. "Raymonde, where did you get white flour?"

She smiled slyly. "I have a friend at the mill in Saint Aignan." She set the unwrapped loaf in the middle of the table. "You have a knife?"

I whipped out the Fairburn-Sykes special that was always strapped to my thigh. Raymonde jumped but then melted with a laugh. "You are always so unexpected."

Busy cutting two thick slices, I made no reply. "None for me," she said. "I already ate."

My challenging gaze didn't budge her at all. Raymonde didn't even blink. "It's for you and Pierre," she said.

"Fine." I could eat plenty, but it felt wrong eating in front of her. We did that too often these days. While the Flamencourts still made omelets whenever we visited, I'd noticed they never joined us, and Nanny Cox no longer poured herself a cup of tea when I sat down with her in her brightly wallpapered rooms at Nanteuil. "Thank you."

"You are too thin," Raymonde scolded.

I broke off a corner and placed it in my mouth almost as reverently as a communion wafer. Closing my eyes, I chewed, mumbling around the soft, sweet spiciness, "Raymonde, this is heaven."

When I finished two slices, she sat me down at the table, covered my dressing gown with the dusty yoga blanket, and colored my hair. "I never really liked myself as a blond," I said, as her fingers worked through my tangled hair. Mother had opinions about peroxide blonds, and I remembered Papa in warm conversations with more than one. Being a horse trader, he'd always known how to talk, and he'd been a handsome man, so I doubt he'd stopped there, not that mother would ever have admitted it.

"Why the frown?" Raymonde asked, bending close to my shoulder. I pushed up the corners of my mouth and met her eyes in the shaving mirror Pierre used, which we'd propped on the table in front of me.

"I was just thinking about some people I know in Paris. Haven't seen them in years. I'd like to, I suppose, but it's just too dangerous."

"I could take a letter," Raymonde offered. "It would be easy. I go back on the afternoon train." She glanced at the envelopes on the table, messages she'd carried from Denise and Prosper, from contacts farther north in Brittany.

"If you gave me the address, I wouldn't need anything else," she added. "Better if I don't know the name."

A radio message to Vera in London was all it would take to reach Jackie. Though I bled inside, wanting to send just a quick word, I knew it was impossible. Even if I sent a message, Vera couldn't relay anything until the war was over. By then, I could—no, would—tell Jackie myself. As for my mother—well, it was possible to reach her in Paris but far too dangerous even to hint that I was here. But a message could accomplish something else.

Don't be stupid, Jacqueline.

"This has sat long enough," Raymonde said, and I followed her outside to the pump. When the cream had been rinsed from my hair, I hurried back inside, to the mirror, but Raymonde reached it first. "Not yet," she said, holding the glass to her chest. "Let me dry and comb it first."

Toweled damp, my hair easily followed her guidance into loose curls.

"Now. Take a look." Raymonde turned the mirror around.

The sight took me by surprise. "I look like I'm trying to be younger," I said.

Raymonde grinned. "Maybe. But it's a striking look, no? And so different from before."

I frowned at my face, paler than usual beneath the dark waves falling across my forehead. The look wasn't complete without smart clothes and a splash of red lipstick, but I might as well wish for the moon. I hardly recognized myself. And I didn't think my mother would either. My idea didn't seem so farfetched anymore. And I'd thought it through. I wasn't being impulsive.

Before Raymonde left, I wrote a letter and sealed it up with a fifty franc note inside. "You don't mind delivering this?"

"Not at all."

"The house is in the third arrondissement. Number 14 Rue Barbette," I told her.

"I'll take it first thing tomorrow," Raymonde promised.

"We'll both be busy passing messages," I said, nodding at the ones she'd brought with her, still lying on the table for me to distribute to Adolphe network. "Just different directions. You'll be safe? Don't deliver mine if there's any danger." My homesick whims weren't worth dying over.

"Of course not. But it will be easy. There are always crowds in Paris. I swim through them, no different from any other fish. It's you who must be careful."

"My knee is just fine," I told her, and we both pretended that was what she meant. "If my clothes dry, I'll take your messages today."

"Take care, Jacqueline."

"You too." We kissed each other's cheeks, and I watched her walk away down the road.

I dressed and hid the letters beneath my blouse, stealing glances at the unfamiliar black-haired woman in the mirror. I tied the scarf around my head, only a few curls waving loose, and tucked my identity papers into my purse with enough francs for a bribe if necessary. After a glass of water and a touch to my thigh to confirm my knife was tightly secured, I went for the door but stopped on the threshold. Raymonde's cake, wrapped in the oilcloth, beckoned from the table.

I nearly always succeeded in stifling premonitions before I went out. *Nothing bad will happen. It's only another courier mission, another drop, another bomb.*

But these days, convincing myself was harder and harder. And the cake was here now. I went back and cut myself a slice. And another. Pierre would want some, I knew, but I couldn't make myself wrap up the loaf. He expected to be home by evening, but there was no guarantee he'd make it back. So far, Theo had always been reliable, but one never knew.

I pressed my finger to a stray crumb lying on the table and brought it to my mouth.

Nothing bad will happen, I told myself again. But I ate the entire cake before I left in case I didn't come home to finish it later.

———

After days of hunting, Theo and Pierre located a new landing field. Pierre wanted two for the next moon phase, but one was better than none. Our next scheduled drop was only two days away, which didn't leave much time if I wanted to burn a day traveling to Paris. I hadn't told Pierre why because he'd never agree to it. Usually, preaching caution was my job, but I didn't look like myself, I answered instinctively to my cover name, and yet I couldn't stop thinking about Jackie, Papa, and my mother.

No one, not Pierre, Souris, or Marguerite, knew who I'd been before. It had felt freeing, but now I felt my own self dwindling beneath my cover. And as week followed week, as the weather turned warmer and the bean and potato plants on the side of the house grew, I worried the invasion might not come. At least, not this year.

Anything could happen between now and 1944.

"I'll be back by dinner," I told Pierre. I'd held back some blank ration cards lifted from the local prefecture, giving me an excuse to visit the *boîte aux lettres* in Denise's circuit.

"You can't put it off?" Pierre asked as I packed the cards and our circuit's latest messages into the lining of my purse.

I shook my head. "Denise will need to make cards for the incoming agents." London's last message was that they were sending us two at the next full moon. And what Pierre didn't know was that there was no point traveling to Paris if I didn't do it today.

"Be careful." He studied me more closely than usual, but I smiled as if I didn't notice.

"You too." Then I was out the door, mounting my bicycle, pedaling to meet the early morning bus.

From there, the train journey was uneventful. By now I knew how to play the odds, choosing busy carriages so I was less likely to be chosen for a random search. At Paris, I left the station and hurried to Denise's letter box. Though there was time to spare, it was easier to breathe without incriminating papers on me.

The blooming Tuileries breathed gently in the breeze, as lovely as ever, if you ignored the sandbags obscuring monuments and the boarded-up windows hiding the denuded galleries of the Louvre.

I found a green metal chair and reclined in the shade,

changing my mind minute by minute. An old man and a bulldog walked past, and at first, I couldn't tell which of them was
wheezing. The dog, I decided, as they came closer. The man
smiled at me and touched his hat; I manufactured a smile in
response, and they shuffled away on bowed legs along the geo-
metrically perfect white gravel.

What if she sees me?

Rehearsed objections crowded around the fear nestled in
the back of my brain, jostling like passengers on the five o'clock
Métro. Still, my fear refused to be displaced. Even though I
planned to keep out of her line of sight, even though my face
and body were thinner, even though my hair was a shiny indigo-
black and there was no reason she or anyone would look for me,
I longed to be seen, not just to see her. Picturing my mother's
frown, then her hand clutching her chest as realization dawned,
I ached for that moment to be real.

But that would cause a scene, and cafés were dangerous. I
couldn't have it, no matter how tempting it seemed. Just stealing a look was foolhardy enough. Selfish. I couldn't explain why
I needed it so badly or why I expected a glimpse of her to ease
my mind and melt the fear freezing my heart.

Of course I was afraid. I had a hundred excellent reasons.
But when I got up from my chair, I didn't descend to the Métro.
I donned my colored glasses and strolled down the Rue de
Rivoli to Rumpelmayer's café.

The famous tearoom was owned by distant relatives of
my mother. She'd often brought me here on weekday shopping excursions to Paris or special Sunday afternoons. I stepped
through spotless glass and brightly polished brass doors into a

world as elaborate as any celebrated pastry confection: cream and gold moldings, pastel-toned murals of the coast, the smells of real coffee and thick pourable chocolate wafting from smooth white china. Miraculously, they served both here. I felt thirteen again, a child in my mother's tow, until a conversation in elegantly modulated German vaulted me back to the present. My hand tightened on the strap of my purse.

"For how many, madame?" The host gave a practiced smile.

"Only myself. I'd like a table over there." My rehearsed words emerged rough and hesitant, as if I'd never tried to pass as anyone but myself before, a sharp reminder that nostalgia could be dangerous. Fortunately, the man was too well-trained or too busy to notice. I followed him past tables of well-dressed women in meticulously turned suits, only the unfaded lines along the seams betraying the garments' age. There was no new cloth to be found, but money still bought the service of excellent tailors. The host led me to an unobtrusive table near the railing on the second floor where I could watch people come and go.

The waiter came and poured me a glass of water while I debated whether to squander a fortune on café au lait or chocolat Africain. As a child, I'd always had the hot chocolate, often with a raspberry macaron. Today it seemed a crime to even think about ordering both.

Well. I wouldn't let that stop me. "Hot chocolate and a raspberry macaron, please." I surrendered a hair-raising number of forged ration coupons with (I hope) convincing blandness. No one dining here could have collected the necessary amount honestly. Mother's favorite tearoom, once the last word in decadent French femininity, was now a den of collaborators and black marketeers.

My chocolate and pastry arrived, and I tore my eyes away from the door long enough to take a bite. The taste and textures were exactly as I remembered, but I found myself unaccustomed to such sweet richness dissolving on my tongue. I sipped from the glass of water, washing the cloying stickiness down my throat. My attention back on the café entrance, I stirred a dollop of whipped cream into my small jug of chocolate.

People came and went. My watch showed twenty-three past two, and though I'd told myself to make it last, I'd consumed every crumb of the decadent macaron (it wasn't hard to reaccustom myself to luxury). The hot chocolate, a meal in itself, diminished a sip at a time from my two-thirds-full cup.

A black-garbed woman, fairylike in her proportions but with movements old and brittle, came through the door. My chest tightened, seeing how she supported herself on a young man's arm. I didn't recognize him, but he smiled and spoke courteously to a second woman on his other side. My cousin. He must be her husband. I knew his name and had seen photographs, but we'd never met.

She'd gotten my letter then. They took a table in the center of the room, half-in, half-out of my line of sight. Maman settled into her chair with a hesitancy—almost timidity—that I'd never seen before.

I wondered what my cousin Adele thought about the letter, the ration cards, and the money—the request from me to take Maman for an afternoon's enjoyment on this particular day, so they could all remember better times. She was scrupulous enough not to simply spend it, but was she too curious? I wasn't sure and couldn't tell. All three were looking about—natural, I supposed, in this oasis of prewar life—but as I busied myself pouring the last of the chocolate into my cup, I prayed they weren't looking for me.

I was only a middle-aged woman, always something of a disappointment to my mother. Especially in my marriage and then my failed marriage. In my migrating from one enthusiasm to another, when I ought to be settled. *Fancies are for young women,* she always said.

All seven of my siblings lay in tiny graves. Perhaps one of them would have turned out as she wished.

My stomach twisted from a surfeit of rich food and familiar old pain, but I reminded myself these slights were not only beyond my power to change, they were also my protection. No matter how strange the letter and the money seemed, Maman would never imagine I could be here, twenty yards away.

I pushed away the breath I'd forgotten, stale from sitting inside motionless lungs. Maman was just the same, though older. Her clothes fit perfectly, though they must have been made long before the war. Her order came—hot chocolate only. I knew, in spite of the shortages, she would only drink half, that her water glass would be emptied and refilled again and again. She had always been ferociously protective of her trim little waist. Growing up, I'd heard the whispers that so many of her babies were born dead because she refused to loosen her stays. *How I survived*—a morbid grin settled on my lips. Perhaps I had always thrived under extreme pressure.

I wished I could hear what they were talking about. Why

hadn't I visited Jackie again, in the last days before departure? It had seemed the wisest course at the time, but I wished I'd inconvenienced her, dragged her to London or persuaded her to meet me in a tacky tea shop for watered-down tea and the bricks we called ration-proof cake. I hadn't wanted her hurt or worried, but now I feared the questions, the emptiness she might feel if I never came back. I should have left a letter, explaining. Vera would have kept one for me.

Even swathed in chocolate, it was hard to swallow the hot lump in my throat. I didn't want to drop out and disappear from my line of women. Someday, when the war was over, Jackie and Ronald would have children.

I'll bring them to Paris. I'll sit with them here, watching them make themselves ill eating too much ice cream.

Maman had done just the same. My cup was empty, but I sat and watched until they finished, until they gathered their things and went out. I wanted to go, but it wouldn't be safe yet. I made myself count out fifteen long minutes before paying my bill, then hurried out at a businesslike pace to the Métro.

CHAPTER 37

———

"Le Meur is in charge of the signals tonight," Pierre said, crouching down on his heels and rubbing his hands.

"Good." I liked Albert Le Meur, the newly married son of a family of local hoteliers and a natural leader among the Chambord group that Pierre and I had collected and nurtured over the past eight months. "He's ready." Albert had joined us on plenty of receptions and designed and built his own signaling lamp from stray household parts. Tonight Pierre and I planned to hang back in the woods, letting Albert take charge. Next time he'd command the reception entirely on his own.

I shifted, easing away from the damp seeping from the ground into my borrowed trousers. They were Pierre's, and though he was small, on me they hung comically large, held around my waist with a double length of old rope. Even after days of unseasonable heat, the ground remained wet here—deep in shade where Pierre and I crouched beneath thick trees—and farther down, the field we'd use for the parachute landing slid gradually into a murk-filled ditch and a treacherous bog. Not ideal ground, but it was close to two roads.

"Georges Fermé? He's bringing his van?" We were expecting

ten canisters, so without Georges's wholesale grocery van, moving everything would be impossible.

Pierre hummed assent but then proceeded to tick more names off his fingers. "Souris and Pierre de Bernard will move in from the south with Madame Bessonier and Bühler and Caillard from Blois…" He kept on, the names flying past too fast for me to count.

"That's far too many!" I interrupted in a fierce whisper. "When I said we needed to train more people, I didn't mean we should invite everyone."

"We can't keep going to all of these anymore," Pierre said, more diffidently than I liked. "We're too tired, and we can't shoulder all the risk all the time."

His point made sense. The more trained people, the more resilient our network. But… "It's too many," I said.

"This is the safest reception for them to watch," Pierre argued. "Easy to come and go this close to the roads."

A flicker of torchlight ended our discussion. I peered through the dark at narrow beams dancing through the grass below. Albert Le Meur and his signaling team. Each point of light a life so easily snuffed out if captured. I shuddered at the number of them.

"Armadine Bessonier is so useful with the canisters," Pierre added.

Again, I couldn't argue. Armadine could carry a full container all by herself. With so many waiting at the fringes of the field, we'd squirrel away tonight's delivery in no time.

"I'm going to have a nap," I said. "Wake me when the planes come." It was too warm to need the worn blanket I'd brought tonight, but it made a dry and softer place to stretch out and close my eyes. I could sleep anywhere these days, in anything. Even at home, I seldom bothered to take off my shoes. Better to stay ready.

———

"It's time." Pierre nudged me awake. I stretched, producing a jaw-cracking yawn, and pinched myself awake, gauging how much time we had by the hum of the engines. Albert's team was already busy telegraphing frenetic messages with their lights. I craned my head back, counting the parachutes that bloomed in the moonlit sky. Seven…eight, no there's nine…

"That's ten," Pierre said with a satisfied nod.

With almost no wind, they drifted toward us as if drawn by magnets. Already I saw runners streaking across the field.

"Let's go." I tugged at Pierre's arm, my eyes fixed on the first parachute, just thirty feet or so from the ground. We left the cover of the trees—

A flash as white as burning magnesium blinded me, blowing me flat onto the ground.

"Pierre." I felt my mouth moving but heard no sound except a buzzing in my ears. My sight, marred by blue and purple afterimages, didn't help. I scrabbled over the ground, feeling for something, and jabbed Pierre in the eye.

"Get off, Jacqueline. I'm fine," he hissed.

"Can you see anything?"

"Give me a minute. What was that?"

"The canister. It blew up before it hit the ground."

Where were Albert and Armadine? Francis, a vet, was also

with the signal team. I strained my ears but couldn't pick out screams or moans from any wounded. I heard shouts though—panicked shouts, echoing into the distance.

"Quiet!" I barked. Not that it mattered. The explosion would have been heard miles away. Already, soldiers must be jumping onto their motorbikes. I pushed to my feet, bracing my hands on my knees. The moment my vision cleared enough to make out shapes, I stumbled across the field.

They're moving. They must be all right, I told myself, advancing through a dark haze of dread. "Albert! Are you all right?" I hissed.

"Jacqueline?" Francis's voice. Not Albert's.

"Yes, it's me."

"Are we betrayed?"

"I think it was an accident," I said with false confidence, not wanting to admit the possibility of sabotage. "But we must get away from here. You're not hurt?"

A darker shadow against a midnight blue sky, Francis shook his head.

"Quickly," I urged. Pierre crept by on my left, helping another signaler to his feet. He moved cautiously but competently enough. Physically intact, I decided, though shaken as the rest of us. I loped awkwardly to the nearest container, draped in khaki parachute silk, and stopped ten yards away. Why had the first canister exploded? What about this one? The eight others scattered around us?

Our codes might be broken. These containers might be booby traps dropped by Germans. Or London could be afflicted by hidden saboteurs. I stood, paralyzed and sweating, afraid to move closer but unable to move away. Time was running out.

Pierre touched my arm. "They seem fine." He nodded toward his left where someone—Armadine?—waddled under a canister's weight. He moved to one end of the canister in front of me. Spurred by the resolve of the others, I hefted the other and we took off for the road at an ungainly run. We'd figure out what went wrong later. For now, we just needed to get everyone out of here.

The van crouched on the track, furtive as a stalking wolf. I didn't recognize the driver, but Georges and Berbert tossed canisters into the back like logs of firewood.

"Careful!" If, as I hoped, the explosion was just an accident, we shouldn't bring on another. But driven by panic, no one took the time to think. "Where's Souris?" I demanded.

"Burying parachutes?" her husband suggested.

I hadn't noticed her in the sprint across the field. "Where was she?"

Berbert jerked his head sideways. "Thirty yards that way."

Closer to the blast than I had been, but still, she should have been far enough away. Unless, at the last moment, she'd moved closer. I spun on my heel and ran in the direction Berbert had indicated. Nothing remained of the container but the marred ground and some charred and fluttering scraps of silk. No time to hide those away. We'd never use this field again anyway.

"Souris?" I called, my voice low.

"I'm over here," she snapped, and relief swelled in me at the familiar impatience lacing her voice.

"What happened? Are you all right?" I slid into the nearby ditch. "I don't see you," I said, scanning in vain.

"Farther back," she said, and I plunged through the knee-deep water, following her voice.

Ahead of me, I glimpsed a silhouette, waving awkwardly, too low to the ground. "You hurt?" I asked, my haste checked even after I waded out of the water by the muddy ground. One foot slid; I caught myself with a hand on the ground and pushed forward. "Souris? What happened?"

"Le Meur ran off like an idiot, crying that we were betrayed. I'd like to slap him," she fumed. Knowing her, this was no idle threat. And if he broke, became a liability… I wouldn't think of that yet.

I approached Souris, but she warned me back with a wave of her arms. She was drenched head to toe in thick mud.

"I was blown back into the ditch," she explained. "I followed Albert, trying to talk sense to him, but he was in no state to mind anyone. He left me and then I realized the ground was too soft—don't come any closer!"

Instinctively, I'd taken two steps forward but stopped now, as my feet sank even deeper with a gurgling squelch. "Don't move," I said. "I'll fetch some rope."

She had sunk all the way to her thighs, but so far, anger seemed to have warded away any panic.

"It won't take a second." I whistled for Pierre. Thankfully, he brought Berbert, and we soon pulled Souris free with the help of a parachute, which we then pushed into the hole she left in the bog.

"It's been almost fifteen minutes," Pierre muttered.

"Georges already left with the van. Francis and Armadine are gone, making their way back to the woods. Are you able to walk?" Berbert asked Souris.

"Of course I am. And I'm too muddy to make it through

a checkpoint anyway," Souris said, stalking away. "I'll meet you at home."

"Stay out of the bog!" her husband called after her. "She'll be fine," he said to Pierre and me. He picked up his rifle. Dressed for hunting, he had a better chance of explaining himself if he were stopped on the way to Nanteuil. "You had better come with me," he said.

I shook my head. "We have to collect our bicycles."

"Come after, then. We need to find out what went wrong."

I nodded. If we managed to get everyone to safety, I'd never risk so many at once again.

As Pierre and I picked our way uphill, back to the woods, I glanced back at the road. No noise, no lights. "Why hasn't anyone come?"

Impossible for the Germans to miss that explosion.

"I don't know," Pierre admitted. But I could tell he liked it as little as I did.

CHAPTER 38

———

MAX SLOUCHED ON THE BACK SEAT OF THE BUS, PRETENDING to doze. Ahead of him, two women bent their heads together in earnest conversation.

"—heard nothing since last night's explosion, but of course it's only a matter of time. Dorothée's boy went out the next morning. Germans beating through the woods and bits of khaki silk caught in the trees."

"A parachute army," the other woman said, nodding sagely. "Getting ready to attack. And how many hostages will the Germans demand from us in return?" She began counting her latest row of knitting. "Reckless fools."

"I had my papers checked on my way into town, at the hospital, and again just now. Three times! They won't be able to hide for long."

"Police will catch them," said the other woman regretfully. "Then there'll be the devil to pay."

Silence, save for the bus chugging uphill. A loose thread from Max's fraying collar tickled his neck, demanding attention, but he ignored it, forcing his body to keep still.

"Do you think…?" One of the women paused. Even through

his closed eyes, Max felt her gaze sweeping over him. "Well. I don't suppose it matters," she said.

The other woman sighed, a tired gust containing all the weary exhaustion of late winter, in spite of it being a fine spring day, filled with sunshine.

"You're tired," her friend said consolingly. "We all are."

"It's just…" Again the hesitation, the careful censoring of words. "I keep wondering, you know." Her voice dropped. Max had to strain to hear. "How much longer?" she whispered desperately.

I wish I knew, Max thought in silent sympathy.

The feeling startled him, vanishing at once with a surprised jerk, which he converted, belatedly, to a swipe across his itching neck. He shifted in his seat, drew his hand farther over his eyes, but the women, like squirrels in the woods, were on their guard now.

For the next twenty minutes, until Max disembarked, they spoke only of rations and knitting.

When he returned to his shabby cover apartment, Max placed a telephone call.

"Paris 7845, please."

There was a pause and a series of clicks as the line connected. "Michel?"

"Good morning, Leo." He and Heinrich were careful not to use real names when there was any chance they might be overheard.

"I'm not getting anywhere," Max said. "We need to stop playing cat and mouse. More checkpoints. More searches. We have those two photographs." And the name from the identity card, though she'd surely changed that by now. Jacqueline LeClair. "It's the only way we'll find her."

There was a pause at the other end of the line.

"Leo?"

Heinrich answered with a soft chuckle. "I think you might finally get your way, Max. There was a cable from Berlin this morning. If Boemelberg doesn't change tactics quick, he's going to have to resign."

Max's breath caught. "I'm coming to Paris."

Heinrich laughed again. "No. Stay there. I want you leading the search."

CHAPTER 39

———

We gathered at Nanteuil the next day, Pierre and I, Souris, Armadine, Georges Fermé, and Albert Le Meur, who'd run off the night before. Albert swore he was calmer now, and so far, I'd chosen to believe him.

Denise, summoned by telephone, arrived by express train from Paris with instructions directly from London.

"They don't know what caused the explosion. They're investigating," she said from the far end of the table.

"Investigating how?" Le Meur challenged.

Denise huffed. "They didn't tell me. It's not like they dialed me on the phone, and there wasn't much time. The detection vans were out again last night." Communication, especially emergency communication, was especially short and haphazard, though bravely conducted by Gilbert, our fugitive wireless operator.

"When will we know more?" I asked, trying to focus the discussion on more helpful topics.

Denise shrugged. "Gilbert is changing safe houses again. I'm sure he'll try and make contact if he has a chance tonight, but…"

Next to me, Souris started drumming her fingers on the table. Pierre was less reticent.

"We're slated to receive another drop tomorrow night, but we can't go ahead unless it's safe," he said.

There weren't many full-moon nights, and lately London seemed intent on sending us their entire arsenal.

"Even if it was an accident and there's nothing wrong with other canisters, it's a bad idea to go ahead now. That explosion kicked the hornet's nest. The Germans know what we're doing. We must lie low for now," Pierre insisted.

Denise shook her head. "London said to proceed. The next drop is in a different location."

"But still within fifteen miles," Pierre said. "What are they thinking? We can't possibly use any more guns."

"They're sending agents," Denise reminded him. "Probably radio operators. That would help."

Souris rubbed her forehead tiredly.

"I told Gilbert to say no," Denise said apologetically. "Just to give you time to catch your breath. Drops this often—well, you had three last month, besides those going to other circuits. Scientist and Juggler both took in supplies too."

"They wouldn't send these arms for no reason. We'll need them soon," Georges Fermé argued. "The Allies must be coming."

"We don't know that," I said quietly. "Not for sure. And the civic center is stacked to the roof. The entire building reeks of subterfuge. Every shed and attic is packed with rifles and bullets. We don't have any more spots to store weapons."

Albert pressed his lips together, his jaw firm. "If an Allied platoon shows up, I will not be the one to tell them we don't have enough ammunition to support them."

Souris's fingertips resumed tapping. I kept my misgivings caged in my chest. While it was true the invasion might come any day, it might also be a year away. And a year was plenty of time for the Gestapo to destroy our entire network, bodies and lives strewn in their wake. An invasion didn't mean deliverance. Last summer's failed Allied landing in Operation Jubilee had done more harm than good, with half the troops killed, injured, or captured. If we rose and fought only to crumble beneath the German boot, I wasn't sure how many would have the courage to fight again. Or be left alive to do it.

But maybe fear—here and in London—was the problem. Only a coordinated liberation attempt would defeat the Germans. Sooner or later, it had to come, and delay wasn't helping.

"Do you have any inside information at all?" Pierre pressed. "An inkling that something big is happening?"

"I know what you know," Denise answered, her words defensive. "If they're risking the planes and our lives to send it, we need it."

Pierre sighed, his brow wrinkling with worry.

"I hope we're about to blow the hell out of them. I get sick every time I pass one of them." Denise's lip curled.

"If it were about passion, we'd win," I conceded. "This isn't about whose cause is just. This is about logistics. We're getting away with too much. I don't like it."

"You want us to be caught?" Armadine scoffed.

"No." I shot her a stern look. "It's just suspicious we had such a clean getaway last night. It took too long to clear out, and no one saw a sign of the Germans until this morning. Maybe they're biding their time, letting us amass more equipment for them to confiscate."

Souris's fingers went still. "You think they are fooling us?"

"I hope to God not. But I fear it," I said.

"I'll return Pierre's question to all of you," Denise said. "Does anyone have any hint of such a thing? Any intelligence or rumor whatsoever?"

Slowly, everyone shook their heads. Souris accompanied hers with a snort. "None of us would keep that kind of knowledge to ourselves. We aren't traitors."

"I know." I laid a soothing hand on her arm, and the nervous beat of her fingertips, a broken cadence of senseless Morse, started up again.

"You don't know anything, Jacqueline?" Denise asked.

I shook my head. I couldn't hedge with a lie. I had nothing but... "Just a feeling that even Germans can't be this stupid. The planes fly right over the château where they quarter their officers. Then last night's explosion. How could they not suspect?"

Albert blew out his breath and ran a hand through his fair hair. He was calmer today, embarrassed about losing his nerve earlier. We'd accepted his apology, knowing he was too young to hold up the fate of so many friends. But weren't we all?

I set my hands on the table. "This isn't moving us nearer a decision, so here's my suggestion. We take the next two drops, fill the stashes we have to capacity, involve as few people as possible. Then we lie low until we know more."

It sounded reasonable, but my stomach objected, twisting like a slipknot.

"If they already know, one more drop is too many," Albert argued.

"Every drop is a risk," Pierre countered. "They have been from the beginning. Every single day, every life involved teeters on the edge. We've kept everyone safe so far. We can finish out the month."

He removed his spectacles and rubbed his eyes. His dark mustache shifted as he frowned. "It's likely we're all getting paranoid. It's been a long fight. We can keep our heads down and keep our cover for the next drop. Next month, if there's more, we'll switch the fields again."

Denise nodded, her concern for me apparent in her fast glance. "They can't possibly know how much we've collected and distributed. And if they come, we fight." She smiled tightly. "We're certainly equipped for it."

So in spite of my reservations, Pierre and I crouched in the dark again the following night, scanning the sky. Two canisters had thumped to a muddy landing, but I held back, the others following my lead, wary of explosions or traps. A third chute, blown slightly off course, headed right for us, floating over the tree canopy. I flinched, but it missed the overhanging branches and settled on the edge of the field with hardly a sound. Something lighter in that one. Beside me, Pierre released a breath.

There were fewer of us tonight, and no new recruits. This job was only for insiders: Pierre, Denise, Georges, and me, so we needed every pair of eyes and arms. Albert, Armadine, Souris,

Berbert, and the others were under orders to be conspicuously visible someplace else, scrupulously observing curfew.

Pierre and I raced to the container and sliced away the cords, but before we hauled it off the ground, something crashed in the trees behind us. I spun around, barely catching a glimmer of silk fluttering through the tangled branches.

"Merde," Pierre muttered. "Go see what that is, will you?" He hefted the container awkwardly and I dashed back to the woods.

"Help!" someone called in a hoarse whisper.

I nearly stumbled. That voice came from the parachute, not the field where my friends worked like demons recovering our supplies so we could vanish in a dozen different directions.

"I'm coming," I called as loudly as I dared—so not much. "Keep still. Keep silent."

My head buzzed, imagining what might result from landing in a tree—bloody gashes, broken arms. Blade in hand, I hurried closer.

In spite of my warning, the person in parachute gear and striptease suit (covering a set of Vera-approved French clothing) was thrashing energetically, dangling well above the ground. A man. At least he'd stopped shouting.

"Don't worry. I'm a friend," I said. "We'll get you down." Pierre, I hoped, would not be far behind. I wasn't tall enough to cut anything from down on the ground. Holding the blade of my knife in my teeth, I hoisted myself up into the tree, shimmying out to the ensnaring branches.

"Be ready," I warned after I transferred the knife to my hand. "Once I cut, you might fall."

"I'm ready." The words wavered, weak and thready—the

voice of a frightened young man, as well he might be, having just plummeted from the sky. "Just get me loose."

I managed two cuts before Pierre arrived. With his help, it went faster. Soon, our arrival dropped unceremoniously to the ground.

"You all right?" I whispered from my perch in the tree.

The first few words were indecipherable—curses, no doubt—but he picked himself up and peeled away the suit. "I'm fine."

Pierre and I exchanged glances, shrugged, and then proceeded to believe him.

"This way," Pierre said.

Georges was waiting beside a car, parked on the verge of the road. "Good. You found him," he said. "The other one is already in the car. Denise said you're to take both agents to Veilleins with you. They'll need transport to Beaugency station in the next few days."

"Both?" Pierre narrowed his eyes at the young men in front of us. Our cottage was hardly more than a shed. We had no creature comforts tucked away—no extra food or bedding.

Georges stepped away from the car. We followed him just out of earshot of the others. "They need to get to Paris, and with all the checks on the road… Your cottage is isolated. It's the safest place. François, the one I found—shorter, with the mustache—tells me he has orders to start a new circuit."

Leading a circuit? He didn't look old enough to vote. And travel to Paris was trickier than ever. Germans had tightened the security on trains everywhere—almost as if someone had been blowing them up. A grin slipped across my face. "Paris is hard right now."

"None of us expect things to be easy," Pierre reminded me.

It wasn't safe to linger here, but I stared at the dark trees, deliberating. May was half-over, warm-weather days slipping like sand through our fingers. If the Allies were planning on liberating France this year, they weren't being quick about it, and they needed every week of fine weather. But maybe they were planning a late start to trick the Germans into relaxing their defenses, sending men away from our coasts and into Russia. I just didn't know.

And now we had these men—green as spring sprouts—to deal with.

"We'll take them," I muttered. Where else would they go? I wasn't going to be a coward and an obstacle like Raymond Flower. "But once they are on their way, we halt operations until I send a message to London. They need to know what's happening here." And I needed to know why they were ordering drops and deployments with so much urgency.

We walked back to the car. "Wait a few days if you have to," Georges suggested. "And be careful."

"You too," I said.

The young men smiled at us as we climbed inside the car. They couldn't have been more than a couple of years apart. Their unlined faces saddened me. With luck, they'd soon be thin and tired enough to fit in. "I'm Pickersgill," the one I'd cut from the tree said. "We have all our papers. Don't worry, they're good enough to get us past anything."

Pierre's eyes shot to mine, and a panicked look passed between us.

"Papers are half the problem. Speak again," Pierre commanded.

"P-pardon?" Pickersgill stuttered in confusion.

"You'll never pass," I whispered, dread dragging down my words. My inflections raised eyebrows, though I'd spent half my life in France. Pickersgill's demanded interrogation. What was Jepson thinking?

Pickersgill's face hardened and his chest puffed. "Paris is flooded with immigrants. I have a foolproof cover story to explain any accent."

"Is your cover story you're a Canadian spy? Because that's the only one they're going to believe." Pierre's voice rose.

Any other time I would have laughed, but tonight—

"Pickersgill's right," the fair-haired one said, his voice timid, as if trying to hide his French from scrutiny. "I've studied five languages at Oxford—"

Pierre's look of horror intensified. "Well, I hear all five of them garbled together in everything you say. And studying in England isn't helping your case. You sound worse than him." Pierre pointed violently over his shoulder. "We have to keep you away from any Germans."

"But they won't know French nuances. SOE told us—"

Pierre raked a hand through his hair. "SOE forgets that every Frenchman is obsessed with his language, and we are crawling with collaborators and frightened citizens who will break under a hard glance. Even if the Germans don't know, French people will tell them." Hope drained from Pierre's face along with his color.

"We'll take them to André Gatignon for several days. Let them talk with him until they're blue in the face. He'll get them as polished as he can," I offered. "It will give us time to devise the safest way to Paris."

"That's if we can even get them there," Pierre snapped. "If we're stopped—"

"I'm married to a Frenchwoman," Pickersgill shot back. "It's my first language now."

My heart thrummed with the same misgivings that had plagued me for weeks. I hid my speeding breath with a curt shrug. "They have a foolproof story."

God above, I hope they are right.

It wouldn't do any good to destroy their confidence. If they were rattled when the Germans stopped us, it would give us all away. "We can pass them off as friends from Normandy if we have to," I lied.

The tall one leaned over the small attaché case that concealed his radio. If Germans searched our car, they'd find two fresh Canadians and one wireless transmitter. Not to mention the pistol hugging my thigh. I didn't have time to meditate or seek out a horoscope, so I settled for a fast prayer. *Just get us home.*

CHAPTER 40

PIERRE AND I AGREED ON ONE THING: SINCE RETURNING McAllister and Pickersgill wasn't possible, the best thing to do was shuttle them on. Their French—while impressive in peacetime—elicited too much suspicion in current circumstances. With so many ears pricked in one densely populated city like Paris, people noticed strange accents, and I wasn't as sanguine as they were about "foolproof cover stories." Citizens were depressed, overworked, and always hungry, and the Germans offered good money to collaborators for turning over suspected spies or fugitives. Trusting a fabricated story seemed as wise as hiding in a hedge maze with a bundle of balloons. Keeping them here endangered the entire network.

André Gatignon drilled them in French customs and idioms—especially the overconfident Pickersgill, with his painful grammar. The tall one with full thoughtful lips fared even worse. His bright blond hair, porcelain cheeks, and blue eyes already stood out in a crowd, without his awkward phrasing. When we checked in with André weeks later, he gave us a shake of his haggard head and uttered, "Did you know they sent us a Rhodes Scholar? He can think his way out of anything, but if he speaks to an unfriendly Frenchman—*mon Dieu.*" Each face they saw, each name they overheard was a domino that, when toppled, could knock all of us down.

As if sensing our predicament, the Germans doubled their searches. There were checkpoints everywhere, more than I'd ever seen before.

A tense meeting with Souris ended in the opinion that midmorning seemed safest for travel and journeying as far as possible by car, despite the increasing roadblocks, was better than dropping them at the nearest station—for all of us. We chose a date, and André moved the Canadians from his home to Nanteuil. Pierre and I would conduct them as far as we could before leaving them to their own luck on the train.

On our way to Nanteuil to pick up the Canadians, Pierre and I stopped in Bracieux to leave messages and supplies with Francis Cortembert the vet. Winding through the white-plastered buildings of the village square, we stopped at a row house with a brass plaque nailed to the door.

The veterinary surgeon waved away a small pack of dogs as Pierre and I took a seat in his parlor and explained tomorrow's destination and mission.

Cortembert frowned and pointed out the dangers of two healthy men of military age walking around as civilians.

"I know," I muttered. "But half the network thinks invasion is imminent." I was less convinced, but I didn't want to be wrong either. And keeping these two men here was too dangerous for our network—a fragile grid of bright lights connecting a score of tiny towns. We'd assembled and trained more than a hundred resistants, but like the power lines we so often bombed, every point, every person, was vulnerable. "Now is when courage counts," I said for both of us.

Cortembert leveled his gaze. "There is no virtue in stupidity."

"I've weighed the risks a hundred times," I sighed. "And this is our best option."

"Be safe," he told me. "We all depend on you."

Behind us someone cleared her throat. Cortembert's wife, who I'd never spoken with, emerged from the shadows of the next room.

"My apologies, Jacqueline, but your clothes have become so worn. They'll stand out in town. Would you like to borrow a suit? It might help you avoid attention."

I rarely managed to share clothes due to my small frame, but Mme. Cortembert was tiny. I scanned my lap, taking in my disheveled culottes, ragged and uneven at the hem from mending and rough wear and washing.

"That would be lovely. And probably necessary," I agreed with a small laugh.

She ushered me to her bedroom, where she pulled out a tweed check suit and a sturdy pair of low-heeled shoes in serviceable brown. To share anything in these times required great selflessness, bordering on love.

"This is beautiful. Thank you." I ran my finger along the neat seams. "I'll return it soon."

I thought of the hundreds of horoscopes I'd read, the many times I'd worn purple, yellow, gray, or blue to attract a little luck. I was no astrologer, but this beautiful brown tweed was a better omen than I'd have hoped for. Everything would be all right. I returned Mme. Cortembert's smile—a promise to each other that we'd do what was necessary. We'd fight together until we won this war.

"*À bientôt*, Jacqueline," she said, clasping my hand warmly.

———

At Nanteuil, we found the two soldiers laughing cheerfully and playing cards with Moune, unaware of the looks passing over their heads. A quiet sigh collected in my chest and escaped with a sad flutter over my lips. Pierre and I loaded them into our borrowed Citroën as they gave cheery goodbyes. Pierre's knuckles blanched on the steering wheel. The load of wireless parts in the back didn't help.

Where the dirt lane met tarmac, he stopped the car, waiting for a goods van to pass. It rattled away down the road, but still he hesitated before shifting back into gear. "Pierre?" I asked.

"We should turn back," he said.

I glanced at the Canadians. McAllister licked his lips. "We have to get to Paris," he said a little helplessly. "If you think a different train station would be better…?"

There were no good stations. Danger stalked every one. The roads weren't much better.

"We should go now," I said. Later on, there would be less traffic to hide in. And checks were more frequent on the late-day trains.

Pierre glanced in the rearview mirror at the empty road and opened his door, jogging to the thick shrubbery at the roadside.

"What—"

He reached into his blazer and retrieved his pistol, placing it in a clump of overgrown weeds. Pickersgill, McAllister, and I watched with surprise as he pulled out his knife and sawed a thick gash at the base of the tree so he could find it later.

"Are you sure?" I asked as he returned to the driver's seat.

"There are a lot of things we can talk our way out of. A gun isn't one of them. Did you bring yours?"

I shook my head. I'd had a similar thought and left mine, reluctantly, with Souris.

Pierre nodded once, sharply, and let out the clutch as he exhaled.

We passed the first towns without incident. But at Dhuizon, a German patrol waved us off our intended route onto one that bisected the center of town.

"Think we'll be stopped?" Pickersgill asked. He seemed almost eager for it.

"This isn't a Beaulieu game," I snapped. No doubt the practice interrogations there had bolstered his confidence to dangerous levels.

"They probably just don't want us on the other road," Pierre said tersely. "Maybe a troop convoy coming through." Not that we needed more jackboots on this patch of ground.

We drove circumspectly down the streets, painfully aware of our ill-assorted party—clearly not a family, not joined by employment either. I wished we could have passed as a building crew or a hospital delegation.

Stick close to the truth. You're a couple, bringing these young men to the train station as a favor to friends.

"The roads are too quiet," I murmured to Pierre. On a Monday morning in the middle of town, there should have been more motorcycles, a fleet of bicycles, even a few cars as people found their way to shops and offices, ready for work. The morning chill refused to lift, condensing beads of water on the windscreen. I folded my arms against my borrowed jacket, reassuring myself with the weight and quality of the wool cloth against my skin.

We followed a lone cyclist around a corner. "Look there." Pierre pointed his chin across the town square to a checkpoint on the road leaving town. "Feldgendarmerie."

Military police.

"Is that bad?" McAllister asked from the back.

"It's usual," Pierre said. "Nothing to worry about. Some little official checks papers, and ours are flawless."

I considered reaching out, putting a hand on Pierre's arm. Even with flawless papers, there were always risks at a checkpoint, and we had a load of wireless parts in the boot. "We could pull in there," I suggested. "Wait at a café until they move on."

Pierre shook his head. "They might be checking papers there all day." We both avoided cafés when we could. Too many eyes and ears. He eased the car forward, a placid look on his face. As we passed the Feldgendarmerie post, the road rose slightly, opening the view ahead. I refused to let my face change expression, but my body tightened. Soldiers lined the road on both sides, a wall of dreary gray made menacing by the picket of machine gun barrels, for now pointing harmlessly at the sky. This wasn't an ordinary checkpoint. Behind us, Pickersgill cleared his throat. "Did we stumble on the route of a parade?"

No one in the car spoke. It would be nice to think it was an honor guard assembled to bolster the self-importance of a passing dignitary, but I didn't feel lucky enough for that just now, even in Mme. Cortembert's brown suit. A low buzz ran though my head, electricity raising the hairs on my scalp. Another uniform stepped in front of the car, filled out by an older man with a heavy scowl who signaled us to stop with his raised hand. His straight row of brass buttons flashed in the slanted morning sun. Pierre stopped, somehow managing to look annoyed and impatient instead of frightened. The Feldgendarmerie officer pointed across the square to the town hall building, making it clear we needed to park there. Behind him a soldier lowered his barrel several inches to emphasize the direction.

Pierre shrugged to show he wasn't happy but wasn't about to disobey and pointed the car toward the building of pale Normandy brick and white plaster. The town clock dominated the center gable, beating relentless time above an empty bandstand that no longer produced cheerful music.

I glanced back at the ranks of soldiers who'd ordered us to turn around and saw a tall cyclist waved through. My gut clenched. They were looking for someone or something specific.

"If we're separated, stick to your stories. No deviation. No ornamentation. No improvisation." I gave the two boys behind me a stern look. "And if they keep us together, let Pierre and I speak as much as possible."

Halfway across the square, a soldier strode from the town hall toward our car, signaling Pierre to stop with a sharp wave of his hand. A submachine gun hung at his side. "You two! Come with me."

I glanced at the boys in the back, but they obeyed the soldier with the impeccable weariness of true Frenchmen. As they were hurried away, McAllister smiled at me, saying without words that he'd soon be back.

Before I could ask Pierre what we should do, another soldier came forward, waving agitatedly. "Move along! Move along!"

Pierre, not needing to feign confusion, gestured uncertainly to the street opening on our right.

"No! No!" The soldier's French was sharp enough to cut. "Park there. Go inside and show your papers."

Pierre nodded and slid us between a van and a green three-wheeled Darmont Spécial. "At least they aren't asking to look in the car."

I'd packed the parts myself, boxing them in auto parts boxes from Grand-Georges and a toaster carton from Roger, but they wouldn't stand more than a brief inspection.

"Let's get this over with." I opened the car door.

Inside the city hall, a uniformed officer with a spotty chin immediately accosted us. He sized us up, consulting a clipboard. "Follow me." He marched us past a long queue of bored townsfolk waiting to present their papers to a rank of harried clerks. McAllister and Pickersgill still hung well back in the line. Neither made a sound or gave any sign of recognition as Pierre and I passed.

Good.

The officer fed us into a much shorter queue, ending with an officer and what looked like a mechanical typist at adjoining desks. I held back a sigh of gratitude that McAllister and Pickersgill were destined for the overworked clerks. "This is my fourth check this week," I said, smiling confidingly at the woman just ahead of us.

"My second."

"I'm winning, then."

Her forehead smoothed and her pressed lips relaxed into a smile. "What's the prize?"

"I'm not sure. But I'm getting so good at this, I think I could make a career out of it."

Pierre snorted, but the grin he sent me was an affectionate one.

"And how many times for you this week, monsieur?" the woman asked.

"I haven't been counting," Pierre admitted. "But she beats me every time."

"Well, I think I look very intimidating," I said.

The woman laughed, but we had no time to talk. The typist rapped impatiently on the desk, and our new friend scuttled forward, opening her well-worn cardboard identification folder on the desk.

The officer picked up her card, examining it under a magnifying glass, but I pretended not to notice, chatting to Pierre. "I told you we should have stopped for coffee. Then we wouldn't be doing this on an empty stomach."

"How about a cigarette for breakfast?" Pierre's eyebrow arched. We'd rolled this week's radio codes into a cigarette. He'd only suggest burning it if—

"I'd love one, dear, but if you share, you'll run out before the end of the week," I said.

"I'll manage." He reached into his jacket and pulled one out of his cigarette case. I took it and leaned forward so he could light it, the orange embers glowing as they slowly devoured our evidence.

"Thank you, Pierre." It had been months since I'd smoked, so I breathed slow, resisting a cough, glad Pierre offered it to me because it occupied my hands. Ahead of us, the German officer was reprimanding the woman for her confused replies.

It will be fine, I repeated silently. *You've done this dozens of times before.*

I took a drag and let it out slowly, the smoke curling soft over my tongue. "Before we go home, I'd like to change my book," I said carelessly, tapping off the ash, burning crumbs of subterfuge. "Is there time to stop at the library?"

"Tired of detective stories?" Pierre asked.

I smiled flirtatiously. "A change would be nice. How about a romance?"

"And have you dreaming of cowboys and aristocrats?" Pierre pulled a wounded face, stepping into his role. "I just gave you my sixth-last cigarette!"

A throat cleared. We turned to the colorless man seated behind the table. "If you are quite finished?"

"I am so sorry, monsieur." I hurried to the desk, whipping my papers out with practiced ease. "The line was moving so slowly, I assumed we'd have more time. Darling? Your papers for this good man here."

The typist looked more astringent than ever, her fingers poised motionless above the keys, but I'd glimpsed what I wanted in the officer's eyes. A remnant of a twinkle.

"I can see you are terribly busy here today, and I hate to waste even a second of your time. And when I think of all the men and women here, waiting for your assistance, and me, delaying you." I smiled as warmly as I knew how. "Well, it doesn't bear thinking of, does it?"

"My dear, you are distracting him. Let the man think," Pierre murmured.

The officer pushed my papers aside. "And these are your documents, Monsieur Corbeau?"

"Yes, monsieur," Pierre said.

"And you work for the Finance Ministry?"

"That is correct, sir. But just now I'm on leave. We were bombed out of Brest, so my wife, Madeleine, relocated to Bracieux. I visit as often—"

"Yes, I see," the officer said. He took a preprinted form, signed and stamped it, and folded it inside Pierre's papers, then repeated the process with mine. "Show these to the guard on your way out."

We chatted nonsense all the way out, hardly able to contain the mounting rush of our incredible luck, until, stunned, we stepped out into sunshine. The chilly mist might never have existed. It was gone.

CHAPTER 41

———

MAX STALKED BEHIND THE ROW OF CLERKS, SCANNING THE lines of waiting people for petite Frenchwomen. Every so often, his heart jumped, but each time the clerk examined her papers and sent her on her way. No one was suspicious here, no one recognized the thick hair, straight nose, and high-cheekboned face of the suspected terrorist Jacqueline LeClaire.

It was the same scene he'd witnessed yesterday, and the day before that: an exhausting succession of checkpoints that demanded too many hours from German soldiers and yielded nothing. If they didn't find her soon, neither he nor Heinrich could justify continuing this intense search. And he'd been so close! He'd found her picture, a used identity card, the fields where she and her people had buried the parachutes that carried their supplies.

Perhaps she'd been injured—one of the fields had witnessed some kind of explosion. He could think of a hundred possible explanations, a hundred chance variations preventing him from catching her. If this—

"Sir?"

Max collected himself and turned to the clerk.

"I've found some irregularities. Not a woman," he amended, perhaps thrown off by the sudden narrowing of Max's eyes. He pointed casually with his stack of papers at two young men waiting in front of his desk. "They don't talk right. Neither of them. No problem with their papers, though."

Max dropped his gaze on them, causing the blond fellow to shift his weight. They were both of military age, too fit to be excused from work detail. If nothing else, he could correct that.

"Ask them to come to my office for questioning," Max said, turning on his heel and disappearing into the requisitioned room where his coat and hat were draped across a borrowed desk.

CHAPTER 42

———

DHUIZON, 2 JULY 1943

THE SOLDIERS OUTSIDE WERE AS ANXIOUS TO GET US TO LEAVE as they had been to make us come. One yanked his rifle impatiently toward the road in a clear gesture for Pierre and me to move off.

We folded ourselves reluctantly into the car. "We can't leave them," I whispered as if the soldiers could hear us.

"We can't stay without looking suspicious." Pierre polished his spectacles with his handkerchief to buy us a few seconds. The soldier at the door furrowed his brow like a petulant child and took a step toward the car.

"Go," I muttered.

The engine jumped to life and Pierre pulled out, gliding slowly onto the road, his eyes stuck on the building we'd just left.

"We can pull over down the block, past the soldiers, and wait and see what happens."

Instead of pointing out the obvious limitations to my plan, he put several hundred feet between us and the soldiers and eased the car over, engine running. Hopefully the sentries would be occupied by the crowd of people coming and going.

"This isn't good," he said through set teeth. "They're going to wonder what we're doing just sitting here."

"Only if they notice us. Think inconspicuous thoughts." Our tight nerves sent palpable waves through the car, like solemn music heard only by prickled skin.

It played on interminably, sweat gathering under my arms as we sat in silence. "We'll give them another two minutes," Pierre finally announced, tapping his fingers on the steering wheel.

"Three," I said, praying it would be enough. We'd waited fifteen already, with no sign of McAllister or Pickersgill.

"They hadn't been singled out when we left," I said to myself as much as Pierre. "But their line was so much longer."

"There were at least half a dozen clerks though," Pierre said. "It shouldn't be taking this long."

I sucked hard on the stub of my second cigarette—this one with no secrets to burn. Another excuse for waiting. Pierre had smoked one already, but if need be, he still had a few more.

But you can't afford to wait.

"Surely they think we are gone by now," Pierre said. "Once they get out, they won't even look for us."

"They're trained for this," I said. "They know how to get around." They both had papers and full money belts. I tossed away my cigarette. "We've got to—"

A shrill whistle blasted behind us, cutting me off. Our eyes whipped to the rearview mirror as the whistle screamed again. Soldiers pounded down the sidewalk toward our car, their rifles pointed.

"You!" one bellowed. "You come back."

"Go!" I shrieked needlessly, as Pierre slammed down the

gas, fishtailing the car as he yanked us onto the road west to Bracieux—still clear.

What had they found? What had the boys said? Panic balled in my chest, cutting off all air as I turned backward to watch the scene, bracing myself against the passenger door. The engine roared and the tires squealed as Pierre zigzagged, already anticipating a hail of shots. "They're already in a car!" How had they managed that so quickly?

He gunned the engine and I tumbled against the back of my seat as the car leapt forward, tearing out of town like a bird flushed from high grass.

"Hurry!" An armored car, full of soldiers, raced in pursuit. We careened around a sharp bend, the rear tires spinning, and for two blessed seconds I lost sight of our tail. But when it reappeared, I saw two—no, three cars hurtling after us, gaining ground. Petrol-fueled and smooth running, they flew past the corners with sickening ease.

"Quick, Pierre! They're getting closer!" Neither of us had a gun.

If they shot out our tires, if they caught us, my necklace, with the L pill, could only protect one of us.

You have your knife. As always, it was strapped to my thigh, waiting. There would be time to... No. If it came to it, I couldn't use my knife to kill Pierre, whatever torture it spared him. I tugged the pendant, snapping the chain, holding it tight in my closed fist. He'd take it if the situation demanded it, if I pushed it at him and shouted loud enough. If I used the knife on myself first.

We launched off a rise in the ground, landing with a

bone-jarring jolt and loud scraping on the car's undercarriage. I tasted blood in my mouth, my tongue trapped when my jaws snapped together on landing. Pierre didn't even notice, stamping hard on the accelerator to carry us across a terrifying expanse of flat open country. The guns in the lead car spat, and Pierre flinched, but for the moment, we were out of range. Bracieux couldn't be much farther. The road would branch there, granting us a little more time.

He doubled his evasive maneuvers, and we hurtled around a curve.

"There's another checkpoint ahead!" Pierre yelped. I whipped my head forward and glimpsed a red-and-white gate, a tangle of barbed wire, a handful of sentries diving off the road. Pierre didn't hesitate. "Hold on!"

I hugged the seat, crouching low, my eyes fixed on our pursuers and their answering shots. A fierce impact rocked the car as we smashed through the barrier. Wood and bullets flew past the windows. The barbed wire clawing our car screamed in my ears; then we were through, speeding away, our bodies whole and our tires intact.

The glass shattered behind me, an earth-rending crack. I curled into myself, bracing for a blizzard of splinters, but none came.

"I can't see!" Pierre screamed. The car veered sideways, but he swore mightily and somehow wrestled us back onto the road.

"Keep—"

My head struck the seat, and a wheel of spinning light filled my eyes, multiplying by twos, by fours, by dozens. Fireworks without sound.

That didn't make sense.

Not fireworks, then. Bombs.

Bombs from the sky and a world of dust and smoke. Shattered glass and the weight of two floors pressing me into blackness.

I'm so sorry, Jackie.

CHAPTER 43

———

NANTEUIL, 2 JULY 1943

THE CLOUDS HOVERED TOO LOW. SOURIS GLANCED UP FROM her strawberry bed, convinced the sky had contracted since the last time she'd checked. Not that she didn't welcome a break from the summer heat, but this humid air and stiff breeze warned of a storm. Beside her, Nanny hummed some English nursery rhyme and stripped away yellowing leaves.

"You always sang that one when we were little." Bette spoke up from the spot where she'd stopped picking strawberries and watched an iridescent beetle attempt to burrow himself into the soil instead. "I always thought your black sheep very accommodating."

Moune laughed and pretended to throw a berry at her sister, not actually sacrificing the precious fruit.

Souris nestled into the sounds of the women around her, lulled by the happy voices of her daughters and Nanny's gentle humming. The berries, some hopelessly misshapen, piled up in her basket. She handled one, debating whether it needed another day to ripen, when the urgent buzz of a motor sawed through the heavy air.

Souris heard it first, but after she lifted her head to the sound, the other women followed like startled deer, still and waiting. Instead of passing on the road and fading away, it growled angrily, growing louder and closer. Just as she got to her feet, an old relic gasogene van skewed sideways and stopped in front of them.

Marguerite Flamencourt jumped from the car, her face blotchy red. Before Souris managed to ask anything, her friend stretched out her hands in terrible supplication.

"Marguerite?" Bette rushed forward.

"Jacqueline and Pierre are dead!"

Souris shook her head, unable to displace the cries of shock behind her. Bette's and Moune's questions clambered on top of each other, unintelligible.

"What do you mean?" Souris managed to ask. "They just left here a few hours ago."

"What about the Canadians?" Moune demanded. She'd taken a shine to the tall fair one.

"What Canadians?" Marguerite asked. "There was a frenzy at a blockade in Dhuizon and I went to see what happened. A Gestapo officer said they'd caught and shot the Jacqueline they'd been looking for, and her accomplice. A little man, they said. With a mustache."

"Been looking for?" Nanny turned horrified eyes to Souris.

Grief tried to claw its way up her chest, but Souris kicked it down. She'd cry later. Now she needed calm. They were all in danger. She ran inside, through the kitchen, the hall, and shut herself in Berbert's study, hand poised over the telephone, collecting her breaths. She rang Paulette Gatignon first.

"Just letting you know that our chickens are ill. We've lost two."

Paulette hesitated. Silence. "Which two?" her voice choked, split.

"The English hen and our small rooster."

A terrible pause while Paulette comprehended her message. "So sorry to hear that."

"Be careful your chickens don't catch the same thing," Souris said. "Goodbye."

A hot tear stung her eye and her hands trembled as she pushed down the receiver and picked it back up to repeat the message again and again.

Souris didn't notice Berbert hovering behind her until she set down the receiver and felt a hand on her back.

"You startled me."

"Sorry, darling." Berbert rubbed the back of his neck like a man twenty years older. Nanny or one of the girls must have told him.

"So far, no one I call has been taken," Souris said, her voice wavering. "But—"

"I know. That's what I came to talk to you about."

Souris felt her heart jump. "What is it? What happened?"

"Nothing, nothing," he assured her, taking hold of her arms. "At least, not yet. But the Germans were looking for Jacqueline specifically. It's not impossible that they might find her cottage soon."

"Good luck to them," Souris said, her voice thick and venomous. "She and Pierre mined all around it."

"Yes." Berbert's look was grave. "But in case they get inside, is there anything there that might lead them to us?"

Almost at once she knew what the Nazis might find in the

low run-down cottage outside Veilleins. "There's a book there. Just a detective novel, but it's stamped like the others in the library." With their home's name and address. Souris's mind sparked, working like a frenzied telephone switchboard as she hurried through the list of things she must do. Everyone to call. How to phrase warnings over the phone. Whether she and Berbert should risk sending the girls and Nanny away via the Gatignon's escape line or whether it was safer to keep them here.

"I'll fetch Roger," Berbert said. "He should know the way through the traps. We can't waste any time."

———

Souris finished her calls before slouching leaden-footed to the stables. She couldn't risk Nanny or the girls seeing her, not until Berbert came back. The only thing she could think to do at a time like this, with her hands trembling and her heart ready to burst, was groom her horse. She began as she usually did, inspecting knees, tendons, fetlocks, hooves as her mare's skin flicked, sensitive enough to feel a fly, thick enough to endure hours in a saddle. Dusting her hands on her trousers, she went for the brushes, selecting the wooden-backed one that, over the years, had smoothed to the shape of her hand, and began drawing circles over Chantilly's withers.

"Maman."

"Yes?" Souris didn't turn around, recognizing Moune's voice and intent on moving with the grain in Chantilly's gray coat.

"It's Dr. Luzuy," Moune said. "On the telephone. He's sorry to call at this hour, but he says he needs to discuss your test results."

"Oh?" The brush stilled. Dr. Luzuy was her doctor, but Souris hadn't had any tests for over a year. Luzuy wasn't a resistant or in their network that she knew, and his message wasn't a recognized code. Working moisture into her mouth, Souris forced a swallow. "Did he say anything else?"

"No."

Souris frowned. "Is he still on the line?"

Moune shook her head. "He said he's at the hospital. He wants you to come."

The brush fell to the ground, causing Chantilly to sidle and twitch her ears impatiently. Souris responded with a perfunctory pat. "I suppose I should call right away, then."

Moune didn't immediately let her pass. "What if it's a trap? We already lost Jacqueline and Pierre."

Souris shrugged. "I'm sure everything—"

"You can't be sure," Moune interrupted.

Souris cupped her daughter's cheek. "You're far too clever for your own good. Watch the drive from the windows. Take the family and run if you see anyone but me. We know what to do in these situations." Her throat tightened, remembering Jacqueline calmly explaining over breakfast what to keep for such an emergency, how to alert others that you'd been taken, how to keep silence for at least two days of interrogation, giving time for others to escape. "I'll be careful."

———

One of the nuns greeted her as she arrived at the hospital. "Dr. Luzuy wanted me," Souris explained. "My blood tests."

"Yes, of course," the sister said. "He's this way."

The tension that had rebounded and doubled on the drive lessened slightly as Souris followed in the sister's wake, soothed by the hypnotic flowing of her dark robes. "Just in here," she said, motioning Souris into a small room. It was dark, lit only by a single bulb.

Souris's eyes adjusted, identifying a rank of painted metal cabinets, all with locks. They were in the dispensary.

"My office here is a little too close to the patient wards," Dr. Luzuy explained as he stepped inside, his face reassuringly honest. "At this hour, I didn't want to disturb anyone."

"Naturally not," Souris said, as if there was nothing extraordinary in such caution.

Dr. Luzuy smiled and smoothed his graying hair. "You know there are no tests."

Souris nodded.

"A patient came to us today. Not one I could discuss with anyone over the telephone. Forgive me, Countess. I am a quiet man. I do my job as best I can under the circumstances. If I am mistaken, please do not be offended..." He stared at his hands, as if the pencil wobbling between his fingers held all the answers to life's questions.

"I would never be offended," Souris said. "We are old friends. The kind who forgive—or overlook—each other's foibles."

The doctor let out an uneven breath. "Good. I thought so. But of course I wouldn't presume."

"Why did you want me here? Who is the patient?"

"The Germans..." He swallowed. "She's with the resistance. They called her Jacqueline."

CHAPTER 44

———

BLOIS, 4 JULY 1943

I TURNED MY FACE AGAINST A THIN PILLOW AND LET OUT A sigh, too tired to remember if this bed was Marguerite Flamencourt's or one at Nanteuil. Certainly too soft to be the cottage. And the light was too bright. Instead of being curled on my left side like usual, my arms and legs rested symmetrically, slightly spread from my straight body, a textbook savasana. I attempted to turn and nestle deeper into the pillow, but nothing happened—as if my mind had cut all connections to my body.

A spurt of panic, weaker than it ought to have been, shot through me, and my eyelids fluttered, making me flinch from the harsh light—and an even harsher voice.

"Sie wacht auf."

A different paralysis seized me. I didn't dare open my eyes, but my other senses stretched out vainly. Nothing familiar here. My mind—electric now, pulsing with panic—accelerated like a plane in a nosedive.

Germans. I didn't know how, but I'd been taken. Was I injured? Pumped full of drugs? What were they going to do to me?

My mind flashed back to Beaulieu, the concrete room I'd been dragged to from my bed in the middle of the night.

Practice, the instructors had told us. *You need to be able to resist for forty-eight hours. Give your network time to escape.*

"Excuse me." The voice was French this time. "She's in distress."

A hand landed on my arm softly. Seconds later, cool metal touched my chest. I sensed the movement of someone leaning over me.

"Be still. Perfectly still or I can't help."

The voice was an almost inaudible whisper, a vain prayer. They weren't sure I could hear.

A signal. I slowed my breath, letting it slide past dry lips, and forced my mind to widen like the sky, to nothingness, where all that existed was breath.

"She may need another shot of sedative," the voice said. "I'll have to monitor for a while."

"When will she wake?" Excellent French from this man, without a hint of accent.

Breathe. Sleep, I told myself.

"I cannot say, Lieutenant. The bullet is lodged in her skull. There is no way to know the extent of the trauma, and I expect the coma to continue for some time. These injuries often cause bleeding beneath the bones and in the brain, causing significant damage."

"But she will wake?"

A pause. I didn't need to see the shrug. It was there, thoroughly French and familiar. If I could have smiled, I would have instinctively. I trusted the body that made that shrug.

"Who can say? You understand, sir, if she wakes again and if she regains her ability to think and speak, we must at least expect severe damage to her memory."

An explanation for me and perhaps advice. I couldn't remember any bullet, but my head burrowed heavy into the pillow, weighted with bandages. I couldn't move, but I didn't feel pain, which according to the Frenchman—a doctor, presumably—I surely ought to. The sedatives?

"Can't you bring her around?"

"I'm afraid not, Lieutenant. Consciousness will return when—and if—the brain is ready. Administering a stimulant at this point would only harm her. I expect she'd be too incoherent to understand us."

"I am not concerned with harming her. I am concerned with questioning her."

An electric chill jolted my spine.

"Be that as it may," the doctor answered in measured tones, "if I rouse her now, she'll likely die before she understands a word you say."

The German answered with a grunt. "Keep a close watch on her."

"She's in excellent hands," the Frenchman said.

For now, I had to trust that promise. I had no other choice, because when their voices floated farther away and I dared a peek through my eyelashes, I glimpsed a torso in field gray standing sentry beside my bed. My memory stretched, straining against confusion, sorting through smells—bleach and soap and something almost like rubber—and sounds—the squeak of shoes on linoleum and a rolling cart. All my memory touched was mist and shadow until my thoughts brushed against Pierre. Something solid. Where was he? In my desire to find him, my finger moved against a thin blanket and that was enough to spend my strength.

Forty-eight hours, I told myself. *Breathe.*

Sleep pulled and I succumbed.

CHAPTER 45

IN THE BLEAK HOUR OF TWO IN THE MORNING, THE REMAIN-ing leaders of Reseau Adolphe gathered in a strained huddle at Nanteuil: Albert Le Meur, Roger Couffrant, Paulette Gatignon, Grand-Georges. Souris relaxed a little with the arrival of each familiar face.

"Where is Berbert?" Albert Le Meur asked even before taking a chair.

"Warning others," Souris said, bridling her worry. He'd brought back the book, but what if his name was next on the list? What if they were looking for him at the checkpoints? "We know Pierre was captured. A man who saw the crash says he was beaten and shot in the leg."

A fast shudder shook Paulette's shoulders.

"He's been in German custody for three days now—if he's still alive," Souris continued despite the catch in her throat.

"And Jacqueline?" Roger Couffrant leaned forward. His eyes warned he wanted truth, without any sugar. His fingers tightened on his battered flask.

"By some miracle, Dr. Luzuy says she'll live. The bullet can stay where it is without causing further harm. Her memory will be affected, perhaps other things as well, but he says that's probably for the best. Until we can get her out."

Albert Le Meur shifted in his chair. "Do you think we can?"

Souris pressed her lips together in annoyance. Jacqueline's rescue wasn't a decision to be weighed and measured. They must pull her out and decide what to do about Pierre. Find him first. Then, if his guards could not be bribed, get him an L pill. Somehow. He'd kept them safe this many hours—she didn't like to think how—but no one could withstand the Gestapo forever.

"I mean, is it safe for her?" Le Meur asked. "Or is it better if she stays in the hospital?"

Souris checked her angry retort. She hadn't considered that, but… "The minute she's sufficiently recovered, the Germans will question her."

"But if her memory is bad—"

"We don't know that," put in Theo Bertin. "If it isn't, she must pretend. For all our sakes."

"Dr. Luzuy said…" Souris swallowed. "Whenever the Germans return, he'll give her an injection. Sedate her. They'll think she's still in a coma, and hopefully if it drags on long enough, they'll eventually pull the guard out of her room."

"That will give us a better chance," Grand-Georges conceded. "And more time."

Uncomfortable silence thickened the air.

"Unless Pierre breaks," Le Meur said.

"He may not have to," Souris said quietly. "The Germans knew who they were looking for. Marguerite's friend said the checkpoints were put up to catch two resistance leaders, Pierre and Jacqueline. They knew both their names and that they head Reseau Adolphe. They might know all of us already."

"I put my son on a train this morning," Grand-Georges sighed. "They captured the fellow he loaned his bicycle to yesterday, and the stupid man left Simon's name painted on it."

Souris pressed her fingers on the table. "It might be wise to run while we still can."

"If we still can," muttered Roger.

Souris nodded. "True enough. But I'm staying here, and I'm going to get Jacqueline and Pierre out. No one else has to."

Grand-Georges snorted. "How thick do you think we are? If any of us were going to hide, we'd have done it already. Tomorrow I'll go to the hospital. I can pretend to change the tires on one of the ambulances and see what it will take to get Jacqueline out. How much money have we got?"

Theo Bertin snorted. "We can try money. But if it were me, I'd want cigarettes."

A low laugh rolled across the dining room table. Souris grinned. It felt strange on her face but good nevertheless.

CHAPTER 46

BLOIS, 4 AUGUST 1943

FIFTEEN MINUTES LEFT UNTIL MY GUARD RETURNED, ALONG with Sister Benita and the midday cup of broth or gruel. Sweat ran down my forehead and back and glossed my shaking arms. I glared at the window, at the beckoning sunshine, as if anger might bring it a yard or two closer.

"Get up," I ordered, as if a command might solidify my jelly legs. I pushed off the edge of the mattress and lurched upright, the room swinging sickeningly around me. Just in time, I caught hold of the metal bed frame and saved myself from toppling. For a long moment I stood, panting, visualizing myself shuffling forward, shifting my weight experimentally. Both legs trembled, weak as twigs, but the right seemed a little better. With one hand on the bed and the other stretching for the wall, I slid my left foot forward.

"Jacqueline!"

A simple head turn would capsize me, but before I could even try, Dr. Luzuy had his arms around my waist and was bearing me down to the bed. I sputtered, swore, gave a weak approximation of a laugh.

"I was nearly there, Doctor," I said, pretending my limbs weren't quivering.

"Stay in bed. You're not fit enough yet. If you fall and hit your head, heaven knows what will happen to you."

"There's no other time for me to try," I protested in a whisper. "My keepers are always here, and you're always drugging me—"

His head whipped to the door, and he glared. "Danger is here now," Dr. Luzuy hissed. "Be patient, Jacqueline. So long as we can allay suspicion, you'll remain safe here. But the minute they think you are at all recovered…" He shook his head. "No one must know you are even capable of sitting. Anyone might have walked in just now—what if it hadn't been me?"

The hurt in his eyes made me drop my own in shame. It wasn't just myself I was risking. If the Gestapo learned he'd deceived them about my condition—plus, I'd had flowers from the Flamencourts and a new night dress from Moune, all marked as "charity" but with whispered messages passed from friend to friend to me. Escape was coming; they were working on bribing guards to free Pierre; they'd blown up another power line and spoiled the windshield of the German car that carried my would-be interrogator while he was visiting my sedated body here in the hospital. If I'd lacked determination to guard their names, this was more than enough.

"Your friends need you," Dr. Luzuy said, as if reading my mind. "Give me your arm."

"You must tell them to do nothing," I insisted as I nestled my head into the thin pillow. "Under no circumstances should they try to rescue me. It's too dangerous." It was more important to protect each other, to keep fighting the Germans.

Dr. Luzuy scowled. "Your arm."

And I must protect them. I held out my arm, counting out the seconds left to me. *Un...deux...* Once Luzuy pressed the plunger of the needle, I never made it past *cinq*.

———

I lay back and stared at the ceiling. I knew, from the slant of the shadows on my wall, that soon Dr. Luzuy would return with his syringe. Later, I'd wake, and my Gestapo interrogators would be gone.

Except instead of Dr. Luzuy's measured footsteps, someone was running, shoes pounding in the corridor. My muscles seized.

"She's not ready. You'll kill her if you take her now." That was Dr. Luzuy, but his voice was as I'd never heard it before. Frantic, furious, afraid.

"We are willing to risk it. She is, after all, a terrorist. Are you?"

"Lieutenant, I beg you—"

"She has conspirators. Those parcels. Those cards you say she cannot wake to read or even understand. Moving her is necessary. You wouldn't want to stand in the way of that, would you, Doctor?"

A long pause.

"Then you have to take her in an ambulance," Luzuy begged. "She won't survive in a car. Go to the desk. The clerk will organize it."

More words, a click of bootheels, then Dr. Luzuy burst into my room, alone, limp as a wet rag, his face white and sweating. All at once, the clamminess on my skin was gone.

"Jacqueline—"

"I heard. Don't be upset. There's nothing you can do." My voice didn't sound real. It echoed far too even, eerily calm, perhaps numbed. *Thank God for that.* I didn't want to cry or gibber.

"They'll be back soon. I can—"

"No phenobarbital." The name of the drug came easily from nowhere, still in that impossible monotone. "I need my wits about me." If I had managed to keep hold of anything, it was the strange moods of destiny—a bomb missed me, just like those bullets missed my plane. Another bullet hit my head but didn't kill me. If fickle fortune wasn't on my side, what else explained it?

Fate might present me with a chance to escape if I could stay awake and keep myself ready.

"I can pretend without the drugs. Tell my friends not to worry. Their names are safe. So is yours. Pass this along—I order the network not to attempt any rescue. Forget me and look after the others." The death's doorstep act would simply continue a little longer.

"Shh, they're coming." Dr. Luzuy clutched my hand.

I closed my eyes and let my mouth fall open, silently marking the footsteps approaching, the German voices and another other doctor spouting one objection after another.

"*Nein.*" They stamped the word on the air and marched into the room.

My bed jerked, slewed to the side, and my head wobbled. Even with my closed lids, the pain made streaks of light.

They picked me up and thumped me onto a stretcher, forcing out a groan; then I was in motion, speeding down the hall. I opened my eyes, floating my gaze blearily at the few faces gathered to see me go—the sisters, a broken-looking Dr. Luzuy.

In the back of the ambulance, they jostled the stretcher until it locked in place, a German cradling his gun in the corner across from one of the hospital doctors. I'd seen this doctor before. He sat opposite the German, his hands clasped and his head bowed. The ambulance lurched forward and swayed on the unkempt roads.

I fought the lulling movement of the speed, the hushed sounds of the tires on the road as I mapped the injuries I must feign, the carefully crafted signs of confusion to display. But we couldn't have traveled far before the guard hollered to the driver.

"I need to get out."

We swerved to the side of the road and he bolted out the back and started retching before we even stopped.

A soft hand touched my arm. "I slipped him something to make him sick," the doctor whispered. "Back at the hospital. We have a few minutes."

He reached into his pocket and took out a syringe. "Dr. Luzuy said—" He paused and drew a deep breath. "I should offer this to you. Morphine. Enough for another kind of escape."

His eyes blinked rapidly, but the needle held steady, hovering between us, inches from my arm.

Ahead of me, only places I did not want to go, suffering undefined, weaknesses not yet discovered. My breath sped as I pictured Souris, Nanny, Paulette, Roger—faces of the people I'd betray if I buckled under torture.

Not so long ago in London, I would have stepped, friendless

and forgotten, from the bridge and drowned. Such resolve for a woman whose life wasn't even in real danger. Such drastic measures for someone responsible only for herself. Maybe that was the difference. Once I'd been trusted with a mission, I'd taught myself to swim.

I swallowed the lump thickening in my throat, unsure if it was a sob or a laugh. "I'm not ready to stop fighting yet," I whispered. "No one will die because of me. I'll hold them off until the end of the war." I smiled, giving him resolve I willed myself to share. "It won't be long."

"Are you sure? They—" He glanced at the open doors, gauging our time left. "I don't know what they will do to you."

I wavered, the fear gnawing, devouring my certainty bite by bite. "I'm sure." We needed to keep fighting, especially now, when giving up felt easier.

He slid back into his seat. "Be strong, then." His next words dragged under the weight of his own oath. "We'll come for you before too long."

———

I held on to that promise, but after we arrived in Paris, I knew *long* would be longer than expected. There were no friendly doctors and nurses here, no gifts or parcels. Sometimes daily, sometimes weekly, in the afternoon or the dead of night, Germans came to question me. I clung to the pretense of damaged memory, my life ring, my only escape from the thumbscrews and the baths of icy water. Sometimes they wheeled me past these instruments of torture; each time I blinked my eyes and pretended not to understand. I told myself, if they tried them, I'd endured worse pain already. I'd fought, and bested, the fear of being drowned.

I'd made a promise to protect my network. None would go to prison or die because of me.

Most of the time, I thought I could manage it, but there was one German—persistent, cold, and cunning—who frightened me. My most frequent questioner. They called him Max.

Each time he came, I pretended I'd never met him before.

———

"We know their real names, madame." Max tugged his lieutenant's jacket straight again, keeping the seams of his uniform meticulously straight. "We have John McAllister and Frank Pickersgill. We captured them with you." Though he spoke in French, he pronounced the English names perfectly.

I peered at him, squinting through the magnesium glare of too-bright lamplight. "I don't know who you mean," I said fretfully. "You say you know me, but I've never seen you before."

I remembered the two Canadian boys, though not how they'd been captured. The only memory I'd truly lost was the one I most wanted—how did I get a bullet in my head and what had happened to Pierre?

The German sighed and pressed his fingers on the desk, leaning forward. Demonic in the lamp's dramatic shadow, I focused on the flaw that made him human, his left eyelid with its intermittent twitch. All this past week—sometimes three interrogations a day—that twitch, like a dot of Morse, had grown more frequent.

"Rubbish. Tell me the truth or it will go badly for you and

for everyone you know. What were you doing in a car with them and a known criminal, Pierre Culioli?"

I smiled up at him hopefully. Inside, I readied my next serve in this tennis match. Though I'd lost count of how many times we'd played, I'd never been defeated. "I know a doctor named Pierre." He was, in fact, a physiotherapist in the hospital here, and his examinations had yielded the information that, with rehabilitation, I should be able to walk without help. Well, I walked now, but they still brought me to these daily interrogations in a wheelchair.

"Pierre Culioli, madame. He's no doctor."

I let my face fall into a confused frown and silently counted the power lines I'd blown up, the derailed train, the supply drops received, and saboteurs I'd trained. The agents I'd delivered safely. All but two. "I'm so sorry. I don't remember," I said, silently chanting, *I am strong enough to reveal nothing.*

"You were in a car with him, madame," Max said, his syllables clipped and sharp. "That is why you are here. Your companion drove through a checkpoint and crashed into a house while evading police."

"I know." I nodded, blinking extravagantly. "Cousin Gui was always a terrible driver."

Max slammed his hand on the table. "There is no Gui, madame! This is not a case of dangerous driving. You were in company with Canadian spies, with a carload of illegal wireless parts!"

I smiled hesitantly. "I'm sure you're right, sir. I should not have been there. Monsieur McAllen"—I mangled the name—"should not have stolen those things. I didn't know about the boat."

Max rolled his eyes.

"Is it possible to adjust your lamp, sir? The glare is very uncomfortable."

"No, it is not possible!" he shouted.

Another explosion. Hiding a smile, I savored the sigh and dramatic flinch that forced him to massage his temples. I glanced away, into the dark recesses of the room's corners, a natural place for my eyes to rest and a safe distance from the English book Max had left open a foot away from me—no doubt watching to see if my eyes would inadvertently scan the lines.

He switched to English, another of his favorite tests. "We found your family, Jacqueline. We've sent assassins to kill every one of them. Will you save your life and let your children die for you?"

Children?

Sloppy lies.

I drew my brow together, troubled. "*Pardon. Je ne parle pas anglais.*"

"You are Jacqueline," he demanded as he leaned forward. "I've found your name in their radio transmissions."

My spine froze, brittle as an icicle, but I kept my face smooth. "*Oui.*" I nodded eagerly and tapped my chest. "Jacqueline."

He blew out an exasperated sigh as I gave him another confused smile.

"Is it lunchtime yet?" I asked in my politest tone, knowing perfectly well that I'd dined on soup and a bit of sausage less than an hour ago. Max's mouth twitched, and I glanced at my hands again, to hide my satisfaction at his growing irritation.

But Max had not advanced to his post by quitting. He carried on for the full hour, at times bellowing curses in English, once yanking my head backward by the hair and telling me in detail what they did with terrorists and spies. I cowered, let my tears fall, apologized.

"I'm sorry, sir. I did not mean to be a terrorist. I will stop." Unnervingly easy to play a desperate innocent.

"Your Pierre told us everything about you while he was screaming. He cares nothing for you."

My stomach clenched. "The doctor?" I asked in confusion. "Why did you torture my doctor?" I whimpered and let tears fall, silently praying that Pierre was safe. And silent. I could hide behind a damaged memory, but what of the others?

I let my sniffling swell to sobs, an indulgence, but one I needed. Max, clever enough to see that these were real, threw his chair over and called in the German guard. I'd won our game. Again.

"You are finished with her?" The guard—too young for his uniform—seemed surprised.

"We'll get nothing useful from her. Nothing." Without looking at me, Max opened a manila folder and scrawled something on the typed form inside. "Send her away."

I swiped my streaming eyes, masking a desperate surge of hope.

"Release her?" The guard was incredulous.

"No." Max snapped the cap on his pen vindictively.

"Back to Fresnes." The guard held out his arm to lead me back to my usual prison. The numbness in my hands and the beat in my temples started again.

"No, you idiot. Read!" He jabbed the paper. "I suppose she may spend another day or two there. I want her on the next train. East."

The guard nodded and snapped a salute.

East. He hadn't said where, but he must have meant another prison.

As he wheeled me into the hall, the guard sighed. "Let's get you back, Jacqueline."

I was used to hearing the name, but this time, it resonated like a chime, an omen. I closed my eyes, a habit now, to keep my thoughts to myself.

What a good thing I'd taken this name, not some alias with no meaning. No matter what my enemies took or where I went, my talisman came with me. And soon, the Allies would come. My friends were still fighting. They would be ready to help. I would too, even if all I could do was guard my secrets.

As the wheelchair coasted through the halls, returning me to my cell, I drew a long breath, falling into the comfortable certainty of a well-worn mantra.

Be strong, Jacqueline. Keep fighting.

CHAPTER 47

―――

This is the lesson: never give in, never give in, never, never, never.

　　　　　　　　　　―Winston Churchill, 29 October 1941

"I DON'T ENJOY THIS, YOU KNOW."

Three yards away, treading water, Denise laughed. "But you can do it. Don't tell me you don't enjoy *that*."

I grunted, but because she was right, I stayed treading water for another minute before pushing through the ripples to shore. "Our last swim together," I sighed. "You're off to parachute training." To someone else, I would have confided more, but Denise always turned gruff and impatient when people thanked her. Anyway, she knew.

"I wish I could come along," I said. Most wouldn't think this way, but to me, after learning to swim, what was there to stop me from leaping out of a plane?

"You're such an idiot." Denise picked her way across the

small sharp rocks surrounding the pond. I'd beaten her to our towels, left safely on the grass, because my feet were too numb with cold to complain. "Here."

I tossed her towel. She caught it with ease.

"I think you get the better end of it," Denise said. "You're going to France. Within days. The first one of us. Don't bugger it up."

All of us—Denise, Prue, Christiane, me—were willing and ready. Except for parachuting, which I wasn't allowed to try, we'd passed all the tests. So when I went to France, I had to succeed, not just for France and the war. I couldn't let Denise and the other women down. "You'll be in France before long," I promised. "Maybe we'll see each other there."

Denise paused her toweling off. "I'd like that."

"Me too."

I tugged on a thick wool jumper and waited for Denise to be devoured by an overlarge man's coat. Together, we trudged back across the lawn to the house, all dark except for the library window. Jepson and Vera were still in conference with our instructors. I wondered where they would send me. What my mission would be.

"Have you thought of how it could end?" Denise asked.

"Not when I can help it," I said lightly.

"I'm serious," Denise said, catching me by the arm. I let her, though I could have seized her, levered her over my back, and slammed her hard against the ground. We'd both done it to each other in practice. "What if they catch you?"

"I won't break," I said.

"Everyone does. All the instructors say so."

My wet hair, stuck to my neck, sent an icy droplet between my shoulder blades. "I know. But they also said it's possible"— *imperative* was the word they'd used—"to resist for forty-eight hours." Denise and I had both practiced that too.

"So?"

"So I'll just start again every forty-eight hours." Brave words. I wasn't sure, if it came to it, that I would deliver, but I knew I'd give everything I could. If forty-eight hours seemed too long, I'd fight for the next hour, the next half, the next ten minutes. I'd never been a mathematician, but I'd loved someone—I smiled, remembering Henri—who'd tried to explain some to me. Even working by halves, if you cut something smaller and smaller, there would always be something left—small and infinitesimal maybe, but that speck would always remain, all the way to infinity. If every session with the Germans cut my courage and resolve in half, I'd never run out.

"If you and Christiane and Prue needed me to keep my mouth shut, I would," I said aloud. I looked into her young face and saw for a moment Jackie's dark eyes. If Jackie's safety depended on my silence, I'd never breathe so much as a sigh. "Wouldn't you?"

Denise nodded once, sharply. Her eyes blinked hard and her lips pressed together. "Yes. No matter what."

I caught her hand, and we started walking again through the dark. "Then no matter what," I echoed. "We'll do it."

CHAPTER 48

―――――

Dear Mrs. J. Pepper

You are much like your mother, you know. We never had a more persistent recruit. I know your wait has been a long and anxious one, but with so many conflicting reports, the search has taken much longer than expected.

I am very sorry to inform you it is now established that your mother died of exhaustion after the liberation of Bergen-Belsen, about the 23 of April 1945, and beg to offer my sincere condolences, along with those of all my staff. Interviews with your mother's resistance allies and fellow prisoners have yielded the following facts, which I hope will answer your questions about her war work.

Ensign Yvonne Rudellat was landed in France by sea in 1942. For nearly a year, she carried out highly dangerous duties, assembling and leading a resistance organization in northern France. She was a network liaison, a combat instructor, and a saboteur, conducting numerous clandestine operations, including bombing of the Chaigny power station, a railway tunnel, and the derailment of a locomotive. She was captured with a local French resistance operative, Pierre Culioli, in June 1943.

I have spoken with M. Culioli, who was sent to Ravensbrück after interrogation and torture but who was liberated in 1945. He informed me that at the time of your mother's arrest, she'd suffered a gunshot wound to the head. Interviews with personnel at the Blois hospital who treated her confirmed that the injury was relatively superficial. Feigning memory loss, she avoided arrest for some months, until Germans learned of a plot to liberate her and imprisoned her first in Fresnes Prison and then Ravensbrück camp.

It appears that concern for her resistance network inspired her to maintain the charade of memory loss. For the remainder of her life, she continued to use your given name, Jacqueline, though she recognized and rekindled friendships with two of her allies who were also eventually imprisoned in Ravensbrück camp, Countess de Bernard and Mme. Flamencourt, who report that she remembered them and the work they accomplished together. I have spoken with both women, and it was their information that led me to another friend of your mother's, met in camp, named Mme. Renee Rosier. Mme. Rosier was sent with your mother to Bergen-Belsen, about March 1, 1945. Mme. Rosier was recently repatriated to France via Sweden. She had hopes that your mother still lived, and indeed she was listed among survivors on April 18, 1945, but her name is absent from any subsequent lists. I am sorry to inform you that it appears she must have been buried in a mass grave with other victims.

I know these facts offer little comfort after your many months of anxiety. I wish I could have given more hopeful news. The only consolation I feel able to offer is that her work and sacrifices for the Allied cause will not be forgotten by all who knew her both here and in France. She was loved and admired by her friends and will be sincerely missed. I was told that even in prison, she swore she would see the end of the war and the liberation of France. In that, and in her work for the Allied cause, she certainly succeeded.

Yours sincerely,
Vera Atkins

AUTHORS' NOTE

I like to think that Regina and I are comfortable with history. We love research and the conceptual construction work that allows us to step away from our smartphones and spend time with imaginary friends in times long past. Our hearts quicken when we are poring over an archived memo with a correction in the type or a penciled note in the margins. When we talk about flying and sailing without GPS (I almost never drive without it), our words come faster, and we add extra punctuation (exclamation marks, mostly) with our hands. People's eyes start to glaze over, but we are too far gone to notice.

And somehow, I've procrastinated writing this note for months. The weight of responsibility is heavier because Yvonne Rudellat is real, not a composite creation. So are most of the people in this book. Though we imagined her thoughts and feelings, nearly every episode in this book is from her own story.

In 1942, she was lonely, overlooked, and left behind, but in the summer of 1943, she was leading a subcircuit of one of France's largest and most effective resistance networks, with numerous acts of sabotage under her belt. According to the surviving documents in her SOE file and the accounts recorded in her 1989 biography, she really did rappel into a railway tunnel to blow it up, derail a train, and lose her cat in the London bombings. She was vegetarian but uncomfortable asserting it, she practiced yoga, and she did complain, frequently, about the one set of ugly underwear she owned for most of her time in France. She was likable, brave, and funny. And when she was captured, she really didn't give up anyone.

As a subject, she is both exhilarating and terrifying to write about. Though our interpolations came easily, we tried hard not to guess too much for fear of getting things wrong. And so far as we can discover, so much of this story is true.

Pierre Culioli was a prisoner of war, and his young wife, Ginette, was killed by German bombing. The field where he and Yvonne and others received parachuted supplies really was that close to a German-occupied château. Souris de Bernard was knocked back into a bog by an exploding canister, and Pierre and Yvonne boarded with an elderly man who died, naturally and suddenly. Edouard and Marguerite Flamencourt really did farm chickens. André and Paulette Gatignon really did float downed pilots to safety in their wine barrels. As much as possible, we have represented Yvonne's friends accurately and honestly, using their real names—which is why the book has two Georges, Georges Fermé and Grand-Georges Duchet.

Max, the German Abwehr agent, is our invention, with a made-up persona and name, but the Abwehr (German military intelligence) really did steal a suitcase from a train containing a list of the entire CARTE network.

At the time of Yvonne's arrest, her cover name, Jacqueline, was known to the Germans, and they were actively searching for both her and Pierre. After the war, many were accused and tried for betraying her and the Prosper and Adolphe networks, but no one was ever convicted, and many of the accusations were wild and implausible. Pierre Culioli was tried and exonerated twice, but given what we learned of his personality, his torture and imprisonment, and his lifelong friendships with the surviving members of the network, Regina and I concluded, like his fellow resistants, that the accusations were bogus.

It is true, however, that he revealed stores of supplies and names to his Nazi captors, who drove him around as he was covered in bruises and was walking on a broken leg. Nearly everyone in the network was eventually arrested, their cover blown as more and more of their friends were taken and tortured.

The history of the resistance in France is tragic and heartbreaking. They fought against terrible odds. Many died. Many, like Pickersgill and McAllister, were sent into the field with no chance at all. But Allied pilots were still sheltered and conducted to safety. Nazi resources were destroyed, distracted, and dispersed. Intelligence was conveyed to the Allies, and when the landings finally came, an army of equipped fighters rose up behind German lines in France.

There are many excellent books, online archives, and museums that can tell you much more than we can, but one of our favorite books on the subject is *Mission France: The True History of the Women of SOE* by Kate Vigurs. Please read it—the women who trained and served alongside Yvonne are worth knowing.

What impresses me most about Yvonne Rudellat is that she gave her best, even when people consistently underestimated her. She knew she had more in her, and she gave it all. She didn't give up, and she kept her word.

She inspires us all to do the same.

READING GROUP GUIDE

1. Yvonne feels an immense amount of guilt for the injury of her child. How do you think this influences her decision-making in the future? Do you agree with her decision to leave France for England?

2. Yvonne is told that she, as a woman, is too old to assist with most war efforts. She was forty-four years old. Why do you think that women are told they are too old at that age, yet men are generally seen as capable and experienced?

3. Yvonne is thrown into a hostile environment in her beloved France. Have you ever found yourself no longer comfortable in a previously known location?

4. Yvonne faces a certain amount of hazing during her training. Why exactly do you think she was treated that way? How did she overcome it? What would you have done?

5. As part of her training, Yvonne must face her deep-set fear of water. What do you think inspires her to keep

facing that fear and continue on with her training, rather than backing down? What things inspire you to face your fears? And what relationship does facing fears have with supportive friends and colleagues like Denise?

6. Yvonne becomes the head of a large team of saboteurs in France. What prompts her to step into that role? What responsibilities does she have to the team? What responsibilities does any leader have to their team/subordinates?

7. Consider Yvonne and Pierre's friendship: How does it build, and what trials must it go through? How would you characterize their relationship?

8. This book is based on the true story of Yvonne Rudellat, whose accomplishments helped the Allied efforts in France during WWII. What do you think we can take away from her story of bravery and of the people others might overlook or leave behind?

A CONVERSATION
WITH THE AUTHORS

Why did you decide to write Yvonne's story in particular?

Yvonne wasn't the only "unlikely" candidate recruited by SOE, but she was the one we fell in love with, perhaps because so many people had written her off. Even more so than today, success for women was defined by an enduring marriage, happy and accomplished children, and skilled (or at least competent) domesticity. Yvonne didn't check these boxes and knew that people considered her a failure, but when she was offered the very slenderest chance, she took it and excelled. She was brave and persistent and cunning, and her courage and lighthearted personality won her friendships, respect, and admiration that she'd never had before. It's such a compelling difference. Who wouldn't want to write her? In fact, it astonishes us that more haven't already!

Can you discuss your decision to add multiple perspectives to the narrative? What do you think Max's sections add to the story?

We actually included even more perspectives in early drafts—scenes from Yvonne's daughter, Jackie; Yvonne's husband realizing she's gone missing (London police told him she must have died in a raid, while she was blowing up power lines in France); Jepson debating with his team about Yvonne's merits as a recruit. There was so much material to work with, but it got unwieldy, so we had to cut back. It was a good call. The perspectives that remain are the truly essential ones: Souris's POV is very helpful when Yvonne is sedated in hospital, and Max's reveals the knife-edge quality of the resistance movement—the near misses, the lucky breaks, and the domino-toppling disasters.

You have written multiple books together. Has your writing process changed at all during that time? What does it look like?

Every book is different, so it's kind of hard to say, but one thing that has been consistent is that we are both in up to our elbows at all parts of the manuscript. Even when we "assign" scenes, we edit indiscriminately, treating all the words as if they were our own and cutting, adding, or revising until we are both happy.

Besides the dueling perspectives, there are also multiple timelines in this book. How did you choose to split up the timelines and position them throughout the novel?

We originally wrote the story in chronological order, but it took so long to get to France that way that splitting the timeline and starting when she takes on the identity of Jacqueline felt very natural.

What do you hope readers take away from this story?

In some ways, this book is a superhero origin story, featuring an ordinary woman who, encountering a challenge, does extraordinary things. Except Yvonne wasn't bitten by a radioactive spider. She wasn't given a super-suit. I know I fixate on this, but she wasn't even given enough underwear! She was super because of what was inside her—the belief that she could do more than others thought she could. Her story also highlights the danger of discounting so-called "unlikely people" and the mistakes we often make assessing an individual's success or potential. SOE's first choice was Raymond Flower, but Yvonne was the person they needed.

ACKNOWLEDGMENTS

This story does not exist without the courageous men and women who envisioned and formed SOE (Special Operations Executive) and the French citizens who risked their lives to support them. In the dark days of war, they stepped into danger and envisioned new methods of victory despite crushing losses. To the agents, especially, who snuck behind enemy lines, and the resistants who endured in the worst of times, we acknowledge not just the debt of this story but our very freedom to write it.

We gratefully acknowledge our outstanding agent, Jennifer Weltz, who reads with keen perception and always goes to bat for us, as well as Ariana Phillips, for bringing our stories to more readers worldwide. Outsize thanks to our talented editor, Jenna Jankowski, for making this project possible (and infinitely better). We also send gratitude to the ever-supportive and encouraging teams at Sourcebooks and JVNLA, including Cole Hildebrand, Cristina Arreola, Jessica Thelander, Gretchen Stelter, James Iacobelli, and Tara Jaggers.

We owe a very special thank-you the British historian and writer Paul McCue, who has dedicated much of his life to studying SOE agents. Paul provided us with the entire government file on Yvonne Rudellat and generously telephoned from

England in the middle of his night due to the time differences. He also introduced us to Julie Clamp, the granddaughter of Yvonne Rudellat. Though Julie never met her grandmother, she agreed to speak with us and faithfully told us what she knew about Yvonne, as well as her mother, Jackie. We have tried to capture the courage, as well as the idiosyncrasies, of her incredible grandmother. We thank her for trusting us with stories of her family.

We relied heavily on the research of dedicated historians and writers. The most comprehensive story of Yvonne's life is found in *Jacqueline: Pioneer Heroine of the Resistance* by Stella King. We also turned to *Mission France: The True History of the Women of SOE* by Kate Vigurs, and other excellent books.

And to our families, and, most notably, our long-suffering husbands, Jeff and Justin, we freely acknowledge your love and support keeps us going and imagining and writing. We are so grateful to you. And to our children, whose teenage years helped us write more realistically about combat, we love you anyway (wink). You truly are our greatest masterpieces.

ABOUT THE AUTHORS

Audrey Blake has a split personality—because she is the creative alter ego of writing duo Jaima Fixsen and Regina Sirois, two authors who met as finalists of a writing contest and have been writing together happily ever since. They share a love of history, nature, literature, and stories of redoubtable women. Both are inseparable friends and prairie girls despite living thousands of miles apart. Jaima hails from Alberta, Canada, and Regina calls the wheat fields of Kansas home. Visit them online at audreyblakebooks.com and on Instagram @audreyblakebooks.